THE BLOODSTONE REBELLION

Book Five of The Crystal Halls

Thomas K. Carpenter

The Bloodstone Rebellion

Book Five of The Crystal Halls

Hardcover Version

by Thomas K. Carpenter

Published by Black Moon Books

Cover design by
G&S Cover Designs

Discover other titles by this author on:
www.thomaskcarpenter.com

ISBN-13: 978-1-958498-22-4

THE CRYSTAL HALLS
Shadows in Amber
The Emerald Eclipse
The Sapphire Stratagem
Chains of Obsidian
The Bloodstone Rebellion

The Hundred Halls Universe
SEASON ONE

THE HUNDRED HALLS
Trials of Magic
Web of Lies
Alchemy of Souls
Gathering of Shadows
City of Sorcery

THE RELUCTANT ASSASSIN
The Reluctant Assassin
The Sorcerous Spy
The Veiled Diplomat
Agent Unraveled
The Webs That Bind

GAMEMAKERS ONLINE
The Warped Forest
Gladiators of Warsong
Citadel of Broken Dreams
Enter the Daemonpits
Plane of Twilight

ANIMALIANS HALL
Wild Magic
Bane of the Hunter
Mark of the Phoenix
Arcane Mutations
Untamed Destiny

STONE SINGERS HALL
Song of Siren and Blood
House of Snake and Tome
Storm of Dragon and Stone
Sonata of Shadow and Thorn
Well of Demon and Bone

THE ORDER OF MERLIN
The Order of Merlin
Infernal Alliances
Tower of Horn and Blood

Other Series:

The Dashkova Memoirs
Revolutionary Magic
A Cauldron of Secrets
Birds of Prophecy
The Franklin Deception
Nightfell Games
The Queen of Dreams
Dragons of Siberia
Shadows of an Empire

The Kingmaker Saga
The Stone Tree
The Crystal Bard
The Ghost Tower
The Champion's Prophecy
The Shadow Labyrinth
The Autumn Empire

The Alexandrian Saga
Fires of Alexandria
Heirs of Alexandria
Legacy of Alexandria
Warmachines of Alexandria
Empire of Alexandria
Voyage of Alexandria
Goddess of Alexandria

THE BLOODSTONE REBELLION

One

Six weeks earlier

The stylized poster near the stage had drawn a crowd. Valor Drux cradled his beer, eyeing the commotion with curiosity. He'd seen a woman tack it onto the wall, then take a seat at the bar. She had spiked green hair, shaved on the sides, and the markings of a waku—the formidable martial artists that used the strange crystals only found in the Undercity. He'd heard rumors of their existence from his home in Seward where he ran a small fleet of fishing boats and taught Jin Jutsu during the long, cold Alaskan winter. The idea that those without magic could suddenly gain the abilities that previously only the top Halls could muster had convinced him to buy a ticket to the city of sorcery. After a week of exploration, he'd been sent to the Goblin's Romp, a seedy bar that was run by the criminal gang that controlled the Undercity. It was his second day at the bar, and his inquiries into purchasing a faez crystal had resulted in blank stares.

Valor motioned to the bartender, an odd-looking character with orangish skin, a slit nose, and crinkled ears that marked him as some sort of non-human. He wasn't a fan of the refugees from other realms, but since it wasn't his city, he wasn't going to make a big deal about it. Better that the trogs stayed here rather than muck up his hometown.

While he waited for his drink, Valor approached the poster, leveraging people out of his way. Even the largest of them hesitated when they saw him barreling through the crowd. That was the way he liked it. Most people knew instinctively when they met a superior being, and if they didn't recognize it right away, Valor was more than happy to give them a sample.

Standing a head taller than the other onlookers, Valor examined the poster, which displayed a trio of fighters in ready stances. In bold, movie-style letters, the header read: Undercity Tournament of Champions. The date was two months away, but that wasn't the part that piqued

Valor's interest. Below the three fighters was a section explaining that the top finishers would receive bloodstones—a faez crystal that Valor hadn't heard of despite him reading everything he could about the Undercity happenings—and the winner would earn a black diamond. A secondary paragraph suggested that those not confident in their abilities could apply to join the Alliance clan, which he suspected was the real reason for the tournament. A recruitment ploy.

"I promise I won't hurt you too bad if you get matched with me," said Valor, enjoying the way the crowd shifted away from him as if they could sense his internal power.

Back at the bar, he collected his beer and found a spot near the woman with the green hair. She wore a sleeveless jean jacket and gave him side-eye. She'd be attractive if she bothered to fix herself up.

"Don't worry, I'm not here to hit on you. You're not my type. What's your name?"

"Go fuck yourself," she said, then finished her beer.

"I plan on entering the tournament. I figure I have a good shot at winning."

The bartender approached, gesturing towards the empty mug. "Hey, Adrena, you need another?"

Adrena grumbled under her breath, but nodded.

"Adrena, huh?" said Valor. "Sounds like it's short for something."

"It's short for none of your fucking business, unless you'd like to stop breathing through your face holes and start breathing through a hole in your chest."

"I'm not intimidated by women like you," he said magnanimously, spreading his palms to show how open-minded he was. "In fact, I've thrown down a few times when the moment's right, if you know what I mean."

"Make it two, Donnie," said Adrena, holding up her fingers.

The trog bartender nodded, grabbing a second glass and filling it to the brim. She took both and left the bar, which Valor didn't understand, because he could still follow her.

"I need information."

"And I need a hangover," she said with her back to him, finishing one of the beers as she headed into the back of the bar.

"I'm looking to purchase a faez crystal. I figured you're the woman to talk to. On skills alone, I'm sure I'm the best who'll enter your tournament, but I recognize that those little magical baubles would make a king out of a jester."

"Good for you."

She set the empty mug on the table of a couple who were eating greasy burgers and headed into the women's bathroom. Valor grabbed her arm before she disappeared past the door. He could be forward, but he wasn't going to be *that* rude. He had a good grip on her forearm, years of working his fishing boats and training in the gym having given him the kind of working strength that often surprised those that mistakenly tangled with him. But she yanked her arm out of his hand so quickly and easily that it actually made him stutter to a stop.

"If you touch me again I'm going to skin you alive and wear you as a hat."

It was the first time he'd really gotten a front-facing view of the Alliance waku. Her eyes were smudged black and there was a deep sadness in her gaze that reminded him of his buddies from the military who'd seen too many of their friends die. She placed the second mug against her lips and drained it while she stared him down, shoving the glass into his gut and disappearing into the bathroom. Valor returned to the bar, a little stunned from the encounter.

"What's with her?" he asked the bartender, congratulating himself internally for not adding "trog" to the end of his question.

"She OG."

Valor checked back over his shoulder. "Her? She barely looks twenty-five."

"Adrena from old Razor, then Drops, before she had to join Alliance. She was born with blade in her fist and probably killed more people than the plague. To live in the shadows is to live with death every day."

"Which faez crystals does she have?"

The trog bartender's slit nostrils flared. "That's dangerous question to ask a waku, but since you new here, I tell you anyway. She topaz and amber stones."

"Stones," repeated Valor. "Strength, speed, and sensing. A formidable combination. Thanks, Donnie."

"Stones only part of equation for OG like Adrena," said Donnie, nodding sagely. "The best can run up walls, or dance through the air like a zephyr, other things you can barely dream of. A waku who knows their stones can kill a dozen weak ones without breaking a sweat."

Before he'd left for the city of sorcery, Valor had read up on everything he could about the waku and the Undercity. He'd thought the

accounts were exaggerations, especially the cheap comics he found online, but he suspected there was a kernel of truth to them. Not enough to disabuse him of his confidence, but enough that he knew he couldn't blindly rush into the Undercity.

"You gonna join tournament?" asked Donnie.

"Join, no. Win, yes," said Valor, shooting the bartender a victorious smile.

Back in his hometown he was used to his fellow residents responding to his confidence, but the bartender only nodded and continued wiping the surface down with a rag.

"Good luck."

Valor sipped on his beer, considering his next move. He hadn't seen Adrena come out of the women's bathroom yet. For all he knew, she'd gone in to throw up. She'd looked like she was in a bad way.

"You seem to know a thing or two, Donnie," he said to the bartender. "Who might my competition be?"

"Hard to say, since the competition was just announced, but I know at least one." Donnie gestured to the back area where a wall of booths was set up near a couple of pool tables. "Big man in the corner. Broke a brick with his bare hands a few nights ago for a bet."

Valor spotted the person—no, trog—that Donnie was speaking about. Had to be around seven feet tall with umber skin and an ugly mug, sporting a single snaggletooth.

"What…?"

"Brodarian," said Donnie, squinting. "They're—"

"I know who they are," said Valor. "I subscribe to *Soldier of Fortune*."

The idea of testing himself against races from other realms had him intrigued. He was certain no humans could best him, so maybe he needed to be concerned about the foreigners in the tournament. But first, he needed to acquire stones of his own. Valor pulled out a large bill and slid it across to Donnie.

"You don't happen to know where one acquires a faez crystal? I'd be more than happy to pay a finder's fee for whoever can help me out," said Valor with a wink.

Two

Sobbing came from the back of the cavern. Choo-Choo had been inventorying their supplies. Since they'd left the Terreno, they'd had to keep a tight control over their food. Not that foraging wasn't possible, but one grew pretty sick of eating crickets and tasteless mushrooms for weeks on end. Yara was sitting across from him, sharpening her blade. Tick was around the front, providing lookout with Koro.

"Are you gonna…?" asked Yara, nodding towards the sobbing with a surprising amount of pity in her gaze.

Choo-Choo left their supplies organized in neat piles and climbed over the rise to the spring-fed watering hole. The air was cooler near the water. His sister, Vasilisa, was sitting against the wall, arms squeezed around her chest, cheeks glistening with tears.

"Vasy..."

The blank, empty stare barely flickered with his arrival. He stood near her, unsure of how to provide comfort.

"Is there anything I can do? Do you need something to eat?"

His sister grunted, scrunching up her face and looking at him like he'd asked her to eat a demon's liver. She pulled herself into an even smaller ball, rocking slightly on her rear. Choo-Choo wished their mother wasn't in the city above. He could use her soft touch. Choo-Choo approached his sister and when she didn't bite, he sat next to her, resting his forearms on his bent knees. She leaned over, putting her weight against him. Choo-Choo didn't say anything, mostly because he didn't know what he could say that would make Andelei's death less painful. It was her first real relationship, and she'd had to watch him be murdered before her eyes.

"What was he like?" asked Choo-Choo.

Vasilisa wiped away wetness near her eye using the inside of her thumb.

"I hated him at first," she said, speaking into the ground. "Because he was Alliance and everything they'd done to our clan. But he was kind.

Sometimes it was hard for me to believe that he was a waku. I couldn't imagine him killing anyone. He was polite to everyone, even the weird vendors in the Terreno, greeting them as if they were old friends. Najani even liked him and she doesn't like anyone."

Choo-Choo put his arm around his sister and pulled her tight. "I would have liked to have met him. In another life, we could have been clan brothers."

Vasilisa tensed. He chided himself for saying something so stupid, reminding her that if they hadn't been opposing the Alliance, then he would still be alive and she'd still be happy.

"He cut him down for no reason. He didn't have to. That murderous fuck."

Deacon. She couldn't even say his name. The former Crow would have killed them all except for Tick's intervention.

"What are you going to do about him?" asked Vasilisa, staring into his face with the intensity of a supernova.

Choo-Choo hadn't thought about it since the day at the Terreno. Getting away and surviving had been enough for the moment. Even when they'd had more resources available, they hadn't considered tangling with Deacon. Their two encounters with him had each ended with them barely escaping with their lives. But the need in his sister's expression, that while Deacon still lived, she would be in pain, had him speaking before he considered the odds.

"I promise you on Dad's grave that I'll gut that wayhos. Make him pay for what he did to Andy, and the Drops, and hell, even Razor."

He surprised himself with the last part, but after years with Tick and Yara, he no longer thought of Razor as his enemies. The past was rearranged in his mind, where the two clans were like a bickering family.

"I will hold you to your promise," said Vasilisa.

Her cold stare sent a shiver through Choo-Choo. She couldn't ever be a waku, but she had the heart of one. No stone and no hand wouldn't make a difference as far as Choo-Choo was concerned.

They turned their heads at the same time when a pressure shift in the cavern made them aware that something had happened. He felt electricity in the air, and rose to his feet as he reached for his blades. Vasilisa joined him at his side with a knife of her own—it was never safe to be unarmed in the Undercity.

The Great Arch was a man-made structure at least thirty feet tall built in the early years of the Undercity when few dared to live in the shadows. No one knew who had made it, but most speculation centered around a renegade mage of the Halls, performing forbidden magics in the protective darkness. The construct was imposing even if it'd proved benign, or at least without magic they had no way of affecting it. But it wasn't the only unusual thing in the area. A glossy black pillar of obsidian lay not far from the archway, a portal for the mages of the city, probably put in place by the very same mage that had created the arch. During their months camping nearby, they'd never seen anyone coming or going through it, though once they had some evidence that it'd been used while they'd been on a raid.

A white mist had formed like a miniature cloud, flat and growing like a disc above the pillar of obsidian. Tick came running from the front with Koro weaving above him. Choo-Choo knew the mages of the city used the portals for travel around the city, but he'd never heard of clouds forming during their use.

"What is it?" asked Tick, horrified.

"Be ready. We don't know who or what's coming through." He turned to his sister. "Stay behind me if things get bad."

Vasilisa made no move to retreat, keeping her blade outstretched. Choo-Choo hoped she wasn't being suicidal in her grief. It was a thing that happened to waku after losing too many of their friends.

The crack of electricity followed by a flash of light had him putting his arm up, even if it passed quickly. As the afterimage faded, he spotted two figures in the gloom, standing on either side of the pillar. His gut tightened the moment he recognized the chalky-gray skin of the mae-trie. The woman wore expensively tailored clothing that marked her as a noble. The man on the other side was stocky, carrying a wicked mace on his hip, dressed as if he were a personal bodyguard. Choo-Choo had a good idea the pair were friends of Dominion, which meant they were enemies, even if they'd never met. He reached for his topaz, preparing to sprint into battle, knowing that Tick and Yara would be at his side.

As he switched to an underhand grip in his left hand, Choo-Choo sensed two things that made him hesitate. First, there was something familiar about both figures, even as he knew he'd never seen them before. The second was they both wore shocked expressions, and despite his side producing weapons, it'd not triggered the same response.

"Yara? What are you doing here?" asked the stocky bodyguard.

Yara's stance softened. "How do you know my name?"

"It's me, Kuma." He gestured to the other side of the pillar. "That's Pandora."

"How? Why?" asked Yara.

"Don't put your blades down," said Vasilisa. "It could be a trick." She looked ready to take them both on at the same time.

"Hey Vasy," said the maetrie woman, the harsh exterior mixed with the friendly demeanor making Choo-Choo feel dizzy. "I used to beat you playing that board game your family made called Undercity. You always came in a close second."

"Pan?"

"I'd show you our real forms, but it takes a lot of energy and it's been a rough afternoon."

Weapons returned to sheaths. The two sides met halfway, embracing tightly.

"I wish I could see your true face," said Yara, grabbing her cousin by the shoulders.

"What are you doing here?" asked Pandora in breathless awe. "We expected to find an empty chamber."

Choo-Choo had a hard time rectifying the honey-mixed-with-glass voice and that it was his friend beneath the illusion. He reached out and pinched her face.

"Sorry. I had to check."

"Check what? It's a transformation. It's not a mask."

He gestured to the small camp nearby. "We're living in the lap of luxury. Can't you tell? What happened to you two? After we leapt into the waterfall, we kept expecting you to show up, and then after a few months we thought you must have died."

"I think we have a lot of catching up to do. A lot has happened since we've been gone I can see," said Pandora. "Is this place safe?"

"As anywhere in the Undercity."

The six of them settled around the makeshift camp. By virtue of being the last to sit, Choo-Choo was looked upon to explain their side of the nearly two years since the unsuccessful raid on the Alliance complex. He didn't think it was going to take long as most of their time had been spent hiding out in caves or in the secret room above Club Onyx, but between the regular clarifying questions and the addendums from his companions, it took nearly two hours to fully explain their side of the story.

When he was finished, he was struck with a realization that their experience had been fairly fantastic, and they were lucky that all three of them had survived with their lives. Which made it all the more painful that his sister's boyfriend had lost his life on the day they'd tried to rescue her. He wouldn't ever be able to forgive himself for allowing that to happen.

The other side of the story—the one about Pandora and Kuma's experiences in the Eternal City—put their meager rebellion to shame. The tale took much longer as even the smallest detail required an explanation. How do things made of concrete and glass live? What do you mean there's no directions? You met the Queen of the Ruby Court and lived? How can an entire realm be kept in a weapon? And so on.

The stories about Hylakane, the Steel Sun, interested Choo-Choo the most. He almost didn't seem real, but their transformation made it clear they hadn't been resting on their laurels in the endless city. Choo-Choo thought he'd been catching up to them in ability, but something about the way they carried themselves now suggested they'd ascended to another level. In his younger years, this would have angered him, but now he saw their return as a chance for them to make a real difference against the Alliance and Dominion Thule.

"Can you really change into anyone?" asked Vasilisa, eyes wide with wonder, her grief momentarily forgotten.

Kuma threw a pebble into the center. "Theoretically, yes, but it takes a toll. The energy for transformation is not cheap, and I'm exhausted afterwards."

"But you said Hylakane could do it effortlessly," said Vasilisa.

"He has the Zhinzi to draw on."

"Not to be rude," said Yara, "but why did you come back?"

"To stop my grandfather," said Pandora right away.

Yara had been playing with her knife. She twirled it in her palm absently.

"Maybe if you'd come back like this when it first happened, but I think the chance to stop them is long past. We've only been trying to survive this last year, and we only tangled with them again to free Vasy."

"Yara's right," said Choo-Choo. "We can't defeat them head-on. They have everything and we have nothing."

"I don't plan on destroying the Alliance," said Pandora. "You're right. It's too late for that. But that doesn't mean that he's not vulnerable."

"Where? We couldn't even put a dent in Deacon," said Tick, stroking Koro's back as she snoozed in his lap.

"That's what I mean to find out. As Lady Saha and her bodyguard, we'll be able to go where otherwise we wouldn't be able to. I don't know my grandfather's long-term plans, but as a minor noble adjunct to the Jade Queen he'll want to court my influence, or at the very least use my skills as a warrior." Pandora hung her head. "It's all very theoretical at this point. Most of it will have to be improvised."

"It'll be much easier than that," said Vasilisa, raising her head. She'd been tapping on her knee and frowning with thought, but an idea had sparked, and she became animated again. "The Alliance is hosting a tournament and offering rare stones as prizes for the top finishers. I think it's meant as a coming-out party for the clan. Legitimizing its presence now that it has complete control of the Undercity. Lady Saha and her bodyguard should enter the tournament as a way to infiltrate the clan."

Stunned silence followed. He could see from the others that they thought it was as great an idea as he did.

"He's probably using it as a recruitment tool," said Yara.

"But for what?" asked Tick. "He has control of the Undercity. Why keep bringing in new waku? He doesn't need that many to run his operations, and all that additional manpower has got to be expensive."

"Tick's right," said Vasilisa, shaking her head. "I've been running parts of the clan's logistics for the last year and a half. I never really thought about it, but there are a ton of new waku coming in every day. More than the clan needs. I supplied some groups with equipment for exploring the far edges of the Undercity. Maybe he's trying to expand the mines? Bring in more cash?"

"Money isn't my grandfather's driving force, but power. While he needs the cash to facilitate his plans, it won't be his main focus," said

Pandora.

"The Undercity is filled with old artifacts and arcane projects from the Hall mages who used to come down here to practice their craft in secret. This arch is proof of that," said Tick.

"Or he wants to take over the gangs in the city," said Kuma.

"That's the problem," said Choo-Choo. "We don't know what he wants or what his long-term goals are."

"Then I'll join the tournament," said Pandora. "It'll give me a reason to hang around and find out what my grandfather is really after. Once Kuma and I figure it out, we'll bring you in."

"Any way you can teach us that transformation trick?" asked Tick.

"I wish we could," said Pandora.

"What are you talking about, Tick?" asked Yara with a smirk. "You pulled off a pretty convincing hostess in the Terreno. I'm sure we could come up with disguises for each of us."

"I'm not sure," said Kuma. "Isn't that risky?"

"We lived in the Terreno for nearly half a year without incident. We had more problems when we were in the caverns. I can't say I'm looking forward to living in a camp again," said Yara.

"She's right," said Choo-Choo. "We can't stay here. It's too risky. Once we freed Vasy, we were planning on heading to the city, but if we're gonna stay, I'm not living like a vagabond."

"We don't have the materials for a believable disguise for all of you.

I don't see how this works," said Kuma.

"We need them," said Pandora suddenly. "Not only to help figure out what's going on, but Lady Saha needs a retinue now that she's in the city of sorcery. Traveling with her bodyguard across the realm is fine, but she would hire or coerce servants once she arrived at a location. And she wouldn't come in through the Undercity, but from above."

"Can you get us up through the portal?" asked Yara.

"No, I only know this one and the one in my grandfather's complex. Getting to the Eternal City was hard enough and only possible because of my heritage. We'll have to find another way."

"There aren't any others, except the one the Halls control, and that might give us away," said Choo-Choo.

"There is one," said Kuma. "It's partially blocked but I bet the group of us could clear it enough to reach the surface."

"The tournament is in a little over a week. Doesn't give us much time," said Vasilisa.

"Then we'd better get started," said Pandora. "Everyone agree?"

When no one spoke, Pandora rose and everyone followed. After days of sitting around the camp, Choo-Choo found a renewed sense of purpose and saw the same in his sister. She was no longer focused on Andy's death, but on getting revenge for his killing.

Three

Removing the rock that had blocked the passage into the city proved easier than Pandora had expected—and nowhere near the challenge that clearing the fountain had been. Between the five waku, their stones gave them a decided advantage in physical labor, and Vasy proved to be quite inventive in helping them design chutes to remove the rock while they worked. The hardest part had been stabilizing the looser sections, and more than once, minor collapses had caused injuries. Nothing they couldn't handle.

Three days later, they ascended through the basement of a fancy restaurant, coming out in the morning during kitchen prep time. The staff froze, a few grabbing butcher knives. Pandora surged forward, letting her otherworldly appearance put doubt in their actions. Except for the encounter with the Ruby Queen's henchman, she hadn't a chance to step into her new persona. She reached into her past, dredging up memories of all the arrogant maetrie she'd had to deal with as a child.

"I would suggest that you not mention our passage," she said in the silk-and-gravel voice that the maetrie were well known for. "If I'm forced to return I will be displeased."

A few blank nods later, they were striding into the city street. The warm daylight was a shock to their systems. Between the years in the Undercity and then the Eternal City—a place of endless gloom—she hadn't seen the sun in what felt like most of her adult life. The group of them, despite the oddness of the city of sorcery, looked like a troupe of performers waiting for the bus.

"Does everyone know their part of the plan? If you need something, now's the time to bring it up," said Pandora.

Even though her friends knew who she really was beneath the Lady Saha disguise, they still reacted as if she truly were the maetrie noble, catching themselves averting their eyes and deferring to her decisions.

"Then we'll see you in the first ward this evening."

The two groups split up.

"I hate leaving them so soon," said Kuma, checking over his shoulder.

"This is the most critical part of the plan. If anyone sees us together, then our ruse later will be undone."

"I know, I know. I just worry is all." He squinted. "I thought you said a long time ago that you don't have a maetrie aura."

"I don't. Why?"

He frowned. "Sure seems like it, the way the kitchen staff looked like they were going to throw themselves to their knees when you gave them a command. Even the others seem weird around you."

Part of her hated to hear it, even if it would be useful to their plan. She'd spent half her life fighting against that part of her heritage, but now she had to embrace it completely for the sake of her disguise.

"Let's find the pawnshop."

The owner of Trinket Trades and Pawn was mystified by their appearance, and even more so when they placed the golden bracelets on the glass case. With no plan to return to the Eternal City, they'd decided the enchanted protection was no longer necessary and their best way to acquire funds in a short time. The stack of bills they received was much taller than she'd expected, and as they left the shop, Kuma gave her an eyebrow raise as if to say, "See."

Flush with cash, they made a few other stops, picking up a prepaid cell phone and debit card. This gave them access to the taxi system, which brought them into the center of town. The Grand Arcane was two blocks from where her grandfather and mother lived in the first ward. The hotel staff collapsed around them like drones around the queen bee, ignoring their weapons and traveler's belongings.

"Your best suite, facing the Spire, and I'll need your concierge in two hours."

Feeling like royalty by the bowing and scraping, Pandora couldn't help but smirk at the blank-eyed stares the other guests gave them. After years of scrambling to survive, it was a shock to her system to suddenly have everything she asked for.

The hot shower nearly made her sob with relief. There were many days, weeks even, in the Eternal City when she thought they'd never see the next morning. To be in the suite of the Grand Arcane, letting the dust wash off her gray-skinned body, was something of a revelation. The bottom of the enormous shower swirled with old dust. She let the water from the multiple showerheads run off her body, examining the scars and imperfections she'd endured in the Eternal City. A thousand what-ifs kept her beneath the steaming impact as she wondered if she was making the right choice. Why not leave the city entirely? Use the gifts she'd been given by Hylakane to forge her own life without the influence of her family? It was tempting. Who didn't want to escape the reach of their abusive relatives? While the journey through the Eternal City had been brutal, the time she'd spent with Kuma traveling had been revelatory. And now she had everything she needed to become wealthy on her own without ever having to return to the shadows.

But she knew she'd never be able to rest knowing her grandfather and mother were lurking in the city, sending their tendrils into the halls of power. It wasn't that she felt a responsibility towards the city, or the people. But she hated the idea that they ruined everything they touched, twisting it into a pale version of the Eternal City. Look what had happened to that place. It was a ruin. A bombed-out city in which a single explosive had never been dropped. They built, and warred, and schemed, and then moved on, leaving the wreckage and bodies behind. Unchecked ambition was a virus, a curse meant to destroy everything it touched like a swarm of hungry locusts.

But even those concerns weren't enough to get her moving back onto the path of confrontation. If she never went back into the Undercity, never saw her grandfather or mother again, never fought in the shadows—there would be a hole in her life that would slowly suck in the rest. Like a black hole silently destroying a star system. She could ignore them, but it wouldn't mean she would avoid the consequences of her decisions. Pandora couldn't know herself until she'd confronted her family. A blade can never be sharp until it's been hammered, folded, and reheated—over and over—and then finally burnished with a whetstone. She'd be a dull piece of metal, a weak alloy, until that conflict was resolved.

The concierge and her assistant arrived at the appointed time. Pandora slipped right back into her Lady Saha persona, barking out orders so fast they could barely keep up. She gave them lists for clothes, makeup, and other personal items. Another was sent out for a broker to sell the faez crystals Choo-Choo had given them, and a third for a trinket dealer.

The ease at which they fell under her influence, either from the aura she was sure she did not have, or the appearance of wealth and nobility that she exuded, shocked Pandora even as she exploited it. A few times she caught Kuma smirking behind the attendants as they scrambled to make sense of her verbal onslaught. When they finally left, Kuma started laughing, bending over and holding his stomach in a loss of control.

"What's so funny?" she asked, anger rising in her throat.

"Never in a million, trillion years would I have known it was you under that disguise. I thought the one guy was going to have a heart attack when you told him he had three hours to get that massive list completed. I never knew you had it in you."

The irritation receded quickly, leaving her with a touch of embarrassment.

"I guess those years in my grandfather's presence rubbed off on me. It felt frighteningly natural. I hope it doesn't stick."

The others showed up a short time later. They were ushered up by the concierge, who'd been warned they would be arriving later. No explanation was given, only that they shouldn't be bothered and brought up right away.

"What the fuck was that?" asked Choo-Choo, flipping back his hood, checking back to the door after the concierge left. "If I'd asked him to strip and dance like a bag of worms, I think he would have given it his best attempt. What did you do to him?"

Kuma started laughing again. She glared in his direction until he got himself under control.

"I may have overdone it," said Pandora.

"Not at all," said Yara, throwing herself onto a purple divan. "These lighters don't know how good they have it. Nice to remind them that the world is a cruel and unforgiving place."

The description bothered Pandora, but she was too energized to disagree.

"What now?" asked Tick, letting his flying snake out of his back-pack. The winged serpent lifted into the air, exploring the suite like a dog unleashed.

"You four can take the back rooms. They'll be back soon, so you can spend the time getting cleaned up. Everything you're wearing will have to be thrown away." She paused. "Did you find Phillip or Dane?"

"Phillip's dead, but Dane was living in one of the old Drops apart-ments and working at a laundromat. He was surprised to see us, as you can imagine." Choo-Choo sunk onto the couch. "He's putting out feel-ers about my mami. Had no idea they'd gotten out, but he was sure he could find her given a little time."

"What happened to Phillip?" The four of them went silent. "Was it my mother?"

Yara was pulling a beer out of the refrigerator. "They found the hideout a few days after we left them. Dane happened to be out picking up supplies when they burst in, killing Phillip and rescuing your mother."

She cracked the beer and placed it to her lips as a phone Choo-Choo had set on the table vibrated. Everyone stared at it like it was a bomb.

"Well?" asked Pandora.

Choo-Choo grabbed it before Vasilisa could snatch it off the table. His forehead hunched with tension. He didn't speak, nodding occasionally and making grunts under his breath. When he hung up, he said simply, "Dane found her."

"That was fast."

"Too fast," said Yara.

"Dane would never," said Choo-Choo, shaking his head.

Yara took another swig before lifting her shoulders. "I'll trust your judgement."

"We should go," said Choo-Choo.

"What about our disguises?" asked Tick.

"Better we talk to her as ourselves," said Choo-Choo. "Don't want to give away the game if someone's watching her."

"Just make sure you don't have a tail. After you get back, you can work on your disguises. The clothes should be here by then."

"What about your part?" asked Choo-Choo.

"We have reservations at five of the top restaurants in the area. She's got to be at one of them," said Pandora.

"And if she's not?" asked Choo-Choo.

"Then we'll go with the backup plan, but I know my mother. For all her bluster about the maetrie being a superior race, she spends far too much time pursuing the trappings of power without putting in the hard work it takes to get it. And if you're right that she hasn't been sighted in the Alliance, then she's definitely up here spending her father's money and influence."

"There's a back elevator and a garage into the lower streets. Best go that way now that you have a key," said Kuma.

The four disappeared into the hallway, leaving her alone with Kuma again, but before she could consider other activities, the phone rang. After he took the call, he said, "The broker is on his way up. Better get your game face on."

"It never left."

"Do we really need this money if we're headed back into the Undercity?"

"One thing I learned from my grandfather is that money makes a lot of problems much easier. We don't need it, but it means we have to worry a little less about some of the other challenges. And besides, the cash we got for the bracers won't cover this suite. Unless we want Lady Saha to be a deadbeat, we're gonna need them to pay our bills."

Four

The chance that someone would recognize them in the city was tiny, but Vasilisa still felt like they were being watched the whole way across. That fear and the experience of being in the open with no cavern ceiling above her made her forget her mixed feelings about seeing her mother.

"How long it been, Vasy?" asked her brother from the passenger seat of the SUV taxi.

She hesitated, not wanting to speak in front of the driver, an Indian man nodding his head to the low-level music on the radio.

"Back when Mami took us up to see the special celebration in the second ward. The one when the entire area was a huge illusionary battle. I remember the ice cream that made my lip blue and made me feel like I was floating, and the guy that ran into the light pole on his bike because he was looking at the sky."

Those days seemed an infinity ago, yet only yesterday. She felt older than she was. Was it Andy's death? Or the nature of living in the Under-city?

"Is that blue car following us?" asked Yara, craning her head to the back.

As soon as Vasilisa checked, the vehicle turned the opposite way.

"Guess not."

The tension wasn't just her then. The others looked tight. It made Vasilisa realize that despite all the dangers of living in the shadows, it was a life they understood and respected. The city was way less dangerous, but the unfamiliarity made it feel worse. Emilio had them dropped off a block from the address Dane had given him.

"Wait here, I'll go ahead and check. If something happens or I don't come back in ten minutes, head straight back to the hotel."

"We're not leaving you, baka," said Yara with a smirk.

Her brother rolled his eyes as he headed down the sidewalk. Vasilisa had only been with them a short time, and she still wasn't used to the way her brother and Yara interacted. Right after Razor clan had folded into Drops, she'd been sure they'd end up scrapping. Now they were like an old married couple who anticipated each other's actions and words. Vasilisa couldn't quite get over the history between their two families, but she was willing to give it a try based on her brother's actions.

Emilio appeared around the corner, waving them on. Vasilisa had to check herself not to run. It'd been two years since she'd seen her mami. The last time had been right after the maetrie mercenary Titus had stopped them from leaving the Undercity.

The apartment building was right above a laundromat and across the street from a ubiquitous Wizard's Coffee. The Spire reflected the sun, forcing her to keep her head turned away. A guy in a uniform shirt was smoking a cigarette outside the business. He flicked it into the sewer and returned inside as Emilio led them to the entrance.

"What if she's not here?" asked Vasilisa right before her brother knocked. He gave her a shrug and rapped his knuckles twice in a rapid fashion.

Her heart stopped the moment the door unlocked and slid open, barely wide enough for a woman with tight gray hair to peer out. When Vasilisa realized it wasn't her mother, she deflated.

"What you want?"

"We're looking for Triana." When the woman frowned, he added, "I'm her son."

The door slammed, followed by muted conversation, and then the locks rattled. A moment later, her mother appeared, cheeks wet with tears.

"Vasy!"

She was smothered by her mother, who was sobbing and rocking. Vasilisa was surprised to find herself unable to cry. She squeezed her mother back, holding on as long as she wanted.

"Come in, come in," said Triana, wiping her eyes with the back of her hand. "Do you want coffee?"

The question was rhetorical because she was in the kitchen before anyone had answered. The woman who'd opened the door was watching the TV, some program where people shouted at each other. When Yara glared, the woman sheepishly reduced the volume.

The apartment was larger than their place in the Pajot, but it didn't have the same feel. There were none of the knickknacks that made it her mother's space, which made Vasilisa feel like she was visiting someone else's home.

"You don't have to do all this," said Emilio. "We can't stay long."

"What? Why?"

"We came to check on you."

Her mother's eyes bounced between them. "You're not staying?"

"No," said Vasilisa before her brother could answer.

"You're not going back there, are you? I know it was my home once, but it's ruined our family's lives. Why would you go back?"

"It's complicated," said Emilio.

"What's so complicated? They killed our friends and family. There's nothing left for us. Why aren't you staying here? I did as you asked and didn't spend too much money, stayed out of sight. I thought once you found your sister, we'd move to another city entirely. As far away from those murderous gray men as possible."

"I have to go back," said Emilio. "There's business left unfinished."

Her mother wordlessly reached into the refrigerator for a fizzy drink.

"Vasy, why you? I understand your brother, not completely, but I can at least understand, but you? That place has taken everything from you, including your hand. And I don't want to lose you."

The ache in her mother's eyes was palpable. Like getting plugged in directly to her emotional state. Vasilisa had to look away. It hurt too much to know what she was thinking.

"They killed Andy."

"Who?"

"My boyfriend. They killed him."

Mami slapped her hand on the counter. The noise startled Vasilisa.

"They'll kill you too if you go back. Why are you both doing this to me? Why did you come back just to tell me you were going to return? Hasn't my heart been broken enough already? For Val and then the entire clan, and now you're going to make me live as a childless mother?

Don't you know I'm supposed to die before you? Don't you?"

She slumped onto a chair at the small kitchen table, mutely staring at the floor. Emilio glanced over.

"You sure you don't want to stay with her? I won't be able to protect you if we get caught. They'll kill us all and there'll be nothing we can do it about," said Emilio.

Vasilisa thought she'd made up her mind, but seeing their distress, even in her brother, made her second-guess herself. The battle had been so fast, so brutal. Multiple waku had died in the first few seconds. She'd watched her brother put his knife in their chest, and then Deacon had killed Andy, sweet, sweet Andy.

"I'll never not see him dying in my dreams if I don't do something about it," said Vasilisa eventually.

"What about me?" asked her mother. "Don't I get a choice? What right do children have to throw their lives away without their mother's input? Don't you know what you're going to do to me? I brought you into this world. You're not meant to leave before me. Once was bad enough. I don't know if I can take it again."

Vasilisa regretted seeing her mother. It would have been better to leave her in a perpetual state of limbo as awful as that purgatory was.

"We should go," said Vasilisa. "I'm sorry, Mami. We've hurt you all over again."

Her brother looked at her like she'd betrayed them both but then the reason sunk in for him as he looked back to their mother, stunned to immobility on the chair, the plastic bottle about to slip from her fingers.

“If we—”

“No,” said her mother. “You don’t get to say that. If you walk out that door I have to believe that you’re dead. Now and forever. No more hope, no more waiting. I won’t be staying in the city. I’m leaving. This was only temporary. I have to start my grieving now. I’m motherless. Eternally cursed.”

Vasilisa took a step towards her but she made no move to stand, so she left the room with her brother on her tail. Emilio looked at a loss for words. Yara and Tick quietly joined them and before she could think about it, they were outside the apartment.

“Are you two okay?” asked Yara.

“Just go,” said Vasilisa, pushing through them towards the stairs. “We have work to do.”

Five

Pandora sent a hotel worker to the five restaurants with a stack of bills for bribing the hostesses, promising an equal stack when he returned with news of her mother's location. There was a chance that she might not be in town, but Pandora doubted it. Selena wasn't like her father, she was vain and thin-skinned. The decades in the Eternal City being looked down upon as a lesser being had forged her personality. Pandora had witnessed her mother being ignored by the other maetrie, both her father's retinue and the nobles of the courts, who considered her an amusing story, not a serious figure to worry about. That was the part that her mother had never understood. She was always looking to please her father by doing whatever he wanted, but he wasn't looking for subservience. Dominion wanted to see her take down foe like a predator after its prey. Only then might he be proud of her.

The Savage Heights was a five-star restaurant in the financial district. The worker hadn't been able to get a visual on Selena, but the hostess had assured him that she'd just been seated in a private room in back.

"Ready?" asked Kuma before he stepped out of the limousine ahead of her. They wore the clothes that Hylakane had given them, not only because it would make them more recognizable, but because they had hidden pockets for weapons. She didn't expect trouble, but there was no reason to be careless.

"*Srazhasa*," she said in maetrie, which roughly translated to "to battle."

Her appearance caused a stir from the staff. The hostess couldn't speak, staring into her book and blinking occasionally.

"Right here," said Kuma, jamming his finger next to their names. "Lady Saha expects the finest."

"I, yes, there will be, we'll do our best, ma'am, I mean Lady," said the hostess, tripping over herself.

As they strode through the restaurant, all eyes were upon them. While the maetrie weren't an unknown quantity, they typically did not visit restaurants or other public establishments, which was why her mother was in a private room. The hotel concierge could have gotten them more private accommodations, but that had been part of the plan.

The hostess stopped at a table, stuttering for words and holding her hand out, the only thing her muddled mind would allow. Pandora still wasn't convinced she had the maetrie aura but she was coming around to the idea. She spotted the row of doors in the back of the main area where the private rooms were located and made sure she was facing that direction when she spoke next.

"This is an insult," said Pandora in her loudest, accented voice. The words rang through the restaurant like a warning bell. The other guests either ducked their heads or stared with their mouths wide open.

"I should have my body servant beat you for this insolence. I was told I would be treated with the respect I deserve, not placed with the doe-eyed cattle," said Pandora.

"My apologies, Lady Saha," said the hostess, looking delirious and a little nauseous. "There are no other spaces. If we'd known of your arrival..."

"Known of my arrival? And let my enemies plan an assassination? I'll have you know I'm a great warrior with many foes. I've fought Red Company on the Plains of Nethersong, and bested the Champion of the Fallow Wastes. They would like nothing more than to see my body riddled with bloody holes. *Sake ehn faro*!"

The last part meant “you discarded rocks that could have been a building,” which wasn’t as impactful in English, so she’d kept it in the language of the Eternal City. The bulging-eyed look Kuma gave told her that she was overdoing the outburst, but she found herself getting into the role of the arrogant nobility in a backwater realm.

The hostess looked like she might be sick, and two tables near the edge vacated quickly. Pandora suspected the others were too terrified of leaving and accidentally insulting her. A waiter in a black shirt and pants came running up to the hostess and whispered in her ear. They’d come from one of the back rooms—each spot had a personal waiter. If the relief in the hostess’ eyes could have been turned into an elixir, it could have been sold for millions.

“Good news, Lady Saha. Another one of our guests, who hails from the same realm as you, has offered a spot at her table. If that’s acceptable?”

“Who is this mystery guest?” she asked with chin raised.

The hostess approached and spoke in a low voice. “Selena Thule, daughter of Dominion Thule. She’s a regular of our establishment.”

Her voice held pride mixed with exhaustion. The hostess looked like she’d run a marathon even though it’d only been a few minutes.

“I believe I have heard of this Thule. Very well. If it keeps me from having to look at your disgusting human bodies during dinner, I will allow it.”

During the walk to the back room, the adrenaline high of simultaneously making a scene and being taken supremely seriously hit the wall of realization that she would be face-to-face with her mother. It was one thing to play a part for people who knew of the maetrie only in stories and rumors, but her mother had lived in the Eternal City for decades. The only thing that would make this easier was that Lady Saha had been gone on her liebereisen for longer, and the time away would have made her less maetrie-like than most.

When the door opened, Pandora strode through like a queen. Her mother was sitting with a trio of guests, but Pandora barely acknowledged them. Selena wore a golden dress that matched the modification to her arm and head. She looked more like an android than half-maetrie, the chalky gray skin coming off as metallic.

"Lady Saha," said Selena with the off-putting smile that was common in the Eternal City. "Won't you join us for dinner? It would be lovely to visit with someone from the old country. It's been years since I've been back, I would love to hear about recent events."

"I'm afraid I cannot help you," said Pandora sourly. "I've been on my liebereisen for many decades and have only passed through the Eternal City as a way station. The machinations of the courts bore me. It is personal achievement that I value most, not the wielding of power accumulated by someone else."

Selena's mouth twitched with amusement. "Then you picked a

wonderful time to visit the city of sorcery and the Savage Heights. Please join us. I think you'll find this encounter quite productive."

Pandora let out a sigh, trying to keep it from being so deep as to be insulting. She took a spot across from the others and Kuma joined her in the seat next, completing the final two spots at the table.

"This is my body servant Aman. He pledged himself to me on the plains of Brodaria after I bested a warpriest of Ghoghali in individual combat."

The blonde woman to Selena's right whistled appreciatively and spoke in a French accent. "I am quite familiar with the Brodarians. It's something of a personal interest of mine."

Pandora hid her grimace. If the woman wanted to talk about the Brodarians, it might expose her lack of knowledge.

"My apologies," said Selena, inclining her head. "Let me introduce my guests. This is Sandi LaFleur, head of Ares Industries. Her Montreal company is known throughout the realms for its superior weaponry, armor, and magical trinkets. To her left is Lee Travic, owner of Acoustic Excavation, and finally, Barry Williams, who heads the Global Banking Institute. We were catching up on some mutual business interests."

The gentleman, Lee, looked the least suited for the table, staring into his napkin as if it were the latest football game. His suit was expensive, but lacked the stylings of the others, unlike Mr. Williams, who had rich brown skin and a patina of shorn gray hair on his mostly bald head. He looked like the kind of guy who hadn't had a single meal under four figures in decades.

"Maybe I have something that might interest you," said Sandi as she lifted a glass of pale liquid. "My company has a large cadre of mages from the Halls who design the most *wonderful* weapons."

She said the last part as if she were making decorative teacups, not weapons of war. The sneer wasn't hard to conjure. Her years in the clans had given her a different perspective than how people saw things in the light, and Pandora didn't want the woman to get chummy.

"I do not care for magical baubles. The most important weapon is the one who wields it. A proper practitioner can turn a piece of paper into a killing tool. I have spent my journey honing my skills in the art of battle."

The others looked equally impressed, while her mother let the corners of her mouth curl.

"Then what a prescient time to visit the city. You know my father of course, Dominion Thule."

"I think I've heard of him. A minor thug with a talent for survival who exists at the edges of the aphena."

The insult barely registered in Selena's eyes. "He has made himself useful to the courts for a long time. Maybe things have changed since you left."

"It matters little and is why I haven't bothered to return, except as transit."

"What brings you to Invictus?" asked the banker.

"Rumors of an infernal invasion had piqued my interest, but I was disappointed to find out that they'd been felled long before I could make it back. But since we're between wars in Brodaria and the giants of Illithusus have returned to the winter lands, I find myself without opponents to test myself against."

Pandora had been concerned about this part of the plan. Coincidence was never a good opening into intrigue, but the glee in her mother's eyes, coupled with the glances from her table companions, eliminated that worry.

"What a delightful time then to visit," said Selena, holding a hand up to her chest. "My father is holding a grand tournament in the Undercity in a few days' time. Great warriors from all over the realms are coming in hopes of garnering great prizes and being named Champion."

"I care not for prizes, and I doubt any of your pathetic cretins here could give me a moment's challenge unless it was one of your Patrons. I might find it interesting to duel this Invictus, or maybe one of the others I've heard so much about."

"I think you'll find this tournament to be to your liking. One of the aftereffects of the invasion was the discovery of faez crystals, hardened stones of magic, which under the proper usage can turn ordinary warriors into supreme beings of combat. I've seen them myself. They are quite exquisite in battle, or scrapping as they like to say."

"Sounds dull."

Kuma kicked her under the table, letting her know she'd overdone it. She glared briefly, hiding her expression as she took a drink.

"Perhaps I might be interested."

"My father would be quite pleased."

"When does this tournament start?" asked Pandora.

"You're in luck. Only a few days away. I could have my father put you up in one of the better establishments in the Terreno. It won't be anything like what's available up here, but it will be better than what you could find on your own."

"I spent years sleeping in ditches waiting for the next wave of battle. If there are no other accommodations, I will accept what's available," said Pandora.

"Wonderful," said Selena. "I'll send along word and prepare a space for you and your body servant."

"Aman is only my *body* servant. My weapon keeper, food taster, and footmen will require lodging as well. I would prefer to stay in the same extended suite. They can sleep on the floor if necessary."

"It shall be done." Selena rang a silver bell on the table. "Maybe we should order."

"I'll let you do the honors, since I know little of your world's culinary amusements," said Pandora.

She spent the rest of the evening asking her mother's companions questions, feigning interest in anything that was battle-adjacent, which meant that Sandi was the main focus of discussion. The banker tried to engage in conversation while the man on his left barely opened his mouth, looking out of place at the fine dining establishment.

"What does an Acoustic Excavation company do?" she asked, feigning ignorance.

Mr. Lee cleared his throat and fussed with his napkin. "We provide mining and excavating expertise."

"I assume this is more than a casual friendship," said Pandora.

"I'm working with the Thules on a number of projects in the Undercity. Faez crystal mining and other ventures of interest in the more difficult places to access," said Mr. Lee, clearly uncomfortable.

"Is this Undercity a dangerous place?"

He swallowed. "Until the recent invasion it was much worse, but the faez crystals brought in more people and now it's not so bad, but still, one of my crew wandered too close to a restricted area and something dragged him into the shadows. They only found his left leg, half-chewed and covered in a glossy slime."

"That sounds delightful. I would love to meet the creature that did that." Pandora turned to her mother. "Will there be menagerie fights during this tournament?"

"The details have been kept secret, but I can assure you there will be twists as fitting for a grand event like this," she said, eyes sparkling with mirth.

At the end of the meal, Selena gave her contact information. Pandora left, motioning for Kuma to follow. He'd barely spoken during the evening, deferring any questions to her as he his station demanded. When they were back in the limousine, she slumped into the seat.

"That was exhausting."

"Exhausting? You looked like you were having the time of your life."

"I guess not being me made the difference, either because I had to throw myself into the role, or because she treated me differently. I was nervous at first, but it never felt like I was talking to my mother."

"At least it went well," said Kuma. "Hopefully the others didn't have any problems. We have a few days to get their disguises ready before we return to the Undercity."

The Undercity. Talking to her mother was one thing. But her grandfather, Dominion, would not be so easy to fool.

Six

The cavern floor vibrated with machinery, sending trails of dust from the ceiling. Camina waited for the excavation equipment to pass. The vehicles were compact, made for fitting in the tight spaces that existed the Undercity. She imagined if the digging extensions were tucked under, they could travel through the old Razor tunnels. Word was that they were bringing them in through the maintenance shafts near the Lazona.

Camina followed behind the equipment out of curiosity. She'd given the Alliance Academy students the day off, not because they deserved it, but because she was tired of the side brawls and constant mistakes plaguing their efforts. She felt totally inadequate as a teacher compared to Brazio or Duro or any of the others she'd trained with over the years. Intellectually, she knew her methods were sound, and it was the greenness of the recruits taken from the city streets without a speck of training and little ability that was the problem. But she also knew that Dominion was a demanding leader and eventually her failures would come back to haunt her.

So she'd taken a trip to the Terreno in hopes of finding a quiet bar and pouring herself into a glass, but the construction had made her curious. The series of caverns near the Terreno where Pandora and Kuma had dueled so long ago were being turned into the arena for the grand tournament.

The progress shocked Camina as the distant walls had been removed and the ceiling expanded upward another fifty feet. They weren't yet assembled, but she spotted stacks of pallets that looked like they would become bleachers. The central part of the space had been ground flat and filled with black and tan sand. Pillars, hanging bars, and other implements lay on the far side. When it was finished, she guessed it might be able to seat thousands, which was something of a shock, considering when she was a child in Razor there might have only been a thousand, maybe two thousand, people living in entirety of the Undercity. More and more were coming down all the time, and this tournament would be sure to increase that rate. The tunnels between Big Dave's Town and the Terreno were being widened and walled off from the other caverns, with guards stationed at regular intervals to protect the guests that would be traveling through them. There were other signs of construction, as one of the old apartments that doubled as a whorehouse had been torn down, a hotel called the Night House erected in its place.

"You can't be here," said a guy in a hard hat when he looked up from his clipboard.

"I serve Dominion Thule directly," she spat back, annoyed by his assumption.

"No," he said, pointing to a heavy crane rumbling in their direction. "You can't be here. We're putting up the gates to keep the curious out."

Grumbling, she returned to the Terreno, where the crowds had swelled in anticipation of the tournament. She spotted potential participants by their arrogant posturing and the way they surveyed the crowd. There were more otherworldly participants than she expected, but she'd been working with her idiot students nonstop, leaving her ignorant to the changes.

A pair of ladies in sequined dresses outside Club Onyx were beckoning people inside for a karaoke contest. Camina thought about seeing Leesa, but given the Terreno was busier than it had been on its craziest Shade's End, it was doubtful that the club owner was available.

A thick, orange-skinned Brodarian twice as wide as the people around him and at least a foot taller marched through the crowd with a serene smile that revealed his snaggletooth. She'd never seen a Brodarian up close, and he was as ugly as their reputation suggested, with a face that reminded her of a bulldog. She would have thought he'd have to muscle his way through but everyone parted around him as if they were water. Knowing the reputation of his race, she assumed he'd be a tough competitor.

After deciding to hit the Poinsettia, she circled past the Night House. An intense looking maetrie woman was entering, a retinue of bodyguards and servants trailing behind. The woman held herself like royalty and had the stride of a warrior. There was something about her that exuded danger. Camina froze for no reason. Something about the group was familiar. A slight woman carrying a backpack on one shoulder and a bag in the other hand glanced her way, sparking another twinge of recognition. But the woman went into the hotel before Camina could get a second look.

"She looked like Tick's sister if he had one," muttered Camina, but quickly decided it was either coincidental or her mind playing tricks on her. It made her wonder how her friends were doing. She'd heard about the confrontation with Deacon and was relieved they'd escaped. Multiple Alliance waku dead and Deacon's reputation damaged. He'd gone on a rampage afterwards, killing two soldados that had the misfortune of being in the wrong place.

She found a spot at the counter in the Poinsettia, annoyed by the well-dressed men and women sampling the smoke bar that had recently been installed. Alchemical smokes gave inhalers a variety of unique temporary experiences like hallucinations or weightlessness. It was one of the many recent changes to the Terreno, which was starting to feel more like the city above than the shadows.

The dark beer spiced with local fungi reduced the lingering annoyance at the back of her head. She was at the far end of the bar by herself, cradling her cold beer and trying not to hear the inane conversations going on around her.

"You're one of them, aren't you?" asked a guy in a gray suit who looked like he'd just stepped out of a corporate meeting.

"One of them?"

Camina gave him a "fuck off" look, but he was too inebriated to notice.

"From the gangs, a waku." He gestured to the RZR tattoo peeking out of her sleeve. "Right? That's a gang sign?"

"Clan, not gang," she said, turning her shoulders, but he didn't get the hint.

"What's it like?" he asked.

Camina sighed heavily. "What's what like?"

"You know, the stones. Is it as badass as it sounds? Flying through the air, being able to punch through a wall, all the crazy shit I heard you can do." He cocked a smile. "I'll buy you a beer if you can show me something."

"I'm not your fucking entertainment. Go find someone else to bother before I break your fingers off and shove them up your ass."

He held his hands up. "Hey, you don't have to be like that. It's a party. We're having fun. I just thought it'd be cool to get a sneak peek. I'll buy you two beers? Or an alchemical smoke of your choice?"

Camina grabbed him by the tie, squeezing it to cut off his oxygen. He started turning crimson immediately.

"We're not your fucking party tricks or entertainers. I learned how to fight so I could protect myself and kill my enemies. I was looking for some quiet and a nice beer or I'd have already gutted you with my blades and you'd be bleeding out on the floor, wishing you'd never met me. Touch me or talk to me again and I show you how quickly I can cut off parts of your body before you even realize it."

After she turned forward, the entire crowd shifted away from her. The guy in the suit quickly left with his friends. Camina threw back her beer, finding a fresh one waiting when she set the glass down. Despite the constant dangers and the threat of clashes between the clans, she missed the old days. Honing her skills was a matter of life and death back then, while now the young waku were only interested in posturing and looking cool for their friends. Despite only being a few years older, or sometimes quite younger than her trainees, she felt ancient in comparison.

The stupid grand tournament was bringing in more tourists from the light who didn't respect their ways or why they'd existed in the shadows. Living in the Undercity hadn't been by choice. Their families had escaped from those that had preyed on immigrants, finding the dangers of the darkness easier to deal with than the gangs of the city. Now they were being trotted out like jesters and fools, expected to dance for their coin. The worst part was it'd been her idea. But she'd been thinking about a way to hone her students' skills and bring in better recruits. But this tournament wasn't even for the Alliance waku. Only outsiders were meant to enter, and the quality of participants meant that the best would prevail. None of it made sense to Camina, especially giving away valuable stones. Unless Dominion's plan was to turn the Undercity into a tourist destination, but that didn't seem right, given the maetrie's background. Dominion had other goals in mind, but Camina had no idea what they might be.

"Another," she said, waving down the bartender. Figuring out the motivations of the clan leader wasn't her intention as she sipped from her beer, but she couldn't think about anything else.

Seven

The welcome party was being held in the central area of the Terreno where he'd watched Brazio duel the Viper with the black diamond so many years ago. Pandora hadn't wanted him to enter the tournament, but he thought it was better that they both join to increase the chances of figuring out what Dominion was up to, and having a chance at the prized bloodstones.

The space looked nothing like it did even a few years ago. Twinkling lights had been strung up around the walls, and a glittering ball spun lazily at the center. Kuma grabbed a drink from a server, but didn't sip as he surveyed the competition. There were at least a hundred and fifty present, maybe more because he assumed not all would attend, hoping to keep themselves a secret until the tournament began.

Kuma reached for his spike mace, forgetting that weapons weren't allowed. Or fighting. The tournament documents they'd been made to sign upon entering had explicitly warned against brawls outside of their scheduled matches. Doing so could disqualify them, depending on the severity of the infraction.

The crowd was impressive. Kuma shifted through them, purposely staying aloof as not to invite conversation. He needed to get a reading on their competitors. While the tournament was only half of their plan, acquiring the bloodstones would make them individually more formidable and better placed to oppose Pandora's grandfather.

The majority were human with maybe a dozen at most hailing from other realms. Everyone looked formidable, though some more than others. He spotted at least two minor movie stars who were clearly looking to burnish their credentials. Others he knew from when he was younger and they watched pirated videos from the internet. They were either self-taught martial artists, or had some supernatural backer that allowed them to utilize magic.

Then there were the ex-military competitors, men and women in fatigues or the black garb of combat gear. Mercenaries. He spotted both

Blackstone Security and Phoenix Corporation badges, and a few others he was unfamiliar with. A tall, powerfully built woman with bright red hair wrapped into a braid looked like she could wrestle a lion with ease.

Kuma suspected there were Hall mages in attendance. Probably from Assassins Hall, or Protectors, though they were cagey enough to know not to reveal their background. After the first round, everyone would know what everyone was generally capable of, and that would make the later fights more interesting.

"Greetings, mortal. You wear the colors of the priesthood," said a thunderous voice from behind.

Kuma looked up into the face of the single Brodarian in attendance, cursing his luck that the sigils of his outfit had been recognized. Expecting this might happen, he'd read up on the Brodarians but feared his shallow knowledge wouldn't be enough.

"The Lady Saha bested the priest and named me her body servant," said Kuma, touching his fingers to his shoulders. "For siege and sign, I am Aman Crownline."

The creasing of the eyes made Kuma fear he'd been exposed, but the tall Brodarian repeated his gesture.

"For siege and sign, I am Noctus Prime of the Eighth Tower. Your lady must be a formidable competitor if she could best a priest of Ghoghali."

"I hope you have the opportunity to kiss her blade upon the bloody sands, Noctus Prime."

Noctus leaned back, letting out a deep belly laugh that brought concern from those nearby.

"Well said, Aman. How did you come to be pledged to the priest? You look like a Cossack, not the human trenchers that live in the outlands."

"My mother was a member of the Golden Helix."

"The Helix!" Noctus exclaimed. "I fought with them on my left flank in the battle of the Divine Canyons. I remember their captain, Latisha, the Siren of Battle. She was a great beast of a woman with a banshee scream that could freeze her enemies in place. I admit I fancied her, but our tents never crossed. Who was your mother? I knew many of the Helix."

A great pit opened in his stomach. It was even worse luck that Noctus had known the Golden Helix. Unless it was a lie and he was being tested. The Brodarians were known for their cunning and strategic minds, and were constantly testing each other, hiding their intentions and strengths behind their outsized personalities.

"Diana Khant."

"I think you're lying to me, Aman," he said, laughing heartily. "Which fills my heart with the joy of battle. A worthy competitor, one who knows the ways of my realm. I wonder if your mother was Latisha, but your look is different. Maybe one of her Maidens. You have a secret fighting technique? What is your weapon?"

"The dire mace."

There was no harm in admitting it since he would see him fight long before they might be matched.

"A brutal weapon. I fight with a single angerblade and chain shield," said Noctus. "It is good your mistress is allowing you to fight. For only in battle can we truly be revealed. Once this tournament has begun, you should join me for a ceremony of haflwyer."

"It would be my honor, Noctus Prime."

The Brodarian patted him on the shoulder, which was like getting hit with a sledgehammer.

"Keep your weapons sharp, *Aman* Crownline," said Noctus, holding a grin in his teeth as he drifted into the crowd.

The way he spoke had Kuma worried that Noctus had figured out that he wasn't really who he said he was. If he didn't know yet, he'd know at the ceremony. Kuma was aware of haflwyer, a tea-like substance that was drank before a battle, sometimes between the generals of the two sides. Haflwyer was an intense narcotic that came from their world and grew in the fields after battle, nourished by the blood of the fallen. The surface readings of the tea ceremony mentioned the ritual was passed down from warrior to warrior. The priests of Ghoghali were the originators of the event, which meant he should know how to perform it. Theoretically. By asking for the haflwyer, Noctus was signaling he knew, or at least guessed, that he was lying about his identity. The ceremony would confirm it and he had no plausible way to refuse it, as it was a great honor. By offering haflwyer, Noctus was suggesting they were at least close to equals. For the Brodarians, it was less about honor and more about strategy. They were famous for calling chess a child's game. Accepting the invitation was the first salvo in their little war, one that Kuma had not come here to fight.

Eight

The ringing of a bell brought everyone's head around. At the far end of the old dueling grounds, a well-dressed Dominion Thule ascended a stage, looking strangely ebullient with a smile that could curdle milk at a hundred paces. It'd been two years since Pandora had seen her grandfather. He'd mocked her in that back room, informing her that their plan had only helped his cause, which had proved correct. Now he was in complete control of the Undercity, flaunting his little empire with a grand tournament. There were no guards around him. Titus Cabone hadn't been spotted yet. She wondered if she could make the stage and finish him off before someone could stop her.

It wasn't just a question of tactics, or ability, but will. Could she kill her own flesh and blood? Was she truly a maetrie in body and mind? The thought remained in her throat like a jagged rock.

"Good evening, competitors. Welcome to the Terreno, the Vegas of the Undercity, though try not to let the comparisons grow too similar. What happens in the Terreno can and will come back to haunt you," said Dominion with a playful smirk that she would never have thought he could pull off.

To Pandora's surprise, the crowd laughed. The threat wrapped in a joke mattered little to the competitors. Like all high achievers, they thought the downsides wouldn't apply to them. Much as the heads of the Alliance clans thought they were bringing in a silent backer, not a murderous city fae who would eventually dispose of them. Realizing she was scowling, Pandora softly patted her hands together and gave her most derisive smile.

"For decades, the Undercity has been a home to the shadows, a place where literal evil lurked in the form of demons that slipped through the barrier from the Infernal Realm. The invasion changed everything. Not only because of the discovery of the faez crystals, but in the plugging of that passageway. No longer are we beset with teeth and claws in the Undercity. It is becoming a safer, better place for all."

Pandora couldn't quite understand the message. She'd thought it was an opening to the tournament, not a politician's stump speech. She checked around to see nodding and smiling. It was only when she realized there were cameras filming Dominion that it made sense. The competitors were not the only ones in the Terreno. There were thousands of tourists, many of them quite wealthy and influential. He was speaking to them.

"When I ended the bloody wars between the clans, I was able to usher in a new era of peace and prosperity. Without the constant fighting, we've been able to invest in the Undercity. The three jewels of the shadows, Big Dave's Town, the Lazona, and the Terreno, have grown because of these changes. And the unique ecosystem, combined with the heavy influence of faez, has brought in researchers from across the world to study its caverns and understand how such a place was formed. We're embarking on a new world, one in which we will no longer have to fear the shadows."

The transformation was remarkable. She knew her grandfather. Not as well as her mother, but she'd been around him at the estate. He was a stern, emotionless figure. Not unlike the rest of the maetrie. But clearly his decades in the city of sorcery had taught him how to speak to the men and women of this world.

"This tournament is not only a grand competition, a way to showcase the talents of realms in the warrior arts, but it's an announcement to the world that we are no longer a place to be feared. It's why I've agreed, with much reluctance, to offer great prizes for the top eight finishers of the competition." He smiled congenially at the crowd. "Please take your drinks and follow me to the arena, where we'll witness a demonstration. Everyone, please join us. Even you watching remotely in the Terreno. You're all welcome."

A great murmuring grew as they headed out of the old dueling grounds, funneling towards the gates where the competition would be held. While she'd been working on making herself more maetrie, her grandfather had been doing the opposite, except he had no human blood to lean on. She didn't believe it for a second. He was ambitious as the maetrie queens, but without their resources, which made his paths treacherous. It was why he'd come to the city of sorcery so long ago.

When she went through the gate, Pandora couldn't believe the size of the space. She recognized the cavern as being the place where she and Kuma had dueled, but there was little remaining from before except a pair of stubby stalactites. The back walls had been knocked out, connecting multiple spaces into a single enormous arena. The ceiling had been extended upward, turning it dome-like. They were led to a set of bleachers.

The non-competitors flooded in behind them, taking the other seats. The arena appeared to be able to hold many thousands of spectators, but only a quarter of it was filled at the moment. When she'd dueled Kuma, there'd probably only been a hundred people watching. The growth was startling and it would only get bigger. She was starting to see what her grandfather was building, even if she suspected this was only the surface reason.

The urge to stay in back was strong, but Lady Saha wouldn't hide, so she leveraged her way through the crowd until she was at the front. Dominion's eyes creased with recognition and he gave her an imperceptible head nod. She responded to the gesture, even as she worried that her disguise had been penetrated.

The arena floor was a mix of black and tan sand. A few short pillars dotted the area, but weren't significant enough to impact strategy. Unless they were going to put down a surface overtop, the shifting material would make people move slower. Pandora considered a half dozen techniques she might employ to take advantage of the terrain.

"I see by your faces that you're surprised at the size of the arena. I assure you this is only the beginning. We have casinos, hotels, and other attractions planned in the near future. This tournament will be a celebration of—" Dominion paused, clasping his hands. "Excuse me. I don't want to spoil the surprise quite yet. I assure you that it will be exciting.

"But for now, please enjoy this demonstration. I think you'll quickly understand why the bloodstones I'm putting up as prizes will be quite sought after."

From somewhere behind Pandora, someone muttered, "If it's not a black diamond, I'm not sure I care."

She had similar thoughts, but was keeping an open mind. While the black diamonds were most desirable, their extreme rarity made them nearly impossible to account for. The only one she was aware of was the one that Deacon had. At most, she imagined there were a half dozen in circulation, but probably less.

Applause startled Pandora back into the moment as two men and one woman came speeding into the arena. Their blurred movement was familiar. A trick that a topaz or well-trained opal could master. But when they skidded to a stop, she sucked in a breath at the tall, lanky blond-haired waku to the right of Dominion. Navos. She resisted the urge to look for Choo-Choo in the crowd. They'd known that Navos was alive, but no one had seen him in a long time.

Navos wore the emotionless mask of duty.

When Dominion gave them a nod, the three waku flipped into action, each going their separate ways. They moved about the arena at great speed, leaping distances of thirty or forty feet and landing as light as a feather. They moved like they had multiple stones, but she knew that Navos only had a sapphire, at least before the failed raid.

The woman stopped before one of the thick wooden pillars. She had tight curls bound into a bunch, pale skin, and freckles across her nose. She went through a series of kicks and punches at high speed, making great leaps and kicking over the pillar, which was ten feet high.

Then she landed and struck the wooden pole with her fist, sundering it in half. The crack echoed through the cavern, bringing a collective inhale, followed by whistles and applause.

A topaz might be able to knock down a pillar by ramming into it with their shoulder, but she didn't know any waku strong enough to break a pillar of wood a foot thick with a single punch without shattering their bones into splinters. Either it'd been pre-broken, or the bloodstone was truly the master stone of the faez crystals.

Her amazement was furthered when Navos and the other waku met at the center, attacking each other with ferocity. She knew fake fighting when she saw it, and this wasn't it. They were striking at each other with speed and precision while barely upsetting the shifting sands. When Navos caught his opponent with a side kick, he flew through the air, skidding across the sands on his back. The arena erupted in more clapping, followed by Dominion raising his hand. The three waku stiffened to attention, bowed, and disappeared as quickly as they'd arrived.

"I hope you enjoyed this demonstration. As you can see the bloodstone is the most powerful faez crystal we've discovered thus far. It can turn an average warrior into a superstar, and it does it instantly without the attunement issues, making it the ideal faez crystal."

The head nods and agreeable muttering from her competitors told her that they were excited about the prospects of acquiring one. Most of them had joined to earn a faez crystal, after which they'd probably return to the light and use their demonstrable abilities to make themselves famous. Dominion's choice of the word "superstar" was well-placed.

"Tomorrow the tournament begins. There are over two hundred competitors, which means we'll split the arena into four separate spaces until we've whittled you down to a more manageable number. Feel free to walk the floor to get a sense of the sand, but know that things will be changed up for the later rounds, so don't get too comfortable. Lastly, the matchups are listed on the other side, but remember, no fighting outside the tournament or you'll be disqualified."

The entire group surged onto the sands as soon as he'd finished speaking, some of the younger competitors jogging over to the banners listing the matchups that were unrolled on the far wall. Pandora moved slowly and deliberately as Lady Saha would, displaying a mask of annoyance to keep the others from speaking to her. She thought for a brief moment that Dominion was going to approach, as she was the only maetrie in the tournament, but then he shifted towards a group of businessmen and -women who were clamoring for his attention. Relief flooded into her limbs at not having to interact with her grandfather just yet. She knew the time would come, but she wasn't quite ready.

The sands were soft and shifting. She crouched down and rubbed them between her forefinger and thumb. The tan sands looked like they'd come from a beach, not that she'd ever been on one, while the black pieces were smooth and uniform as if they'd been manufactured, not dug up. She wasn't the only one testing the place where they'd be setting their feet. Dressed in a black martial arts uniform, a massive gentleman with gray-touched hair was putting himself through a series of kicks and punches. She could tell even at a glance that he was holding back, making himself deliberately slower. A few others happened to be watching him, smirking with the idea that they were superior to him, but she knew better. They'd be in for a surprise if they fought him. After reviewing the state of the floor, she headed back to the Night House without bothering to check the lists for her opponent's name. For one, Lady Saha wouldn't care as she would consider herself superior to everyone else in the tournament, and two, her body servant Aman would acquire the information. Pandora left the arena first, feeling many eyes upon her stiff back.

Nine

Choo-Choo was last to return to the suite at the Night House. He knew he should have returned earlier, but he couldn't get over the shock of seeing Navos after many years apart. It wasn't even the way the former Drops had performed in the arena, his abilities far beyond what they'd been before, but how he'd looked completely blank. Choo-Choo knew that he'd probably been concentrating on the demonstration, but it seemed like something was missing from his friend. Or maybe it was because they'd spent their entire lives together and he was used to Navos' optimistic outlook.

The door opened after he knocked, revealing a disappointed Yara. He almost didn't recognize her even though he'd been the one to help her put on the disguise, because his mind was so busy reviewing Navos' appearance.

"Where have you been? We thought you got caught or something," she said when the door closed.

He tapped on his ear, but she shook her head. "The blockers are turned on. It's safe to talk."

The others were in the living room of the suite. It looked like they'd been in discussion already.

"Was there a problem?" asked Lady Saha/Pandora.

Choo-Choo had to blink away the urge to genuflect, reminding himself that it was his friend beneath the stern gray-skinned exterior.

"No, I was just..."

"You wanted to see Navos again," said Vasilisa as she fidgeted with her fake hand.

He collapsed on the couch, pulling off his wig and tossing it on the floor. While they'd paid stacks of cash to have facial modifications from a mage who worked on the rich and famous in the city, growing hair in that short of time wasn't an option.

"I wanted him to recognize me." Before they could admonish him, he held up a hand. "I know, I know. We're not supposed to contact anyone else, but I couldn't get the idea out of my head."

"We don't know who's compromised—either they've switched their loyalties naturally, or they might be under compulsion like Garret," said Pandora.

"I'm not going to put us in danger," said Choo-Choo. "I ain't no wayhos."

Kuma tossed him a beer and crouched next to the table. "Anyone feel like they were recognized? Do we need to make other modifications, or you feel like you're good?"

"No one gave me a second look," said Choo-Choo. "Even when there was almost no one in the arena, I walked by a couple of older guards from before the consolidation and they treated me like everyone else."

"Same for me," said Yara, who had blonde hair and looked Caucasian rather than a Japanese-Brazilian mix.

"You look like you should be named Becky," said Tick, chuckling as he stroked Koro's back.

Yara extended her finger as she threw herself on the love seat on the opposite side.

"Thoughts on the announcements?" asked Pandora.

"You're the expert on your grandfather," said Yara. "You tell us."

"On the surface, it sounds very logical and business-minded. The investors he brought down looked like they were salivating over the idea of building up the Undercity. The laws of the city don't apply here, which means they can do whatever they want as long as they don't draw too much interest from the Halls.

"The tournament is exactly what we think it is. A way to put the region on the map. And he gets some recruits from the publicity and maybe a few idiot competitors that decide to sign up. The bloodstones, however..."

"Yeah," said Kuma. "They were more impressive than I thought possible. It's like they're a topaz, emerald, and some black diamond in the same stone. That girl should have come away with a broken hand when she punched through that pillar. Give one of those to someone who knows how to use them and you'd be in trouble."

Nods of agreement were lost on Choo-Choo because he hadn't noticed. He'd been watching Navos the whole time, wondering how so much had gone wrong and if it'd ever be safe to talk to him again.

"If we could get a hold of those bloodstones for ourselves, we could do real damage to the Alliance," said Kuma.

"It can't be the only reason for the tournament. Anyone see anything else that stuck out?" asked Pandora.

"What if it is?" asked Yara. "What if your grandfather's gone legit?"

"Never," said Pandora, shaking her head vehemently. "Power is everything to the maetrie. If you're not cheating, you're not trying. There's something else going on. Maybe it's not in the Terreno. He's working with that excavating company, a big global bank, and a weapons manufacturer. There are probably others. He's not cultivating those relationships for fun. He has something in mind and we need to figure out what it is."

"Do we know where the excavation company is working?" asked Vasilisa.

"No, but that's a good question," said Pandora. "We need to find out."

"I don't think slinking around in the shadows is possible anymore. As soon as we got caught they'd probably figure out who we really were," said Choo-Choo.

"Not that way," said Pandora. "Yara got one thing right about my grandfather. He may not really be *going* legit, but he needs to appear that way. He's clearly courting the business side of the city of sorcery. If there are answers to be had, it's with them. We need to make connections."

"We're warriors not spies," said Choo-Choo.

"I can be a spy," said Vasilisa right away.

Heat rose to Choo-Choo's cheeks, and she gave him an apologetic smile.

"No, you're right, Vasy. I can be a spy too. If that's what's necessary."

Seeing Navos had affected him more than he thought. It was strange. They'd been in the Undercity for years attacking the Alliance and it was the first time he'd seen his best friend. The entire thing felt off.

"What are you going to do?" asked Yara. "It's not like you can ask them *hey, what are you digging down here?*"

"She's got a point. Questions along that line would be suspicious," said Kuma.

The group hung their heads, even Pandora, who he thought would have more answers.

"What if we wanted to open a business down here?" asked Tick.

"That's not what Lady Saha would do," said Pandora. "I've made it clear she's a wandering warrior on her liebereisen. It's a good idea, but it'd look suspicious."

"Then it can't be Lady Saha asking the questions," said Choo-Choo.

"It's too late for that," said Kuma.

"No, it's not. We've still got a lot of cash on hand. Why not leave and come back as someone else? An investor, or potential business partner. Give us a reason to ask questions."

"A mining supply company," said his sister, sitting up and snapping her fingers. "I know a lot about supplies and logistics. I could bore you for hours about everything I know about it."

"I don't know," said Kuma, shaking his head. "Sounds risky. Wouldn't it be easy to uncover that you're not really a company?"

"We wouldn't talk to Dominion. Only the other businesspeople, who aren't going to have a reason to dig into our pasts," said Choo-Choo, nodding at his sister. "Unless you have a better idea."

"No, it's good," said Kuma. "Wishing we would have thought about it before we came down, but it shouldn't be hard to go back up and change."

"We'll contact Dane. He can help with new backgrounds," said Choo-Choo.

"Now that's decided, we need to talk about the tournament," said Pandora. "Who are we fighting tomorrow?"

Kuma leaned forward, placing his elbows on his knees. "I didn't recognize the names, which wasn't a surprise. I'm matched against a Marvin Teller, an MMA fighter who I guess is a world champion in his weight class. I don't think he'll be that difficult unless he has some supernatural abilities up his sleeve."

"And me?" asked Pandora.

"Lee San. No idea about him. Should we send Yara and Tick out to find out more?" asked Kuma.

"Lady Saha wouldn't bother. I'll go in blind, but I'm not worried. If I can't beat some random unknown warrior, then I shouldn't have come back. But during the fights, we'll need you two quietly studying everyone, marking their techniques and everything."

Choo-Choo stood, gesturing towards his sister. “We should go. We have a lot of work to do before we return.”

“The tournament should last a few weeks at least, so don’t rush back. You need your disguise to be shadow-proof,” said Pandora.

Ten

Lady Saha did not attend the opening ceremonies for the grand tournament. Only when it was time for her match did Pandora arrive in the arena looking bored and disdainful of her surroundings. The truth was much further from that false-reality. As she met with the attendant before her match, a wave of unexpected nervousness hit.

I survived two years in the Eternal City, I can win a single match.

Logically, she knew she was right, but when did logic ever weigh in on affairs of the heart? This was more than a reckless plan to take down her grandfather. Her whole life seemed to weigh on the balance of the fight. She covertly checked around the arena, almost expecting him or her mother to be there as if they were proud parents.

As she set aside her extra clothing and stepped onto the sands, she tried to imagine what her father would say to encourage her, but it'd been so long she couldn't remember what he sounded like. The only images she could conjure were of him standing in the kitchen with a spatula, making pancakes.

"Lady Saha?" asked the match judge.

He was an older waku, probably thirty years old, wearing the uniform of the Alliance. Her opponent was watching her strangely, and not only because of her maetrie heritage. She hadn't realized the judge had been speaking to her.

"Get on with it."

"But you haven't agreed to the rules."

Rules. She didn't remember him speaking. Not a good way to start the tournament, but she recalled the papers she'd signed at the beginning.

"Yes, yes. Fight until someone is unconscious, taps out, or leaves the arena voluntarily. I'll try to make this quick," said Pandora offhandedly.

"No killing," said the judge, eyes darting. "You signed the waivers."

"No *purposeful* killing," she said, letting a toothy grin reveal itself. Her opponent, to his credit, did not flinch or look away.

The judge stepped back and her opponent bent at the waist. It would have been proper to return the gesture, but she was Lady Saha, not Pandora, so she flicked her fingers in a dismissive gesture.

"Begin!"

Pandora fell into the casual fighting stance that Hylakane had taught her. Her opponent brought his fists up in an open, upward style that she assumed came from the kung fu lineage. While the clans in the Undercity had borrowed from those techniques, they differed in brutality, focusing on quick kills with a blade rather than extended fights.

Lee San shifted forward like a sidewinder snake across the desert sands. The technique was well chosen for the environment as the shuffling foot made for a solid foundation. A sapphire Push would have been the easiest counter, but she was not Pandora, nor could she give away the presence of her stones. She brought her arms forward in a sweeping wing attack, mimicking the wraithhawk's final wingbeat before landing. The maneuver was a hair late, missing the apex of Lee's ridge-handed puncture strike, knocking them both backwards.

Pandora was disgusted at herself. If she were back in the Eternal City, Hylakane would have knocked her to the ground for her failure. Lee San smirked, a sign that he felt he wasn't outmatched. At the edge of her vision, she realized their match had the largest audience. Fellow competitors along with the business crowd were watching with interest, because they'd probably seen her as a top challenger.

Distracted by the murmuring of the crowd, Pandora almost missed his second attack. Her left hand mistakenly went for a blade while her right managed a deflecting block. They danced through another four moves, and while he never landed a blow, she had to retreat three spaces. When they broke, standing apart for another pause in the fight, she sensed the crowd growing disinterested. They'd thought they would see her demolish her opponent. It wasn't that she couldn't. Pandora was certain she was vastly superior, but she'd let the weight of the moment tangle up her instincts. Now, the only question was how Lady Saha would respond.

When Lee surged forward, he moved surprisingly quick. To the casual observer, it appeared that his technique was flawless. But she saw the gap near his right hip where his arm was protecting his flank improperly. She could have stunned him with a kick, but realized that she couldn't just win. She needed to dominate the match decisively, or Lady Saha would lose face.

Using her opal, she sped past his attack, and rather than hit the obvious target, Pandora struck his knee. Lee went down with a great cry of pain. Before he collapsed, she struck him across the jaw, his eyes rolling into the back of his head and his body hitting the sand with a thud. She turned and bowed to the crowd, ignoring the match judge's attempt to grab her arm for a victory raise.

She stalked away, heart thundering in her ears as the crowd glared at her. She played the part of the villain and they would hate her now.

It hadn't been her intention, but she'd fallen into it instinctively to keep anyone from questioning her Lady Saha persona. Pandora circled the Terreno, the adrenaline from the fight coursing through her veins. Was this how her mother felt? She played a part to keep her grandfather happy? Or did she truly believe in his vision?

Kuma's match was an hour later, but Lady Saha wouldn't care, so she returned to the empty suite. Yara and Tick were observing the other matches and taking notes. The silence angered her, so she went in search of a drink. It was early in the "day" but the bars were packed with visitors. She'd never seen the Terreno so busy, not even on Shade's End. The Amber Glass seemed the least annoying place, so she went in, finding a spot at the secondary bar in the back. To her surprise, they carried arosenthe, which she threw down her throat the moment the bartender passed it over.

"Are the drinks to your liking?" asked a voice from her right.

Pandora turned, readying a volley of verbal spite. She found herself face-to-face with the dark-haired waku who was now one of her grandfather's lieutenants. She knew Deacon by description mostly, but it was easy to see that he'd spent time in the Eternal City. The realm etched itself on the soul, scarring it in ways that went beyond the injustices of the flesh.

"It is not terrible."

Deacon smirked, gesturing towards an empty stool. "May I join you,

Lady Saha?"

She almost missed that he'd switched to her grandfather's language.

"If you dare."

He gave her a cocked grin.

"You must work for Dominion."

Deacon inclined his head. On the surface, he didn't seem to be the cocky traitor that she'd heard so much about. The Eternal City had changed him.

"I serve him as he sees fit."

"As you should," she spat.

"I spent time in your realm."

"I'm not blind," said Pandora. "The city leaves its mark on all."

"It was more than a visit. I trained there."

"They must have felt pity on you."

Deacon rocked on his stool, not quite laughing, not quite angry.

"In a way, I never felt as at home."

Pandora gestured at the bartender for two more shots of arosenthe.

"Then you're a fool. They all are."

He raised an eyebrow. "I heard you were unusual, for a maetrie."

"My greatest enemy is myself," said Pandora, sliding the other shot to Deacon. "They squabble over rubble while I seek perfection."

"I saw your fight. It was decisive."

"It was a farce."

Deacon threw back the shot, never losing eye contact. She matched his gesture.

"I'm sure you'll find greater challenges later. There are many formidable competitors. I would have liked to have joined it myself, but Dominion forbade us from the competition. He didn't want anyone to think it was rigged if we won."

"You think training in the Eternal City makes you special?"

Deacon flexed his fist, shattering the thick shot glass. His hand was bloody but he made no move to stop the bleeding.

"I didn't come here to measure dicks with you," he said.

"Then why did you come?"

"I was curious. Except for those in Dominion's retinue, and a few mercenaries, I've met few other maetrie."

"Kavano."

"You know him?"

"By reputation only," she said. "He carries one of the Tears. It's hard not to know about him."

Deacon reacted strangely, checking back to the bartender rather than matching her gaze.

"Will he be in the tournament?"

He shook his head. "Kavano hasn't been here in years. My boss no longer needed his services. For now, anyway."

"Must have been quite the job to require his expertise. Even I would not dare to challenge him. There is possibly no finer."

"That's what I've heard," said Deacon. "But he was here while I was in the Eternal City, so I never got to see him fight. That's one of the reasons I watched you."

"Without a Tear, I am a pale comparison."

"Are they really made from…?" Deacon lowered his voice. "Never mind. I shouldn't be talking about them."

Pandora couldn't figure a reason for his reluctance, but decided Lady Saha wouldn't care. Deacon rose from the stool.

"I must get back to my duties, but I saw you and wanted to make an introduction."

"For you, or your master?"

He smiled, but it never reached his eyes.

"I'm sure we'll be in touch."

Deacon strode out of the bar as the crowd parted, leaving Pandora to ponder the meaning of the visit.

Eleven

The second time down the long ramp that led from the Goblin's Romp to Big Dave's Town was a different experience. The first time, she was a servant in Lady Saha's retinue, wearing simple clothing and hauling overstuffed duffle bags. Now she and Emilio were dressed as lighters, their faces modified by sorcery for a sum that seemed astronomical, especially since it was the second time in days.

"Quit fidgeting," she said to her brother, slapping his hand as he tugged on the tie around his neck.

"How do they wear these? It's like a noose."

"It symbolizes their slavery to the corporate world," said Vasilisa.

"But we own our own business."

She shrugged. "Better to fit in. Your hair looks ridiculous."

"Shut up, Vasy."

He fussed with the new wig, which was curlier than before. She extended her left hand, which was only an illusion, extending her middle finger. The cuff on her left wrist provided the enchantment, which would interpret her moods accordingly. It was better than the prosthetic that she wore on their first trip, but it would be harder to remember.

The traffic on the ramp was busy. Two golf carts full of people passed them on the upper half. Vasilisa waved down the third, handing over a folded bill for the ride.

"Headed to the tournament?" asked the guy driving the cart. The left half of his jaw had silvery scales and his left arm was wrapped in a cast, but she knew it wasn't an injury. Like a lot of residents of the Undercity that had chosen to live in one of the settlements, they did so to get away from the normalcy of the light. She didn't know if the driver had been cursed or was the recipient of a nasty spell, but it wasn't polite to ask.

"Yes, but not to watch," said Vasilisa, hugging her backpack in her lap.

"What kind of business?"

"Excavation and mining logistics," said Vasilisa, handing over a card. The driver read it while navigating around a group of drunken college students who were drinking from plastic cups as they descended.

"Molly Franks. You look pretty young to own a business," said the driver.

"Magic hides a lot of age," she said with a wink. "My brother, Adam, however, is as young as he looks."

Emilio elbowed her, eliciting a chuckle from the driver.

"Been in the Undercity before?"

Vasilisa shook her head. "No. Anything I should be worried about?"

"Now? Nah. As long as you stay to the settled areas, you'll be fine. Not like it was when I first moved down here. The Alliance expansion has made it as safe, or safer than the city."

"That wouldn't be hard," said Vasilisa, nodding as if she understood.

When they reached Big Dave's Town, the driver dropped them off near the tunnels.

"This is as far as I go, but the Alliance has transports from here to the Terreno, which is where the tournament is."

The wait for a ride from Big Dave's took longer because a crowd had built up. Emilio stayed quiet. He looked like he was working hard not to fidget, which made her smile. They weren't the only people in suits waiting.

"Stop looking so glum, you're scaring people off," said Vasilisa in a whisper when some of the crowd moved away.

When the cart arrived, she and Emilio were stuck on the back. An older gentleman blocked them from climbing into the seats. Vasilisa had to grab her brother's arm when he moved to force his way through.

"This sucks," he whispered as the cart zipped through the old Razor tunnel.

"Can you at least not glower at them? We need to talk to them. If you're scaring them off, this isn't going to work. We're not going to get any *business*," she said.

The Terreno was packed when they arrived. It felt strange to return for a second time in a week with an entirely new disguise, but unlike the first, no one was staring at them. Lady Saha had drawn attention, while they looked like most of the other tourists in attendance. They found a room at one of the smaller hotels.

"Not that way," she told her brother when he moved towards the arena. "That's not our battle."

He stayed on her hip as they entered the Arcanix Club, a newer hostess bar. They were greeted by a woman in a skintight aqua outfit, but Vasilisa informed her they would stay at the bar. The woman was disappointed, as the bar wasn't where the club made its money.

"Looks like they've copied off the Onyx," said Emilio.

She elbowed him hard, and he was about to retort, but he seemed to remember they weren't supposed to know about the Terreno. Her brother shrugged and said, "I read about it a few days ago."

With a drink in her hand, she surveyed the other guests. While she'd never gotten to go to the Onyx, she knew the stories well. It was strange to see an Undercity club filled not with waku and soldados, but tourists and business folk.

A group of three younger men in suits were laughing at the end of the bar, eyeing the hostesses and speaking too loudly about the woman singing karaoke on the stage. Vasilisa took a deep breath and approached them.

"Hey," she said when one made eye contact, the prepared introduction leaving her mind the moment she reached them.

A guy with a bright lime drink gave her a once-over. "You're not a hostess."

"Of course not. I'm here for the opportunities. What about you?"

He nodded towards his friends. "We're here to find some strange."

"Strange what—"

The meaning hit the moment the words left her lips. He started laughing and sipped his drink, leaving her to storm back to her brother, cheeks burning.

"Want me to punch one of them?"

Vasilisa threw back a big swallow of whiskey. "I wish. Fucking lighter wayhos."

"Language," said Emilio, smirking.

"Fuck, I know."

After a half hour at the Arcanix Club, she realized no one was there to talk business. They moved to the High Shadow, which had the quietest music playing on its speakers. After ordering drinks, she leaned back and observed, trying to make herself approachable. Emilio was clearly trying to do the same, but it was like painting a bull to look like a cow. No matter the colors, the horns were still easy to see.

"I'm gonna take a walk around," she said.

In the busy bar, she wished she had an amber to overhear conversations. She found an older gentleman with stylish gray hair swirling his glass of amber liquid and took position near the bar, acting like she was trying to get the bartender's attention.

"Is it always like this here?" she asked as she drummed on the bar.

He gave her a warm smile. "First time?"

"Literally just got here."

"Not at the fights?"

"Not why we came here," she said.

He held out his hand. "Arnold Peters. Dynacore Industrial Enchantments."

Vasilisa shook his hand, thankful her missing hand was on the left. Handshakes weren't the preferred greeting in the Undercity, but Dane had coached her about returning a strong grip.

"Molly Franks. My brother and I own an excavation and mining logistics company."

"Lot of that going on down here," said Arnold. "I have to say, the Undercity isn't what I thought it'd be."

"Heard from our driver that it's changed a lot recently." She lifted her drink. "What does Dynacore Industrial Enchantments have to do with the Undercity?"

"We provide secure protections for all manner of industrial projects. Our enchantments keep equipment from failing, excavations from collapsing, that sort of thing. We were the lead safety contractor on the rebuild of the Portland Zoo a number of years ago."

The way he said it suggested she should know, so she nodded approvingly.

"That's impressive. We're still small fish, but trying to grow. When we heard what was happening here, we put our business on autopilot and came here."

"Smart move. I smell a lot of opportunities," said Arnold.

"You have any advice? We've really grown on word of mouth recommendations, but that's taken a long time."

"Long time?" he asked with an eyebrow raise.

Vasilisa grinned before she took a long drink. "I wouldn't want to give away all our secrets."

Arnold laughed heartily. "Fair enough. Cultivating an air of mystery can be a good strategy. As for advice? They say the man to talk to is Dominion Thule, but fair warning, he's a maetrie. But not like some of the other city fae you may have met, if you've met any. I've heard he's lived in the city for decades, so he understands our ways."

"Talk to him about what? I know little about what they're doing down here, except mining for faez crystals. I was a bit shocked when I saw how big *this* place was."

"The mining operations are a good start, especially if you're into logistics. I'm sure they need more of that." He scrunched up his face and reached into a pocket, pulling out a business card that had scribbles on the back. "You know, I met someone a few days ago. She's in charge of the logistics around here. Maybe she could help you. The name's Elani Perez. Hard woman, but she knows her business. That much is for sure."

It took all of her self-control not to react when he said Elani's name. Vasilisa drank deeply to hide her reaction, relieved he was busy fussing with the card rather than watching her.

"Thanks, I think I can remember her name. Where does she work out of?"

The location he described was her old office in the Terreno. Vasilisa was surprised to hear Elani had been relegated to logistics work, but given the contractors Dominion was bringing in, they might not need her expertise any longer.

"Thanks, Arnold." She finished her drink and set it on the bar. "Before I go, just so I understand the situation, besides mining faez crystals and holding martial arts tournaments, what else are they doing down here? I ask because I've seen a lot of different companies, more than you'd need for mining."

Arnold checked around before leaning in conspiratorially. "Between you and me, Molly, I haven't the slightest idea, but you're right. There are a lot of weapons manufacturers in attendance. Or other companies that don't make sense. Which says to me there's more money on the line than it first appears." He gave her a wink. "Good luck."

Vasilisa grabbed her brother on the way out.

"Where are we going?" he asked when they were outside.

She checked the time, realizing that Elani's shop would likely be closed.

"Let's check out the tournament and then return to the hotel. I'm tired from the long day and want to get up early in the morning to see an old friend."

Twelve

Using a towel, Kuma squeegeed the sweat from his arms and neck. The fight had only lasted ten seconds, but he'd worked up a good lather. The applause had startled him. After a scrap in the shadows, the only thing he usually heard was heavy breathing and the moans of dying waku. His mind equated the physical effort with the strive to stay alive, and adrenaline rocketed through his body.

"That was impressive. Where did you learn that technique?" said a husky voice from behind. He'd heard the woman's approach, but was too busy reviewing the sequence to care. The balanced lightness of her steps suggested she was a warrior.

"On the plains—"

The answer died on his lips when he found himself staring at Camina from three feet away. Her short, dark hair was slicked back and the smudges around her eyes remained the same. He almost blurted out her name until he remembered he was Aman Crownline, body servant of Lady Saha.

Camina sensed his confusion and checked over her shoulder. Her mouth wrinkled.

"Is there something wrong? My apologies for bothering you after your fight. I'm Camina Tanaka, head of the Alliance Academy."

"You...you look like my mother's companion from the Golden Helix. I was startled by the resemblance."

"You mother was a mercenary?"

"She was." Not wanting to get caught up in history which he knew little about, he added, "You had a question?"

Camina startled out of introspection. "Your technique. Part of it was familiar, but the other half was quite foreign. Unexpected. You moved explosively and without regard to the counterattack."

Kuma inhaled slowly, but not because he needed time to formulate his response. Camina had been his friend since he could remember. He knew from the others that she was a member of the Alliance, but he wasn't expecting to come face-to-face. He wanted desperately to reveal himself, but knew that it would be foolish under the circumstances. While she'd passed along information that had helped them with Deacon, no one knew if that had been a trap. As head of the Academy, she'd clearly gained their trust.

"After this round there will be over a hundred competitors. Nearly all will have knowledge of their opponents going forward. There are at least three styles I could have employed that would have been more appropriate for my opponent's grappling techniques, but I found it necessary to win quickly rather than efficiently, to keep others from understanding my capabilities."

Camina's eyes widened with understanding. "That's wise."

"While Lady Saha has taught me fighting techniques and how to harness my inner power, it was the priests of Ghoghali that taught me to always understand the strategic nature of my choices. No fight exists on its own. Success plants the seeds of our future failures. The Brodarians have keen minds, capable of seeing dozens of moves ahead. I'm merely a novice and can only see a handful, but the necessity of my choice for this fight was obvious."

"I see," said Camina, slowly nodding. "I had not thought to the intricacies of a tournament. My history predates the Alliance's control of the Undercity. It was only important to win the scrap you were in, rather than worry about the next one."

Sensing an opportunity, Kuma spoke carefully. "I'm new to this realm and especially the Undercity. What was it like before?"

Camina stared at the wall. "Dangerous. Thrilling. Awful. To be a waku then was to feel like a knife in the dark. Always looking for your enemy, never knowing when the blade was coming for your back. Strangely, I miss it." She stiffened. "I'm sorry. I shouldn't be talking so freely, but I feel like I can admit things to you that I shouldn't."

The hope that the old Camina existed burnished his heart, but there were too many lurkers around to speak plainly.

"I am a stranger twice removed, once from the Undercity and then from the realm itself. Perhaps it makes it easier to speak to me."

"Or maybe I'm just looking for anyone to talk to," she said with a sad laugh.

He saw her hollow loneliness, the ache of losing everything from before. Stuck in the Alliance without friends, knowing that everything they'd worked for had been lost. He couldn't imagine. At least outside of the system, Kuma had hope, even if it was ill-conceived, because he was with Pandora during those trying times.

"Would you, and feel free to refuse, especially if Lady Saha would object, but would you join a training session with my students? The Academy has grown quite large and unwieldy. I fear I'm not able to instill the discipline required to make true warriors out of the chaff I've been given. It might help to have an outsider's perspective into the arts of war."

Kuma bent at the waist. "I would be honored. I will have to confirm with Lady Saha, but if you send a way to get in touch to the Night House, I will tender my response."

"Thank you, Aman."

Camina's face screwed up again, making him wonder if he'd messed up.

"Until then."

"May your enemies grow blind and your allies grow bold," he said, offering the traditional Brodarian departure.

Kuma watched the ongoing fights for a few minutes but decided he would rather return and find a meal. He hadn't been able to eat before his match, despite his confidence about winning. The changed nature of the Terreno made him feel like he was in a different place than he'd grown up. Far too many suits and dresses, way fewer uniforms. The Alliance had a smaller presence in the streets, keeping to the outside for security. It was the peace that his father had always strived to achieve. If it weren't for Pandora's insight into her grandfather, he might have decided the best course was to pledge himself to their clan. Niran had wanted to end the senseless killings and blood feuds, but the clans' intertwined histories had made that impossible.

No one was in the suite when he returned. He ordered room service and jumped in the shower, quietly amused by the ease of acquiring food after the struggles of the Eternal City. The others returned not long after he finished his meal, a roast cricket stew with ghost-eye mushrooms and a heavy spice that was unfamiliar.

"Last match just ended," said Tick as he tossed himself on the couch, whistling for Koro, who'd been hiding in the back room. The androgynous disguise made Tick the least recognizable of the group.

"What's wrong?" Kuma asked Pandora when he sensed her tension with his amber.

He'd learned that most maetrie had a resting scowl, and Pandora in her new guise was no different. He couldn't tell if inhabiting the persona had brought out her maetrie side, or if it was a trick of the change.

"I spoke to Deacon."

The casual vibe of the room stiffened like a student snapping to attention when the instructor walked in. A blade appeared in Yara's hand and she stepped towards the door expecting ambush.

"It's okay," said Pandora, holding her hand out flat. "He was curious because I'm a maetrie and he'd spent time in the Eternal City."

"You should have stabbed him in the heart," said Yara, frowning. "I know, I know. We can't blow our covers, but it would have relieved me."

"That's all he wanted?" asked Kuma.

"I know I'm not an amber, but I didn't sense deception. Though when I asked if this introduction was for him or my grandfather, he didn't respond, which is an answer itself."

"He'll come looking for you eventually," said Kuma. "Are you going to be okay with it?"

"I fear this disguise was a mistake," said Pandora, clasping her hands together tight enough to make her knuckles white. "It brings out the maetrie in me. You saw my fight."

"You put a lot of doubt in your future competitors with that result," said Yara. "You can be sure no one will want to be matched with you."

"But if I lose who I am, then this whole exercise was for nothing," said Pandora.

Kuma wanted to put his arms around her. He could see the tension in her furrowed brow. Hylakane might have trained her to be an alloy—the best of both her heritages—but training ended the moment one got punched in the face.

"In the unexpected meetings, add Camina to that list. She came up to me after the fight to ask about techniques."

"We saw," said Tick, stroking the back of Koro's neck.

"She'd like me to join her in training. I'm inclined to agree, but wanted to check with the group first."

Yara shrugged. "No issues here."

Kuma couldn't decide if he was excited or worried about a meeting. He missed his childhood friend, but so much had transpired in the last two years that he feared his emotions might interfere with their plans.

"How goes the scouting?" he asked.

"With over a hundred matches it was hard to watch them all, but I think we caught all the ones that were important," said Yara.

Tick pulled a notebook out of his pocket, licking his fingers and flipping the pages until he came to a stop. "The way we see it there are about twenty competitors that pose any threat of defeating either of you. The rest are chaff that you can easily beat.

"Of those twenty, there's a smaller group that should be your biggest challenges. The first is the most obvious—"

"Noctus Prime," said Kuma.

"Yes," said Tick, nodding. "Besides being seven feet tall and looking like he could punch through a brick wall, he's frighteningly tough and demonstrated as much in the first round. He had a challenging matchup, a grand master from Korea who was known for climbing Everest without gear or oxygen, and spent an hour at the peak doing handstands and other extreme demonstrations of his ability. The first thirty seconds of the fight, Noctus stood there laughing while the grand master threw everything he could at him. Kicks, punches, choke holds. He might as well have been attacking a pillar of steel."

"The Brodarians are known for their resilience," said Pandora. "Raised to fight from infancy, pushed to extremes during a lifetime of training. Like the maetrie, they live longer than humans, giving them the advantage of time."

Tick nodded. "He ended the fight when he grabbed the grand master's pinky. In a matter of seconds, the grand master tapped out. He left the tournament stunned."

"Hopefully we don't get matched against Noctus until the final eight then," said Kuma.

Tick flipped the paper in his notebook. "The next one to worry about is Valor Drux. Ex-military, MMA trained, heard he's a boat captain in Alaska when he's not teaching. From all appearances, he's picked up a stone or two. Topaz for sure, no idea if he has any others. I don't think he'd be an issue, except for the topaz. He made a mockery of his opponent.

"The third to worry about is a woman named Angel Chen. When she fought, half the crowd gravitated to her match. She appears to have supernatural blood. Her opponent was confused half the time, striking at empty air. Then there are the Botez twins, one male and one female though it's hard to tell them apart, who dismantled their opponents with blurring strikes. The assumption is they're Hall mages, but no one knows which ones. Maybe Assassins, or one of the other physical ones."

"Anyone else?" asked Pandora.

"We only watched one round. A few fights were quick like yours, which means we don't have a good idea of what they're capable of, but I can't imagine they're much worse than the five we identified."

"The next round is in three days," said Pandora. "Let us know how your meeting with Camina goes."

"And yours with your grandfather."

Pandora shook her head. "I don't think he'll contact me yet. He's waiting to see how far I progress in the contest. He won't care that I'm a fellow maetrie if I scrub out early."

While she was competing as Lady Saha, the way she spoke about him was as if it were her in the tournament. Before they'd returned, Kuma hadn't been worried about how Pandora was going to react to her blood relations, but now that they had, he saw pitfalls ahead.

Thirteen

The bell on the door rang as she entered the building, this time not as the owner, but as a woman looking for information to grow her business. Vasilisa had to remind herself that this place, for Molly, was entirely new. She craned her neck in all directions. The shelves had been moved into the front area, filled with crates of materials to be sent to the mines. For a woman of Elani's experience to be dealing with logistics had to be a blow.

"This isn't a shop," said a stern voice from the back. "This is Alliance business."

The bored way she repeated the announcement suggested it wasn't the first time people had wandered in, thinking it a place to buy trinkets or a place to find discount sex.

"I'm looking for Elani," said Vasilisa.

Her brother had stayed behind at the bar, worried that Elani might recognize him despite the disguise. Vasilisa felt more confident since she'd grown considerably since their last meeting, but as she stepped into view the icy glare of the former Drops maintenance head had her concerned that she would see right through the mask.

"You've found her, but if you're looking for new business, find someone else to talk to. I'm neither a business, nor am I looking to start one. This is simply a logistics hub."

The anger mixed with world-weariness had etched deep lines around her mouth and eyes. Vasilisa almost didn't recognize the older woman.

"I'm sorry. I recognize this is an imposition—"

"If you do, then get out."

"A moment's time—"

"Is a moment more than I have. The whiff of money that you think you smell in the shadows is really death. This place isn't for the likes of you lighters. I can offer nothing but heartache."

Elani returned to her bookkeeping, placing her pen to paper under the assumption that her dismissal had been enough to make the intruder leave. Vasilisa hesitated, not wanting to leave, but not knowing what to say.

"I still hear you breathing..."

The steps towards the door felt like failure. Vasilisa let her hand remain on the handle searching for a reason not to leave. Inspiration came like a bolt of lightning and the words were past her lips before she considered their wisdom.

"I met someone you know, a chance meeting, but it's how my brother and I learned the extent of what's going on in the Undercity."

The tightness of Elani's jaw told Vasilisa the impact of her words.

"Triana—"

"Quiet, girl," barked Elani. "That name is best not to be spoken here."

The older woman scrutinized Vasilisa, making her worry that her disguise might be pierced.

"How did you meet her?"

"A mutual friend sent me to her. I paid her well for her information. But she asked that I find you and tell you that she's doing well and not to worry about her." It was all Vasilisa was going to say, but then she threw in at the last moment, "And her children as well. Said they've moved on from the Undercity."

Tension broke from Elani and her shoulders slumped with a big exhale. Vasilisa was glad that Emilio hadn't come since it might have made recognition easier.

"It's as good of news as I've heard in a while." Elani stared hard before closing her notebook. "Fine. I'll speak to you. Briefly."

Vasilisa approached, nervously keeping her hands behind her back as not to accidentally give away the illusionary hand.

"My brother and I own a mining and excavation supply company. We're looking to expand and grow our business. We can provide cut-throat pricing due to some advantageous sourcing, but what I don't know is who to talk to or what exactly is needed. For obvious reasons, none of the businesses already working with the Alliance is willing to give up information."

Elani ripped off a piece from her notebook, then scribbled on the paper before holding it out. It crinkled in Vasilisa's hands as she accepted it, trying to make sense of the words on the page.

"Lee Travic?"

As she said the name she remembered he was one of the people at dinner with Pandora's mother.

"Acoustic Excavation. He's leading the special dig sites."

"Special dig sites? I don't understand."

Elani frowned. "Neither do I. But you wanted someone to talk to. He's your man. You're welcome to use my name. It doesn't mean much but it might help get an introduction."

"You don't know what they're digging?"

Elani gestured to the room of supplies. "All this is for the faez crystal mines which aren't complicated. Whatever they're digging for in the wastelands is much deeper and much riskier, requiring heavy equipment and arcane techniques we don't have access to." Her forehead hunched as if she'd said too much. "That's all I can tell you. You should find Lee in the Terreno at times. He stays here when he's not at the dig site, usually at Club Onyx."

"Thank you, Elani." Vasilisa hesitated. "And I'm sorry."

The older woman screwed up her face. "Sorry for what?"

Realizing that last bit had come from Vasilisa and not Molly, she added, "You seem sad. I hope things turn around for you."

She left before she had to clarify her comment, clutching the paper and wondering how they might gain an audience with the head of the excavation company. The interaction with Elani told Vasilisa that barging into a conversation wouldn't be enough. If this was a special operation, it was likely to be secret and he wouldn't bring in an outside company without careful vetting, which they wouldn't stand up to. If they were going to gain Lee's trust and business, they had to find a different way.

Fourteen

The arena had been split into two fighting areas rather than the four from the first round. Pandora strode into the space, careful to keep her resting disdain, which acted as a shield pushing people away who might get too close. She felt their eyes upon her back, curiosity about the maetrie warrior. The others had already reported the rumors about her fight, which were favorable considering her frustrations with her own actions. They'd interpreted the mistakes as toying with her opponent, which when she looked at the length of the match compared with most others, it made sense. Despite the missteps, she'd defeated her opponent in a third of the time of most matches. It was just that after years of training under Hylakane she had an obscenely high standard for her own actions, which made her understand how Duro and Brazio must have felt towards the end. When there was no one available to challenge you, the only person left was yourself.

The attendant dropped her clipboard upon Pandora's approach, keeping her eyes averted as she fumbled picking it up.

"Welcome, Lady Saha."

The woman had the delirious look that Pandora had seen in others around the maetrie, which made her begrudgingly agree that she had some small aura.

"Is that my opponent over there?" she asked, flinging off her cloak to land gently on the chair. A collective exhale formed in the crowd, which consisted of a few hundred people.

"Yes. Dimitri Voldov."

The man opposite her was not unknown to her, because of Yara and Tick's scouting, but she wanted them to think she hadn't cared enough to bother. He wasn't in the top list to worry about, but close enough that the match had left her unable to eat that morning. But fear was not something that Lady Saha would experience, so she had to wall away those emotions behind a scornful mask.

As she removed the golden bangles from her wrists, setting them in a neat pile, she felt the intense gaze of her grandfather from a high station that overlooked the arena. He stood on a platform, surrounded by the Alliance waku who wore the bloodstones, including Navos. Pandora forced herself not to care, spinning on her heels and focusing on her opponent. Dimitri Voldov had worked for the Phoenix Corporation, and while his name wasn't identifiable as a member of Animalians Hall, that didn't mean he hadn't changed it. Even if he wasn't, the Phoenix Corporation worked across the realms, not quite as mercenaries, but rumors about misdeeds from its members made her suspect that Dimitri could be more than his appearance.

Pandora sized up her opponent as she crossed the sands. He didn't appear intimidated by her, which itself was a concern. Dimitri should be no match for maetrie of her reputation, especially after her first match. Dimitri had experienced a similarly quick fight, knocking out his opponent with an elbow to the jaw, followed by a choke hold. He'd shown no signs of magic, but that didn't mean that he wasn't capable. She had to assume she wasn't the only one holding back during the early rounds as not to give anything away. They'd agree not to use their faez crystals during the fights unless it could be done in an inconspicuous way, which meant she couldn't use her sapphire since its use was obvious. The opal, however, had become second nature and was invisible to the eye.

"Remember that you've agreed to fight until someone is unconscious, taps out, or leaves the arena voluntarily," said the referee. "No purposeful killing. If you're found to do so, you will be barred from the tournament."

The last part felt directed towards her. She made sure to smirk as the warning was delivered, but Dimitri never flinched, staring back with the intensity of a supernova.

As the start of the fight loomed, thoughts about the fight were overwhelmed with the presence of her grandfather. Even though it wasn't Pandora on the sands, but Lady Saha, she felt like it was the former. Either a responsibility as a maetrie, the need to maintain her disguise, or the weight of her grandfather's expectations—or all three—kept her distracted.

"Begin!"

Her hesitation was only a quarter of a second. Barely the blink of an eye, but in a fight that moment of time was an eon. Dimitri kicked up sand and, in the same move, thrust his hands forward, articulating his spell with dexterous fingers.

"Shayut!"

The air condensed into a misty shield of energy, slamming into her like a pickup truck. Pandora skidded across the sands on her back, a cloud of dust surrounding her. Dimitri flew through the air, his knee bent with the intent of crushing her head in while she lay prone. Pandora rolled out of the way, bringing her arm around to block the axe kick once he'd landed. She fought from her back, then thrust up when the space was forcibly given.

"Shayut!"

Dimitri tried a second time, but she was ready for it, anchoring herself with the sapphire. The force washed over her like a crashing wave. The secondary attack came from an awkward angle, since Dimitri had expected her to be further back. She used his momentum to spin him away from her in a tumbling crash. Using his Animalians marks, he got back on his feet before she could land a hit. He blocking the early attacks, but his magical speed was short-lived. Before he could renew the pace, Pandora caught him in the throat with a knife-hand. The rigid strike collapsed him to his knees as he choked for air while she paced away, annoyed by his failure to harden his weak spot.

The crowd had risen to their feet, watching as Dimitri collapsed onto the sands, tapping the ground frantically, which brought the medics into the arena. The referee stared at her fallen opponent until she called out, "Declare me winner or do I have to do that myself?"

After a quick arm raise, Pandora stalked out of the ring, snatching her red cloak while incantations brought Dimitri back to consciousness. She never saw her grandfather leave the platform, but he was standing along her path back to the Terreno, hands clasped behind his back like a benevolent ghoul in a pinstriped silk suit.

"You fight well."

"My opponent was a fool. He never should have entered the tournament. Hopefully there will be more challenging opponents in the next rounds."

The twitch of his lips marked his amusement. "My daughter told me about your chance encounter in the city and I was pleased to see your name on the lists. What will you do after the tournament?"

Sensing an opportunity, Pandora paused before speaking. "I have not yet decided. Perhaps I will lay down anchors afterwards, but that would depend on many things."

Her grandfather arched an eyebrow. "Keep winning and we can discuss options."

"And why would I want to work with you? Lady Kikala is quite fond of me and she is a maetrie queen. And while you're cunning and resourceful, there's not much for you to offer me in this backwater realm."

"I think you'll find the balance of power in the Eternal City has changed much since you've been gone. The Jade Queen was nearly assassinated a decade ago, and her prospects have dimmed since. Make no mistake about this realm—while it isn't the Eternal City, it has much to offer for those ambitious enough."

Before she could make a return quip, her grandfather marched away. Pandora continued into the Terreno keeping her hands hidden beneath her cloak because they were shaking from the encounter. While Lady

Saha might see Dominion Thule as a near equal, Pandora only saw her grandfather as a terrifying figure capable of anything. She went straight back to the Night House, throwing herself onto the couch the moment she entered the suite and burying her face in her hands.

Fifteen

The second round of fights were still in progress, but Kuma had a different priority for the day. A guide brought him from the Terreno to the main Alliance area by way of well-guarded tunnels. He was shocked by the changes when he arrived as the last time he'd been there was the assault on the complex. The space had been filled with hovels and ramshackle buildings spewing black smoke from cheap fires. Now it rivaled the Terreno or Big Dave's in neon signs, with dozens of new businesses built along the high walls of the narrow cavern, stacked on top of each other with metal stairs leading up at numerous points. Kuma had stayed the stoic warrior during their travel, but couldn't help asking questions of his guide when they arrived.

"The construction seems new. Is this true?"

The guide was a younger waku with a prominently displayed topaz stone in his right ear. Kuma thought the placement unwise as a savvy opponent could rip it out, but the Alliance had no obvious enemies left, so they were less cautious.

"Since Master Thule guided our clan to victory over the wretched Razor and Drops clans, the Undercity has prospered. We are honored to have him as our leader," said the waku.

Kuma didn't even have to ask if his guide had been around before, because he'd observed none of the habits long-term residents of the Undercity had, like pausing before entering new caverns, or checking the ceilings for predators or enemies. The kid—and while they were probably only a year or two apart in age, their experiences were vastly different—spoke more freely, giving information about the new additions and explaining the expansions happening elsewhere in the Undercity. Had their two clans not fallen into a war of attrition, this could have been Razor ushering in the new age in the shadows.

The Alliance Academy was adjacent to the main cavern. Newly constructed the year before after walls between smaller spaces had been knocked out, the area reminded him of the Drops Academy rather than

Razor. A large concrete pad was surrounded by low-roofed buildings where students stayed during training. Fungal gardens with ghost-eyes and hooded violets provided color between the paths.

Camina, along with her Academy students, was waiting for him on the concrete pad. A group of waku stood in two lines before her, while the hundred or so others remained on the bleachers surrounding the training area.

"Thank you for joining us, Aman," said Camina. "We're honored by your presence."

"The honor is mine. I am quite curious about the training methods of the waku."

Camina extended her arm towards the two dozen trainees on the field, then made a slashing motion. They broke into groups of two and started sparring using their fists and stones. Kuma placed his hands behind his back and watched passively. He wanted to watch his friend, Camina, rather than the waku, wondering how her years in the Alliance had changed her.

"These are your newest recruits?" he asked.

Her flinch was followed by a pained response. "These are the *top* students."

"My apologies."

"No need," she said. "You see clearly. I am a poor teacher."

"Tell me about your training program."

They strolled around the outside of the sparring matches. The cadence of shouts and impacts was blessedly familiar to Kuma, making him wistful for the days of old when honing his skills was the only thing he had to worry about.

"They start with simple exercises. Many of the trainees come to the Undercity without the physical tools necessary. After a few months of heavy work on their muscles, they begin martial training, followed by attunement at the sixth month. After that, their efforts are split between stone work and continuation of their fighting skills. This continues through the second year, after which they are placed into the ranks of the working waku."

"I do not believe you need me to tell you where your deficiencies are. Two years is barely enough time to learn how to throw a single punch if that's the only thing you worked on. I spent the first ten years of my life learning a single discipline while you're trying to teach them everything in two short years."

Camina's eyes closed momentarily. "Two years is all I'm given. Master Thule strongly requests that they complete their training in this time, but expects more output. I'm afraid I'm not capable of meeting his expectations, which is why I hoped you might provide an outsider's viewpoint on their training."

The compressed schedule made no sense to Kuma. When he'd joined Razor Academy, he'd had a dozen years of physical and mental training before his first day.

"This isn't training at all," he said, offhandedly.

His words had been instinctual, but they seemed to trigger something in Camina. She stared at the sets of sparring partners with a frown hooked to her lips.

"No, it's not."

Sensing the tension in Camina, he asked, "Would you like me to offer them pointers for improvement?"

"We would be honored."

Kuma approached a set of sparring partners, and after observing them, gave them techniques for improving their attacks. He was careful not to use terms or practices he would have learned in the Undercity, sticking to the quips he heard frequently from Hylakane. Most of it was too advanced for the trainees, but he didn't care if they learned a single thing. When he was finished giving advice to all present on the concrete pad, Camina sent the entire class away to be supervised by her assistant trainers.

"You must be quite disappointed in the quality of my students," said Camina as they strolled back towards the main cavern.

"That is not for me to decide," he said, keeping his arms behind his back. "Do you enjoy it here?"

The question surprised Camina. A half smile faltered on her lips. "That's not for me to decide."

Kuma felt her pain. He'd spent his entire childhood with Camina and had never seen her so subdued. He had to know if there was some of her old spirit left, or if the Alliance had ground that out of her.

"Understood. But if you had your choice, what would you do?"

Camina glanced around surreptitiously. "The life of a wandering warrior sounds romantic."

"Ah, yes, sleeping in ditches and learning how many realms have their own version of the mosquito is quite lovely."

"My apologies, I didn't mean to offend."

Kuma held his hand up. He'd forgotten it wasn't Kuma she was seeing, but Aman. His joke had fallen flat. "Nothing of the sort. I was just waxing on difficulties of not having a home. This tournament has been the most excitement I've had in the last few years."

"I would like to give it a try," she said.

They'd stopped in the tunnel. Camina stepped close. Her lips parted slightly.

"Are you…?"

The intent was made clear by the tongue resting on the bottom of her lips. Heat rose to his face as he thought about his friend Camina.

"I'm sorry," he said, stepping back. "While I'm in the tournament, I must save my energy."

Camina squeezed her eyes shut. "I'm so stupid."

"No," he said, placing his hand on her arm. "The fault is mine. I'm unused to such advances."

"Are you and Lady Saha…?"

Seeing a convenient way out of the awkward situation, he said, "We have on occasion to amuse ourselves on the long road, but we're not romantically inclined."

"Oh."

The sweet smile made Kuma wish he'd been more forceful in his rebuke, but he hadn't wanted to hurt Camina's feelings. They'd been friends so long, he thought of her like a sister and couldn't imagine being in bed with her. On the other hand, it might give them a reason to speak again and he wanted to find out if she could be trusted with their secret. He wasn't about to reveal himself yet, but he knew he wanted to. It hurt to hide his true self from Camina.

"I should return. My match is later in the afternoon and I must prepare my mind."

"Understood," she said.

Before he could turn away, she leaned upward and pressed her lips against the corner of his mouth, pulling away quickly and striding down the tunnel alone. Kuma made his way back to the Terreno, catching a ride on a motorized cart filled with Alliance waku on a break. He ignored their attempts to converse with him as he was too busy thinking about the reason why Dominion Thule was rushing the training of his waku. Why continue to recruit new waku if he wasn't going to properly train them? Either he no longer thought them necessary for the defense of the Undercity, or there was some other reason.

Sixteen

Walking into Club Onyx, Choo-Choo was struck by how loud it was. He'd been inside for hundreds of hours during his long sequester, but he'd never been in the club during working time, only after the customers had left. The place was packed. A crush of businesspeople and Alliance waku crowded around the bar. Every booth was filled with well-dressed hostesses and their clients, enjoying hand poured whiskey and casual conversation. Darina was on stage, belting out her favorite tune of "Come On and Pay Me!" to the delight of the men and women arrayed before her.

"May I help you?"

Choo-Choo found a familiar face in Aspen Wu staring up at him.

"Hey—" He screwed up his face. "I mean hello. I was looking for a friend who might be here."

"Oh," she said, half turning as if to lead him into the club proper.

"Lee Travic."

Her arm dropped. "I'm afraid he's in a private room and has asked not to be disturbed."

"He told me to meet him here."

Aspen deflated slightly. "I'm sorry. Mr. Travic has many business suitors who try to speak to him. He would prefer to enjoy himself in the privacy we can afford him in the club. Is there something else I can offer?"

Choo-Choo scanned the club for Leesa, but didn't see her anywhere. "I'll get a drink at the bar."

"Very well. Have a wonderful stay..."

"Adam Franks."

"Adam Franks." Aspen held out her hand. "It was lovely to meet you." She paused, tilting her head. "Have you been here before? You seem familiar..."

"First time. Sorry," he said.

Aspen left, but checked back more than once, making him worry his disguise wasn't good enough. He'd spent so much time with the hostesses of Club Onyx, they would more easily see through his disguise. He hoped that wouldn't be true for others. He'd had Vasy stay back at their hotel since the hostesses could be rather touchy, and if they figured out she was missing a hand, the whole disguise might unravel.

Reaching the bar took forever. He was used to being in the club without customers, climbing under the bridge, and making himself a drink. He wanted to use his topaz to push himself through the tightly packed crowd, but Vasy had told him not to use his stones under any circumstances or it would give him away. Once he had a drink in hand, he loitered by the stage, contemplating how he might gain access to the head of Acoustic Excavations.

Choo-Choo figured there were two places that he might be, either in the back rooms with one of the hostesses, or in a private room on the opposite side. He made a circuit past the sliding paper doors, using his amber to listen to their conversations as he feigned studying the architecture. The five private rooms were each filled with rowdy groups singing karaoke or having drinking contests. Two of them were clearly Alliance waku on a night out, while the other three were lighters. He'd half convinced himself that Lee had to be in the small rooms on the opposite side until he heard someone say his name. It sounded like he was entertaining his workers with the help of Leesa, which explained why he hadn't seen the club owner yet. As he was a partner of Dominion Thule, she was making sure he was treated with extra care.

The door slid open suddenly, giving Choo-Choo a glimpse into the room. He spotted Lee along with other tough looking men and women who clearly worked for him by their matching attire. Before Choo-Choo could move away, Leesa stepped out in a glittering silvery gown.

"Can I help you?" she asked as she closed the sliding paper door.

"Admiring the architecture."

Leesa gave him a flat smile. "Or perhaps you're wanting to speak to one of my guests who would prefer his privacy. I'll ask you to leave if you disturb him."

She brushed past and he blurted it out before he could think through what he was going to say.

"Leesa."

The way he said it must have been familiar, because she turned slowly, forehead hunched, then checked around them.

"Do I know you?"

Choo-Choo knew he had to choose his words carefully because in a world of waku, someone was always listening. Especially to the owner of the club.

"No. I'm new to the Undercity, but a friend said I should stop by and say hello. This was his favorite club, right up until the end."

"Who?"

"Doran."

It'd been nearly a year and a half since they'd rescued Leesa and the other hostesses from a group of rogue waku. He'd worried that she wouldn't remember his name, but she immediately tensed. Leesa stared at him as if she were trying to see inside his soul.

"I remember him. We haven't spoken since. Shame he never comes around anymore. We had so much *fun* back then."

"I'd love to reminisce, if you have time."

Leesa checked over her shoulder. "I have some things to attend to, but if you're interested, you can buy me a bottle of Lone Magus in an hour when I'm free."

"You can count on it."

The bottle was expensive, but they were still flush with cash after selling all the stones. He paid for the bottle, which brought a raised eyebrow from the bartender when he said who it was for. Choo-Choo couldn't sit still while he waited, putting back more whiskey than he thought prudent considering the situation. He hadn't seen Leesa since he'd revealed himself, which made him worry that she'd decided to turn him in for a reward. He had no idea how much the Alliance was paying, but he was sure Leesa could get anything she wanted for his life.

"Adam?" He turned to find Aspen smiling. "Come with me."

She led him into the guarded hallway. Two Blackstone security guards stood outside the runed doors. He stepped into an empty room with a bottle of champagne in an iced bucket.

"She'll be along soon."

When Aspen left, his heart rate soared. Had she lured him into this room to be ambushed? He thought about making a run for it, but decided that he'd already ruined his disguise with Leesa. He had to know for sure, even if it put everything in danger.

The door opening had him snapping into a fighting stance, only to see Leesa's concern.

"What are you doing back?" she asked once the door was locked.

"I don't want to get you mixed up with what's going on. You did more than enough before, but I need to find a way to get in tight with Lee Travic."

Leesa crossed her arms. "I know you don't want to hear this, but there's no point in continuing whatever you have going on. I'm not sure I want to help anymore. I felt responsible after you saved us from Doran, but I think my debt is paid. Things are going well with Club Onyx. I'd rather not screw things up. I almost didn't come back here. The only reason I did was I thought you deserved an answer."

He wasn't expecting her to refuse him. "I'm not going to screw things up."

"Where are the others? Are Tick and Yara lurking around here? Did you get your sister out? I was really hoping you'd stay up top, sell the stones you took and put the shadows behind you."

"That was our plan, but then we ran into some old friends," he said.

"What? Really?" Her eyes widened. "You mean…?"

"I don't want to say more, but I assure you that Dominion Thule doesn't have good intentions for the Undercity."

"You could fool me. He's done more for this place than all the clans before him. I know it was painful, but there's peace now. People are making money, having good lives. And this tournament has been a major boon. I've got investors who want to open another Club Onyx in the city. They love what I've done here."

"I get it. I'd probably think the same if I were in your shoes, but I really need to get in with Lee Travic. I'm not going to kill him or anything like that. I just want to find out what they're working on. His project has nothing to do with the faez crystal mines."

Leesa leaned her head back, moaning with frustration. "Why do I always want to help you? I must be an idiot."

"Because you know everything that's happened in the Undercity since Dominion Thule arrived hasn't been right."

"Do I though?" she asked.

"Can you help or not?"

Leesa pulled out a pocketknife, which made Choo-Choo put his hands up, eliciting an eye roll.

"Really? Like I'm going to do anything to you with this," she said, unfolding the blade and grabbing the bottle of bubbly, using the edge to break the seal. "I figure if I'm going to screw myself again, I'd better have a drink."

"We won't betray you."

"That's not what I'm worried about."

Leesa shoved the bottle under her arm and yanked the cork out. The loud pop was followed by the splash of golden liquid onto the table. She continued the pour, filling their glasses and then throwing it back before he could take a single drink. She collapsed on the couch and poured herself a second.

"Lee and his crew are careful not to talk about work around us. We laugh, sing karaoke, and play stupid drinking games when they visit. But once when they were deep in their cups, one of the crew babbled something about not wanting to go back to that bitch Persephone. Lee kicked him under the table, but the message was clear. I don't know what Persephone means, but maybe you do?"

Choo-Choo downed his glass, holding it out for a second pour. "Unfortunately, I do know what that means. It's not a person, but a company. Persephone Inc. It's an old company, predating the clans, that was searching for something in the wastelands to the southeast. There's old equipment near the canyons. The few times I know that my clan explored those areas, they lost people to creatures no one had ever seen before, or never came back."

"What's there?"

"No idea, but explorers have been seen heading that direction for decades. Few return. The lower areas are filled with massive colonies of tumblers, or the infernal creatures that never made it to the surface. If they're digging down there, they're probably looking for something old that was left, or purposely hidden."

Choo-Choo leaned forward, resting his elbows on his knees, cradling the champagne glass in his hands.

"What could they be looking for?" he asked.

Leesa tapped on her glass with a fingernail. "When I was a younger hostess, I remember the time I first met a maetrie. There were a pair of them. They'd stopped in the Terreno looking for a guide that was a regular. When they told him where they wanted to go, he refused and called them crazy, but then later on, I saw them all leaving together."

"It was the wastelands, I assume. Did you ever see them again?"

"No. Neither the maetrie or the guide."

"Do you remember their names?"

A short laugh slipped out. "I could barely keep my thoughts straight around them. But I'd never seen them before or since."

"Was this guide a mage?"

"Explorers, if I recall."

Choo-Choo leaned back on the couch. "This would have been about ten years ago?"

"About."

"I can only assume Dominion sent some of his lackeys into the depths. I doubt they found what they were looking for since he's got an excavation company working for him now. Or they found what they were looking for, but it'd collapsed and now they need someone to dig it up, but they couldn't do that before since the clans controlled those areas," said Choo-Choo.

"Are you suggesting Dominion only took over the Undercity to be able to dig for whatever was lost down there?"

"No. Maybe. Clearly the faez crystals are a huge prize, but maybe not the only prize." He sighed. "The more I learn, the more I understand Pandora's concerns about Thule's intentions."

"I don't like what this implies," said Leesa. "We've been through enough upheaval. I'm over it."

"What could it be?"

"You know as well as I do this place is filled with artifacts left by the early explorers from the Halls, or made by them in the secrecy of the shadows. Even the Alliance maybe only controls a third of the physical space down here now. The northwest and southeast sections are mostly untamed. Even if a fifth of the stories I've heard are true, this place is still a minefield of old magics."

"I need to take this back to the group. It's a lot to process."

Before he reached the door, Leesa said, "I'd stay away from Lee and his team. They're not letting anyone into their inner circle, and when they leave the Terreno, it's with a large cadre of Alliance waku. Good ones. Not the trash that they're promoting now."

"Thanks, Leesa. Take care."

"You too. Give them all my love. I miss the old days when you and Kuma wanted to kill each other. Things seemed much simpler back then."

Choo-Choo missed those days too, but he knew no matter how much he wanted it, they were never coming back.

Seventeen

Watching the second round of the tournament made Yara want to claw her eyes out, mostly because she knew she could beat ninety percent of the participants. Instead, she had to pretend she was just a servant for Lady Saha, observing and taking notes on her mistress's future opponents. At first, she and Tick had sat together, discussing their analyses until they realized others were listening in. So now they watched separately and only compared notes when they'd returned to the suite.

The match she was watching concluded with a knockout, eliciting applause from the crowd that was drinking and laughing. Yara didn't bother writing anything down since the winner wasn't remotely good enough to make it past the next round. They'd only advanced as far by being lucky with their matchups. It was strange to be sitting in the space that had once held the duel between Pandora and Kuma, but now was a huge arena.

The second round had revealed a few more interesting competitors, ones that had hidden their talents during the first round, much as Pandora's opponent had. Nothing significant, but as they went deeper into the tournament, those little edges would add up.

Yara checked back to the observation deck. Dominion Thule had been there earlier in the day, surrounded by his personal guards. He'd left an hour ago, but in his place stood a brooding figure dressed in all black. Deacon. The pen snapped in her fingers.

"Fuck."

The murderous urges she normally felt when she saw him were tempered by the results from their last encounter. Not only did they barely survive, but Vasy had lost her boyfriend when he'd gotten in Deacon's way. The idea that they could defeat him—considering his training in the Eternal City, the black diamond, and the strange metal attached to his body—had long ago left her mind. Maybe Pandora could now, but even then, Yara had her doubts.

That didn't keep her from staring at him across the bleachers. He seemed different from the last time they'd seen him. Thinner. Gaunter cheeks. Was he becoming like the maetrie? Or just not eating as much these days?

To her surprise, the black-clad Titus Cabone strolled into the cavern, climbing the stairs to join Deacon on the observation deck. It was the first sighting of the mercenary captain in a long time. His normally arrogant demeanor seemed tempered by annoyance as if events hadn't been going his way. She sent her amber in their direction, but the cheering crowd made listening to their exchange impossible. Yara moved from her spot, picking one closer in hopes of hearing their conversation, but by the time she got near enough, Deacon climbed down, shaking his head while Titus returned the way he'd come. She froze when Deacon headed not back to the tunnels that led to the main Alliance area, but towards her. He had his head down, mumbling to himself, so he didn't see her transfixed in his way. She managed to sit next to a rowdy group of drunken businessmen as he passed, then slipped in behind once he was a good distance ahead.

Yara knew it was unwise to follow him. Her disguise was good enough to fool casual observation, but if he suspected something, it'd be easy to figure out who she really was. But whatever had transpired between him and Titus made her curious. More than curious. She kept other tourists between them, using the way people unconsciously avoided Deacon to not lose him.

He went into Club Onyx. Yara hesitated outside, since it'd be more obvious that she was following, but she felt the risk was worth it. One of the hostesses she didn't know was leading Deacon to one of the private rooms when she arrived. Yara spotted Lee Travic, the head of Acoustic Excavations, inside with a bunch of men and women in company branded overalls.

"...the left side collapsed. Titus' men just came back. At least a half dozen injured, a few critically, and the retaining wall's no longer there. Two weeks of work down the fucking drain and you're here drinking and having a grand old time. Do I need to remind you how important this fucking job is to my boss? Fucked doesn't quite match the level that you're at right now with Thule."

"I'm sorry, we needed a break. This dig ain't easy. What with the wards, the guardian. Everything. It ain't been the simple project your boss made it out to be when he hired me. One of the hardest things I've had to work on, what with the conditions. Not sure I would have taken the job if I'd known the specifics."

"It's a little too late for that," said Deacon. "You'd better get your ass back to the dig site and find a way to make it through that wall."

"What if I can't? I never expected all that leftover sorcery down there. It's like trying to weasel out of a truth bond. It ain't happening. And six out? I'm already running a skeleton crew. I'm gonna need more workers."

"That ain't my problem. Get the fuck through that wall, or not only are you not going to get paid, but you're probably not ever leaving the Undercity."

Yara managed to step away from the sliding door when Deacon came bursting out, a murderous glare in his eyes. He went straight for the busy bar, which parted for him. She deposited herself in the crowd, working her way up to order a drink, casually spying on Deacon. Up close, he looked worse than expected. The dark circles around his eyes made him look thirty years older. As he drank his whiskey, he kept rubbing the part of his chest where they'd managed to blow off one of the metal attachments. Had that upset the magic that made him stronger? Or was it the enchantments from the Eternal City doing a number on his body?

A short time later, Lee Travic and his team left the private room, looking haggard and suddenly sober despite the litter of old beer bottles on the table that she'd seen when she caught a peek inside. Yara wanted to follow but decided it was too risky with Deacon on the prowl. He finished a couple of whiskeys and left Club Onyx.

As Yara finished her drink, she spotted a familiar broad-shouldered Choo-Choo leaving the private area with Leesa. While his disguise was solid, she'd spent the last two years with him and knew his mannerisms. There was no sign of Vasilisa, which meant he'd come to the club alone.

Yara followed Choo-Choo when he left, catching him in the hallway that led outside. He froze when he saw her.

"We need to talk."

Choo-Choo checked behind him. "I was thinking the same thing."

"Find a way into our suite without being seen. I know. It's a risk, but we have big things to discuss."

"I'll get Vasy and meet you there."

Yara waited a minute before following Choo-Choo out of the club, then headed straight for the Night House.

Eighteen

Pandora had been in the suite practicing her breathing exercises when everyone returned. As Lady Saha, she found it difficult to move around the Terreno without being the object of attention, so she'd stayed in the suite, relying on the others to figure out what was going on. Yara entered first, followed by two faces she wasn't expecting to see: Choo-Choo and Vasilisa.

"What the fuck are you doing here?" she spat angrily. "You're risking everything."

The rebuke washed over them as they glanced between themselves until Yara spoke up.

"We have to talk. Something's not right."

Everyone froze when the door opened again, revealing Kuma, who stuttered to a stop.

"Uh-oh. I assume this means something's wrong." He paused. "Where's Tick?"

"At the tournament. We'll have to catch him up later," said Yara.

Heat rose to Pandora's face. "This whole thing will blow up in our faces if anyone followed you here. We're being watched. At least by our top competitors, and possibly my grandfather. What could be so important as to risk everything?"

The flinches and hurt in their eyes told her she'd gone too far, but her veins were filled with hot lead and she needed to get rid of the heat somehow.

Kuma's face broke with sympathy. "Pan..."

Hearing her name rather than Lady Saha's reminded her that she'd fallen back into her maetrie ways. It was hard to wear another's skin and not become them, especially when the persona was one she'd been trying to avoid.

"Get on with it."

Over the course of a half hour, Choo-Choo and Yara went over what they'd learned about the dig site and Thule's past search for artifacts in the Undercity. When it was over, they looked to her.

"I know he collected them. That's it. Not much more than that."

"Come on, Pan," said Yara. "Don't hold back. You know him best. What could he be looking for?"

"Hold back? You think I'm holding back? You have no idea what it was like growing up under his thumb."

Yara staggered backwards as if she'd thrown a Push. The downcast looks from the others made it clear what had happened.

"Fuck," said Pandora, pacing towards the kitchenette. She scratched at the gray skin on her arm, wishing it'd peel away. When she returned, no one except Kuma would meet her gaze.

"He wants power. In whatever form it exists. I guess if the Undercity is filled with old artifacts left over from the early years of its existence, then he might be searching for something like that."

"We need to learn what it is," said Kuma.

"Like we weren't thinking that already," said Choo-Choo, frowning. "But after talking to Leesa, I don't think there's a way to get in with his crew."

"Sounds like there is," said Vasilisa. "Based on what Yara learned, they're going to be desperate for help."

"Are you planning on strolling down there and joining his crew?" asked Choo-Choo, crossing his arms.

"Something like that," said his sister.

"There's another thing going on with Dominion that I don't like." Kuma leaned against the couch. "When I met with Camina, she wanted tips on how to improve the training, but I told her there was nothing I could do. She's given two years to turn them into experienced waku, and these aren't like the old days. The trainees are fresh from the surface and not worth a damn. Why bring all these old gang members down here if you're not going to train them? Why does he need so many?"

No one answered. Pandora's stomach did backflips. She knew her grandfather was planning something, but she didn't have a clue to what it was. Was this about the Eternal City? Was he making a move there? Or was this about the city of Invictus? Dominion had never been one to reveal his plans, even to those closest to him. She wished she'd known some of this when they'd talked the previous day. Maybe she could have pried loose a fleck of information.

Their silence was interrupted when the door opened, revealing a disguised Tick. He took one look at the room.

"Uh-oh."

"Matches done?" asked Yara.

"Last one completed about twenty minutes ago, but that's not why I hurried back. They announced the new rules for the third round, which will start in two days."

"New rules?" asked Pandora, stepping forward.

"After the first two rounds, there's about seventy competitors left.

For the third round, it'll be a grand melee. Top thirty-two that survive move on."

"Grand melee?" exclaimed Kuma. "Some of the weaker warriors could gang up on the better ones, knocking them out. This could be a bloodbath."

Unlike the others, the announcement hadn't surprised her. The structure mimicked the cutthroat ways of the Eternal City, which she was well accustomed to.

"There's only one answer here. We need to find allies."

Nineteen

"This is a terrible idea," yelled her brother from the bathroom. "It's going to get us killed."

"Then you shouldn't have brought me down here," said Vasilisa, attaching the sheath to her calf and letting the pant leg fall over it.

"You think that's going to save you?" asked Emilio as he pulled a shirt over his broad shoulders.

"Better than not having anything at all."

"I still think this is a terrible idea," he said.

"I think I recall more than one story of yours that involved similar stupidity, so I think your opinion is rather flawed."

"Figured you'd actually remember those stories," he said.

"I idolized you. You were my big brother, one of the best waku of his generation. At least until Pan came along."

Emilio hesitated as he considered the bowie knife they'd bought in a Terreno shop. They'd agreed not to use any weapons that might tie them to the clans.

"Past tense?" he asked.

"I assumed you knew what the hell you were doing, but after the last two years, I realize that everyone older is just making things up as they go along."

Emilio wagged his eyebrows. "The illusion of adulthood."

"I wish someone would have told me," she said, throwing on her leather jacket.

"For the record, I still think—"

"I'll put it on our gravestones if you're right."

The wash of people in the Terreno was heavy, forcing them to fight through the crowd. The announcement of the grand melee had brought more tourists from the light. It was easy to pick them out by the way they stared at the glittering lights attached to the stone ceiling, or gawked at the Alliance waku striding through the passages. Vasilisa wanted to stop and tell them those idiots were posers, and the real deal was standing right beside her.

"Who are we looking for?" whispered Emilio in her ear.

"I'll let you know when I see them."

She led them near the eastern entrance, the one that came from Big Dave's Town. Two carts of tourists were unloading while talking too loudly and wearing too much perfume. Wearing anything that smelled in the Undercity used to be a death sentence as multiple critters hunted by scent, but those days were long gone. At least around the Terreno.

A half dozen Alliance guards looked bored at the gate, performing cursory checks for unauthorized weapons. Nothing more than a pocket-knife was allowed, unless they were a competitor. Vasilisa picked out the guards standing to the side, chatting quietly, and strode up from behind.

"Hey—"

The words died on her lips when they turned. She recognized one of them as a friend of Andy's. Her entire face went numb and the words trickled off her lips unsaid.

"I'm not a guide. Bugger off," he said, turning back.

Emilio put his hand on her arm to pull her away, but she shook him off.

"We need a ride."

The guard screwed up his face. "Do we look like the fucking ticket booth? The taxi between here and Big Dave's is over there."

"Not to Big Dave's. To the big dig in the south."

She heard Emilio's in-breath behind her, but ignored it.

"What the fuck did you say?"

The guard gestured towards the others and suddenly they were surrounded.

"I fucked up," she said.

"You're damn right you did. We might have to take you up north for some questioning."

Before her brother could do something stupid, she stepped in his way.

"We just got hired by Lee Travic. We're excavators. They have a problem and we're supposed to be joining the team, but my stupid brother forgot to set the alarm and we missed the caravan down there." She pulled out a wad of bills. "I'm paying for a guide and protection. Half now, half when we get there."

The anger on their faces turned to greed with open mouths and calculating eyes. The guy that had been Andy's friend, said, "I don't know. I don't want to get in trouble."

"You won't because you'll be dropping us off with Lee and his team. If we're lying, you'll find out then. Either way, you get a big paycheck."

The guards conferred for a minute before returning with an answer.

"We'll take you, but you have to listen to us, and if you do anything to put us in danger, I'll cut your throats and leave you for the predators in the shadows."

"Understood."

The guard pointed his finger over her shoulder. "Tell him to stop eyeing me or you're not even gonna make it that far."

"Adam," she said, pulling him away.

They settled on four guards to come with them, which told Vasilisa that the Undercity was still dangerous outside the guarded areas. The guards searched their backpacks and patted them down, but made no mention of their knives. The rest of it was standard exploration gear like headlamps, food, water, and nylon ropes.

Not long after they left the Terreno, heading south, the familiar darkness brought a sense of comfort and attention, and she returned to the habits that one learned growing up in the Undercity.

"Don't worry," said one of the guards to her brother when he spotted him checking the upper areas of the caverns they passed through. "You're safe with us."

The guards made hand signals, which were easy to interpret, despite the differences between the clans. She bugged her eyes out at Emilio not to react when they started talking about her ass and making bets about which one of them she'd take to bed.

Twice during the journey, the guards made them stop and huddle against the wall while two of them scouted ahead. She assumed one of them had picked up a noise with their amber. Emilio did a good job hiding that he had the same abilities, which she was thankful for, since he wasn't known for his subtlety.

The guards didn't take them by routes she knew, but after three hours of careful travel, they arrived at the dig site. Floodlights revealed large canvas tents. Generators hummed from another area while men and women in hard hats hurried around the space like cockroaches in the light, tension in their hunched shoulders and harried expressions. She spotted Lee Travic angrily gesturing to a group of workers.

"Here's your other half. Thanks for the guided tour. We'll check in with Lee now," she said, holding out the wad.

She knew they were in trouble when the guard was staring over her shoulder as he took the cash. "I think we'll wait and make sure everything's as you said it was."

Emilio gave her a look, but she responded with a tight shake of the head. They weren't going to get out of their situation with violence.

"Who the fuck are you and what are you doing on my dig site?" asked Lee, marching up, red-faced and looking like he hadn't slept in days. She assumed after a hard day of drinking, he'd hurried back and hadn't slept.

"We were sent here to help with the dig," said Vasilisa, holding out her business card. "Molly and Adam Franks."

Lee stared at the card as if it might be explosive. "Who sent you?"

She could feel the eyes of the guards who'd brought them on her back.

"Elani Perez. She sent us a message at our hotel that our services would be needed."

As soon as the guard spoke, she knew they were in trouble. "I thought you said you were expected."

"What's this?" asked Lee.

"She claimed she was expected at the site to help," said the guard.

Lee grabbed her arm and got in her face. He smelled like day-old whiskey.

"You better tell me who the fuck you are, or should I throw you over the edge? Tell me what the fuck is going on."

"Okay, okay," she said, holding her hands up. "I lied about Elani sending us here and that you were expecting us. We're new to the Undercity and hungry for business. We can be a big help."

"Sounds like bullshit to me," said someone to her left.

"No, it's not," said Vasilisa. "Think about it. Why else ask to be delivered right to you, Lee? I knew it wasn't going to be pretty, but I hoped we could show you that we can be valuable. We know excavation and we're pretty clever when it comes to new projects. We can be an asset. I swear. Give us a chance."

Lee glowered. His cheeks were bright red. "You're right. You *are* going to be a big help."

"That's great," said Vasilisa, exhaling with relief. "I'm glad you un derstand. I'm sure you were young and ambitious once too."

Lee gestured to the guards. "Grab 'em. We're taking them into the pit. They can help us figure out how to get past the wards. And if not, then they're not my problem anymore."

Twenty

"Lady Saha? Yeah, fucking right. I'd rather dip my dick in glass and jerk off," said the enormous warrior in black martial arts robes as he turned back to the rest of the group at the bar. The guy had to be at least five hundred pounds. Yara had watched his last fight. He'd grabbed his opponent by the belt, tripped him, and landed on him with his full weight, breaking ribs and leaving him unable to continue.

The others in his circle clearly didn't want to discuss alliances. As Yara shifted away, one of the women grabbed her arm. "We saw what that maetrie bitch did in the first two rounds. We're gonna put her out of the grand melee like she deserves."

Yara yanked her arm away from the woman, stalking towards the bar in frustration. It'd been the same everywhere she'd been. No one wanted to ally with Lady Saha, or Aman by extension. The brutality of the first two rounds had shown the competitors that she needed to be eliminated. The only bright spot was that it identified her as one of the top warriors in the competition. Which wouldn't be a consolation if they both got knocked out. If they were going to acquire a bloodstone, they needed to get into the top eight, which meant making it through the grand melee round.

After getting a drink at the bar, she leaned against the wall and surveyed the crowd, looking for competitors she hadn't already talked to. It was the third place she'd been that day. No one trusted Tick, and Lady Saha would never be seen inquiring for allies herself, so it was left to her and Kuma to find them.

She saw Deacon when she circled around to the back, finding him standing alone at a smaller bar made to look like it existed on an island. Something about Deacon elicited pity rather than anger. Despite his power, he looked reduced. Broken. The urge to speak to him overcame her fear of being identified. She'd fallen hard for him when he'd been a Crow training in Razor lands and when he'd betrayed them, she'd wanted nothing more than to gut him from balls to throat. As she approached, she feared some part of her still had feelings for him and wanted to find out. It felt like edging up to the precipice of a cliff, anticipating the vertigo that came with the view.

Deacon glanced up from his drink, forehead hunching with confusion as she approached. Yara's heart doubled in time. *This is the bastard that killed my family.* A part of her wondered if she could stab him through the heart before he could react.

"Lady Saha sends her regards."

The words came out of her lips unconsciously as if some part of her brain was trying to keep her from getting killed. She had to remind herself that she looked nothing like Yara with blonde hair and pale, milky skin. In fact, if the old Yara could see who she was now, she probably would have spat on the ground and tried to pick a fight.

"She sent you?" he asked, eyebrow raised.

"She's rarely so direct, but she did speak of you, which is unusual."

"You know her well," said Deacon, gesturing to join him at the bar.

"Not that long. She hired me after she entered the city. My name is Greta. I'm a professional assistant for mages."

"And a tournament scout?"

Yara let a grin rise to her lips. "I've a second degree black belt in Tae Kwon Do. I wouldn't, of course, last a single round of the tournament, but it was part of the reason she was willing to hire me. That and the grizzly bear trophy on my wall."

She was pleased how easily the lies flowed over her lips. It was the first time she'd had to use the backstory they'd come up with for Greta.

"You hunt?"

"I kill."

"I can see why Lady Saha hired you." He set his glass on the bar and nodded towards the empty space between him and the others. "You're not afraid of me."

"No offense, but I've worked with beings significantly more powerful than you."

"Probably not as fucked up," he said, flatly.

"Oh, you'd be surprised. Magic does a lot of strange things to people, either directly from the faez, or indirectly from the limits removed from their lives."

He placed the drink before his lips. "I'm not the same person I was a few years ago." Deacon closed his eyes briefly. "I'm not even sure I'm a person."

He looked away and she could see how gaunt his cheeks were in the dim light of the bar. He looked like a cancer patient deep into their chemo treatments.

"You'd be surprised how many of my clients have said the same thing." She cocked a smile, thinking about the years of hiding and battling the Alliance patrols. "Even I've had my moments, getting lost in the job, putting the needs of my clients above my own. You start to wonder where your responsibility ends and you begin."

Deacon held out his glass, and she clinked hers against it before throwing back the amber liquid.

"I want to have regrets, but that would only invite weakness." He shook his head, glancing at her through his fallen black hair. "I don't know why I'm telling you all this, but I feel like I know you."

"Maybe we knew each other in a past life," she said.

The familiar hunger in his eyes said she didn't have control of the situation. While their conversation was waking echoes of their past relationship, she had no desire to engage with Deacon again.

"Hey..."

Yara cleared her throat. "How do you find working for the maetrie?"

The question stopped his in its tracks, leaving Deacon briefly confused.

"I'm not sure what you mean?"

"How do you know if you're doing a good job? It's the one area Lady Saha is different than most. I never know what she's thinking. I always feel like she's testing me," said Yara.

"She is." Deacon stared into the distance, painful memories reflecting in his eyes, which looked black in the dim bar light. "Everything is unchecked competition to them. Everything is a test. If you're not climbing over the carcass of your friend, you're falling behind."

"Seems like your boss isn't so bad," said Yara softly. "I was pleasantly surprised when we got down here. I was expecting glorified holes as fighting pits, not Vegas underground. Much smaller obviously, but bright lights big city, nonetheless."

Deacon stilled. "Everyone's playing to win, but Dominion has an entirely different game in mind."

He looked like he had more to say, but he stared into his glass instead.

"I have to go." He rubbed his chest absently with the grimace of ache. "If you have time, maybe we could..."

"I'm flattered, but you know how demanding the maetrie are. I think firing would be the least of my problems if I blew off finding allies for Lady Saha."

"Good luck." He brushed past, gently resting his hand on her shoulder. "Be careful what you agree to with the maetrie. Every gift has a hidden curse."

Deacon disappeared into the crowd, leaving her alone at the bar. She contemplated his words as she finished her drink. Spending time in the Eternal City had burned the cockiness out of him, leaving him a pale shadow of his former self. But it wasn't just that. She sensed a finality to his outlook, which didn't make sense, given his position within the

Alliance and the clan's hold on the Undercity. Deacon should be jubilant, not a sullen, brooding warrior long past the ideals of his youth. The change in him, more than anything, left Yara concerned that they were missing the big picture in the Undercity.

Twenty-One

The Poinsettia felt different to Kuma than the previous times he'd seen the bar. When he was a young man in Razor, it was enemy territory, a building that he might spit on if he thought no one was looking. Later on when he first became a waku, he remembered the way the Drops leadership stood on the balcony, watching the duel between his uncle Brazio and the woman from Demon Dogs with the black diamond. He wondered what they were thinking about the fight. When he lost his clan and became a Drops, he never had the chance to visit and had thought the bar had likely been rebranded. Now, standing inside, it felt smaller than he expected. The bright flowers of poinsettias matched the décor of the interior, which had none of the nods to the Drops. Nor were there any waku with tattoos on their faces, or even Alliance uniforms. The bar was filled with tourists in suits and dresses, sipping colorful designer drinks. Even though the Drops had only been his clan for a short time, and had been his enemy for much longer, the commercial nature of the place felt like sacrilege.

It wasn't hard to find Noctus Prime. At seven feet tall, he stuck out especially when seated at a table covered in chessboards. Even if Kuma had been blind he could have found him, given the deep belly laughs coming from that direction as Noctus moved his pieces on three separate boards against different opponents. His ochre-brown skin glistened with sweat in the crowded bar. Despite his ugly mug, Noctus' eyes glimmered with fierce intelligence.

"Brother Aman!" exclaimed the Brodarian upon sighting.

"Noctus Prime. I didn't know you were a chess master."

The enormous warrior kept his eyes on Kuma while moving pieces on the boards, much to the frustration of the bar patrons who were clearly losing. A couple of them were conferring with their friends between moves.

"I learned the game a week ago. It's marvelous in its mimicry of war, though there are a number of flaws which make it limited in its educational properties. However, it's simple enough to keep me occupied between matches." He glanced down to the board in the middle, pushing a rook forward. "I believe this is checkmate."

A group of men in collared shirts erupted, consoling their representative with pats on the back. After a round of raised drinks, they left the bar in search of other distractions.

"A week? I find that hard to believe," said Aman.

Noctus raised an eyebrow.

"It's similar enough to a game we call Kings and Queens. Our board is larger and has more varied pieces, but I suspect they might have been influenced by each other in the past." He looked down at the board. "Ahh...checkmate again."

"Have you lost yet?"

"Earlier I played a grand master and he dismantled my position in fewer moves than I would have preferred, but his brutal attacks gave me a new insight into the game. I should hope to play him again."

"Not looking for allies?" asked Kuma.

"Preferably ones that won't attract overwhelming numbers," said Noctus.

Kuma kept his face neutral but he groaned inside. "So you've heard."

"Most of the competitors would prefer if your mistress were not in the competition."

"And they would you?"

"I'm comfortable with my position," said Noctus. He checked to their surroundings. "It appears my third opponent gave up. What an unfortunate result of my previous games. I was rather enjoying this one."

Kuma snorted softly under his breath. He didn't know much about the Brodarians, but from what he'd read, he knew they were cunning strategists. Tick had reported that during his fights, Noctus had stood motionless, letting his opponents attempt to injure him for a minute or two and then once he'd seemingly grown bored, he grabbed them as if they were a child and gently choked them out. Not only were his wins convincing, they would serve as a warning to all who might tangle with him in the grand melee. Kuma wasn't sure he could beat the Brodarian.

"We'd be a strong team," said Kuma.

"The goal isn't to win the round, but to survive to the top thirty-two."

Kuma exhaled. "You believe they'll ignore you for easier targets."

"In all battles, overwhelming numbers triumphs against quality, but if they choose me as their target, they will lose far more of them for the price of eliminating one opponent."

Noctus Prime watched keenly. Kuma sensed he was being judged, which meant the possibility of acquiring him as an ally was still open. But how?

"Interested in a game?" asked Kuma, gesturing towards the board.

"You play chess?"

"Not chess. Something else. If I win, you join our side," said Kuma.

The broad smile made Kuma think he was on the right track. "What do I get when I win?"

"Whatever you want," said Kuma.

"What if I asked you to leave the contest?"

"You wouldn't. That would mean there's a better chance of them deciding you're the biggest threat."

"Whatever I want... Having a maetrie warrior at my beck and call might be interesting. Maybe I'd ask you both to return to Brodaria and serve in my army," said Noctus.

Kuma bowed. "If that's what you wished."

"Very well. But what game shall we play? Care to wrestle with arms? Or perhaps a match of tako-blades?"

Kuma had no idea what the second game was and feared it was something he should know based on Aman's background. The other would be a quick loss as Noctus outweighed him by hundreds of pounds. The far window had a view of the outside. He caught the glittering lights of the Bogo through the gap.

"How about a game of pachinko?"

"Pachinko? The annoying rattle in those ugly lighted boxes?" asked Noctus.

"The very ones."

"There seems to be no skill with them. You would leave your fate to chance?"

Kuma shrugged. "Choosing a game that both of us know would mean one of us would likely be better, leaving the game to be the choice itself, rather than the contest. And since most of the games we might both know would come from Brodaria, where I know you'd be at an advantage, it seemed safer to pick a game neither of us have played before."

"Maybe you've been spending your time in these parlors and have acquired an advantage, Brother Aman," said Noctus Prime, his grin revealing bunched together teeth.

"Maybe."

"Or it would be smarter for me not to play at all if I believe that I would be stronger alone during the grand melee."

Kuma smiled. Had he not read about the Brodarians' penchant for battle in all forms—physical, mental, warfare, anything really—he might have gotten discouraged by the deflection, but he saw Noctus' desire to engage in a contest and refused to give up.

"If you thought you were stronger you wouldn't have considered my offer for a contest," said Kuma.

"Or I'm seeking information about an opponent, one who has given up much in this short exchange."

Sensing he was losing Noctus, he said, "Play a game of pachinko to decide who picks the game."

"Isn't that the same as winning based on your logic before?" asked Noctus. "Sometimes the best battles are the ones we don't fight."

The way Noctus stared at him suggested there was a second part to the line, one that he should know based on his history in Brodaria. Fearing that he was not only going to not acquire Noctus as an ally but expose his false history, Kuma bent at the waist.

"Your words are wise."

Kuma left the Poinsettia. When he stopped outside, he found Noctus by his side.

"I will play your game of chance, but the loser gets the opportunity to refuse the contest."

"Agreed."

Kuma almost offered his hand for a shake, until he remembered that Brodarians saluted each other by banging their fists together.

The pachinko parlor Bogo was noisier than he remembered. He didn't know how Tick could stand the racket. A third of the machines were occupied by men and women sitting in chairs, some smoking, nearly all drinking, holding a silvery dial that controlled the speed of the balls coming out of the machine. Boxes of pachinko balls sat by some of the players, while others had only empties. No one gave them a second glance as they were too focused on their machines.

He found two adjacent machines and put equal bills into them, giving both the same starting point.

"Whoever has more balls at the end of ten minutes is declared the winner."

"That sounds fair," said Noctus.

Settling before their pachinko machines, Kuma pointed out the clock on the wall. When the second hand was completely vertical, he said, "Begin."

Kuma grabbed the round knob that controlled the silvery balls' speed of being launched into the machine. He'd played a few times in the past, only as a curiosity, unlike Tick, who had an obsession for the game. The first ball sped into the vertical field, clacking through the nails, missing the scoring holes, and falling through the center, which meant he'd earned no new balls.

"Ha! This is easy," said Noctus.

Kuma saw a dozen silvery pachinko balls come streaming out of the bottom into a tray. Noctus had managed to get his first ball into a scoring hole.

Focusing on the game put Kuma into a trance as he adjusted the speed, and therefore the height, of the balls. They bounced through the field, jittering back and forth, until they either scored points or disappeared into the bowels of the machine. When he ran through his money, he took the tray of balls he'd acquired and dumped them back in.

Noctus was ahead of him, laughing gleefully as the pachinko machine made noises and lights. The ten minutes went by quickly. Kuma went on a good run, piling new balls in his tray until the final seconds counted down.

"End."

Noctus pulled his hand off the dial as the final ball slipped through the center. They drained their machines, placing the trays next to each other. After a careful analysis, Noctus announced, "I believe you've won, Brother Aman. That game was more intriguing than I would have given it credit for."

The idea that the Brodarian might be addicted to pachinko gave him amusement. He pictured Noctus Prime at the machines like the older players, staring into the bright lights like an automaton as silver balls flew past his vision.

"What game do you propose?" asked Noctus.

Kuma had an idea of the contest he wanted, but was afraid that Noctus might suspect the advantage and pass on it. He knew trying anything with detailed strategy would be in the Brodarian's favor, which left the simpler contests as the best option. The game had to appear fair on the surface while giving Kuma the better chance.

"A contest of swimming."

Noctus gave a belly laugh. "Not concerned that I'm a much better swimmer than the history my race suggests? Maybe I sought advantage by learning a skill that others did not possess."

"Then say yes."

"I pass," said Noctus. "While I can swim better than most, I know you humans are agile in the water. Next game."

"Tight rope walking."

"Interesting, but pass."

Kuma feigned deep thinking. He knew what he wanted the game to be, but knew that getting Noctus to agree would be challenging.

"High jump."

Noctus crossed his arms, cradling his chin in his palm. "Are you attempting to subvert the law of threes? I would assume you know this law, which means you're either baiting me by placing this choice in the most favored position, or trying to trick me. On the surface, it appears a fair contest. While I'm more powerful in the thighs, my weight makes the jump harder. What you don't know is that I fight with the single angerblade and shield because it encumbers me less, allowing me to make great leaps in battle, appearing where my foes do not expect me.

"On the other hand, humans are small and can leap surprisingly high despite their size. Yet, I cannot imagine that you could leap higher than twice your height, which puts me at the advantage." He smiled, revealing his mangled teeth. "I accept."

The arena was closed. They were making adjustments to the field in preparation for the grand melee. Kuma didn't want to reveal his abilities, so he led them into a cavern off the main drag. The Alliance guards started to deny them passage until Noctus put an enormous hand on their shoulders.

"How shall we proceed?" asked Noctus when they reached the secluded cavern.

Kuma spotted a wall of connected stalactites and stalagmites that reminded him of the structure he'd burst through in his duel with Pandora. The ceiling was at least forty feet high in that area.

"We take turns leaping, touching the stone as high as we can. Failure to jump higher means you lose."

"Simple enough. Who shall go first?"

"Since I won the pachinko game, I think it should be you."

Kuma didn't know if Brodarians required limbering up, so he was surprised when Noctus made a standing leap, touching a spot at least fifteen feet high. He landed surprisingly soft, reducing the impact by bending his knees and dipping into a squat. The gravel beneath his feet shifted with the shock.

The ease at which Noctus achieved that height made Kuma worry he'd picked the wrong contest. He wasn't sure how high unaided humans could jump, but he suspected that the Brodarian had leapt higher than any could on their own.

Kuma took his spot along the rock wall, taking a moment to stretch his limbs. If he had both an emerald and a topaz, the contest would have been laughable, but with only the first, he could only make himself light.

He calmed his beating heart with long inhales and exhales. Only when he felt completely relaxed did Kuma cycle to Light and leap upward, soaring vertically like a human rocket until he touched a spot at least five feet higher than Noctus'.

When he landed, Noctus burst into laughter, holding his belly and bending at the waist. He went on for a minute until he finally calmed, grinning at Kuma as if they were old friends having shared a good joke.

"I knew you were deceiving me. I'm pleased to find I was right." The Brodarian put his arm around Kuma's shoulders. "I concede the contest. You've played your part well. I suspect there's more to you, and probably Lady Saha by extension, but I'll leave you to your secrets. Come, let us return to the flower bar and enjoy a round of drinks together to celebrate our new partnership."

Kuma had planned to continue the search for allies, but in joining with Noctus, realized that the three of them might be enough to hold off the masses that would come after them. He let the Brodarian lead them back to the Poinsettia.

Twenty-Two

The guard shoved Choo-Choo in the back, making him stumble towards the elevator cage along the cliff. If his sister wasn't with him, he would have fought back already, but he feared she'd get shot in the chaos. Vasilisa had no stones to protect herself. That had to be him. Their mother would never forgive him if he let her die, so he clamped his lips shut and kept moving forward.

The area was different from when they'd gotten caught by Deacon and had to jump off the cliff into the water filled with dangerous Cthulhu-jellies. Further northeast, he guessed, though it could be close enough they used the water pumped from the lake.

"Into the cage, face the wall, keep your hands behind your back," said Lee.

"They're cuffed, you idiot," said Vasilisa.

He smacked her in the back of the head with the butt of his rifle. Choo-Choo threw himself between them, receiving a knee to the stomach for the interference. After catching his breath, Choo-Choo stumbled into the elevator. He spotted a huge chain hooked to the ceiling and other mechanical gearing.

"Be lucky you don't have to walk. We put this in last month," said Lee.

At least five automatic rifles were pointed at them. Choo-Choo leaned his head against the cage wall as the doors were shut and it lurched downward, the steady clink of chains rotating through the gears drowning out all but the loudest noises. The cliff quickly fell away. Electric lamps revealed a meandering path cut into the curve further up where a mechanical cart filled with rock and led by two men in hard hats crawled up the slopes. The elevator went down for much longer than he'd expected. Even the fall from the edge into the lake had only been a hundred and fifty feet or so. After a minute of steady downward progress, he thought they were at least three times that distance below. The cutback path had gone the other direction. The lamps were dim, but they gave him an idea of the scale as he looked up through the cage material.

"What's down here?" asked Vasilisa.

"Shut up," said Lee.

"If you were going to kill us you would have already done that. You want our help, even if it's at gunpoint. Giving us a little information might make success possible," said Vasilisa, yelling over her shoulder.

Facing the cage, Choo-Choo grinned at his sister's argument. She could be relentless about a subject when she thought she was right.

"Fine," said Lee. "The locals call it the Wastelands, but that's the broader wild area that has resisted taming due to the prevalence of dangerous critters. The area we're heading into is named the Dark Depths by the earlier explorers from the Halls. It's not dark, as you'll soon find out, but it is in the depths. Unlike the other parts of the Undercity, it's not close to the infernal realm and it has a high concentration of faez which made it ideal for certain kinds of experiments."

Around the time Lee paused, a faint illumination far beneath made his comment about the name clearer. The rock seemed to glow a bluish light which made the air muted.

"Most of those experiments involved great magics, or the attempt to make powerful artifacts. Old workshops and other remnants of their activities still remain, some more resistant than others to exploration."

Lee quieted for the final descent. A cluster of electric lights revealed the secondary settlement at the bottom of the elevator. Steel walls patrolled by guards with guns provided a barrier. Choo-Choo always knew that the Undercity held more secrets than even a local like himself had ever dreamed of, but this was grander and more frightening than he'd expected.

When the cage hit the cavern floor and the accordion door was slammed open, Vasilisa gave him a flat look as she followed the guards out of the elevator. Not a single person wasn't armed. Choo-Choo spotted multiple guards dressed in the black gear associated with Titus Cabone's crew, though he didn't see the maetrie mercenary leader himself.

"This isn't what I expected," said Vasilisa.

"Neither did I, Molly. Neither did I," said Lee.

"I was expecting it to be hotter," said Choo-Choo as he hurried to keep up with his hands cuffed behind his back.

Lee chuckled. "If this were normal underground, you'd be right. But this is beneath the city of sorcery, a place so drenched with faez that it changed the nature of the earth beneath it. As far as past researchers can tell, this region isn't completely in our realm at all. We passed that line about four hundred feet above us."

"We're not in our realm?"

The words fell out of Choo-Choo's mouth as he struggled to wrap his mind around the idea. He craned his neck as if he could see that invisible line. Traveling to other realms had always seemed like a foreign idea, even as he knew that some mages and others did it quite frequently.

Even Pandora and Kuma had experienced another world recently.

"Yes and no. Don't think too much about it. The key part is that this nebulous region allowed mages to perform some pretty sketchy stuff, some of which still exists. My boss is a collector it seems and is searching for a particular piece down here."

"What's that?"

Lee laughed. "It doesn't matter. What matters is we can't get past a certain area that has vexed all our attempts to bypass it. I don't know if it's possible, but we're going to keep trying."

"Or you might be the one in cuffs," said Vasilisa.

"I don't think I'll get that lucky," said Lee soberly.

Making a deal with the maetrie seemed akin to shaking hands with the devil. Choo-Choo never thought much about the maetrie, but Lee's comment reminded him that they were fae—and the fae existed on rules entirely different than humans'.

The cuffs were removed before they left the protection of the steel partitions. Four guards armed with automatic weapons and wearing runed Kevlar armor joined them, spreading to the four points as they moved through piles of rocks at the bottom of the pit. The absence of a ceiling made Choo-Choo feel like he was on the surface during the night.

They walked for twenty minutes, stopping frequently as the guards verified corners. Choo-Choo wondered if he could take the rifle from one while he was distracted and kill the others in time, but then that would leave them at the bottom of a pit they didn't know how to get out. It would also leave them ignorant of whatever Dominion Thule was digging for in the darkness. Better to keep going and learn what it was before he tried to escape.

When they left the piles of rocks and crossed a relatively flat section, Choo-Choo sensed they were nearing their destination. Floodlights bloomed in the darkness, revealing an archway covered in strange runes that looked like angry slashes on the cavern wall. The writings were familiar, then he remembered that Pandora and Kuma wore clothing with those markings.

"Maetrie writings," said Choo-Choo.

Lee turned his head, shock on his face. "You know it?"

"How to read it? No. I just know that's what it is," said Choo-Choo.

"It's a gateway and a warning," said Lee, extending his arm to indicate portions of the writings. "The maetrie version of Stay Away, No Trespassing."

"Sounds like an invitation to me," said Vasilisa.

Lee shook his head. "You and your sister aren't as cowed by this as the others I've brought down here."

"I told you we're young and ambitious."

Lee nodded slowly. "I truly hope you'll be able to survive this."

The pronouncement tightened Choo-Choo's stomach. Lee led them through the archway. The ambient blue glow made headlamps unnecessary. After a short transition, they entered a large room, partially collapsed with a hunk of glossy stone that had been broken into pieces lying at the center.

"Obsidian?" asked Choo-Choo.

"A portal. We believe that's how the maetrie that created this were accessing the area without having to travel on foot. But it was destroyed when the wall collapsed. That's been our biggest issue, the instability. Whatever magics helped hold the structure together are breaking down.

In a few years, a decade maybe, this entire thing would be buried beneath thousands of tons of rock."

As if to prove his point, a faint rumble spit dust out from the rock wall to their right. A few pebbles bounced between their feet. Lee stared at them as if they were live grenades.

"Let's move."

Steel retaining beams littered the next section, holding up walls near collapse. The path opened up, revealing a larger interior space than Choo-Choo would have expected. They met up with a team of workers at a tertiary site. Everyone was wearing hard hats and carrying lights. Dust motes filled the air. Lee had them wait while he talked to the others, and he returned with hard hats for them.

"You wanted to help, now you get your chance," said Lee, leading them to a narrow hallway, the walls braced with horizontal support beams. "Down that way is where the maetrie were doing their secret work. If you can get past the wards and figure out what's beyond it, then maybe we can talk about leaving the Dark Depths."

"Wards?" exclaimed Vasilisa. "We're not mages. We work in mining and excavation."

Lee stared back flatly. "I have my doubts, but I'm willing to be convinced. Figure it out or don't, but remember, you came to me."

A guard shoved him in the back with his rifle. Choo-Choo saw an opportunity to fight back, but Vasilisa grabbed his arm, tugging him towards the passage. He gave her a look, but she shook him off. Choo-Choo followed his sister beneath the retaining beams as the earth rumbled like a giant in disturbed slumber. Dust fell upon their shoulders as they slipped into the darkness.

Twenty-Three

A ziggurat had been built at the center of the arena. Made of wood and steel, it rose four levels above the sands. At the top, a red sheet covered a large cube. Pandora, along with the other sixty-seven competitors, gawked at the structure, wondering how it would affect the grand melee.

"Now we know what all the hammering was about," said Kuma in maetrie.

The others around them frowned at the unusual language.

"It seems our host has a surprise planned," she said curtly. Pandora spotted the imposing form of Noctus Prime, grinning at the updated arena like kid staring through the glass at a room full of puppies. "Are you sure we can trust him? Brodarians aren't exactly known for being loyal."

Kuma's non-response left her stomach in a twist. They'd been over this point numerous times since he'd come back with the announcement of cooperation. He probably didn't want to rehash the same arguments. As the competitors filed onto the sands, they joined Noctus near the corner of the enormous structure.

"Lady Saha. I look forward to fighting alongside you."

The nearby competitors went wide-eyed with surprise, which was probably his intent, though Pandora couldn't figure why he would reveal it before the grand melee. A taller warrior with pockmarked cheeks shifted towards another group to warn them of the alliance.

"Any ideas? A knockoff of an Eternal City competition?" asked Kuma.

"Nothing I recognize. But I can assume that there will be a twist," she said.

The Brodarian crossed his arms as he studied the structure. "It will require us to climb the ziggurat. Maybe a Lord of the Mountain game." He put a massive hand on Kuma's shoulder, making him lean under the weight. "Your excellent jumping ability should prove decisive."

They didn't have to wait long to find out, as Dominion climbed onto the viewing platform. Pandora sucked in a breath when she saw her mother joining him. Noctus Prime checked back at her reaction, but said nothing.

"Who's the hottie golem?" asked a competitor from behind, eliciting a round of laughter from those nearby.

Her mother stood defiantly on the platform. The half of her head that had been replaced by silvery and gold metals glimmered in the warm lights of the arena. On the surface, Selena was striking. To many, she would be beautiful in her own strange way, but not to Pandora. She knew the why, and that made the changes perverse. Her mother wasn't changing for herself, but to please her grandfather, who couldn't care less. Pandora had watched Dominion ignore her mother back at his estate, treating her like a child who was being tolerated at the adult table.

"Greetings, competitors, and congratulations on winning your first two rounds!" announced Dominion to the cheers of the packed audience. The entire arena was filled. People were standing in the aisles. Pandora wasn't sure that many people had ever been in the Undercity in one place. It was a sign of how much it had changed.

"Here in the shadows, much like my birthplace, the Eternal City, warriors are prized. We live in a hard world. As the Halls experienced only a few short years ago, peace and prosperity can be threatened by forces beyond our control. It's up to us as men and women of action to prepare ourselves for that eventuality. We cannot trust anyone but our own flesh and bone."

A smattering of applause came as the crowd tried to make sense of the hard turn. Her grandfather seemed to sense the mood and shifted into a brighter tone.

"That is why we are celebrating the power of will with this tournament. The third round will be a little different than the first two. Now that we've whittled the competitors down to a more manageable number, we're going to let them battle it out for the final thirty-two spots in a grand melee!"

The crowd cheered as he raised his arms in triumph.

"But to keep things interesting, and to make sure that not everything was decided before," he said, chuckling, "I've added a kink into the competition."

When he raised his hand, invisible wires yanked the crimson covering from the top of the ziggurat, revealing a flat piece of steel mesh, beneath which hung dozens of rods.

"Thirty-two," she said right away. "There are thirty-two rods."

"To pass the grand melee, one not only has to survive your fellow competitors, but you must retrieve a rod from the ziggurat and bring it to the red gate beneath the platform."

Pandora hadn't noticed before, but there was an exit to the arena floor as he described. Walls had been built around the entire sand area. The nature of the game would force them into close combat with each other. Their group of three seemed laughably small compared to the other allied teams.

"Before we can start, every competitor must move to the outer wall. Once everyone is in place, there will be a short countdown and then the grand melee will begin, continuing until thirty-two rods have been carried through the crimson gate."

Pandora jogged to the outer wall with Kuma and Noctus Prime. There was at least a hundred feet between them and the ziggurat. A cluster of fifteen stood to their left and another group of eight was to the right. There were similarly sized teams along the circumference of the arena. They were the smallest team at three, the next biggest being the group to their right and the groupings numbering seven. A few of the teams had added colored arm bands to their uniforms to make their allegiances clear.

"Watch out for the team to the right," said Kuma. "Valor Drux recruited some of the top competitors—most of them have real-world experience. Mercenaries, ex-military, a few Hall mages, including the Botez twins. Avoid them if possible. The other one I'm worried about is headed by Angel Chen. She has a few on her team that have been quietly effective during their matches. The other teams are made of the chaff."

"This setup is quite interesting," mused Noctus as if he were deciding which brand of tea to drink. "Shall we attack the rods immediately, or wait until the chaos has reduced?"

"We could wait by the gate," said Kuma.

"No," said Pandora right away. Lady Saha would never take that approach. It was too passive. "We'll set up on the platform beneath the top and prepare to make our move when the time is right."

"Lady Saha is wise," said Noctus, grunting with approval. "Perhaps we can eliminate some of our opponents."

Dominion Thule raised his hand. "The competition will begin in five, four, three—"

"Good luck," said Kuma.

"—two, one, begin!"

Some of the competitors started running before the final command was given, but it was too late to have them start over. Half the teams made a mad rush for the ziggurat, climbing up the angled platforms or leaping onto them with supernatural strength.

By the time Pandora reached the edge, three teams were battling on the top, including Valor Drux's group. They fought like a well-oiled machine, keeping in formation and striking hard at nearby opponents. The mesh holding the rods was much higher than anticipated, forcing those on the top to use each other to climb up. Each rod was wired to the mesh, so it took time for the teams to remove them.

"There's a team at the gate," said Kuma, checking over his shoulder. "The largest, but weakest group."

Pandora's blood pumped with excitement. She wanted to get into the mix, but the chaos at the top had competitors getting knocked off as there wasn't enough room. Two of the groups had taken control and were removing the rods. As they pulled them down, other groups attacked their flanks, but the high ground made it difficult to break their ranks.

As it appeared the first group led by Valor Drux had gathered enough rods, other teams collected beneath their position, preparing to attack them during the escape to the crimson gate. A straggler got knocked off the top, sliding down to rest at Noctus' feet. The Brodarian calmly knocked him out with one punch, much to the cheers of the crowd. Kuma took the unconscious competitor and pushed him over the slope to the second level.

"We shouldn't wait much longer," said Pandora. "Once there are few rods it will only get harder."

Valor Drux's team rushed down the slope, smashing into the team waiting for them. She thought about joining in, but decided there was easier prey.

"I have an idea," said Kuma.

"Does it involve revisiting our contest?" asked Noctus.

"Come on, Lady Saha. We can bypass the battle beneath," said Kuma.

She saw what they were intending. Noctus crouched, holding his hands in cupped form. Pandora placed her foot in his hand, facing the hanging rods while Kuma joined her.

"Ready," said Pandora.

A wave of lightness hit her as Kuma extended his emerald. "Ready!"

Noctus threw them upward, grunting despite their negligible weight. Pandora flew upward, almost too high, landing hard on top of the mesh. A small number of rods had yet to be claimed as the melee beneath was pure chaos. Feet and fists found any exposed flesh. At least a few competitors were unconscious beneath the all-out brawl.

She threw herself to her knees, reaching through a gap to grab a rod. The wire was easy enough to snap with a good tug. She was about to go for a second when Kuma held up two. He tossed one down to Noctus and they prepared to leap when the whole structure shifted, knocking them off their feet. On the right side, a group had grabbed the edge of the mesh and their collective weight was forcing the structure to lean. The metal groaned, and her only warning of the collapse was the snapping of wires.

The entire structure flipped up, sending them rolling down the side into the mass of combatants, followed by the mesh landing atop them. The entire group fell over the side, sliding down to land in a collective heap, trapped under the structure. The wires smashed against her ear, sending flashes of pain through her vision. Someone punched her in the throat, and fingers gouged for her eyes. She fought back but the mass of people scrambling for the rods made picking out a single enemy impossible. It wasn't fighting, but mass wrestling. Pandora didn't know when she lost the rod, but it was no longer in her hands. She was trapped near the center of the pile and feared that there was no way to get her rod back.

Twenty-Four

"May the shadows keep us safe."

Vasilisa found herself mumbling the saying as a ward against the dangers ahead. Lee Travic and his gang were back a hundred feet, past the retaining walls. The rocks groaned, threatening to collapse. Shifts sent streamers of dust into the passageway.

"I can't believe this is another realm."

She turned to her brother. "That's what you're thinking about?"

Emilio shrugged. "Better than thinking about what's ahead."

Around the corner, the rocky terrain turned back to the runed-covered walls they'd seen at the entrance. The sharp angled lines that made up the maetrie language matched their spoken words and the alienness of their fae backgrounds.

"Do you feel that?" asked her brother, grimacing.

She nodded. A high-pitched whine, almost too high to hear, made her squint.

"It's awful. Sounds like a motor that's off-balance and going to fail soon."

"Worse," said Emilio, shaking his head. "Like that, but much, much worse."

"What do we do?" she asked, shifting her backpack off her shoulders and digging inside for a headlamp. The ambient bluish lighting had faded. After clicking on the light, she examined their surroundings, checking above them.

"It looks like the earth collapsed on this structure, burying part of it," she said.

"What do you think the maetrie were doing here?" asked Emilio.

"I think we'd have to ask Pandora about that."

"I doubt she'd know. This is old. Well, old for us, not the maetrie."

Vasilisa approached the wall with her hand out, palm flat and vertical.

"What are you doing?" asked her brother.

"I don't know. They said there are wards. I was hoping I might be able to feel one before it blew up on us, or whatever they do."

"You're trying to get past them?" he asked.

"Got a better idea?"

"Like escaping," he said.

"I doubt we can get out from here. Or they wouldn't have let us come back this way," she said.

He exhaled deeply. "I hate that you're right."

"Hard to know that your little sister isn't so little anymore?" she asked.

"I blinked and you became a young woman." He hung his head. "I know I've said it before, but I'm so sorry about what happened with Andy. I would have liked to have met him."

She tilted her head. "Emilio. We're not going to die."

"What?"

"None of this last comments bullshit. Focus on getting us out of here," she said.

Emilio pursed his lips. "You're more and more like Val every year."

"What do you think?" she asked, holding her hand a few inches from the wall. "Safe to touch?"

"How would I know?"

"Use your amber, you wayhos."

Her brother blinked twice, before sighing and approaching the wall.

He crouched down, examining the structure with the intensity she recognized as use of his amber.

"That humming is coming from deeper. I don't sense anything here except some water running in the rock."

Vasilisa brushed the stone with her fingertips, pulling back as if she were testing a live wire. The rock was dusty. Once she'd confirmed it was safe, she ran her fingers across the markings.

"If there were wards here, they're probably long gone. The collapse broke whatever magic they contained," she said.

"You don't know that, but come on. Let's see what's ahead."

The passage was wide enough they walked side by side. As she studied the formations, she saw how this entire area had been a larger complex, but then the ceiling had partially collapsed. Around a corner, they found an area marked off by Lee's team. Caution tape wrapped around iron rods drilled into the ground demarcated a space before a wall that seemed newer than the others.

"No dust," she said. "It looks more recent. The wards must be active."

Vasilisa held out her hand, but there was nothing to indicate the latent, and probably dangerous, magic. She held out the illusionary hand, the one generated by the metal cuff on her left wrist, out of curiosity. The verisimilitude of her fingers broke down as they entered the invisible field. Her flesh bent awkwardly like light refracted through water.

They went wide around the caution tape. The way split into three directions. Her brother pointed to the leftmost passage.

"I can hear that noise again, coming from this way."

They found a skeleton in the next hallway. A shoulder and arm partially stuck out from the bottom of a wall that had collapsed long ago.

"Maetrie bone?" asked her brother.

"Would make sense. No one else knew this was here, and if they were using a portal to get in and out, then a city fae would be likely."

After wandering through the partially collapsed tunnels and narrow passages through the rocks, they were surprised when they came upon an intact room with an opening leading deeper into the complex. The section leading up to it appeared like it'd been excavated recently, with scratch marks on the stone from digging equipment.

"I feel it," she said, seeing Emilio's scrunched-up expression.

"It's like having a hive of bees in my head. It's awful."

Vasilisa grabbed a small rock and tossed it ahead. It bounced along the floor, coming to rest near the wall. After the pebble test, she extended her illusionary hand and cautiously shifted forward, looking for signs of change. When they passed through the opening, they were greeted by a larger space with strange equipment she didn't have words to describe.

"What is this?" exclaimed Emilio.

On a large table lay a metal golem as if it were a patient in a hospital. A crimson gem glowed faintly in its chest.

"I don't like the looks of that," he said.

"No dust on the floor," said Vasilisa.

There were two openings out of the room. The equipment along the wall looked like stone boxes covered in maetrie writing with metal knobs and levers. After confirming no wards with her illusionary hand, Vasilisa examined the golem up close.

"Don't touch it," said her brother.

"I'm not stupid."

She marveled at the construction. She knew the mages of the Hundred Halls made arcane constructs or modified beasts for their own perverse purposes, but she'd never seen one. While faez crystals had changed the Undercity, they'd done so in an almost invisible way, unlike the flashy and sometimes catastrophic magics of the Halls. Or the maetrie, it seemed.

"Check out this next room," said Emilio, sticking his head through the opening.

"You should let me lead. I can check for wards," she said, holding out her illusionary hand.

The ruby in the golem's chest surged with light for a split second. It happened fast enough she wasn't sure if it'd been her imagination or not, but it made her want to move on quickly. She joined her brother in the next room, which contained more strange equipment, but no table or golem.

"The noise is coming from that direction," he said, pointing through an opposite opening. "It's making my teeth hurt."

Vasilisa massaged her own jaw. "It's making me nauseous."

The excitement of wandering through an old maetrie complex deep in the Undercity was tempered with the idea that ancient magics might rise up and kill them.

The next room had more old arcane equipment that gave no clue to its function. It appeared that some stuff had been looted, by the faint outlines left on the walls and floor. A wide crack let in a puddle which covered a corner, but grew no larger because it was tricking through another crack in the stone.

"The water is louder here. Must be a stream wandering through the rocks above us," he said.

"What if it isn't a stream?"

Emilio stared back blankly. Their silence was interrupted by a rumble in the earth. Barely a shiver, but it put a squeeze on her gut.

The next area had Vasilisa wanting to double over. "That noise. It's awful. What is it?"

"No idea."

Before her brother could move forward to investigate, she held him back.

"Let me check."

She used her illusionary hand to confirm no wards ahead. She wasn't sure it would work for all kinds of magic, but at least it was better than nothing.

"Is this where they were checking?" asked Emilio.

"What do you mean?"

"They said something about a retaining wall collapsing. This area seems clearer than the others. I think they were working in a different section." He looked over his shoulder. "Should we go back?"

"Let's explore a little further while we're here," she said, leaning her head through the gap in the wall. A heavy trickle meandered down the stone. It'd worn down the rock, which showed how long the maetrie complex had been in the Undercity. Vasilisa craned her neck, spotting the curve of a pipe through the hole about ten feet above her head.

"I think I found the source—"

She leaned out of the crack at the same time a heavy thud startled her to silence. Emilio was in the next room, but he hurried back, shining the handheld flashlight into the opening that led the other way. When a second, unmistakable footfall sounded, she knew they were in trouble. Ponderous footsteps followed. The massive golem that had been on the table stood in the doorway, its ruby gem bursting with crimson light. The construct raised its fists menacingly before charging.

Twenty-Five

Pandora couldn't breathe. A knee was jammed into her gut, restricting the ability to inhale. People were shouting, lashing out at each other. The blonde warrior with the broken nose next to her was unconscious. But the pain wasn't the worst part. She knew while they were trying to free themselves, valuable rods were being whisked through the gate. Passing the grand melee was slipping out of reach every second she was trapped. She used a sapphire Push, but the mesh was too fine to impact.

When black dots started forming in her vision, the crushing weight of the mesh structure lifted away. She fought her way through the crowd and mistakenly stepped off the edge, tumbling down to the second level. A hand grabbed her neck and she punched upward until she realized she was looking into the snaggletoothed grin of Noctus Prime.

"I lost my rod."

Kuma came stumbling from around the corner, also missing his prize.

"Thanks for getting us out, but we're fucked," she said.

Noctus used his rod to salute them. "I'm sorry, my friends. I should make my way to the gate before they decide to come after me. Good luck with your rods."

He was jogging towards the gate before she could think of saying anything that might change his mind. Pandora didn't blame him for abandoning them. At least he'd gotten them out of the pile of people before he left.

When she checked back to the sands, she saw a massive melee near the gate. The few remaining rods were being fought over by a large group. She had no idea if her rod was one of those or if it had already gone through.

"How do you want to approach this?" asked Kuma in maetrie as the others that had been trapped beneath the structure were joining the battle with them.

The answer was as plain as the bloodlust of the crowd, cheering as the remaining competitors mauled each other trying to acquire the last few rods. But once again, it would mean leaning into her maetrie heritage. She checked to the platform to see her mother and grandfather watching the carnage with unrepentant glee. The expressions were familiar. The joy of city fae enjoying unchecked competition was the same as human kids watching puppies play.

"Position ourselves between the melee and the gate. We need to reduce the number of competitors."

"Really?" asked Kuma, aghast.

The shock in his face made hating herself easy. "Not killing. Unconscious. We can't take on so many at once. We need to even the odds."

Kuma blinked. "Yes, of course, Lady Saha."

Except for a few on the ziggurat that were too injured to continue, the rest of the competitors were clustered together in a massive knot of fists and feet, fighting over a handful of remaining rods. No more than five, but it was hard to tell in the chaos.

Pandora knocked out the first competitor the moment Kuma pulled them from the pack. They turned with their fists up, but too late, catching an extended kick to the jaw. When they tried to stand, Kuma knocked them out with a punch to the head then dragged them to the side. The crowd quickly became incensed by their cruelty, shouting jeers and calling them cheaters. Debris rained down from the bleachers, but guards put a stop to the trash projectiles.

At first, no one in the melee noticed their strategy. They'd incapacitated eight competitors before a tall warrior with blood all over his face grabbed his friends, who disengaged from the edges and came after them five on two.

"Thank you for volunteering," said Pandora, giving them a short bow that the crowd interpreted as mocking. Her comment had been honest. A face-forward fight was preferred.

"I'm gonna knock the gray from your skin, you freakish bitch," said Bloody Face.

The five warriors moved forward in harmony to each other. She remembered them as ex-military mercenaries who had clearly fought together in the past. The crowd was on its feet, cheering the side battle.

"No visible stones," she said in maetrie.

Kuma gave her a short nod. Bloody Face gestured to his companions, a fist twisting, which was returned with various finger motions. She wondered if she were making a mistake, not using their faez crystals.

Bloody Face attacked first, an obvious feint, which she avoided by shuffling back, readying for the flanking maneuver. The others did not disappoint, curling around to attack in tandem. Sensing an opportunity to educate the competitors that had claimed their rods and were watching from the gate area, Pandora struck out with speed, grabbing a wrist and breaking the locked elbow before sending her knife hand into the other's throat. Both attackers were reduced to curled positions. She turned to help Kuma, finding he'd knocked out the first and was soundly beating the second. Pandora advanced on Bloody Face, grabbing him by the back of the hair when he tried to flee into the melee. She punched him hard enough that his knees gave out and he slumped to the sands.

The cluster of fighters had been reduced by half from when they'd first approached. Men and women were unconscious or crawling away from the fight, too injured to continue. With a dozen warriors left, and three rods lying in the sand, the standoff was tense.

Pandora went after the rear warriors, attacking without regard for their attention. Bones broke and blood splattered as she tore into them, keeping an eye on the three rods. In a matter of moments, the remaining warriors realized none of them would be walking through the gate unless they could take care of her and Kuma. Leaving the rods alone, they attacked in a group. Had it been the earlier teams, the fight might have been interesting, possibly even weighted in their opponents' favor. But Pandora saw their feeble attacks as children trying to take down an elephant. She made every one of them pay for the slightest mistake. A fist to the jaw. A foot to the knee. Pandora threw one over her shoulder into two others attempting to attack her from behind. The final sequence was a blur. When she had a moment to reconcile the carnage, there were only four competitors standing.

"Which one of you is the better warrior?" she asked the pair across from her and Kuma.

A broad-shouldered black woman with her hair in braids, a few of them broken loose from the fighting, and a short red-haired man who looked like he could run through a brick wall stared back with equal menace. The red-haired warrior opened his mouth as he puffed out his chest.

"It's me, I'm—"

Before he could finish what he was saying, Pandora locked him in place with a sapphire Pull and threw her foot through his jaw. He flew backwards, landing on two other unconscious competitors.

"Good luck in the next round," said Pandora as she snatched her rod from the sands.

Side by side, she and Kuma walked through the gate with their rods to utter silence. The only sound in the cavern was Noctus Prime's belly laugh. Pandora checked back to the platform to see her grandfather staring down with a perverse smile on his lips. He gave her a slight head nod before applauding them.

"Congratulations to the victors of the grand melee!"

The rest of the crowd took up their host's example, but it lacked the enthusiasm of a sporting event. Pandora saw the faces of the men and women filing out of the arena. They were sickened by the abject violence. What had been an exciting two rounds of the tournament with thrilling matches had turned into a brutal bloodbath. The question in everyone's minds now was how much worse could it get?

Twenty-Six

The living construct went straight for his sister. She was trapped in the corner, frozen without a way to escape. Choo-Choo reacted instinctively, shoulder-charging the golem to knock it from its murderous path. The impact stopped him in his tracks. It was like he'd run directly into a mountain.

He looked up in time to see a metal fist coming for his head and rolled behind the silvery body, finding his feet in time to see the golem reorient itself on him.

"Emilio, run!"

The golem moved faster than he expected, but it was no match for his topaz speed. It put a fist deep into the wall, sending shards of stone in every direction. Choo-Choo tried to yank it off its feet by grabbing it behind the knee and leveraging it over, but the construct was too heavy and strong.

The room was small, no more than twenty by twenty, making escape impossible while his sister was stuck in the corner. Choo-Choo bounced off the walls, using them to change directions rapidly.

"We have to get back to the others," said Vasilisa.

"Then they'll know we're not who we are," he said as he ducked beneath a head-hunting punch.

When the golem tried to pivot in a puddle of water, the metal boot slipped slightly, giving Choo-Choo an idea.

"We need more water in the room," he told his sister as he evaded the golem.

He didn't get to see if she'd understood him as he was too busy trying not to get his head caved in, but then he heard rocks being smashed. Vasilisa had climbed into the crack and was kicking the fragile edges, clearing more space for the water to spill onto the floor.

"Not enough, we need more," he said, trying to keep himself behind the golem. The construct kept turning each direction, but was unable to spin fast enough.

Vasilisa was deep into the hole, so he couldn't see what she was doing but he could hear her smashing rocks together. After what felt like a long time, a gush of water spilled into the room, covering the floor.

"Ha! It's working," he said, right before he slipped, tumbling to the waterlogged floor. He managed to get back to his feet in time for the golem to clutch his arm. The construct grabbed him by the shirt and threw him into the wall next to the crack. The impact broke loose more of the structure. Choo-Choo managed to regain his feet, but the golem cut off his escape routes. He climbed into the hole, hoping the rushing water and debris would keep the massive construct from reaching him inside.

"What are you doing?" exclaimed Vasilisa, soaking wet with water spraying in her face. She had a rock in her good hand.

The golem reached the gap and shoved its hand into the hole. Choo-Choo kicked it away, but knew that strategy wouldn't last long.

"Climb!"

Vasilisa pulled herself higher into the space. It appeared a large pipe ran past the room and sometime in the past had been damaged, which was where the leak had originated. His sister had opened it up some but the gap was only a few hands wide.

Choo-Choo kicked out hard then leapt up, pulling himself against the top of the space. The golem couldn't fit, so it smashed its fists against the wall, opening the hole wider. Bracing his body against the rock, Choo-Choo kicked out against the pipe. In four hard blows, he managed to smash the outer portion of the pipe. The flow of cold water became a flood for a few seconds until it settled to an equilibrium.

"Climb in."

"Climb in?" she responded.

"Got a better idea? This thing is going to break through the wall in about a minute and I'd rather not be here."

His sister, looking like a drowned rat, muttered curses as she pulled herself through the hole, climbing into the pipe which sprayed water in his face. Choo-Choo followed her after smashing the gap wider when his shoulders wouldn't fit. He pulled himself inside right before the golem broke through the wall and started attacking the pipe.

"Climb!" he told his sister, but she was already ahead of him. The pipe went up at a forty-five-degree angle. Moving up required pushing both hands on either side and avoiding the flow of chilly water that covered the bottom few inches. Vasilisa climbed with surprising speed despite the stump.

When the golem's attacks grew muted, Vasilisa paused above him. He'd lost his headlamp in the fight, but his sister's rotated back and forth. They were soaked and shivering from the cold water.

"I want out of this pipe," she said between breaths.

"We have to go up. It'll keep us warm."

"What was that thing?" she asked.

He frowned. "You saw it the same as I did. Some sort of maetrie guardian."

"I liked it better when Razor was our enemy. Whatever this crap is, it's bigger than our little rebellion."

Choo-Choo didn't have an answer. His sister started working her way up the pipe, so he followed. Every time she got her knees in the flow, it sprayed water in his face. After a fifteen-minute climb, the pipe evened out. They no longer had to climb but it was harder to stay out of the cold water.

"I can't feel my hand," she said.

Choo-Choo's lower lip was quivering. He could barely muster

speech.

"Mine are numb too."

"We have to get out of the pipe soon, or we're not getting out at all."

Choo-Choo banged on the curved wall. The material provided a dull echo.

"I think we're still in the ground. If this water is coming from the lake near the well, then it'll have to cross the huge opening eventually. Keep climbing."

"What if it goes around the gap, staying in the earth?"

"Just climb," he said, not wanting to consider what she'd said.

Every ten feet, he stopped to hammer his fist against the wall. His hands were so numb it felt like hitting it with someone else's limb. Then after a painfully long time, he struck the pipe to hear a higher pitched ring. Choo-Choo placed his back against the curved wall and started kicking, unconcerned about who or what might hear. If they didn't get out soon, they'd never get out. If it hadn't already, hypothermia would set in. Choo-Choo kicked with both legs like a pair of pistons. He gave it everything he could until the first crack formed then he kept hammering that location. When a small piece broke away, he stuck his eye to the hole, hoping that they weren't over a deep drop. The bluish illumination he'd seen during the long elevator ride down made distances hard to distinguish, but he didn't see any artificial lights, so he kept kicking.

His foot burst through the side, sending a large chunk of the pipe to smash on the rocks about fifteen feet below. The pipe was crossing a gap and returning to the earth. If he'd waited another five feet, he'd have missed the opportunity to escape.

"It's a drop. I'll lower you down."

Using the straps of her backpack, Choo-Choo let his sister drop to the slope. He followed her out, the freezing water cascading over his body, until he landed hard, nearly tumbling over a secondary cliff. Vasilisa grabbed his arm, steadying him.

They stood on a ledge overlooking the eastern part of the deep canyon. Reflected artificial lights shone in the distance, marking the location of the elevator and winding ramp. Still shivering from the water, they rubbed their arms and stomped their feet to get the blood flow back into their limbs. Vasilisa sat on the edge, found a couple of food bars in their backpacks, and handed one over. He joined her, relishing the warmth of the Undercity air.

"How are we getting out?" she asked after finishing her food bar. "The elevator is guarded and the ramp is fully lit."

"Let's worry about it after we rest some. My legs and arms are tight from the cold water."

He knocked the crumbs off his lap and set his pack on the rocks. The sharp stone made it uncomfortable, but he managed to fall asleep for a short time. He woke to find Vasilisa sitting against the wall.

"Okay?"

"Warm. It's enough for now, but I want out of here."

"Let's get down then."

The cliff was the first obstacle. It was about thirty feet down. Vasilisa wasn't comfortable climbing with only one hand, so they spent the next hour tearing apart their backpacks, making an improvised rope. It wouldn't get her all the way down, but close enough to drop safely. He held a knot he'd made at the end while she shimmied to the bottom, then he followed by climbing down the rock face.

The way after was a mix of scree slopes and rocky traverses. They managed to make it to the canyon floor, which based on the lights, he assumed was on the same level as the work camp. Most of the guards were right inside the wall, which made observing from a distance easier.

"Ideas?" he asked.

"What about those carts?"

His sister pointed to the vehicles that carried material to the top of the Dark Depths by the ramp.

"Won't that be obvious?"

"If we act like we know what we're doing, maybe they'll assume we're a set of workers. There's no reason they should think we escaped, and I doubt they went and checked, given the murderous golem. It seemed like they were working in a different area than we went."

Choo-Choo hated the idea, but it was the only plausible one that might work.

"Go now, or wait?" he asked.

"The ramp looks empty."

Using the piles of rock that littered the empty space, they moved up to the cluster of powered carts for transporting materials. It took a few minutes to figure out how to start one. He was unused to the pull-cord, but managed to get the motor running after a good yank. With the engine rumbling, he was certain they were going to get caught. They followed the cart into the open space. The beginning of the ramp was a hundred meters from the camp, too close as far as he was concerned. The whole way across he kept expecting to be challenged. One guard waved to them, so he waved back.

The cart engine increased in tenor as they climbed. Vasilisa guided it from the back using the handheld remote. It was painfully slow. Choo-Choo wanted to leave it behind and run up the ramp as fast as possible.

Reaching the top took an hour. It came out in an area filled with debris and other carts. They turned off the engine and after confirming no one was nearby, headed into a tunnel leading away. Back in the part of the Undercity he knew well, he had his sister turn off her headlamp. After their eyes adjusted, he led her through the connecting passages, using his amber to keep watch.

A half hour later, he entered a familiar looking cavern, and after tracing back and forth, found the escape hatch for the Razor tunnels.

He opened it using the stainless steel wheel and had Vasilisa climb down first.

"Are these the Razor tunnels?"

"Yep."

"How'd you know it was here?" she asked, switching on her head-lamp.

"We used it a few months ago when we tried to find Elani. It hasn't been used, so we're okay," he said.

"Hasn't been used? Why are there tire tracks then?"

He saw what she was pointing to with her headlamp. It appeared they were using the hewn tunnels now, which made their passage perilous as there was nowhere to hide if one of the carts came through.

"I'd rather chance it here than try to move through the caverns. Too many patrols these days." He unsuccessfully tried to identify how recently the tire tracks had been made. "Let's keep a good pace."

Choo-Choo took the lead, jogging at a rate his sister could keep up. She wasn't used to running, so she tired easily, especially after a long climb out of the Dark Depths. He willingly passed two exits wanting to get closer to the Terreno before they surfaced, but at the third, he felt they'd pushed their luck too long. He climbed up first, checking their surroundings before letting her come up into a space lightly illuminated by fungi. They made it through two caverns, before he heard voices ahead. Choo-Choo had his sister stay back while he crept into listening range.

"Are you sure it's this way? We've been through three caves and I haven't found the damn entrance."

"It's the one with the ghost-eyes. The wheel's in a cubby in back. What's the big hurry anyway?"

"Something about needing more manpower at the dig site. They had a breakthrough. Something about an old construct that went wild and smashed through the wards."

"Wild."

"Prefer if we didn't have to go. Was hoping to catch the next round. After that grand melee, anything could happen."

Mention of a breakthrough due to the golem had Choo-Choo wanting to hear more, but he had to move Vasilisa before the other group stumbled on them. He made her hurry and they crossed to the other side of the cavern before the large group of men and women detoured through the spot they'd just left.

The next few hours he kept them from the random patrols that grew more frequent as they neared the Terreno. When they stumbled upon the passage that went between the Terreno and Big Dave's Town, he had them wait off the trail until a new group was being led through and then joined the back of them. There was a chance they could be iden tified returning to the Terreno, but he decided it was worth the risk as it was unlikely the same guards would be at the entrance gate. When they reached it, they were quickly ushered into the noisy, crowded space, and went straight for their hotel, collapsing on their beds the moment they were inside.

Twenty-Seven

Camina stood at the front of the platform waiting for Instructor Gomez and his team of second-year waku. The sounds of grunting drifted over the low-roofed buildings. The other groups were busy working through their exercises. She couldn't figure out why Gomez hadn't appeared yet.

When the dark-uniformed trainees came running onto the concrete pad, Camina immediately knew something was wrong. Instructor Gomez approached with his chin dipped towards his chest.

"Where's the rest of your team?"

Gomez stared back with his mouth half open. He checked over his shoulder before answering.

"You don't know?"

Anger formed in her belly. "Don't know what?"

Gomez swallowed. "Titus came and got half about an hour ago. I assumed you already knew. It's why we were late. We were rearranging the bunking situation under the assumption we'd be getting new recruits to fill in those that left."

"Titus got them? To take where?"

"He didn't say."

Gomez couldn't meet her gaze, which meant he'd been too afraid of the maetrie mercenary to ask questions. Or gobsmacked by his aura.

"Damn city fae," she muttered under her breath.

He gestured towards his team. "Should we begin our review?"

Camina barely heard him. She was thinking about why Titus might have coopted her trainees. This was one of the better groups as Instructor Gomez had proved to be an inspired teacher despite his inexperience.

"I need to find out what's going on. My apologies, Gomez. I was looking forward to this. Your team always performs above expectations."

His brown face brightened with a hesitant smile. "Thank you, Instructor Camina."

She left him as he led his team back to the other training area, heading for the main cavern where the Nest was located. It wasn't the first time that her trainees had been taken for mysterious purposes, but it'd always been in ones and twos. Grabbing half of a group, twenty entire trainees, deserved more than the non-explanation she'd gotten.

As she reached the other cavern, a few people recognized her and started to say hello, but quickly sensed she was in no mood. Camina went straight for the elevator at the base of the cliff. She hadn't been up it since she'd raided the location as a member of the Drops. The area had changed, that much she knew, because it'd been under construction for years. But it was the one place she knew she could find Titus Cabone and get an answer for what he'd done.

"You're not authorized," said the guard at the bottom of the elevator. "I'm sorry, Instructor Camina."

"Red?"

The guarded nodded, a partial smile trying to form. She remembered him from training. He gave it his best effort, but wasn't worth a shit. He punched like a wet noodle and looked like he was going to fall down every time he got hit. She would have never let him don the uniform of a waku had it not been for the directive to pass all her trainees.

"I run the Alliance Academy, Red. I'm authorized, whether or not they ever thought to mention it," she said.

He checked to his fellow guard, who clearly didn't want to be involved. She jabbed her thumb into the button.

"If they ask, tell them you tried to stop me," she said.

When the door opened, she stepped inside. A moment later, it lurched upward, giving her a good view of the bars and other businesses that had been given a home in the cavern. Only Alliance members were allowed in this part of the Undercity, but given how large the clan had gotten, it meant the place was packed at all hours of the day and night. The expansions to the west had been to put in stacked apartments to compensate for the newcomers.

The elevator opened revealing a completely different view than she'd expected. Except for the high-tech vault door, the complex had been utilitarian, barely above corporate offices. The ceiling had been raised and the entrance pushed back. Pillars led up exquisitely made stairs to a set of marble doors with scenes of battle carved into the front. She felt like she was wandering into ancient Greece, but instead of warriors in togas and holding spears, a pair of maetrie guards stood on either side of the door.

The first step was the hardest. She felt like she was pushing against an invisible membrane and a heady dizziness made it hard to think, but she managed to make it to the top and approached the guards. The black fitted armor looked like it was made with large overlapping scales and enchanted with fell magics.

"I need to see Titus."

Neither guard acknowledged her existence. They stared forward with a blank stare. Frustrated by the lack of response, she surged forward with her hand out. Her hand never touched the door. Without remembering how she got there, she found herself standing at the bottom of the steps, staring at the elevator. She recalled the guard speaking to her, but not what was said.

"Dammit."

She marched up the stairs only to find herself back where she'd started, a hazy cloud dissipating from her mind. Between the maetrie aura and the conditioning she'd received when she'd been made to join the Alliance, she felt incapable of controlling her actions around them.

Reluctantly, she climbed back into the elevator and returned to the ground floor. The human guards at the bottom were smart enough not to ask, or make a comment. She wasn't finished. Camina wanted answers. But she wasn't going to get them in the Nest.

The neon sign of the Eleventh Gonka buzzed in the cavern. While it wasn't "evening" there were three shifts of work for the Alliance, which meant the bars were filled at all hours of the day. She didn't think any matches for the tournament were going on, which meant most of the clan would be staying around the area. She went into the bar, which felt like nighttime due to the dim lighting and drunken relaxed faces inside. A group of sapphire waku were playing a game that involved pushing a shot glass around the table. Pandora found who she was looking for at the back bar, sitting alone, cradling a glass of amber liquid between his hands.

"Hey," said Deacon with half-lidded eyes. He looked ready to fall off his stool, which surprised her. His cheeks were cavernous.

"You okay?"

"Do you know how I joined the Crows? Well, not how, but why I didn't have anything better to do?" he asked.

"I came to ask a question."

Deacon chuckled under his breath and continued unabated. "I had a family once. I wasn't more than six or seven when they died. Some city mage accidentally blew up an apartment building. Killed 'em both. If I would have stayed around, maybe I would have been put in the system, but I'd been playing with my friends and I knew I didn't want to stay there. Didn't want to see them pulled out in body bags, or under white sheets, whatever. Lived on the streets after that until I joined the Crows. I've always been a survivor. I ain't giving up now."

He touched the right side of his chest as if it hurt, then downed the rest of his whiskey, sliding the glass to the bartender, who automatically refilled it.

"Something wrong?"

Deacon burst out laughing. "Wrong? No. We won." He seemed to remember who he was talking to and screwed up his face. "Sorry. I really liked being in Razor clan. Sometimes I feel bad for what happened."

"I don't really want to hear this," she said.

"You came to me."

Camina fell silent. She couldn't decide if she felt pity or anger, and after the failed attempt to get answers from, or even find, Titus, she was in a foul mood.

"They took my trainees."

He seemed to come out of his daze. "Took your trainees?"

"Yeah, half of Instructor Gomez's group. Twenty new waku soon to graduate the Academy. Didn't tell me or anything. I get that I serve at the whims of Dominion Thule, but I've been working hard. Don't I

deserve an answer?"

She knew it was more than that, but it was the only part of it she was willing to admit.

"Don't ask questions if you don't want to know the answer. I wish someone would have told me that two years ago," he said.

"What do you mean?"

"Isn't it obvious?" He held out both his arms, spilling whiskey.

"Not you."

"You don't think Thule has bigger plans than the Undercity? He's city fae. When you can live to be thousands of years old, you can play the long game."

"What are you talking about?" she asked.

"I wasn't the first and I won't be the last," he muttered as he placed the glass to his lips. After finishing half his whiskey, he slammed it down and put a finger in her chest. "Don't. Just don't."

"Don't what?"

"Exactly." He shooed her away. "Begone. Don't..."

The words trailed off as he rested his head on the counter. He was still talking but she couldn't make sense of what he was saying. The two events, the loss of her trainees and Deacon's comments, left her uneasy. She'd thought that Dominion Thule had taken over the Undercity for the faez crystal trade, but now she worried that it was only the beginning. What could he be planning? And did it matter if she figured it out? It wasn't like she had friends anymore. As far as she knew, Yara and the others had left the Undercity. Which meant she was alone. Maybe it was time for her to find a new path. She wasn't sure if the compulsion would allow her to leave, but she thought it might be worth a try.

Twenty-Eight

Kuma sat on the back of the couch, resting his elbows on his knees. He found it hard to believe the tale that Choo-Choo and Vasilisa had returned with, even as he knew they were telling the truth. Pandora paced along the back side of the room. As Lady Saha she wore a terrifying visage even as he knew who was beneath the disguise. The others kept glancing back to her as if they expected her to burst into uncontrollable rage.

"Tell me again about what you felt when you were in the labs. Every last *detail* down to how it made you feel," said Pandora.

Choo-Choo spread his arms. "Haven't we gone over it enough?"

"Tell her," said Kuma, sensing what she was thinking. The idea was making his stomach hurt.

"It was like being around a generator that was unbalanced and going to explode soon," said Vasilisa, shaking her head softly. "I didn't like it. Made me feel a little ill. Nauseous. I know this sounds weird, but I thought whatever it was, it felt hungry."

When Pandora closed her eyes, inhaling through her nose, Kuma said, "You don't know for sure. It could be a lot of things. You said it yourself many times. Your grandfather collects artifacts. The Undercity has a lot of old magics hiding in the shadows."

Her eyes burst open as she shook her fist. "It wasn't just *any* area of the Undercity. That was a maetrie compound. They probably placed the portal there so they could come and go as they pleased from the Eternal City until something happened."

"Are either of you going to explain what the hell you're talking about?" asked Yara.

When it was clear Pandora was too angry to speak, Kuma said, "I'm not saying this is what it is, but there are these weapons. Maetrie weapons."

"Abominations," said Pandora, continuing to pace.

His friends stared back with concern. "Tears of the Gods. *Plazk-*

abog in their language. Made from obsidian and magesteel. They were made for, I don't know why they were made, but they can destroy an entire realm. Trap it inside and give its power to the wielder. Hylakane had one. Zhinzi. The assassin Kavano has another. Supposedly there's another in the city."

"And now another," said Pandora, her jaw pulsing with anger.

Kuma clasped his hands together. "We don't know that."

"We know it was stolen and it disappeared. What if the thief took it here, escaped through the portal and then destroyed it behind them, but fucked up and the entire place collapsed on him," said Pandora.

It was what he'd been thinking, but he hated speaking it out loud because that might make it true.

"Am I getting this right?" said Vasilisa. "The maetrie can make weapons that will destroy an entire realm? What the fuck. How can we compete with that?"

"They can't make them anymore. The knowledge is lost to time, but there are eleven of these weapons. Four of them haven't been used yet. The artifact in the Dark Depths could be one of them. If that's what it is."

Pandora had her eyes closed and her fingers massaging her forehead. "I always knew my grandfather was ambitious, but he's not like this. He's not a mass murderer."

"You said Hylakane had one?" asked Tick quietly.

"He did. I never liked being near it."

"He was your teacher?"

Kuma wanted to convey that he wasn't like that, but he could understand the disgust on Tick's face.

"He regretted what he did and then his Court was wiped out by one of the Tears. If any of them have paid the price, it's him."

"Fuck me," said Yara. "This could be worse than the invasion."

"We don't know he has designs on this realm," said Pandora. "Why destroy what you've been working so hard to subdue?"

"That doesn't exactly make me feel good," said Choo-Choo. "And you don't know that, Pan. I'm sorry. I know he's your grandfather, but we can't take that chance."

"What can we even do?" asked Tick.

"We have to kill him," said Pandora suddenly.

"Kill. Him. Your grandfather?" asked Tick.

Pandora's eyes were wet. "Yes." She swallowed. "Taking over the Undercity is one thing, but acquiring a Tear. An unused one. There are no good things that can happen with it. Even if he never uses it here."

"We don't know he has it yet," said Choo-Choo. "Maybe soon, but I don't know when."

Kuma shifted off the couch. "Could we take it from them?"

Choo-Choo and his sister shared glances before they both shook their heads.

"Both camps, above and below, were armed to the teeth. And if they're near, that means Titus will probably be on site with his crew. We don't have the numbers, or the firepower," said Choo-Choo.

"What about another hit on the Alliance HQ?" asked Tick.

Kuma shook his head. "When I visited their Academy, it looked upgraded. It was hard enough last time, and that was with Duro and Brazio. I don't think we have enough for that either."

"Then we're fucked," said Tick, slumping into the couch. "The whole city, above and below, is fucked."

"I've already said what we need to do," said Pandora tightly.

"Yeah, but how? He's surrounded by guards at all times," said Tick.

"We have to win the contest. Or at least get into the top eight. There'll be a ceremony," said Pandora, eyes darting all directions. "The winners will have access."

"Are you sure?" asked Kuma. "Despite everything we know, he *is* your grandfather."

"Family isn't the people who gave birth to you," she said, staring into the distance as she mumbled under her breath. He wanted to put his arms around her and tell her everything was going to be okay, but he couldn't do that in front of the others. Nor was he sure he believed it.

"We don't have to decide anything now," said Kuma. "We're still trying to win the contest and we know that Dominion is planning something. Might not have anything to do with our realm, but either way, we don't like it. For now, let's focus on what we can deal with, namely, the contest. Tick. Yara. What's the word on our opponents for tomorrow? And do we have an idea what's going on with the arena?"

Tick pulled out a notebook, licked his finger, and paged through it as he crossed one leg over the other.

"First is Lady Saha. She will be matched against Adriana Kuinin. She was the one who got the last rod. Nigerian born. Like everyone who's left in the contest, she has some supernatural abilities. Moves fast, hits hard. Probably hiding her real powers, but hard to say. You should win, but don't take her lightly."

Pandora looked like she was barely listening. She startled slightly, nodding in Tick's direction.

"Now for Aman Crownline. Your match is against the person who goes by Dream. We don't know much about them. The only thing I can say about the matches is they appeared to be more about the Dream's opponents making stupid mistakes. I worry what that means."

"I'll figure it out when I get there. What about the arena?"

Tick looked to Yara, who frowned. "The gates are blocked so you can't see inside, but I did see them hauling large round beams through the back entrance. There were boxes and other crap that gave me no clue to what's inside, but I have a feeling they're going to add obstacles to the arena."

Kuma thought back to his training with Instructor Kaz when he'd first gotten his emerald. He'd run the course hundreds of times until he could do it with his eyes closed.

"I think it's time to use our stones."

Twenty-Nine

The platform above the packed bleachers was empty. The Alliance banners hung on the front railing. She felt stupid for expecting either her grandfather or mother to be there, as if they were proud parents about to watch their child compete in a meaningless competition.

"Lady Saha?"

"Don't talk to me."

The attendant took a step back and shook his head before hesitantly opening his mouth.

"Your match is next."

"Match? Yes, of course. Lead the way."

The competitor area was on the edge of the arena. Her match was the third of the day. The stands were full, everywhere except the platform. She checked back to see if they'd arrived before removing her crimson cloak with a flourish and tossing it on the bench.

As she stepped onto the stands, she knew she should have been paying attention to the previous matches. The scenes had passed before her eyes, but she'd barely registered them. She'd been too busy thinking about if she could kill her grandfather should the opportunity present itself.

"Twenty-nine pillars. Thirteen rings."

"Excuse me?" asked her attendant. "Did you say thirteen rings? There are fifteen."

Pandora checked back to the arena. She knew the attendant was correct. The ziggurat that had been the focus of the grand melee had been deconstructed and replaced with an obstacle course of pillars, rings, seesaws, and other objects that would make the battle unusual. They stopped at the head judge for the match. Her opponent, Adriana, was waiting, shaking out her arms and stretching her neck like a boxer before a match.

"I'll go over the rules one more time before you begin. The object ball is at the center of the arena. Competitors will begin on the blue and red pillars on opposite sides. When the horn blows, the contest will start. It'll last five minutes, or until someone is unconscious for more than thirty seconds. The competitor with the object ball at the end of the five minutes or thirty seconds of unconsciousness is the winner."

"What if my opponent is dead?" asked Pandora.

Everyone but Adriana reacted with horror. The head judge cleared his throat. "Purposeful killing is outlawed and you will be removed from the contest. But if the death is accidental..."

"I understand. Let's get this over with," said Pandora, marching towards the blue pillar before the judge had dismissed them. Her behavior was chalked up to the peculiarities of Lady Saha, but Pandora knew that wasn't the real reason.

"Get your shit together or you're going to lose this," she muttered under her breath.

The crowd was clearly on her opponent's side. They were already chanting her name. Pandora took her spot on the pillar as the judges moved into their positions. She'd given little thought to her strategy for the contest.

"Begin!"

Pandora was caught in her thoughts, and left the pillar a quarter second after Adriana. A series of posts led to a hanging platform at the center where the object ball was waiting. To Pandora's surprise, her opponent skipped across the obstacles at great speed and snatched the heavy ball off before she'd even reached the platform. Adriana leapt to a hanging ring and with the agility of a squirrel bounding across the branches in a forest, reached the highest level of the arena. The speed at which Adriana moved left Pandora concerned. She followed the path that her opponent had taken, but by the time she neared her position, she'd already traveled to the other side of the arena. The jeers from the crowd burned in Pandora's ears.

She quickly regretted not spending her time memorizing the arena's obstacles. Adriana moved through them as if she'd already scouted the best ways to escape. While Pandora knew her opponent was no match in a stand-up fight, what would it matter if she could never catch her? The cat-and-mouse game continued unabated, with Pandora rarely coming within thirty feet of her opponent. The first two matches of the day had been grueling brawls on the main platform until the last thirty seconds, when one of the competitors grabbed the ball and fled for the remaining time. She'd mistakenly thought her match would be the same.

Pandora pushed the limits of her stones—opal for speed and sapphire to give herself boosts as she leapt. But Adriana was faster. The woman moved like lightning.

The match clock read less than a minute. Pandora paused on a lower post while Adriana rocked on a ring forty feet diagonal from her position. If she was going to catch her, it had to be in the next sequence. There wasn't enough time remaining for another shot.

The crowd's chants broke through Pandora's concentration.

"Saha Sucks! Saha Sucks!"

She recalled the duel with Kuma years ago. While the cavern had changed—only the base of the stalactites remained on the ceiling where Kuma had run through—the mood was drastically different. The duel had been one of honor and the crowd had been silent, waiting to see who would emerge victorious. This was a spectacle. It burned to think how the clans of the Undercity had been cheapened and turned into sideshows at a carnival.

Pandora reviewed the paths that Adriana had followed. She'd picked her paths well. There were three major routes she regularly took. Pandora saw there was no way to catch her. She was too quick and knew her terrain well. Pandora tried not to think of the harsh words spat from Hylakane's lips for her failure to imagine more than her victory. In a fight between knavth and faeila, it's the terrain that decides the winner. She'd thought she was neither, a wraithhawk flying over both, but now she knew she was as dumb as a dolgant wandering into a cloud of the sharp death. Or had this been self-sabotage? The cruel and comfortable skin of the maetrie had worn well. Maybe it was best to lose and forget the Undercity forever.

"Saha Sucks! Saha Sucks! Saha Sucks!"

She ground her foot upon the sands. This was not the way she wanted it to end. Not when her grandfather was poised to do unspeakable things. The paths of her opponent danced in her mind. She saw the routes like strings. *If I run here, she goes there. If I take this path, then she uses this to escape.*

Pandora was running before her mind had caught up with the strategy. When Adriana took the route that would lead them to cross paths, albeit her opponent would do it thirty feet above on the tops of a pillar, Pandora veered left, building up as much speed as possible. At the precise moment Adriana's foot touched the top, Pandora flung herself at the wooden pole, using her sapphire to Push off like a rocket. Her feet hit the heavy structure like a missile. The crack was like a bomb going off. It snapped at the base, exploding into splinters, leaving a jagged spike. The stable pole Adriana was expecting fell away from her foot at the last possible moment, the heavy ball flinging from her hands. She tipped awkwardly, hitting the falling wood and pinwheeling her arms as she dropped directly onto the sharp remains.

The death would be accidental. Despite her words at the beginning of the fight, Pandora felt no ill will towards Adriana. If she died, it would only make her opponents fear her more. It was what Lady Saha would do. It was the maetrie way.

At the last moment, Pandora sent a sapphire Push, deflecting Adriana's falling body to spin away from the tip of the spear. As her opponent hit the sands hard, Pandora scrambled to the leather ball, which had rolled nearby. The bright horns of the match ending left the arena in stunned silence. Medics ran onto the field to care for Adriana, who was bleeding from the mouth, a clear sign of internal injuries, as she coughed and sputtered.

As Pandora strolled from the sands, handing the ball to the judge, she saw a figure upon the platform. Her grandfather stood like a sentinel, a crooked grin announcing his pleasure about the match. He gave her a nod as she exited the grounds, taking her position on the bench next to her body servant. Kuma wouldn't make eye contact, which hurt worse than the knowledge that she'd almost lost.

Thirty

Pandora's match lingered in Kuma's thoughts as he watched Noctus Prime and his opponent, Lars Wagner, settle onto their pillars. Given the size of the competitors, both in excess of four hundred pounds, Kuma thought they'd likely stay to the platform as half the other matches had.

It didn't help that the pillar Pandora had destroyed had changed the field. Not considerably, but it made one of the routes harder to navigate. The wooden spear had to be removed before the fourth match. He'd wanted to talk to her, but there was no way to do it surrounded by the other competitors. He was the only one sitting near. The others had gotten up and moved away, signaling their collective displeasure. To the untrained eye, it appeared that she'd almost killed Adriana, but Kuma knew she'd thrown a last-second Push to keep her from being impaled.

"My money is on Lars if any one of you chickenshits wants to stretch your balls," said one of the Botez twins. A few other competitors nodded in agreement.

Valor Drux pounded his fist on the railing. "Never bet against a Brodarian in battle. I'll take your bet. Five grand for the match. Another five that it doesn't last longer than a minute."

The Botez twin—Kuma couldn't tell which—looked apprehensive about the number.

"That's more than I got liquid, mate."

"I'll wait. But I always collect," said Valor with simmering intensity.

"Fine."

The ex-military warrior had become a favorite of the crowd and the other competitors. He'd assembled the best team during the grand melee and had won each of his matches decisively. He'd fought the match after Pandora's, proving to be a tonic for the crowd after the near-fatal result. Valor had offered his opponent the choice between the platform or a chase between the rings. For the first minute, they'd scrapped on the platform, Valor clearly showing he was the better warrior. Even without the stones he'd acquired, Kuma thought he was formidable, but the addition of the faez crystals gave him the edge he needed against opponents with supernatural abilities. When his opponent grabbed the leather ball and tried to lead him on a chase, Valor easily caught him, demonstrating speed and quickness that rivaled Adriana's. The crowd cheered thunderously when he won the match. Kuma suspected that after Noctus, Valor was the next most difficult opponent.

When the signal was given, the two massive competitors lumbered onto the platform. Both ignored the heavy leather ball. Noctus Prime's grin could have swallowed the moon. At seven feet tall, he was a head taller than Lars, who was a champion in world's strongest man competitions and had fought as a mercenary in other realms. It was the fight everyone had been looking forward to that round.

Lars stomped his foot like a bull readying to charge. The enormous warrior broke into a run that would have made a sprinter proud. Noctus made no move to avoid his approach. The impact became inevitable. But at the last moment, the Brodarian shifted to the side, catching Lars and throwing him over his hip. The German flew through the air like a lead blimp. When he hit, the impact was thunderous. Lars struggled to his feet while Noctus watched passively. He could have taken his opponent out when he was briefly stunned, but he gave him a chance to return, beckoning him with the curl of his fingers.

The second approach was more cautious. Lars shuffled forward, hands ready to grapple. Noctus tilted his head as if he were examining a flower or child's drawing. Then he struck, ramming his knuckles into his opponent's forehead. The big man crumpled to the ground, eyes rolling into the back of his head. Noctus put his foot on the leather ball while the unconscious count was given. The cheer for the non-human's victory was surprisingly robust, but Kuma figured they were entertained by the old warrior's superior display.

"You cheated."

The Botez twin jabbed his finger at Valor, who held his hands out passively.

"It's not my fault I can see who is the better warrior. Don't worry. I won't make you pay up now, but we can work out a schedule for later." Valor shrugged. "If you make the top eight and earn yourself a bloodstone plus whatever else he's offering, you'll have more than enough cash to pay me."

As the field was cleared for the next round, Kuma stood and stretched out his muscles. He wasn't going to make the same mistake as Pandora or some of the other competitors who had underestimated their opponents. Given the scouting report, he knew how he planned on approaching Dream, whether it was a stand-up fight or a chase through the arena. Kuma preferred the latter as his experiences training with Instructor Kaz would give him an edge, but since Dream's previous battles had been surprisingly uninspiring, he wasn't sure what to expect.

Kuma gathered near the judge for final instructions. While they were given he tried to pierce the veil of mystery that his opponent had cultivated in the tournament thus far. Dream was an unassuming figure, with dusty brown hair and an unremarkable face that made it hard to remember. He was neither big nor small. He was the embodiment of the word average and had won his previous fights mostly on the backs of his opponents' mistakes, so there was little to understand. Using his amber, Kuma found it hard to penetrate his opponent's demeanor, as if he hid in a cloud, mist obscuring his true self. As Kuma returned to the pillar for the start of the match, he grew worried that Dream was more than he appeared to be. The lackluster fights compared to the rest of the tournament potentially revealed a darker reason.

When the horn sounded, Kuma burst into movement, beating Dream to the platform. He planned on grabbing the leather ball and making a run for it, but when he leaned down to scoop up the object, his foot kicked the ball over the edge into the sand. Before he could follow it over, his opponent had cut off his advance.

The simple, unforced mistake had Kuma staring over the edge, trying to figure out how it'd happened. Dream had his fists up. His form wasn't all that tight. Kuma shook off the accidental kick and prepared to engage his opponent. He should be able to beat him in a scrap.

The first punch went wide. Kuma didn't even see Dream move. It was as if he'd thought his opponent was in an entirely different location. Kuma resisted the urge to stare at his traitorous hand, but he knew that wasn't the issue. A second attack was met with a block and a counter kick, knocking Kuma back a few steps. This wasn't going as he'd planned. He threw himself at Dream, only to find his attacks missing, or landing as glancing blows, then catching solid hits to the jaw or midsection. The hits weren't particularly intense, the strike of a younger warrior, but collectively they were adding up.

When Kuma went for a roundhouse only to find himself on his back, having caught an elbow to the jaw, he worried he was losing the match. As he popped back to his feet, he saw Lady Saha's incredulous glare as if she couldn't believe he was losing either.

Two more attacks. Two more counterblows, leaving Kuma staggered. Something was wrong. Deeply wrong. Dream was messing with his head. He didn't know how, but there was no way he'd become this shitty of a warrior.

Kuma burned his amber, using every ounce of his energy to flood Dream with his senses. The initial burst of information staggered Kuma with overwhelming details. A spate of vertigo shot through his gut right as Dream caught him in the ribs with a side kick. Kuma retreated before his opponent could follow up with a second attack.

The world didn't make sense to Kuma. It was like looking through two screens, each one showing a different image. The differences were giving him a headache. He thought back to his training in the maze when he first got his amber. This was similar, except that the darkness was one-sided.

When Dream came at him again, he sensed the difference between the two realities. Dream's footfalls didn't match the sound of his approach, nor grunt of his attack. Kuma ignored the Dream he was seeing and blocked the one he detected with his other senses.

Dream frowned.

His hands dropped for a second, even as Kuma found new resolve. Ignoring the visuals, Kuma threw punches and kicks where his amber told him Dream was located. Half his attacks went wide, but he managed a couple of solid blows, leaving his opponent scowling. Encouraged by the result, Kuma threw himself at Dream, forcing his opponent backwards and landing more hits. Kuma saw his chance to knock Dream out of the competition, but then he heard the sound of footsteps rapidly retreating. He followed the sound, running with his eyes closed not to be distracted by false realities, and leapt at the edge of the platform, catching Dream in midair and landing with his full weight on his opponent. Ribs cracked upon impact. Kuma dared to open his eyes to find a different opponent than the one he'd stepped onto the platform with. Tiny bumps covered his face and exposed flesh. Dream was groaning, struggling to remain conscious. Kuma helped him by rabbit punching him in the forehead.

Back on his feet, he had all the time in the world to collect the leather ball to the applause of the crowd. They weren't near as rapturous as the other matches, but he figured that either the scrap hadn't appeared that interesting due to the illusions from Dream, or his connection to Lady Saha made him a less appealing figure.

When he reached the competitor area, Pandora asked him in maetrie, "What was that about? You looked drunk."

"I'll explain later."

He grabbed a water bottle and chugged the contents. Another match in the books. One more for the top eight. Dominion Thule might have turned the Undercity upside down, but Kuma bore a kernel of hope that they could take it back.

Thirty-One

The jacket didn't fit the way Pandora wanted it. She turned as she stared into the mirror, scowling at the woman on the other side. It no longer looked strange to be Lady Saha. She marched back into the other room.

"It's all wrong, isn't it?" she asked a stunned Tick who'd been whispering quietly to Koro.

Camina looked up from her beer and frowned. "You look fine."

"It's not fine. I'm supposed to be a minor noble of the Jade Court, not a traveling huckster. My grandfather will see right through this disguise at the dinner."

"Didn't your mentor give those to you?" asked Camina.

Kuma stepped into the room wearing the same clothes he'd worn on the journey back, except they'd been cleaned by the hotel.

"You look like you're supposed to look, Lady Saha. You're on your liebereisen."

"I'm just not ready for this fucking dinner. This is a mistake. He'll figure out that I'm not who I say I am."

Kuma approached and put his hands on her upper arms, staring her straight in the eyes. A million numbers careened through her head as her heart thumped in her chest.

"We have to go. It would look worse if we declined. Suspicious even. You said it yourself, these kinds of events are as much a battle to the maetrie as the ones in the arena."

The world narrowed. "But you know what we have to do..."

"Not today," he said, shaking his head. "Today is just a nice dinner with our fellow competitors. I'm sure Dominion has a surprise or two for us. Nothing bad. A kink in the competition, but he wants to preen before his guests."

Pandora left her weapon in the suite despite her instincts. The invitation had said not to bring them, but she'd thought about trying to sneak in a short blade. With Kuma at her side, they strolled through the Terreno as visitors gave them a wide berth. She ran through the details of her past, the fabricated history that Hylakane had helped her construct, but each item felt thin and easily exposed.

The dinner was being held at a newer restaurant in the Terreno called the Infernal Kitchen. The place looked like it belonged in the first ward of the city, with attendants opening the door and an expensive brushed steel and polished darkwood exterior. The sign had a real fire burning at the center of the "a." The hostess led them into the back where a private space had been set aside for the competitors. Two of Titus Cabone's mercenaries stood outside with automatic weapons to keep the curious away.

The inner door opened revealing that most of the other guests had already arrived. The towering Brodarian, wearing a stiff military uniform of black and crimson, had a gaggle of admirers who were laughing freely at his battle stories. The other locus was Angel Chen, wearing a voluminous white dress that shifted around her lithe form like wings, reinforcing her name. She looked like the embodiment of a gentle breeze.

"Aman—"

She hadn't realized Kuma had moved away until she'd spoken, but should have anticipated it. They'd discussed how they might approach the evening, and splitting up to learn more about their guests was the plan. The hope was to cautiously suss out potential allies should they take their fight with Dominion into the open.

A waiter who couldn't meet her gaze approached with a tray full of artisanal glasses. She snatched one and marched to an empty part of the room as the way the others turned their backs made it clear they had no desire to speak to her. She hadn't realized that there were others besides her fellow competitors until a voice made her stiffen.

"Lady Saha. What an honor to see you again."

Pandora would have chewed through her glass to avoid speaking to her mother, but as a minor noble, she had no choice but to meet with her host.

"I'm sure you are." She gave her a once-over. "Your dress matches the gleam of your skull, Selena."

Her mother touched the side of her head nervously. "It requires an extra flourish when it comes to fashion. On the good side, the metal absorbs the most wonderful enchantments."

Pandora chewed her words until they were unformed mush. Her mother stared back before sputtering into conversation.

"Your matches have been quite extraordinary. I'm rooting for you to win."

The compliment bounced off Pandora's forehead like a rubber ball. She wasn't even aware that her mother had the capacity, yet here she was, offering kind words to a woman she barely knew, and who was the most hated of the tournament.

"I believe you're the only one," said Pandora, nostrils flaring.

"Quite the contrary. My father is thrilled with your performance, and there are others. Of course, it's not acceptable to cheer for you because you are different and do not bow down to their pathetic niceties. We know the real war. The one that requires never backing down. I believe you have more admirers than you might guess."

"I'm not here for their fawning."

"Of course, Lady Saha. You're a winner. A true warrior." Selena lowered her voice. "Not like most of the others. Sure, there are a few that understand what it takes, but most are just pretending. Playing a part, but soon they will be exposed."

"You presume too much," said Pandora, hoping her mother might find someone else to bother.

"You're right, Lady Saha," said Selena, inclining her head. She faced the party, sipping from her glass. A moment later, an exquisite sigh slipped her lips. "I wish my daughter was here."

"You do?"

Pandora took a drink to hide her shock and the way her voice had cracked, not at all maetrie-like, but her mother was deep into her own thoughts and had missed it.

"I was not aware you had a daughter," she followed up.

"Pandora. She *was* a warrior and held much promise, but she proved to be a catastrophic disappointment. When things got tough, she disappeared. I supposed that comes with having too much human blood. We can't all be predators."

A numbness overtook her entire body. To hear her mother speak about her unbidden by familial bonds was like getting stabbed in the heart. Pandora couldn't speak or move. If someone would have bumped into her, she might have fallen over.

"I'm sorry," said Selena. "You probably don't care about my daughter. Apologies for bringing her up. I don't know why I did that. I barely think about her these days."

"She *was* a warrior?"

Pandora wasn't sure why she'd asked the question, except that it was a scab that she wanted to pick at.

Selena sighed. "A member of the Drops clan. Held multiple stones. In the battle for the Undercity, she chose the losing side, a mistake I cannot understand. Why would she turn against her family? We're all she has."

A cutting laugh slipped out. Selena turned beet red.

"A true warrior sees their own path and takes it regardless of the consequences. Maybe she was disappointed in *you*, Selena Thule," she said, turning on her mother.

Selena's jaw slowly dropped, then snapped shut with fear cascading through her expressions.

"I do all I can for my father. Dominion is a great leader. A visionary." Selena stared at her silvery metal arm. "I was not gifted with the ability to fight, so I find ways other ways to support his vision. You should consider joining with him. His plans are much grander than one might expect, given his position in the Courts. He's going to—"

Her eyes widened as she sensed she'd said too much.

"Going to?"

Selena squeezed her eyes shut as her mouth curled into a rictus of pain.

"No, Selena," she muttered under her breath. Her mother looked up and smile. "Excuse me, Lady Saha. I have to check on preparations."

Her mother marched away, heading through swinging doors in back that led to the staff area. Pandora finished her drink and grabbed another from a tray. She felt lucky that her mother had interpreted her ill-chosen words as admonishment, not the angry rebuke of a spurned daughter.

"Lady Saha, may I speak with you?"

Valor Drux swaggered over with a drink in his hand and a salesman's smile on his lips. Pandora hid her disgust with a drink, hoping he'd get the hint, but he settled next to her as if they were old friends.

"You fight like a demon," he said, gesturing with his glass as if it were a salute.

"I fight to win."

"As do I. I plan on winning the competition. A bloodstone plus a black diamond. I could do anything with that. Easy to be famous with that combination."

"I'm not here to be famous."

"Oh, but you could be," he said. "That's why I wanted to talk. You might not know it, but videos about the competition have blown up online. Do you know what our internet is?"

"I'm not a fucking idiot," said Pandora, using a maetrie word as her curse.

"Sorry about that. I'm not up on the comings and goings of the Eternal City."

"Get on with it," she spat.

"Right. A woman of action. I like it."

She was glad he didn't wink like she thought he would. She would have had to deck him.

"But anyway. Like I said, everyone in this room is famous. I was thinking about putting together a traveling tournament afterwards. A team of warriors like this would make a killing. We could rival the Mystique. Perform superhuman feats, show them how real warriors fight. I know this might not be the typical interest of the maetrie, but I figured since you were on this travel adventure thing, you might consider it." He threw in a wink. "I bet we'd really enjoy getting to know each other."

If it weren't the middle of the party, she would have grabbed his balls and crushed them, not as Lady Saha, but for herself.

"I'm not interested."

Valor opened his mouth as if to add more to his argument, but then he nodded, clearly sensing her simmering animosity.

"Got it. The lone warrior." He clucked his tongue. "You do your thing, Lady Saha, and good luck. I hope we face each other in the finals."

Her chest felt cavernous. The other fools were trying to carve out a name for themselves while she was fighting a hidden war against her grandfather. She watched them laugh together, oblivious to the real battles. It made her feel even more like an outsider. Kuma had joined the group around Angel Chen and was chatting like old friends, while she'd been forced to interact with the parent who'd given up on her. Never had she missed her father more than in that moment. The doors leading out of the party enticed her forward until she heard the tapping of silverware on glass.

"Good evening, my fine warriors," said Dominion at the head of the large table. He wore a black pinstriped suit with a purple tie and managed to make his normally ghoulish expression congenial. "Why don't we all take a seat and break bread together. I've spent almost four decades in your beautiful city, and one of my favorite endeavors has been the gathering for meals."

As she settled into her assigned seat between one of the Botez twins and Angel Chen, waiters spilled from the back room with trays. In a matter of moments, a feast was displayed upon the table, barely enough room to eat.

"Please, everyone dig in."

Pandora wasn't hungry, but she took a few slices of roast pig, not bothering with the greeneries or other delights, while the others dumped huge portions onto their plates. The room returned to its previous volume as conversations, new and old, rose to fill in the silence.

"Your fights were amazing," said Angel as she slipped a hunk of steak between her generous lips.

"My efforts have been lackluster. I have much to improve in this tournament."

"A true warrior never accepts their results as the final word. There's much to admire," said Angel in an easy manner.

"You've fought well too," said Pandora begrudgingly. Pandora wanted to like her, but as Lady Saha she kept her disappointed mien.

"There are no easy fights left. I wonder what kind of surprises our host has planned for the next round. It's the hardest one. The fight before the prize. Imagine how terrible the losers will feel." Angel leaned in conspiratorially. "But I don't think that'll be an issue for you or I."

"I do not fight for prizes."

"You city fae are a strange lot," said Angel, eyes glittering with amusement. "I should like to visit the Eternal City someday."

"You would not like it. It's not a vacation. It is competition incarnate. Death lurks around every corner," said Pandora.

Angel leaned in close, tongue resting on her teeth. "I'm not afraid of danger. It thrills me in fact."

She wanted to call her a fool, but caught Kuma staring. He forced his lips into a fake smile and intensified his gaze.

"I'm sure you would do well in the Eternal City," she said after a pause.

Angel leaned back in her chair. "I thought so too. It's nice to have that confirmation. Has Valor pitched his idea yet? I thought I saw you talking before our host arrived."

"I'm not interested."

Angel placed her hands on her arm. "You should consider it. Think of the fun and adventure. We'd make ourselves filthy rich and more famous than the city mages while having a grand time."

Pandora hesitated because the idea was enticing. To set aside the burdens of her life and learn what pleasures were offered outside the Undercity. The muscles of her chest relaxed and she felt herself breathe more easily. Before she could answer, a waiter leaned in her ear.

"Lady Saha. Mr. Thule would like to speak to you. Sophia Botez has agreed to change places."

At the end of the table, her grandfather raised his glass in salute. The illusion of freedom she'd been contemplating shattered.

"Of course. It would be an honor."

Pandora rose from her chair as staff swept in and changed their places. The spectacle was not lost on the rest of the competitors. Her grandfather could have placed her at his side from the original seating, but making a scene about the move was meant to put a thought into their heads.

"Dominion," she said with an incline of her head as she settled into the chair.

"I can bring something else, if this human food is not to your liking," he said, gesturing towards the mostly untouched pork lying in a pool of pink juices.

"I'm not hungry."

"When was the last time you were at Jade Court?" he asked.

"Decades ago."

"Much has changed since you were there last."

"Nothing stays the same," she said, switching to maetrie. It was a commonly used aphorism. The Eternal City was in constant turmoil. To expect it not to change was akin to keeping your eyes closed.

He continued in their shared language, much to the annoyance of those nearby who'd been planning on eavesdropping.

"Your matches have been...interesting."

She let the insult wash past her untouched. "I've underestimated my opponents, nearly to my demise. They're much stronger than I give them credit for. I'd always considered the humans a lucky race to have been born at a nexus between realms and with an uncanny access to the old powers."

"It is understandable," said Dominion, chuckling as he scooped up his drink. "I've made that same mistake myself, more than once. Their short lives make it easy to see them as inferior, but with such a small window to affect the world, they burn bright. In a way, our longevity is a curse. It makes us complacent, thinking that long, careful strategy will overcome any resistance."

"You admire them."

He quirked his mouth. "Understand them. Some more than others. There are those within their society that have the same zeal for dominance that our kind does."

"I do not care for them."

"Yet you keep one as a body servant."

His twisted smile spoke volumes.

"Aman is useful."

"Is he loyal?" asked Dominion with eyebrows raised.

"He was bred to be a war slave. Compliance comes naturally," she said.

Dominion stilled, which attuned her to his mood.

"After the tournament is there any way I could convince you to stay and join my retinue? I think you'd find my ambitions are not small."

"I seek personal improvement."

He smiled, smoothing the table covering with the flat of his hand.

"I can offer that. You might remember my association with a certain freelance warrior."

"Kavano."

"We've an agreement. I employ him from time to time. I'm sure I could ask him to train you, if that was your wish."

The offer was astronomical. As Kavano was considered by his peers to be the greatest warrior of the maetrie race, the proposal was on the same level as the stones themselves. What Dominion didn't know was that she'd already been trained by one of Kavano's equals, but that wasn't something that Lady Saha would have in her history.

"An intriguing idea."

She scanned the table as she waited for Dominion to continue.

"Just intriguing?"

Pandora leaned her head lazily in his direction. "The Courts, the nobles, they're like riding a stelynka without a saddle. No matter what position you end in the race, you're left a bloody mess."

"I would not think you afraid of a little battle."

"I like to know how badly I'll be cut," she said.

His nostrils flared. "Are you suggesting I'm merely a mount to be ridden?"

"I don't recall *you* ever signing up to ride. You made your living as a stelynka salesman. Are you telling me you're entering the gonka?"

Her grandfather leaned back in his chair as he surveyed the table. She leaned in close.

"I fought for the generals in Brodarian. I've taken bounties in Danir, hunted dragon salamanders in Caer Corsydd, and survived the death cults of Normadia. But only when I understood the stakes." She grabbed her drink. "This tournament belittles your ambitions. If you can tell me what you're truly after, I might consider it."

Dominion speared her in his sights. The end of the table near them had stilled as if they sensed the tension. He seemed to recognize his outward disdain and let the corners of his mouth twitch into the semblance of a smile.

"You see clearly. But I'm afraid I cannot elaborate. You'll just have to take me at my word. I assure you that I treat my friends well."

"I will think on it."

He raised his glass towards her. "That's all I ask."

As he nodded, he rose suddenly, holding his drink and switching back to English.

"I would like to propose a toast to the fine warriors in attendance. There's a saying in my lands. Vyagragot. It means heads I win, tails you lose. It's not a kind strategy, as those of my people never are, but it's one reason that I came to your world. I prefer the idea that we can all profit together. This tournament has helped put the Undercity on the map, and I must thank you all for that. I'm aware that some of you are discussing a traveling martial arts show, and if you would like I can help fund such an endeavor, but I would leave such a decision up to you."

The table erupted in applause as everyone looked around at each other and nodded while Pandora sat quietly. She saw the greed in their eyes. Already they were spending the money they had yet to earn, and that would come with hidden strings.

"We can save those business decisions for later. For tonight, I wanted to meet with you all, share bread, and announce the format for the next round." He paused, looking to each as he kept his glass in hand. "As great warriors you each excel in many arts. We've seen thrilling hand-to-hand battles, chases across uneven terrain, and a brutal but entertaining grand melee. What we haven't seen yet is how you each fight with your preferred weapons."

The table erupted in chatter while Pandora's gut twisted into a knot. While she was an expert with the short, curved blades favored by the clans, she'd barely begun to learn the weapons that Hylakane had given her. The others at the table had more time and experience with their tools of war.

"I can see by the conversation that the next round excites. I know it will be the best round yet. To help you prepare, I'm here to announce the matchups."

Dominion placed his hands behind his back.

"There will be eight fights over two days. Four per day, spaced out to give our crowds ample time to enjoy each one. I know this round means much to each one of you. A bloodstone is on the line, and for the eventual winner, a black diamond. Know that there are few of those stones in existence. I'm offering a priceless prize that I look forward to handing over *personally* during a private ceremony after the final match. I hope you will fight accordingly."

He lifted his glass, a gesture echoed by the rest of the table, before letting his mouth wrinkle with the semblance of a smile.

"The first fight will be Valor Drux versus Simon Botez."

The older warrior saluted the younger one, who'd been sitting to her left previously. Pandora was glad to see this matchup as it would eliminate one major contender.

"The second match will be Angel Chen versus Laird Green."

The applause that followed was not enjoyed by Angel's opponent, who cleared recognized the mismatch of skill.

"Third match will be Darian Orpheum versus Sophia Botez."

More applause but by the appraising nods, most thought the match would be more equal than the previous.

"The fourth and final match for the first day will be Lady Saha versus Jack Sugihara."

Pandora glanced across the table, finding her opponent nodding in her direction. He was a handsome gentleman who had entertained the crowd with his smooth style. She raised her glass as she was glad to find that she hadn't been matched with Kuma. It would have been bad for their plan to have one of them knocked out before the top eight.

She was thinking about what she knew about Jack Sugihara as the other matches were called. She hadn't been paying attention to who had been named, only that it wasn't Kuma. But when the third match of the second day was called, the rest of the group started smiling and laughing. She looked down to Kuma, who stared back with wide eyes.

"The last match of the round will be between the two that have seen action on the Brodarian plains. Noctus Prime versus Aman Crownline."

Thirty-Two

Kuma stepped to his right, swinging the dire mace overhead, only to shatter the designer lamp hanging from the ceiling. Thin shards of glass fell across his shoulders as he let the weapon relax at his side.

"This is pointless," said Kuma, knocking the pieces from his clothes. "We need to find an open cavern for this."

The tight confines of the suite, despite having moved the furniture into the master bedroom, did not provide much practice space. Choo-Choo rested the plastic angerblade on his shoulder. They'd made it from trays they'd stolen from the kitchen, cutting them to size and melting them together to form a facsimile of Noctus Prime's preferred weapon.

"There are too many eyes about, and you know I can't easily leave the Terreno."

"I know, Choo-Choo. I need to get my mind right about this. Otherwise I'll never have a chance at beating him."

His former rival smirked. "Let's talk through the strategy. Your muscles should remember how to swing a weapon."

Kuma wondered what Hylakane would have suggested as a strategy, but given his skill, he might not have even considered the match worth a single thought.

"Let's do it."

Choo-Choo held up the plastic weapon. It looked like an enormous cleaver with a short handle. The real version weighed around seventy pounds.

"Remember, under no circumstances can you allow yourself to be hit by his weapon. It cleaves through armor and will take your limbs off as easily as pruning a shrub. The key will be to wear him out, never letting him near until you can knock him down with your dire mace."

Kuma laughed. "You make it sound so simple. And when have you ever pruned a shrub?"

Choo-Choo grinned. "Despite his size, he's quick. Don't let him bait you into a counteract early in the fight. Especially not into his chain shield, which is perfectly suited for capturing your weapon. He has more reach too. Your best bet will be to keep him turning. He's fast front to back, but doesn't rotate well. If the terrain is uneven, then that strategy will be even better."

"What if it's a cage, or something I can't escape from?"

"Then you're fucked, Kuma. If you value your limbs, you'd probably want to tap out quickly."

A knock on the door startled Kuma. An attendant stood outside with a letter in his hand.

"This invite is for Aman Crownline."

"That's me," said Kuma, accepting the thick parchment and closing the door.

"A letter?"

"Invite," said Kuma, settling onto the arm of the couch against the wall. The front had his false name written in beautiful calligraphy. The card inside revealed a short message written on card stock with the hotel logo.

"He used the gift shop," said Kuma, chuckling. "I would have liked to have witnessed that purchase."

"Who?"

"Noctus," he said, handing it over to Choo-Choo.

"Please accept my invitation for a ceremony of haflwyer at Club Onyx at your immediate convenience." Choo-Choo looked up. "Haflwyer?"

"Brodarian tea ceremony. Haflwyer is a narcotic. They drink it before big battles. Sometimes generals meet halfway and drink together before returning to their separate sides," said Kuma.

"You're not going, right?"

Kuma frowned. "I have no choice. To refuse would be a great insult. On the other hand, I suspect he knows I'm not who I say I am and this will only confirm it. There is almost no literature about the details of the ceremony."

"This will put the whole plan in danger."

The risk was real, but Kuma didn't think he could refuse. Not and face the seven-foot-tall warrior in the arena with his angerblade and chain shield.

"I don't think so."

"Why?"

Kuma thought about his interactions with the Brodarian. "He's here for the tournament. Exposing me would only knock me out, and I believe he is more interested in the fights than winning."

"I thought Brodarians loved winning more than anything else."

"Competing, not winning. They just happen to be really good at winning. I don't know much about them, but Hylakane told stories about Brodarian armies meeting on the battlefield, fighting for days, and then returning to their homelands content that they'd waged the war with honor."

"And I thought Razor clan was weird," said Choo-Choo.

"It all seems like a dream now."

Choo-Choo furrowed his forehead before nodding, a wry smile on his lips. "I miss the days when you were my mortal enemy."

"I as well. Simpler days, man. Simpler days."

After changing into his travel clothes, Kuma headed to Club Onyx. When he stepped through the inner door, a flood of memories hit him. The lights and sounds made him feel like he'd come home—a place that didn't exist anymore. The booths were packed with tourists enjoying conversation with their elegantly dressed hostesses with bottles of bubbly or whiskey at the center of the table. A couple of drunken businessmen were singing karaoke on the main stage to the applause of their friends, while the bar was layers deep.

"Welcome to Club Onyx, Aman Crownline."

Kuma's mind blanked when he realized that Leesa was standing next to him in a silvery dress that hung on her lithe frame, exposing her collar-bones. Her hair was a mix of red and blonde.

"I'm looking for Noctus Prime. He's a—"

"We're well acquainted with Noctus. He's a regular guest when he's not competing. Follow me. He has a private room."

She led him to the party rooms on the opposite side of the stage. The paper door slid wide, revealing the enormous Brodarian. A stylish tea set with a cherry blossom motif sat at the center of the table.

"Aman! I am quite pleased that you accepted my invitation. Thank you, Leesa, for bringing him."

"Shall I send for drinks or food?" she asked.

"Today my friend Aman and I will be dining on conversation and tea."

"Very well."

Leesa left and he took the spot opposite Noctus.

"A bittersweet match at the cusp of rewards," said the Brodarian.

"I would have preferred to meet you anytime rather than this part of the tournament," said Kuma, truthfully.

Noctus' ever present smile faltered. "You fight well, but it won't be enough, my friend."

"Was this invitation to intimidate me?" asked Kuma.

"Not at all. I wanted to share tea as is customary before a big battle."

He grabbed the pot and began to pour two cups.

"You brought haflwyer?"

"It does not travel well. This is green tea, which I thought would be more appropriate for you."

Kuma froze for a second and when Noctus' lips curled into a grin, he knew he'd made a mistake.

"You know."

Noctus let out a belly laugh. "The knot for the dire mace is wrong, haflwyer ceremonies are never offered outside my race because it's often fatal to outsiders, and when we had our day of competition at the pachinko parlor, you moved around the streets as if you'd been born here."

"Was it that obvious?"

"To me, yes. To others, I cannot say. Who are you really? I've met shapeshifters before, but you do not seem like a true changeling."

Kuma sipped his tea. The bitter flavors warmed his belly.

"I'd rather not say."

"Secrets are heavy burdens."

"This isn't to blackmail, is it? I drop out or you expose me?" asked Kuma, cradling the warm cup in his hands.

"I would not dishonor our relationship with such a strategy. I do not know why you hide your face, but I expect it has to do with our host, Dominion."

Kuma glanced towards the paper door, which prompted a laugh from Noctus. He pulled out a black box and set it on the table.

"I do not like to be bothered. I picked one of these up in the city before I entered the Undercity. We're safe to talk." Noctus gestured towards the colorful teapot, which Kuma shook off. "I assume Lady Saha is also not who she appears to be, though I have to say I have not found any cracks in her armor."

Kuma's gut tightened with the thought that he'd been the one to blow their disguises.

"I wish I could say more, but I cannot."

The Brodarian took a sip of his tea as he contemplated the situation.

"Given the knowledge of the Terreno, I suspect that you're a former member of the clans. Probably out to seek your revenge for what happened years ago when our host took control of the Undercity. Do I have it right?"

Kuma sighed reluctantly, which encouraged a smile from his counterpart.

"Do not worry, friend Aman. I do not seek to expose you, only to satisfy my curiosity. This problem has been a burr in my mind. Knowing the truth, even if incomplete, will help me sleep better at night." He let out a belly laugh. "Do you know the best way to defeat a Brodarian?"

"What?"

"Give them an interesting problem that he cannot solve easily," said Noctus, continuing to laugh. "There was a famous battle a few centuries ago that halted halfway through the melee when a strange flash of light fell upon the bloody fields, followed by an explosion in the nearby mountains. The two sides stopped the battle and sent a combined expedition party to discover the reason, only to find it was a meteor. Once they'd returned and the combatants understood why, the battle resumed its fever."

"Who won?"

Noctus quivered even as no noise came out. "No one remembers as it wasn't as interesting as the mystery."

"Or are these stories to confuse your enemies?" said Kuma, lifting his cup.

The big Brodarian winked before taking on a serious mien. He set his hands flat on the table, on opposite sides of his cup.

"I am concerned about our fight tomorrow."

"That you might lose?" asked Kuma with a smirk.

"I wish it were more even, I truly do. Maybe if we fought with fists, or the construction of the arena were different, but the angerblade was developed in the gladiator pits, where death was the loser's reward. I do not wish to hurt you, my friend."

"Use another weapon."

"I cannot. It is not in my blood to give up an advantage," said Noctus.

"And I must win this round and reach the final eight."

"The prize is important to your plans. The bloodstones." Noctus narrowed his gaze. "What do you plan, friend Aman?"

"Please do not ask me that question," said Kuma, shaking his head.

"Fair enough." Noctus' head dipped towards his chest before rising again. "Let us set aside these weighty matters and enjoy our tea in broth erhood. The universe hums its own tune. Let's sing together awhile."

Kuma lifted his cup in salute, taking a sip which the Brodarian matched. Noctus set his down as a grin spread across his enormous face.

"Let me tell you about the time I stole into the Arch Imperator's highland palace and slept with his bonded sister during the Seven Empire Battle..."

Thirty-Three

Pandora stayed in the suite during the morning of the fight, receiving updates from Tick, who returned after the first two fights. Valor Drux defeated the male Botez twin after a twelve-minute duel that had delighted the crowd and solidified the winner as the fan favorite. The second match between Angel Chen and Laird Green proved less enjoyable as she won in a short twenty-second contest that ended with her saber in his shoulder, after which he tapped out.

She intended to watch the third match, but hadn't mustered the energy to get up from the edge of the bed. The ornate box holding the wraithhawk mask sat next to her. She pulled it into her lap, running her palm across the smooth wood before unclasping the metal latch and lifting the lid with both hands.

The mask was an exquisite work of art. She gently fit her fingers beneath and pulled it out before cradling it in her hands. The material was unknown to her, but it was warm and the edge shifted with shadowy purpose. It was an ancient maetrie artifact. She imagined Hylakane standing in his garden surrounded by the ethereal creatures wearing the mask.

"Do not forget from which it came, or why it was made," she repeated, hearing Hylakane's stern voice in her head. It was a gift to help with her grandfather, though he'd never elaborated why. Was he afraid of wraithhawks? Pandora didn't think so. She'd never heard of such a fear, and in truth, all maetrie were wary of the strange birds due to their untouchable existence.

After caressing the mask for inspiration, she returned it to its home, closing the box and readying herself for the match.

She carried the stalbyka in its sheath and wore the metal-lined crimson cloak as she walked through the Terreno. The crowd parted around her, whispers rising like wings. She felt weighed down by the expectations of the fight. Her opponent, Jack Sugihara, was an expert swordsman with a past that suggested unusual magical origins. Videos of him running up thin wires or across short stretches of water made it clear that it would be no ordinary fight. She had every intention of using her sapphire, but feared her relative inexperience with her weapons would prove decisive.

The arena was packed. She bypassed the heavy crowds standing outside the gate hoping for someone to leave so they could take their place. The guards let her through a side door. The judges were preparing the floor for the third match. This round the terrain was simple. A flat wooden platform that extended a good distance, providing ample area to scrap.

On the way to the competitor area, she briefly spied Dominion and her mother, standing on the platform with the mercenary Titus Cabone. For once, seeing them didn't bring a tightness to her chest, but she was so focused on the upcoming match, the larger concerns felt distant.

Pandora took her spot next to Kuma, who was sitting at the end of a bench by himself, bouncing his knees and looking more like he was the one about enter the arena. He inclined his head, but said nothing. A lot rested on them reaching the next round and earning bloodstones.

The two competitors took to the wooden stage. Darian Orpheum in a dark blue uniform reached it first, idly spinning a metal staff with the ease of a master. He took his position on the far side, performing a series of intense, speedy maneuvers and flips with his weapon, before tossing it high into the air and catching it behind his back to the applause of the crowd.

In contrast, Sophia Botez marched onto the platform like the headsman preparing for the first beheading of the day. She had the intensity of a live bomb. Unlike Darian, she held her sword stiffly at her side, performing no tricks, not giving the crowd any indication of her skill. The simmering anger seemed in reaction to her twin's earlier loss, leaving this match as the only chance for them to earn a bloodstone.

Bets were being thrown around in the crowd and amongst the competitors, with Darian receiving the higher totals, but Pandora wasn't sure that was correct. The stylish tricks that worked in performance competitions weren't the same as a real fight. On the other hand, the staff was a good weapon against a single saber. The smooth metal bar had more reach and attacked faster, making it like a dual weapon and single weapon in the same breath.

"Begin!"

The start of the match had her heart climbing into her chest, despite not being on the stage. The two competitors approached cautiously, Darian spinning the staff while Sophia stared back with the blade at her side. Pandora didn't see what triggered the start, but they threw themselves at each other, saber and staff ringing against each other in a furious display of attack and defense. The pass lasted five seconds at most, but involved dozens of parried strikes.

Having tested each other's defenses, the two circled like predators looking for a weakness. The next attack came from Sophia, leaping high with what at first looked like a blindly aggressive attack that left her open to counters. But when she landed on the opposite side of Darian, he touched his chest, pulling away his hand to reveal it was covered in blood. The crowd, ripe with tension, erupted in applause. A minor cut, but a cut nonetheless.

Darian wiped his hand on his pants before facing off with Sophia. She slammed her foot on the wooden platform, sending a ripple of energy through the surface. The wave put Darian off-balance as she threw herself forward, blade in a high strike position. He spun his staff to block, but the undulating floor kept him uneven. When his staff clattered onto the wood, a gasp shot through the crowd as they saw the saber deep in Darian's chest. He fell to his knees, mouth agape, the life quickly draining from his expression as medics ran onto the stage. Pandora had seen what had happened though it'd been so quick that it made it hard to process.

Everyone in the arena was standing as the medics fell to their knees to work on a prone Darian. Flashes of magic bounced over his fallen form, but Pandora knew exactly where that blade had been thrust, making it unlikely he would ever get up. In the matter of half a minute, the medics stopped their attempts to revive him. A sheet was laid over Darian.

"There will be a thirty-minute break before the next match."

Sophia returned to the competitor area without her weapon and sat by her twin. No one moved until Noctus banged his fists together.

"For Darian Orpheum. May he never lose another battle."

A few matched Noctus' gesture, or added ones particular to them. As Pandora contemplated her fight, it wasn't the prospect of death that concerned her. She'd faced worse in the shadows of the Undercity, or the streets of her grandfather's home. What concerned her was that everything she'd done thus far might be nullified by a failure in the arena. Only with a bloodstone and then a black diamond for winning the entire tournament could she even conceive of a world in which she could take down her grandfather's rule.

The time passed painfully slow. She'd expected to step into the arena not long after the third fight, but Darian's death had changed the timing. She felt bad that she was more perturbed about the delay than his death, but in her eyes, more than one life weighed on her reaching the final eight. The crowd stayed in the stands during the wait, no one wanting to give up their seat.

When the body had been removed and the blood on the wooden platform cleaned as best as possible, the judge ushered her into the arena. She kept her weapon in its sheath, crossing to her appointed spot. Jack Sugihara stood opposite her. Their weapons were of similar nature, a curved blade made to kill and not get trapped. But she came with an additional weapon, the metal-weighted cloak that acted as both shield and distraction.

Unlike during her previous matches, Pandora felt completely attuned to the battle. She watched the rise and fall of Sugihara's chest, felt the calmness of her heart, and prepared herself for the fight.

"Begin!"

Pandora met him at the midpoint, blades clashing in a testing advance. They struck and defended cleanly. She sensed his strikes were superior, but not so much that she felt outclassed. The second pass was a high-low stratagem that she saw clearly. When Sugihara followed with the cut towards her legs, she threw a block, but at the last moment, he twisted his hand and a gust of wind punched her in the gut. Her block glanced against his blade, which still sliced through the fabric of her pant leg. She retreated quickly to assess the new information.

The corner of Sugihara's mouth curled upward. He'd hidden his ability thus far in the tournament, but she could see in his gaze that he was angry that it hadn't been the decisive blow that he'd hoped.

When they met again, swords clashing, their bright sounds ringing through the air, she waited for his hand to twitch and slammed him with a Push at the same time, following up with an angled attack. He stumbled backwards, barely getting his weapon up in time, but she switched to a Pull on his legs. The blade kissed off the other and caught him in the upper arm. Sugihara retreated to open space, checking his arm when he saw that she was not pursuing. The crowd whistled and softly applauded at the exchange.

The third pass began cautiously. Sugihara approached, clearly apprehensive about her surprise.

But she wasn't finished.

He blasted her with a wave of air that felt like getting hit by a mini-hurricane. Squinting through the wind, she knew he was coming too fast, so she let the gust twirl her backwards, flinging her cloak into a high arc. The metal-lined material slammed into his blade, and as she curled around, she hit his legs with a heavy Push. Sugihara stumbled to a knee, and she continued through the spin, halting with her blade against the back of his neck.

"Do you yield?"

Sugihara's eyes closed and his chin dipped towards his chest as he exhaled with disappointment.

"I yield."

She pulled the blade from his neck as the judge announced her as the winner. The applause was muted, but she didn't care as she returned to the competitor area under the watchful gaze of her grandfather and mother.

Thirty-Four

Camina gave the students at the Academy the week off to watch the rest of the tournament. She wasn't sure if she didn't care after Titus raided her students, or if she thought they were too distracted to be effective learners. Originally, she had no intention of going herself, but as she sat at the edge of the bed in her little room at the Academy, knees bouncing with a lingering annoyance in her gut, she decided braving the crowds was better than being alone.

The Terreno was more packed than she'd ever seen it. She had to jostle with men and women in business attire, or drunken college students with neon plastic cups full of alcohol in their fists. The change in five years from when she'd first come to the neutral ground as a new waku made it feel like an entirely different place. A guy with a wave of blond hair and a salmon-colored shirt spilled sticky liquid across her arm when he stumbled into her. He opened his mouth to say something pithy, but the look she gave him had him swallowing and hurrying to catch up to his friends.

She lingered near the entrance of Club Onyx. A few hours of having someone listen to her problems sounded like a nice diversion, but seeing Leesa would only make her homesick for the old days, which didn't exist anymore. Instead, she headed towards the arena where the first fight of day two was due to begin soon. Long lines led up to the gate, with people pushing and shoving to get in before the arena was full. She'd heard there were people camping out the night before. A death on the previous day had tripled the price of the tickets.

"Hey, lady, you can't butt in line," said a drunken guy with a lazy gaze and an enormous neon mug. He reached out to grab her upper arm, so she sent opal energies into his hand, making his flesh heat up immediately. "Hey! What the fuck. What did you do to me?" he asked, pulling his hand away and shaking it furiously. "You're one of *them*, aren't you? That was a neat trick. Can you do another?"

Camina leveraged her way past him, aggressively pushing through the crowd and ignoring their complaints. She reached the gate and the guard started to tell her that she couldn't come in until he saw who she was.

"Instructor Camina. Please come in through this side gate. There aren't extra seats, but maybe you could use the platform."

She said nothing, heading inside to get away from the sea of eyes on her back. She found a spot along the wall in back partially opposite of the platform, which was currently empty. The arena was a marvel. Nothing as large as the stadiums in the light, but for the Undercity, it was huge. She immediately spotted the stain where the competitor had died the previous day. It'd been a huge topic of discussion at the Academy, with many of her students asking if they'd shut the tournament down because of it. At first she'd been surprised by their comments, but then she remembered most of them had never seen a dead body, let alone been the cause of one.

Movement across the arena clued her to Dominion's arrival. The gaunt city fae took to the platform to scant applause. He seemed unfazed by their lack of adoration.

His arrival signaled the start of the second day of matches. The two competitors took the field, but Camina was barely paying attention because she'd spied a familiar face on the platform with Dominion. The pale-haired Navos was a personal guard, staring over the crowd with a stoney expression, nothing like the cheerful waku she'd come to know during her short time in the Drops. But the change in personality wasn't a surprise, given her own experiences in the Alliance.

She wondered if they'd given him the same course of drugs and conditioning that she'd received after she was captured. Curious, she stared intensely at Dominion and found her thoughts weren't as scrambled as they'd been in years past. She tested her theory by imagining stabbing him through the heart. It brought a wave of vertigo and blurry vision, but nothing like the complete shutdown that such thoughts created previously.

Rising cheers and applause signaled the start of the match. She wasn't expecting to be impressed, especially since she'd heard most of the best warriors had fought on the first day, but the two combatants threw themselves at each other with their signature weapons—twin kamas and a long spear. The second weapon had the reach, but the kamas were effective at blocking and trapping the extended attacks. The match went on for a few minutes, each combatant catching their opponent with glancing blows. The end came when Winchester Caine overextended his spear and Bo Kan trapped the shaft between the kamas and yanked the weapon away. Bo Kan was declared the winner once his opponent yielded with blades to his neck.

The next two matches were less interesting. Camina barely paid attention, even though the entire tournament had been her idea. She checked back to the platform occasionally. Somewhere during the second match, Selena Thule joined her father. She almost expected to see Deacon, but he'd been scarce as of late. The same with Titus Cabone. She understood the latter as she heard there were breakthroughs at their dig site in the Dark Depths. No one explained what it was they were looking for, but she assumed it had to be extremely valuable given the money and manpower that had been devoted to the excavation project.

When the fourth and final match was announced, Camina paid attention. The seven-foot-tall Brodarian was considered by some to be the best warrior, while others named Valor Drux, Angel Chen, or Lady Saha. Camina felt sorry for his opponent. Aman Crownline was outmatched with his heavy mace, compared to the frightening looking weapon called an angerblade held by Noctus Prime. It looked like it was part of a massive machine press meant for cutting thick pipes rather than a weapon to be wielded by a single individual.

The two competitors stood side by side as they waited for the arena surface to be cleaned of blood from the previous match. Aman stared curiously at the ceiling, making her wonder what was up there. She assumed it had to do with his strategy, given the importance of the next few minutes, but found he was only staring at a truncated set of stalactites. The line of limestone extensions had been first destroyed years ago during a duel between Kuma and Pandora, but then shaved down to stubs during the construction of the arena. Why would Aman stare at the old stalactites? Especially at a time like this. She reviewed their conversations at the Academy, but found nothing to illuminate her concerns. Her curiosity deepened as he stepped forward when his name was called, waved briefly to the crowd, and then went through a series of stretches. Something about his mannerisms were familiar. So familiar that she felt like she was seeing double. As Noctus Prime was announced to the crowd, the roar of applause drowned out her thoughts, but did not dissuade her from the idea that somehow, some way, she knew Aman Crownline.

Thirty-Five

He was the first person Choo-Choo noticed when he entered the arena midway through the first fight. He'd waited until the crowds were thickest to reduce the chance of being identified. Not that he thought they were looking for him or his sister. They were probably assumed dead from the maetrie construct, but he didn't want to give them that chance. The ticket price had been astronomical, but they still had cash to spare. Vasilisa had stayed back at the hotel, claiming a headache, but he knew that the fights only reminded her of Andelei.

"Can you hurry up?" asked a guy from behind, shoving him from the back.

Choo-Choo had stilled when he'd seen Navos on the platform. The guy behind him tried to nudge him forward, but he lacked the leverage. Choo-Choo stayed a moment longer than necessary before continuing along the passage to reach his seat. He ended up about a hundred feet from the platform. Seeing Navos only reminded him that their raid on the complex had been a disaster. He missed Navos more than he allowed himself to contemplate. The tall, blond waku had been the cheerful counter to his morose moods. But now he didn't look the same. He had the blank countenance one might expect on a statue.

Applause startled him out of his thoughts as the first match came to a conclusion with Bo Kan as the winner. Choo-Choo hadn't cared who won, as he thought both competitors had little chance of beating any of the others in the top eight. He wished that Kuma had been in one of their spots so they could have two bloodstones. Choo-Choo didn't give much hope to his former rival's chances against the seven-foot-tall Brodarian.

Halfway through the third fight, Choo-Choo sensed movement on the platform. He caught Titus Cabone in his black gear ascending to join Dominion and his daughter. The arrival of the mercenary leader made Choo-Choo want to leave the arena and at the same time, get closer so he could hear what he had to say. An attempt to listen with his amber proved fruitless as the crowd's energetic chanting was covering up anything said on the platform.

Choo-Choo rose from his seat and made his way closer, hoping to get in range before the conversation ended. He kept his head down while he watched their expressions, catching Dominion looking unhappy with what Titus had to say. Fearing he was going to miss it, Choo-Choo barreled over a couple of attendees to make it to the outer ring, where he hurried near the platform, feigning looking for his seat.

"I don't care what you have to do. Throw more men at it. We're too close to give up now," said Dominion.

"It's proved more resistant than expected," said Titus.

"If you have to personally acquire it for me, I suggest that you do so. I'm not paying you these considerable sums for your constant failure. Maybe I should have had Kavano stay. He might be a pain in my ass but he's reliable."

Titus glowered quietly, but bowed his head. "You'll have it by the end of the tournament."

"That's better."

The black-clad mercenary left the platform. Choo-Choo lingered as he watched Navos stare out across the crowd with a blank expression. *What did they do to you?* He'd never known his friend to be still. Ever.

Whenever he bunked over, part of the reason they stayed up all night talking was because Navos fidgeted like a kid after the candy store. There was no point in sleeping.

A hand grabbed his upper arm, startling him. “I know you.”

Choo-Choo froze. He’d been recognized from the trip to the excavation site by one of the guards. He knew it. He turned slowly, formulating his escape out of the arena, which would only work due to the heavy crowds.

The Alliance guard uniform had Choo-Choo wondering what stones he might have in case he had to quickly disable him. Choo-Choo didn’t recognize him, but there’d been other guards at the entrance when they’d made the bribe. The tense standoff had the guard furrowing his forehead as if something wasn’t as expected. Choo-Choo squeezed his hand into a fist, preparing the first blow.

“I saw you push those people over back there. I don’t know what you think this place is, but we don’t tolerate that kind of behavior.”

The unexpected admonishment had a curt laugh slipping from his lips. The Alliance uniform, which had at one time brought concern as a rising power in the Undercity, looked more like a janitor’s outfit.

“I’m sorry. I won’t do it again,” Choo-Choo said. “Now if you would excuse me, I think I remembered my buddies are in a different section.”

Choo-Choo slipped past the incredulous guard, working his way back to the other area. He reached it as the third fight ended, leaving the final match between Kuma and Noctus Prime. As he settled into his seat, he hoped that Kuma at least survived with all his limbs.

Thirty-Six

The first three fights blew by in a dream. Kuma found himself on the platform next to Noctus Prime all too soon. The nervousness reminded him of his duel with Pandora, prompting him to check the ceiling for the truncated stalactites that he'd run through to surprise her and force a yield. He wished the battlefield had more obstacles, giving him a better chance. The straight-up fight, dire mace versus angerblade and chain shield, was not in his favor.

The judge called them to the center, where he gave a brief rundown of the rules, which hadn't changed, so Kuma was barely listening. He took position across from the enormous Brodarian. Kuma had never fought someone so large.

Noctus wore padded leather armor with strips of metal sewn into the sections. It was protective without being overly heavy. Kuma had hoped he would be wearing the heavier armor common to the Brodarian battlefield, but without guns in play, his opponent had chosen mobility over protection.

"May your blade stay sharp and your shield never shatter," said Noctus, inclining his head.

Kuma almost said, "May the shadows keep you safe." Until he remembered who he was. He switched at the last moment, repeating Noctus.

"Begin!"

Noctus' grin split his face, exposing his snaggletooth as he hefted the angerblade and chain shield. The latter's shifting metal made it sound like a miniature waterfall. Kuma circled slowly, keeping his distance from the big warrior, knowing that he could close the distance in an eyeblink.

"If you're not going to fight, you should yield," said Noctus.

"You haven't attacked yet either," smirked Kuma.

Noctus lunged forward. The angerblade was like an industrial scythe cutting a field of wheat in one swing. Kuma leapt over the weapon, swinging his dire mace at his opponent's hand. The brutal spikes clanked against the handle, barely missing flesh. A kick forced Kuma to retreat, but Noctus kept coming, wielding the enormous blade like a dining utensil. Kuma ran out of room as he neared the edge of the platform. Getting knocked off would be an easy way out of the fight, but he had no intention of giving up.

Switching to Lightness, he leapt thirty feet to a safe spot away from the Brodarian. The space gave him room to cycle Heavy before Noctus found him again.

“A nice trick, but it won’t save you.”

Noctus attacked again, but Kuma didn’t engage. He ceded territory and leapt away when nearing the edge. This repeated a few more times before the restless crowd started jeering.

“You’d make a poor gladiator,” said Noctus.

“It’s a good thing I’m not one.”

Noctus surged forward, but instead of bringing his angerblade around, he kept his weapon and shield in a ready stance. Kuma resisted the urge to counterattack, knowing it would only get his dire mace tangled in the shield. The lack of engagement left their encounter to consist of the pair of them shuffling around the platform in a one-way dance. Seeing that Noctus was prepared to match his strategy, he flicked his mace towards the angerblade side in an attempt to catch the Brodarian’s hand, but he blocked with a shift of the weapon and counterattacked with the chain shield.

The heavy links caught Kuma across the shoulder. It felt like getting whipped by a chain link fence and had enough weight to knock him off his feet. Kuma rolled with the fall, coming up on his feet, but Noctus was right there, bringing his angerblade in a slashing arc. Knowing that he couldn't block cleanly, or risk his weapon getting sheared in half, Kuma deflected it. But the Brodarian kept coming, swinging his weapon in a crossing X and keeping close enough that Kuma couldn't leap away, showing the reason why the angerblade had gotten its name. Thin holes on the back of the thick blade let air pass through them, creating a wailing sound.

Kuma had to back away in a circle or get trapped against the edge. Sensing an opening in an otherwise flawless assault, he struck the angerblade as it went past, giving it more momentum than Noctus expected and using that overcorrection to escape again.

As Kuma caught his breath, he saw that Noctus was barely winded. The Brodarian was not only supernaturally strong, but had stamina as well. The battlefield was a keen teacher. This left Kuma with fewer options than he'd hoped when stepping onto the platform. He'd hoped to wear out Noctus, but that seemed unlikely.

"Do you yield, friend Aman?"

"No."

"Then the battle continues," said Noctus, jogging forward with his weapons in a high ready position.

Kuma shifted to his right, putting himself on the chain shield side, which would make the angerblade attacks have to travel further. The big man made nimble adjustments, matching the slide. When Noctus brought the angerblade around, Kuma planted his right foot and threw himself the other way, ducking under the attack and striking at his opponent's thighs with the dire mace. The metal strip in the heavy padding on Noctus' legs deflected the worst of the hit, but it managed to rip a gash in the leather. Kuma retreated to the opposite side of the platform while Noctus investigated the cut, holding up his fingers covered in dark wetness.

"First blood." Noctus held up his angerblade above his head in a battlefield salute. "Well done, my friend."

From anyone else, the comment would have been arrogant, but Kuma knew how much better Noctus was in the fight. It'd felt like sparring with Hylakane.

Kuma laughed. "Another three hours of this and I think I can take you down."

Noctus grinned in response, loping forward with weapons up. When Kuma started to shift, Noctus slowed his advance and rotated with his movement. The grin plastered across Noctus' face showed how pleased he was with his tactic. At the edge of the circle, Kuma was expending much more energy to keep away, while Noctus only had to move slightly. If the battle did go on a long time, stamina would matter. Kuma halted, letting his arms rest at his side.

Edging closer at a measured pace and shifting each time in mirrored directions trapped Kuma at the corner of the platform. Then Noctus closed the distance and attacked with a fervor that had Kuma defending for his life. The angerblade sung with battle song, whistling through the air, or ringing loudly against the dire mace. No one that big should be able to move that fast, or swing for that long. Kuma kept up his blocks, hoping Noctus would tire soon. He looked for gaps to counterattack the Brodarian's hands, but it took all his skill to keep from losing a limb. Kuma managed an artful block that opened an escape route to the opposite side while the crowd cheered.

"You'll wear out eventually," said Kuma as Noctus approached.

"Will I?"

Noctus halted at the center of the platform and with the dexterity of a juggler switched which hands held his angerblade and chain shield. The display had the crowd raising their arms and cheering loudly.

"Nice trick."

"A tired warrior is a dead warrior. On the plains of Vedun, the battle was three days of constant fighting. It was a war of exhaustion."

"I wish you would have told me that tale at the Club."

Noctus came at him like a singing whirlwind. The angerblade was blurred steel. When Kuma tried to block it, his dire mace almost came out of his hand. He circled hard, keeping Noctus sidestepping, eventually trapping him against the edge of the platform and forcing him into purposeful blocks that left the dire mace vibrating from each hit. Kuma feigned a counterattack, inviting a mid-body strike. As the angerblade swung around, Kuma kicked out at Noctus' forward knee as he attacked the weapon with his mace. Using the combined strikes, Kuma shoved the overbalanced warrior over the edge of the platform. Noctus pin-wheeled as he fell flat on his back on the sands.

The crowd erupted as Kuma raised his arms in victory.

"No win! No win!"

The judge ran to the edge, swiping his hands apart.

"Leaving the platform has to be voluntary. The match continues."

Kuma tried not to feel disappointment. He'd hoped the entangled attack might look voluntary, but clearly they were looking for an obvious absconding. Noctus hauled himself back onto the fighting floor, knocking the loose sand off his body. The Brodarian's jovial mien had disappeared, replaced with an intensity that worried Kuma. The judge ushered them to the center and then gave them the go-ahead to resume their fight.

Noctus attacked immediately, forcing Kuma into an all-out defense that stretched his abilities. Only Hylakane's training and the foresight of the amber stone kept him from getting split in two by the angerblade. The swinging had to be tiring, but Noctus looked neither winded nor concerned. An attempted counterattack was easily blocked, but not by the chain shield, which had almost become forgotten in his hand.

An idea formed for Kuma, who saw a chance, not to win, but to even the odds slightly. Pulling it off would be tricky as purposely getting his mace entangled in the chain shield would leave him open to evisceration. Kuma baited Noctus into overextending, and rather than counterattack, which was expected, he ducked underneath, circling around and forcing his opponent to turn quickly to maintain his defense. In the ensuing turns, Kuma struck out at the chain shield, catching it with his dire mace and flinging it out of Noctus' hand. The defensive shield slid across the platform and dropped into the sand.

The shock of losing his shield registered not as anger, but as laughter. Noctus backed away, his belly laugh filling the cavern with its echoing mirth.

"You continue to surprise, friend Aman. I couldn't have asked for a better fight."

Kuma used the break to catch his breath and shake out his tired limbs. The fight was nearing its tenth minute. The longest of the round. Burrowing his amber into his opponent looking for clues, he found that Noctus' muscles, especially the forearms, were quivering from the long effort. Sensing an opportunity, he closed the distance and invited attack as not to let Noctus find respite.

The next exchange taxed Kuma's limbs as he withstood constant battering, but he had to stay close enough so that Noctus would continue his assault. His idea would only work if his opponent's arms were tired. Otherwise, he'd probably end up split in two.

When he didn't think he could withstand it anymore, Kuma retreated, creating space between them. The sudden change surprised Noctus. His opponent looked ready to enjoy the chance to recharge his tired limbs, when Kuma leapt forward into a sprint. One, two, three steps—and then he leapt high into the air, cycling Light to reach an apex twenty feet above the Brodarian.

As he arced downward, Kuma switched to Heavy, making himself weigh as much as a boulder. Noctus brought his angerblade up, but a rising attack was less powerful, especially in the arms of a tired opponent. Kuma slammed his dire mace down with both hands, putting everything he had into the strike.

The impact exploded the shaft of the dire mace. The head careened off his shoulder, tearing flesh before spinning away. Kuma avoided the rising angerblade, but hit the platform like a meteor descending from the heavens, cracking it and sending him tumbling like a rag doll. Pain wracked his body. He tried to get up but all his bones and joints felt like they'd been shaken for an hour.

Then Noctus was standing over him. He rested the angerblade against his chest.

"Do you yield?"

Kuma closed his eyes and nodded.

"I yield."

The crowd erupted, but their voluminous praise was no salve to his mood. He'd lost. Noctus helped him to his feet. Everything hurt. The Brodarian placed a hand on his shoulder.

"Had the shaft not broken, you might have won," said Noctus. "That was a fight for the ages, my friend."

The Brodarian left Kuma at the center of the platform to bask in the adoring cheers of the crowd. He felt numb from head to toe and wished he could magically teleport back to his suite. Rather than return to the competitor area, he headed through the crowd towards the exit, while people reached out and patted him on his back.

Thirty-Seven

The suite was still torn apart from Kuma's training, with couches and other furniture pushed against the outer wall and shards of the ceiling lights scattered on the expensive carpet. Pandora stood at the center, rotating slowly, taking in the expressions of her fellow rebels. Since Kuma's loss a few hours ago, no one had wanted to discuss the fact that their situation had grown more difficult.

"Not everything goes as planned. We need to make adjustments," she told them.

Yara lifted her head, eyes creasing with thought. The others seemed less enthusiastic.

"I don't want to give up," began Choo-Choo. "But I don't know how we pull this off. The bloodstones are great and all, but they don't even the overwhelming numbers."

"We don't have to fight the whole alliance, only my grandfather's personal guard."

"You really think we can take him down during the final ceremony?" asked Tick, leaning back on the couch with his legs crossed.

"It's our best shot to finish what Duro and Brazio started. But there's no guarantee that Kuma will be allowed anywhere near the stage. We need more warriors to overwhelm the guards and even the odds," she said.

"We need the old crew back," said Choo-Choo intensely. "We need Navos and Camina."

"And Adrenalynne," said Yara. "I saw her at the teriyaki place earlier. They could get into the ceremony since they're Alliance. Maybe."

"Can we trust them?" asked Pandora. "They've been working for the Alliance for a couple of years now. They might not want to give up where they're at. Look at Camina. She's head of the Academy."

"And not happy about it, by my conversation," said Kuma. "They're not really allowing her to train, which doesn't make sense."

"Why train? They're just glorified security guards," said Tick. "Even

I could beat them."

"You could beat five of them with your hands behind your back," said Pandora.

"Don't forget Elani," said Vasilisa from her perch on the dresser. "She has no love for the Alliance. I know she'd help."

"I think Noctus Prime might as well," said Kuma, his face pinched with concern.

"Noctus?"

"He knows I'm not who I say I am. Pandora too. He guessed at the reason too."

Choo-Choo rose to his feet. "He knows? There's no way we can go through with this. He could blow this thing up for us."

"I...I don't think so. The Brodarians love strategy. He'd be more likely to want to see how this all plays out. But maybe, just maybe, I might be able to convince him to lend a hand." Kuma shrugged. "He already knows, so what's it hurt to go a little further?"

Choo-Choo shook his head. "Except if he's a stooge for Dominion, then we'll be giving him the exact timing of the rebellion. How the hell did a Brodarian even end up in the contest? Seems too big of a coincidence."

"I won't talk to him then, if that's what the group decides," said Kuma.

"Pandora?" asked Vasilisa.

"Yeah?"

"Do you really think you can take him down if Deacon and Titus are there?"

A pit formed in her stomach. "It won't be easy."

"What if they're not there? Or at least Titus? Maybe some of the other top waku? The ones from before. What if they weren't around during the ceremony? Because they're almost always there now. I notice we never see the new waku guarding the platform. It's always the ones like Navos, or the other bloodstone wielders."

"What are you thinking?"

"We need a distraction. Something that'll keep Titus busy and away from the Terreno."

A grin rose to Pandora's lips. She remembered when Vasy had been the smart mouthed younger sister in the Pajot, but now she was a woman in her own right. She might not be able to attune to a faez crystal, but she was still formidable.

"What are you thinking?"

"If we can get Elani, that would give us access to explosives. We don't need to go down into the pit. If we blow up some equipment around the top, hit their generators and elevator, they'll be forced to move resources to protect it. From what my brother said earlier about the conversation with Dominion, Titus will make it his personal role to protect the excavation project. Whatever it is that your grandfather is after, it's an important part of his plan."

"When did you get so devious?" asked Choo-Choo with a smirk.

"When? I always kicked your ass when we played Undercity, you wayhos," said Vasilisa, laughing, which brought a more relaxed mood to the group.

"Okay. An explosive distraction is on the menu," said Pandora. "I'll leave it to you, Vasy, to contact Elani and make a plan. The tournament will be over two days from now. Two fights tomorrow and then the final on the following day. The ceremony will be that evening after the final match. It's not going to be open to the public. That's when we have to be ready."

"Then we'll want to hit the excavation site before then. The day before the finals but not too early," said Vasilisa.

"Who's going to contact the old gang?" asked Pandora, circling slowly.

"I'll talk to Camina," said Kuma. "Our earlier interaction should give me cover."

"I've got Navos, of course," said Choo-Choo.

"How will you get to him? He's always around Dominion, or not around at all."

Choo-Choo frowned. "I don't know yet. But I'll let you know when I do."

"I've got Adrena," said Yara. "Based on her resting scowl, I'll assume that she's an easy yes to join us."

"What about you?" asked Yara.

Pandora tilted her head. "Me?"

"The tournament."

"I reached the level I needed for the bloodstone," she said.

"What about the black diamond?" asked Yara.

"It'd be nice, but it won't come into play for what we're planning. You heard my grandfather on that first day—the bloodstone attunes instantly and perfectly. I'll be able to use it right away. While the black diamond is like the old stones. It could be a week, or not at all before I attuned to it."

"That's not what I was thinking," said Yara, lips curled downward.

"I don't understand."

"Think about it. The bloodstones go to the top eight. He'll probably give all those stones out first, giving you a chance to attune. The black diamond will probably be saved for last, giving you the best access to Dominion. But *only* if you're the winner."

The weight of what she was suggesting settled onto her bones. "Yes. I see. You're right. That would be the best time." She sighed. "Have we heard who my first-round opponent might be or what the changes to the arena are?"

Yara shook her head. "The arena is blocked off. No chance of peeking and you won't know who your opponent is until tomorrow. The only thing we know is that you won't need your weapons. After that, it could be anything."

"Anything," repeated Pandora. "And knowing my grandfather, it's going to make the match exciting."

Thirty-Eight

A guy with bleached tips and a T-shirt that read "Waku Do It Better" nearly knocked Vasilisa over. She reached for the blade hidden in her jacket as she shouted, "Watch where you're going, you wayhos!"

He barely noticed as he was stumbling drunk. Vasilisa glowered at his back with her hand on the smooth hilt. "Fuck." She looked around, realizing she'd used an Undercity insult, but no one had noticed. The Terreno was a mess. The lines outside the noodle shops went around the block. There was a velvet rope for Club Onyx with thick-necked bouncers outside turning away underdressed potential customers. The place was insane.

The old shop was down a narrow alleyway in the part of the Terreno used by enterprising prostitutes. A crowd of them were standing at the end of the passage. Vasilisa shook her head at their offers. A woman with a tail brushed up against her.

"I'm not in the mood," she said.

The prostitute shrugged and focused her attention on the rest of the crowd. The old shop was the last door on the right. No signage indicated the purpose, which made Vasilisa worry that Elani had been moved from the Terreno to make room for other properties. She pushed the door open, triggering a bell as she entered. The interior was packed, shelves brimming with equipment and supplies. The one to her left had boxes spilling with climbing harnesses and carabineers.

"This ain't a hotel. Go find somewhere else to pluck your fancies," said an angry voice from the back.

Vasilisa stepped into view. Elani was sorting through a box, marking a paper on a clipboard. When she looked up, she recoiled.

"It's you...how did you? I heard you and your brother were dead."

"A waku isn't that easy to kill," said Vasilisa.

"You?"

"No. My brother."

Elani screwed up her face then recognition hit her. "You're not

Molly."

"And he's not Adam."

"I should have figured it out when you said you knew Triana."

Her gaze flitted to the illusionary hand. Vasilisa switched off the enchantment, eliciting a gasp from the older woman, followed by the wetting of her eyes. She came around the desk and threw her arms around Vasilisa, much to her surprise.

"I'm so happy to see you're alive, Vasy."

"I'm...thanks. Me too," she said, prompting a laugh from Elani.

"How?" she asked, holding her at arm's length.

"It's a long story, but not important right now. You remember back when the Alliance first took over and we were trying to resist?"

"All too well," said Elani despondently. "The only thing we did was get some good people killed."

"There's a chance we can still take them down," said Vasilisa.

Elani tilted her head. "Now? No way. They're too dug in. Like a rock tick that burrowed in good."

"I'm not kidding. There's a chance."

"Who? It can't just be you and your brother. Shadows below, it'd have to be an army."

"It's not just Emilio and me, but it's not an army either. But that's all I want to say."

"What do you want from me? You know I can't fight and neither can you."

"We need explosives. Don't worry, it's not for the Terreno. It's a distraction."

Elani leaned against the desk with a heavy sigh. "If I give them to you, they'll know who it was. This isn't the Alliance of the early days. They've gotten more organized. I'll be at risk if you don't pull it off."

"I know. It's a lot. But we need those explosives. There isn't much time," said Vasilisa.

Elani closed her eyes and inhaled slowly. "Fine," she said, opening them. "How much?"

Vasilisa gave her an amount that brought a low whistle. "Must be some distraction."

"It's gotta be."

"Give me a few minutes. I'll be right back," said Elani, pulling a set of keys from a wall hanger.

Vasilisa pulled herself onto the desk and fiddled with the zipper of her jacket while she waited. The bell on the door rang. She sat up straight, glancing towards the inner door where Elani had disappeared to. Panic set in since she had no reason to be in the Alliance logistics area, but before she could scramble off the desk, two fresh-faced waku appeared from around the shelves.

"Hey Elani, you got some extra water bottles around that we might use?" asked the Alliance. He tilted his head. "You're not Elani."

The second screwed up his face. "How do I know you?"

No words would come. It was the guard she'd bribed to take them to the excavation site. Recognition bloomed in his expression. He marched over and grabbed her stump arm before she could think about trying to run. Not that it would have mattered. The only thing running through her mind was the threat of being bound to a chair and tortured with an opal until she revealed their plan.

"You're the one who lied to me about knowing Lee." He frowned at the desk. "You're working with Elani."

A pit formed in Vasilisa's stomach. Not only was she going to get herself killed but the older woman too. The others would have to flee the Undercity. Everything had fallen apart. She thought about the blade in her jacket, but the guard was right on her.

"It's not what it looks like," said Vasilisa, even though she was pretty sure that it was.

"It ain't for me to figure out, but you'll be talking to someone, real soon. Especially the part about you and your brother not dying in the Dark Depths. Be a lot of questions on how you managed to pull that off."

"We got lucky—"

Elani entered the room with a big box in her arms. "This is the first one..."

Her voice trailed off when she saw the Alliance waku. Then her expression faltered, the corners of her eyes tugging downward.

The waku holding her arm turned towards Elani. Vasilisa yanked the blade out of her inner pocket and shoved it into his neck. He gargled blood, shocked by the reversal.

"Hey!"

The second guard was reaching for the handgun on his hip when Vasilisa pulled the blade out of the first waku's neck and threw it. The blade stuck right in his solar plexus. He looked down, surprised by its sudden appearance, and the gun slipped out of his fingers and clattered to the floor.

"Oh no..."

Elani joined her in staring at the two bodies leaking blood into the wooden floor.

"Nice throw."

"Thanks. I guess some skills never leave you."

Elani turned to her with a sober expression. "I guess I'm in it now. Let's get rid of these bodies first and then we'll get the rest of the explosives."

The bodies were warm. It took the two of them to drag them in back and use tarps to wrap them up and store them on a back shelf, placing boxes in front to hide potential discovery. The blood was harder to clean up as it soaked into the wood.

"Don't worry about the stain. I've been meaning to paint the floor.

Let me put the explosives on a cart."

"I can't push boxes labeled explosives through the Terreno," said Vasilisa.

Elani frowned. "You're right. I've got a better idea. You know that cavern to the southeast near the old Razor tunnel? The one with the formation on the wall that looks like a fat man taking a dump?"

"How could I forget."

"I'll have them delivered there tonight. Does that work?"

"Won't that be suspicious?"

"I'll repackage and pack them with mundane stuff," said Elani.

"Seems risky. But I don't have a better idea."

"I'll put labels with Titus' name on them. No one will even think about pilfering a single item. Trust me. The average Alliance waku shits himself when they hear his name."

"That reminds me. Have you heard where all the young waku have been sent? Dozens of them. The ones not yet finished with their training at the Academy?" asked Vasilisa.

Elani shook her head. "No idea."

"Not getting sent to the excavation site, are they?"

"No. I'm fairly certain of that. I get the invoices for the groups heading that direction. Half my job as of late has been resupplying Lee and his crew."

"Okay, thanks," said Vasilisa. "What about after this? What are you going to do?"

Elani laughed, holding up her hands, which still had blood on them. "Getting the fuck out of the Undercity until this is over. I've been thinking about it for a while anyway. I can blend in with the crowds heading back to the surface. No one will notice."

Vasilisa pulled a wad of bills out of her pocket, then wrote an address on a piece of paper.

"This is where my mami lives. If we're successful, I'll send word right away. If you don't hear anything in four days, I would leave the city for a while and find new lodging."

Elani approached and put her arms around her. They hugged for a long time.

"Good luck. Kick their asses for me."

Vasilisa left the shop feeling like it was the last time she was going to see Elani.

Thirty-Nine

Kuma had wanted to meet Camina at Club Onyx, but the place was too busy, with velvet-roped lines that snaked down the street. His role in the tournament and especially the fight with Noctus had made him famous, knocking out other popular spots in the Terreno. He could barely get through the streets without people wanting to take selfies. A noodle shop on the second level near the back provided a quieter venue. He gave a couple of college-aged kids a wad of bills to vacate a booth and another to the waitress to keep people from bothering him. He ordered a bowl of spicy ramen and a beer when Camina didn't show up at the appointed time. He'd never received a confirmation for the letter he sent to the Academy, so he was thinking about how he might contact her when she slid into the booth opposite him.

"I'm sorry. I ordered food and drink when I didn't think you were coming."

Camina hung her head. The shadows around her eyes had deepened since he'd seen her last. A world of thoughts passed behind her eyes, making Kuma check over his shoulder to make sure he wasn't about to be attacked.

"I almost didn't come..."

The waitress interrupted her thought. She ordered the same as him. Kuma dabbed the sweat on his forehead with a napkin before tossing it back in his lap.

"I saw your fight," she said.

"I'm disappointed."

"You shouldn't be. No one gave you a chance. I saw the betting lines. They were overwhelmingly in Noctus' favor. You gave a lot of deep pockets a heartache making it that close."

"There are no second chances in battle," he said. "If that'd been real, I wouldn't be speaking to you right now."

The waitress showed up with the beer and bowl of steaming ramen.

"The world is full of second chances," she said, picking up her chopsticks.

"And the optimistic dead."

Camina snapped up a wad of noodles and held them before her mouth. "I had a friend who was an optimist. I miss him."

Kuma raised an eyebrow. "A good friend?"

"The best."

She swallowed her noodles and washed it down with a gulp of beer.

"I saw him fight in the same place you lost to Noctus once. Many years ago back when the shadows were at war."

"Tell me about this duel."

She smirked. "I never said it was a duel."

"You're right," he said, responding with a grin, glad to see that she'd figured out that it was him without having to say it out loud. After checking to make sure no one was around, he slid his hand across the table. Camina captured it and gave it a squeeze before pulling hers back. The corners of her eyes were wet and she gave a heaving sigh.

"I—"

He shook her off and pulled out a pad of paper and a pen he'd taken from the hotel. Kuma wrote out a note as he spoke aloud.

"How goes the Academy training? I hope my suggestions helped improve their fighting prowess."

The note read: *Finish what we started two years ago. You in?*

A smile cracked her lips as she scribbled a response.

Yes. Who else?

"They're much stronger now. Thank you, Aman. It's always good to bring in extra eyes."

Everyone who survived plus a few others.

"I'm a poor teacher. I should have learned more on the plains of Brodaria, but Lady Saha came and took me away."

They're using my trainees somewhere. Not at the excavation site. Not in the Undercity. Do you know?

Kuma shook his head as he sucked down the broth. He wiped his mouth and signaled another beer from the waitress, which prompted Camina to finish her first and hold up two fingers.

No idea. DT has bigger plans we think, but no idea what.

Camina tapped on what he'd written, nodding her head.

When?

Awards ceremony.

Camina wrinkled her nose.

Lady Saha?

Kuma cracked a smile as an answer, which prompted an incredulous shake of her head.

I'll be there.

Others?

Camina shrugged and flipped over the pad when the waitress appeared with their beers. When she was gone, Camina wrote on the paper.

See Navos and Adrena sometimes, but no talk.

"Maybe you could ask to stay for a while," said Camina. "I could use the help at the Academy and I'm sure my boss would allow it."

Be ready. Will need everyone.

"I'm afraid Lady Saha has plans for us after we're finished here. I don't know where we're headed next. Otherwise, I would love to stay, but I wanted to meet again before we left. With the tournament nearing its conclusion, the next few days will be hectic."

Kuma took the pad of paper and shoved it into his pocket. He'd burn the notes in the hotel suite.

"That's a shame. Maybe I'll see you at the matches tomorrow."

He threw a wad of bills on the table as he stood up.

"May the shadows keep you safe," she said.

He inclined his head. "May your blade stay sharp and your shield never shatter."

Forty

The atmosphere in the arena was at a fevered pitch when the competitors entered. Pandora was in the middle and Valor in the lead, but she wasn't paying attention to the crowd. The fighting floor had been changed. It looked like a mix of the platform and obstacle course. Pillars rose above the sands, sometimes as high as thirty feet, and some of them had wooden stages on top, no larger than fifteen feet in diameter.

"Hope they made 'em strong enough to hold me," said Noctus with a laugh.

She glanced back to see her grandfather and mother on the special platform in back, along with Titus Cabone and Deacon. The bloodstone guards, including Navos, stood guard at the corners, not that anyone would think to attack them.

Three more fights, she told herself.

The eight competitors stopped at their area next to the arena. The long benches had been removed, replaced with individual stations with their names. As they settled at their spots, Valor turned to the group.

"Good luck. Fight well and I promise I won't hurt you too bad if we get matched up."

"Go fuck yourself," said Sophia.

The next part Pandora barely heard because she was studying the arena, memorizing the locations so she didn't have to think when she moved around during her fight. She didn't realize her name had been called until the crowd erupted in applause and Angel Chen was staring her down.

"I was hoping I'd get matched with you," said Angel as she strode onto the arena floor leaving Pandora to follow. She hoped her inattention had been interpreted as ambivalence. A set of wooden steps led to the central platform where the judge was waiting.

Her opponent was as beautiful as she was dangerous. A flash of golden light filled Angel's eyes, but quickly disappeared. A warning. It wasn't the first time the illumination had been spotted during a fight.

Pandora suspected she wouldn't hold back, unleashing her abilities now that they were in the final eight.

"Begin!"

Pandora yanked Angel forward with a Pull, attempting to knock her out in the first seconds of the fight. Her opponent's block was followed by a knee to the gut. Pandora deflected it then grabbed Angel's silky ponytail. Angel spun around but rather than attack, her eyes exploded with golden light.

The world disappeared as Pandora's vision turned to a sea of white. She blasted a heavy Push, knocking Angel away, knowing that was only a temporary solution to her sudden blindness. Switching to the sapphire radar she'd relied on in the shadows of the Undercity, she "saw" Angel approach from a different angle on silent feet.

The crowd gasped when Pandora blocked a kick to the head from the side, spun through a punch, and then retreated to the opposite side in hopes of her vision returning. Using her radar and the memory of the arena, she plotted an escape route when Angel came running. Leaping to the platform ten feet above and to the right, she stopped at the edge, daring Angel to make the attempt.

Pandora's only warning was the increased brightness in her blinded vision. A wave of golden energy tumbled Pandora backwards and nearly off the edge of the platform, giving Angel space to advance. A twisted Push-Pull knocked Angel sideways before she could advance, giving Pandora a second chance at a head-hunting blow. An angled elbow block, followed by a kick to the stomach, left Pandora flying backwards over the edge. She Pulled herself back to the original platform, landing heavily in her haste not to fall to the sands, vision coming back as blurry shapes.

Angel came flying over, golden light surrounding her like a wave of force. Pandora found her feet and blasted forward with a heavy Push. The two energies impacted, exploding outward. Pandora was knocked onto her back, but found her feet quickly, while Angel struggled to stand. Before her opponent could muster a defense, Pandora tackled her, keeping her eyes closed in case of the golden light. She pummeled Angel from atop her, striking through the attempted blocks. Golden light flashed out, pressure pushing her upward, but Pandora had anchored herself with the sapphire. At the tenth strike to the head, Angel went limp. Pandora held her fist above the unconscious woman's head until she was certain that it wasn't a ruse.

Back on her feet, eyes stinging from the earlier blinding light, she raised her hand in victory as the crowd applauded with restraint, acknowledging the result.

Angel woke a short time later and followed Pandora back to the competitor area, a scowl on her lips. The others congratulated Pandora as she slumped onto her seat, drained from the fight.

While Pandora recovered, drinking water and regaining her vision, the next match was called. Valor Drux versus Bo Kan.

Pandora was expecting a longer match, but the tall ex-military Valor quickly dismantled his opponent with speed and agility that had the rest of the competitor group glancing amongst themselves wondering if anyone could beat him.

"Fucking cheater," said Sophia when Valor returned. "You didn't move like that before."

He flexed his arm and kissed his bulging muscle, winking at her when he was finished. When the next match was called, Sophia stood up and made a throat cutting gesture at Valor, despite her opponent being Dorcheski, who looked annoyed that he wasn't being taken seriously. Despite the disrespect, Pandora didn't give him much of a chance, unless he was hiding supernatural abilities. Her instincts proved correct when Sophia knocked out her opponent thirty seconds into the fight with a brutal kick to the head.

The last match of the day involved Noctus Prime versus Jackson, who was clearly outmatched. He made a valiant attempt to take the fight to one of the smaller platforms in hopes of knocking Noctus off and letting gravity do the hard work, but the enormous Brodarian caught him in a headlock and slowly choked him out, letting Jackson sink to the platform unconscious.

After her grandfather gave a short speech, hinting at further changes to the arena for the semifinals matches in the afternoon, the competitors were given a lane out of the arena. As they rose to their feet, Valor chuckled.

"No more easy fights left."

A runner came down from the platform, stumbling into their area with two notecards. He looked apprehensive about approaching until Noctus gently removed them from his hand.

"What is it?" asked Valor, trying to peer over the Brodarian's shoulder.

"Next round matchups."

The way Noctus stared left a stone in her gut.

"Don't keep us waiting," said Sophia.

"You'll get your wish," said Noctus. "You're battling Valor in the first fight."

Pandora was hoping for either of the others. To her, Noctus was the one to beat. Before she left the competitor area, she inclined her head.

"I'll see you on the battlefield."

Forty-One

The boxes of explosives sat in a neat pile near the rock wall, covered in pale crickets crawling over the containers. Choo-Choo knocked them off with his hand, flicking the larger ones into the air.

"How the fuck are we going to carry all this?" he asked Vasilisa.

"It's not all explosives. She filled it with other stuff in case anyone peeked into the boxes," she said.

"There's four of us. We should be able to haul it just fine," said Yara, nodding to Tick, who was stroking Koro's back as she was wrapped around his neck.

After disassembling the boxes, removing the explosives and triggering mechanisms, then carefully situating them into their backpacks, the four of them started moving.

"Tick on point. Everyone keep your sensing on high, and for shadows' sake, try not to get into a firefight if we run into a patrol. If someone gets a lucky shot, we're going to be paste on the walls."

The passages were surprisingly quiet. Usually they had to avoid patrols after Koro spotted them, but they made their way to the old Razor tunnel without incident.

"Where is everyone?" asked Yara once they were safely in the tunnel.

"Maybe they're at the Terreno for the semifinals today," said Tick.

"I don't think so," said Choo-Choo, shaking his head. "I wonder if this has anything to do with Camina's missing trainees."

The implications brought a heavy mood to the group. Choo-Choo couldn't figure out where they were going, but it seemed bad, either way. The level tunnel made travel quicker than normal, though it still took a few hours. They climbed through the hatch into a fungus-lit cavern. Moving through the Undercity had never bothered Choo-Choo, but after the escape from the excavation site last time, he had a new appreciation for the shadows.

"We're about a half hour away. Keep your weapons ready and your senses on high," he said, reconfirming his blades with a touch.

"Stop right there! Hands up!" came a voice from twenty feet behind them.

The dim light revealed a young man with a big gun clasped between two quivering hands. His hair was matted on the side, suggesting he might have been sleeping, which was why they hadn't sensed him when they came out of the tunnel. His Alliance uniform was dirty and the front was tied incorrectly.

"Hey, man," said Choo-Choo, raising his arms. "We're bringing supplies to the site. No need to point that at us."

The guard screwed up his face. "No. You're not supposed to be here. They stationed me here to keep an eye on this hatch and they said anyone who comes through it is against us."

Choo-Choo cocked a smile. "You got it all wrong, man. No one told us about that. We thought it'd be easier to move through the tunnel rather than the normal routes. We're part of Lee's crew."

"No you ain't," he said. "I heard about you two from the others. I thought you were dead, but I guess they were wrong. I'm gonna take you back and let Titus' men deal with you."

Choo-Choo thought about throwing a blade, but the curved fighting ones weren't the best at range.

"I wouldn't do that," said Yara from his left. She said it low and mean. The guard trained his gun on her, the shaking growing more pronounced. "Look. They left you out here by yourself. And look at your hands. You can barely hold that gun level. Maybe you get one of us, but if you shoot, you're a dead man. We're faster than you. Better if you put down the gun and we'll tie you up and put you in the tunnel until we can retrieve you later. It'll suck, but at least you'll be alive."

"What? Why would you say that?" asked the guard, shifting his weapon.

"Because you're out of your element," said Yara. "You look like a nice kid who got excited about the idea of becoming a waku, but now you're hiding in a cavern without a clue of how dangerous it is to fall asleep."

"I didn't fall asleep!"

"Either way. You know you shouldn't be here, but you're too afraid to leave now that you have a few stones. They probably told you they'd hunt you down and skin you alive if you left."

A sob slipped out of the kid's lips. He barely looked fifteen. If he'd been born in the shadows, he'd be a fit, fighting machine, but the kids they brought in from the light were only skilled in petty crime and drug sales.

"How about we—"

The flutter of wings was the only warning. Koro sunk her fangs into the kid's neck. The gun exploded, the bright flash temporarily blinding before he dropped to the ground, foaming at the mouth.

"Emilio..."

His heart sunk when he saw the darkness spreading across his sister's chest. A dark hole went through the strap of her backpack and into her shoulder. He caught her as she sunk to her knees.

"No, no, no," he said, pressing his hand over the wound as he slipped the pack off. "Fuck."

Vasilisa's eyes were unfocused as a headlamp shone in her face. "I'm not going to die, am I?"

"Get the fucking first aid kit," he told Yara, but she was already handing it over. "Why can't one of us have an opal? Why?" Then to his sister, "You're gonna be okay. You're gonna be okay."

Her shirt was soaked. Blood was coming out of the wound fast. Yara wadded up gauze, which he shoved into the hole on the front and back of her shoulder. He had no idea how much blood she'd lost already, but his hands were covered.

"You can't die, Vasy. Mami would kill me. And then it would break her heart and then it'd only be me left. You can't die. You just can't."

Her chin sunk towards her chest as her eyes threatened to close. He pressed his hand against her forehead, pushing it up.

"No sleeping. Stay with me. You have to stay awake."

"Why?"

"I don't know, but you do," he said as Yara wrapped bandages around his sister's shoulder, holding the gauze in the holes. The material immediately darkened from blood.

"More, wrap more," he told Yara.

"That's all the bandages."

"Cut that asshole's shirt then. He doesn't need it."

Using the dead guard's shirt, they applied additional bandages to the wound.

"It's slowed, but I don't know if she has internal bleeding or not," he said.

"Use your amber," said Yara.

He'd never tried to analyze a gunshot wound. He pressed his hands against her shoulder, keeping them there even as she winced. The body was a confusing place of unfamiliar sounds, overridden by the thudding of her heart. He listened for a long minute before pulling away.

"I couldn't hear anything. I don't know if that's good or bad."

"I'm feeling better," said Vasilisa weakly.

"You look like shit," he told her. "Pale as Leesa's white ass."

"What do we do now?" asked Tick, frowning.

"We have to take her back so Pandora can heal her with the opal."

"She might not even be available. She's still in the tournament, hopefully," said Yara.

"I'm fine," said Vasilisa with half-lidded eyes. "Go. Blow up some shit. I'll wait here and you can take me back."

"I can't do that, Vasy."

"You have to," said Vasilisa. "There's not enough time to take me and then come all the way back. It was hard enough sneaking out of the Terreno through those old passages. You might not be able to make it in, and especially not with me. I can't crawl very good right now."

"Vasy..."

"You know I'm right, older brother. If I was a waku and we were on a mission, you'd leave me. The only reason you're not is because I'm your sister."

He grimaced, but couldn't bring himself to agree.

"She's right," said Yara. "I'm sorry. But she is. We can't bring her back *and* cause a distraction."

"I could take her back and you two could go on," said Choo-Choo.

"I'll be fine, Emilio. I'm feeling better already. Just move me to that dead guy's spot and I'll stay here until you get back," said Vasilisa with a forced smile.

"You're not lying to me? You're not just saying this so I'll leave?" His heart was bouncing around in his chest.

"Emilio...go..."

"We should listen to her," said Yara. "Pan can heal her when we get back. Another hour or two isn't going to be fatal. And you might not even have access to Pan if we went back now. She'll probably be in the second match of the day by then."

"Tick?" he asked angrily.

"You won't be mad if I'm wrong, will you?"

"Tick, just tell me your fucking opinion."

The diminutive waku swallowed. "I agree with them. We have to go now. Without a distraction, Titus and some of the others will be at the ceremony. We have to thin their numbers or we'll never get a good shot at Dominion."

Choo-Choo closed his eyes. He could hear his mother screaming at him for letting Vasilisa die just like his older sister. For the first time in his life, he regretted ever being a waku. He wondered what it would be like to live in the city with his family alive and happy, not covered in blood in the darkness.

"Emilio, you have to go," said Vasilisa firmly.

She looked him in the eye as she pushed him away.

"Let me move you first." He picked her up, cradling her to his chest as he relocated his sister to the matted sleeping bag behind a rocky crenellation. He kissed her on the forehead after he set her down.

"I'll be fine. Just kick ass and hurry back. I'd really like to visit Mami with you. See her smile when we both walk in the door."

Choo-Choo rose to his feet hesitantly. It was hard to take steps away from his sister in her condition. What if she wasn't alive when he came back? Could he ever forgive himself? He didn't think so. He'd burn the world down if that happened.

Forty-Two

The arena floor had changed in the few hours they'd been away. Additional pillars had been added in the spaces between the platforms, which had been changed out for smaller versions, leaving an uneven fighting space. The worst part was the spikes driven into the sand, sticking up and making any falls perilous. The crowd was humming with excitement behind them, while the four competitors stared at the new obstacles.

"It'll be worth it for the black diamond," said Valor, cracking his knuckles.

"Not when I knock you onto one," said Sophia.

The promise of a traveling martial arts show that had brought a moment of solidarity between the competitors was absent with so much on the line. Valor and Sophia were called to the arena, leaving Pandora with Noctus. He pulled over his chair, settling next to her as the introductions were given for the first match.

"Our host certainly knows how to make a spectacle," said Noctus.

"He's had plenty of training in the Eternal City."

Noctus chuckled lightly. The crowd was on their feet as the two competitors settled onto the main platform.

"Who do you want to win?" he asked, leaning over.

"I don't care."

"Ahh," said Noctus. "I think we both know Valor's the better warrior."

She raised an eyebrow in his direction. "On that we can agree, but I'm not counting Sophia out. Her anger might carry her when skill alone might not be enough."

"I find anger to be counterproductive," said Noctus.

She stilled as the match began in earnest. Without much room on the main platform and the danger of the spikes if they fell, the two combatants stayed to the middle, testing each other's defenses. When Sophia was knocked to the edge, she retreated by leaping to the uneven poles and finding a new platform.

"Why do you want the black diamond, Lady Saha?"

The way he said her name reminded her that he knew she was an imposter.

"Does it matter? Why do *you* want it?"

Pandora expected a lighthearted quip, but the way the Brodarian settled into his chair with a heavy sigh suggested deeper motives.

"The wars of Brodaria have been in constant motion for centuries since the Breaking of the Haran. It is our way, our life. To cross blades on the battlefield and feel every cell of your being raging against death is the greatest drug our people have ever known."

Noctus' chin dipped slightly, an epoch of doubt in comparison to his normally bright mood.

"All this changed a few decades ago. I heard rumors for years, but then they came for my kingdom."

"Who?" asked Pandora, leaning forward.

"War has never been about territory, or ownership. We fight to settle disputes, or to test ourselves against superior foes. To improve. To see the haflwyer blooms like a bright wound spreading crimson across the rolling hills. It is our way. It defines us as a people.

"But then I started seeing foreigners in the ranks of my opponents. Black-clad mercenaries carrying *seitizak*, or forbidden weapons."

He said the word like an insult, the hard consonants coming out as if he were spitting on the ground.

"What weapons?"

"The kind made in your world. The ones that kill fast and without regard to honor. We've known of these weapons for centuries, but chose not to make them. Same with your magics, but at least those we are resistant to. The others, they ripped through our ranks, cutting down warriors without regard to their histories, leaving them honorless in the mud."

Pandora jutted her chin towards the platform. "Titus?"

"No. He seeks easier prey. These mercenaries are ones that come from the Halls, or at least their master does. Blackstone." His hand squeezed to a fist. "Two years ago, I met Marduk Prime on the Onolo Wastes. I'd heard rumors of his conquests. His name was anathema, said with great disdain, and sometimes with a blood curse.

"He refused the ceremony of tea and attacked in the night. I was ready for him, but the *seitizak* weapons and the ranks of Blackstone mercenaries ripped through our side. My warriors fought valiantly, but we were crushed without the opportunity for *asaide*. They killed nearly every warrior. I escaped by leaping into the burning mud pits until they'd stopped searching for my body."

The crowd exploded to their feet, and Pandora, having not been watching, thought there might be a winner, but it'd only been a great display of physical ability when Victor had caught himself on a pole after being knocked from a platform. He monkey-climbed back to the top and rejoined the battle with Sophia in earnest. His opponent looked strangely unsteady on her feet, but she was too interested in what Noctus had to say to pay attention further.

"You want the black diamond to protect yourself from their weapons. You seek revenge."

"I seek vengeance."

"You want me to lose so you can retake your empire."

"No," he said. "I would never ask a fellow warrior to give up their rights of battle. But I tell you so that when I win, you understand that your failure was like the haflwyer blooms. They can only happen when the blood of defeat has been spilled."

Pandora leaned close so only Noctus could hear amid the delirious applause.

"I seek vengeance too. I hope you understand."

His serious demeanor broke into a broad smile as he squeezed her shoulder like an old friend. Before he could speak, a change in the arena interrupted his thought as a great collective in-breath locked the entire crowd into stasis. Valor Drux had Sophia by the neck from behind at the edge of the tallest platform. He could drop her off and she'd likely die as she was nearly unconscious. He was trying to get her to concede, but she was fighting through the pain, trying to kick him even as he had her legs trapped. Pandora sensed that if he wasn't in front of a crowd, Sophia would be dead already. He kept up his choke hold until his opponent went limp, and he gently laid her on the platform to rapturous applause.

Noctus winked in her direction as he rose in preparation to take to the arena.

"To glorious battle."

Forty-Three

The somber quiet as they advanced through rocky passages was not just out of necessity, but from the weight of Vasilisa's injury. When it was clear that Choo-Choo wasn't capable of directing the group, Yara took over, making the hand signals required to keep them moving as a unit.

It was a comfortable return with the three of them, reminiscent of the years of guerilla warfare against the Alliance. If they were successful in the next few days then she'd either no longer care because she was dead, or she could finally return to the life she'd known before Dominion entered the Undercity.

When they neared the wastelands, she slowed their advance, not wanting to rush into a firefight that would leave them outnumbered. It meant sending Koro ahead to scout while they stayed back, huddled against the cavern wall. She felt alone in those times because Choo-Choo was staring at his feet, clearly thinking about his sister, and Tick was linked to the flying snake.

The excavation site was heavily guarded upon their return, requiring backtracking until they could find a spot unguarded. The camp was at the corner next to the cliff where the elevator was located. They were looking down from the opposite corner, the edge of the camp at least thirty meters across a nearly flat wall. Floodlights made the idea of sneaking through the shadows impossible. Guards stood at every conceivable entry point, including the top of the ramp that went into the Dark Depths. Generators rumbled from multiple points.

"Any different from last time?" she asked Choo-Choo, waking him out of his stupor.

"More guards. More lights. They split up the generators, or maybe I'm remembering them wrong." He squinted. "Is it just me or do they seem happy? Last time it was like I'd walked into a funeral."

Yara exhaled. "I hope that doesn't mean they found what they're looking for."

"Probably not found, or they'd be closing up shop. But close. Might have a shot at shutting them down then," he said.

"We're here for a distraction, not to stop them from finding whatever they're looking for," she reminded him.

"Yeah, I get it," he said.

"We're not actually going to try to sneak over there are we?" asked Tick. "This is ten times worse than before. Every passage into the camp is guarded with triple the numbers, and not with those stupid new waku that seem to be everywhere else. These are Titus' gang, or real waku that were around before Dominion."

"They're not guarding every passage," said Yara with a smirk.

"What?" asked Tick, then realization set in. "No. No way. I did enough climbing back when we were preparing to hit the Alliance complex, and this time the fall is, I don't know, forever?"

Yara angled her arm towards the cliff wall between them and the camp.

"If we climb down from here and then over, staying below the edge, we could come up near that generator building which isn't too far from the elevator. If we blew those up, that would set them back and surely bring Titus and more guards down," said Yara.

"It could be done," said Choo-Choo.

Tick's face was pale. "We should have brought harnesses and climbing gear."

Yara put her hand on his shoulder. "Don't worry. We'll need a lookout, and Koro provides a flying guard should someone discover us."

"It's not that I don't want to go," said Tick. "But I don't have a topaz like you two."

"We should get moving," said Choo-Choo. "Every second we delay is a greater chance that—"

The words died in his throat. He swallowed with nostrils flaring.

"You go first," said Yara. "If I fall I can switch to Light and you can catch me. The other way around, well..."

He didn't wait to answer, swinging his leg over the edge. Yara let him continue before following. She preferred climbing up as you started at the safest spot and grew more dangerous over time. Starting at the top meant one was faced with the worst-case scenario. Yara steadied her nerves and shifted her weight over, using a lump of connected rock as a good handhold.

Once she was moving, focused on the next hand placement rather than the yawning expanse beneath, she forgot about the danger. To stay out of sight, they had to climb down for sixty feet, then move lateral, staying under the edge of the cliff. She couldn't see Tick hiding on the ledge, but knew that he would keep a lookout. Halfway across, she remembered that they'd left some of the explosives in Tick's bag, but decided the extra weight would have been too unbalancing.

The rumble of the generators grew louder as they neared the other side. Yara could see Tick peering over the ledge. He gave her a thumbs-up. She made a point of checking back every few feet now that they were nearing the top of the cliff. Yara stopped next to Choo-Choo once they were directly beneath the edge. The elevator was about thirty feet to their right, but the outer casing blocked sight from the cage, so they were safe, even if someone decided to use it.

Peeking over the edge revealed canvas tents and a single building with a lock on the front. She spotted four guards within fifty feet. Two stood at the top of the ramp, which was on the opposite side of the elevator, and the other two were standing to the left on the other side of the building, resting their arms on the automatic weapons held around their necks with a strap. The two men were chatting quiet enough not to be heard over the generators. Workers moved through the camp in hard hats, and further out there were more guards. If something happened they'd have a dozen men and women with guns on them in a few seconds

"Let's pack half the explosives on the elevator and the other half on that building. Set the timer for ten minutes. That should give us enough time to get back to the other side before they explode," she told Choo-Choo.

He looked distracted, but eventually nodded. His mind was on his sister's injury. She hoped he could pull it together for this last bit. When he started to climb over the edge, she tugged on his arm and pointed to the elevator. As he started climbing to the right, she pulled herself over, checking each direction to make sure she wasn't spotted.

Reaching the building without incident, Yara unzipped the bag and pulled out the bricks of explosives. She didn't want to leave them out in the open. The flat roof had an overhang which had space to hide the explosives using sticky tape to hold them upside down. Four bricks would turn the building into splinters, obliterating every tent within a hundred feet, and hopefully, bring part of the ceiling down. Yara set the timer for eleven minutes to give her a little extra room since she was further from the edge and locked the settings, which would prevent anyone from turning it off should it be discovered. She was going to return when Tick signaled her, pointing towards the elevator. The door opened up twenty feet to her left, leaving her exposed. Yara started to cross the open space but saw that the guards on the other side had turned slightly.

Yara thought about making a run for it, but once they were on the wall, it'd be easy to bring them down with a well-placed shot. Not even Koro could save them.

The elevator lights flashed, signaling the doors were about to open. Through the front cage material she could see at least four people in the lift.

As the doors prepared to open, Yara switched to Lightness, leaping onto the building roof and lying flat. The noise of the generators hid her impact. The four workers left the elevator, three men and one woman, but stopped right outside, continuing their conversation. Using her amber, she could hear them discussing the excavation site at the bottom. They seemed excited about the new dig.

In Yara's head the timer was counting down. Even with the extra minute, she was running out of time to escape the explosives. She peeked over the edge to see the workers hadn't moved.

Forty-Four

The sounds of the crowd faded away as Pandora took the central platform across from Noctus. He was a giant compared to her. The truncated fighting space made avoiding his fists impossible, and he was clearly the stronger warrior. The sapphire would have to be the difference.

The earlier friendliness displayed in the competitor area was absent. Noctus stared at her like the headsman sizing up how hard he'd have to swing to take her head off. She returned his expression with a mean mug of her own, but felt it lacked the same intensity, especially since he knew that she was not actually Lady Saha.

"Begin!"

Noctus burst forward like a sprinter after the starting gun, crossing the space between them in an eyeblink. She blasted him with a heavy Push, attempting to knock him off his feet. The Brodarian stiffened upon impact, but withstood the blast like a powerful oak weathering hurricane winds.

The minimal effect of the Push left her almost too stunned to escape. She'd hoped the stones would give her the advantage she needed, but as he closed the remaining distance, she remembered him mentioning that Brodarians were resistant to magic.

A right hook nearly took her head off. She avoided the first three punches, but the misses corralled her towards the edge. Pandora escaped by diving through a gap, rolling over and onto her feet, but Noctus was upon her the instant she regained her feet.

Burning her opal to reach peak performance, Pandora countered his flurry of attacks. It was like fighting with a machine. She managed to catch him with a few kicks, but they had the impact of a puff of wind. Once again herded towards the abyss, Pandora backflipped to the next platform, landing with her hands up and ready to fight.

Noctus grinned at the escape, the first sign she'd seen of the jovial warrior, before his lips curled back to intensity. He made a standing leap to her platform, landing like a boulder, shaking the entire structure. The space was smaller. He cut off her escape routes in two steps. Punches came like missile strikes. If she hadn't seen him fight in earlier matches, she might have thought he'd wear out, but his endurance was legendary. He'd kept up swinging the angerblade during the entirety of his battle with Kuma, which meant he could throw punches for hours.

Using her sapphire, Pandora managed to annoy Noctus with Pushes and Pulls. They weren't as impactful as normal, but deflected his attacks keep her from getting annihilated.

When the assault grew too much, she escaped to a higher platform again, using the breather to adjust her uniform. Noctus leapt after, but rather than giving him the space to land, she surged forward with a sundering kick. He punched the bottom of her foot, sending her flying backwards. She nearly tumbled over the edge, but used her sapphire to anchor herself.

While she could use her sapphire to slow her fall, the numerous spikes would make it difficult to avoid injury.

Seeing that a stand-up fight was considerably in his favor, Pandora leapt to a series of individual poles that reminded her of the training with Hylakane. She hoped the smaller foot space would make balancing harder for Noctus, but he leapt after her with the grace of a dancer, his lips wrinkled with a fateful smirk.

While he did not seem uneasy on the pole, the tighter constraints made her defense simpler since he couldn't anchor his punches with a wide stance. At over seven feet tall, he could easily become unbalanced, so she used her sapphire against his legs, trying to exploit the change of terrain. Pandora grew hopeful that this new tactic might lead to an opportunity for victory. Noctus was visibly annoyed by the difficult circumstances. She was setting him up for a counterattack when he leapt straight across the gap. The enormous Brodarian caught her by surprise. He extended his arms, punching her with both fists in the chest, throwing her backwards off the pole.

Forty-Five

Seven minutes.

The timer was counting down in Yara's head and the workers still hadn't moved. Between the explosives in the building and on the elevator, she wouldn't have enough time to escape the blast radius. If she was on the wall, even with her topaz strength, she'd get knocked unconscious into the abyss and her emerald wouldn't be able to save her.

Six fucking minutes.

She was going to die because of a group of chatty engineers. They were blathering on about load calculations and the tensile strength of support beams. Yara wanted to scream. She scooted to the edge under the assumption she had to move now, or be turned into a bloody pulp.

A cry of surprise from the workers had them scattering. The flying snake had appeared by the elevator. Before she could hop down, the two guards came over to investigate, but Koro was already gone. When they neared the edge, Yara checked to make sure no one was in sight range. The workers were still running the other way and the two guards near the ramp were looking into the massive chasm.

When Yara saw a hand reach up from the edge, grabbing the guard's black pants, she rose to her feet and using Lightness, made the thirty-foot leap, kicking the second guard with both feet. In the blink of an eye, both went tumbling into the yawning expanse, their screams devoured by the distance and the rumbling generators.

Yara scrambled over the edge. Five minutes. It wasn't enough time. The abundance of caution that had safely gotten them over was thrown to the winds as they moved like frightened monkeys across the cliffside. Yara didn't bother checking back to see if the guards had spotted them. Dead by bullet or explosion, either one she could do nothing about unless she reached the ledge where Tick was waiting.

"Hurry! One minute!"

The call from Tick came down to them, but there was still too far to go to reach him. She risked a glance back to see the other guards near the elevator and still more headed that way. They needed somewhere to hide from the blast. Looking down and to their left, she spotted a large crevasse running up the wall at an angle

"Choo-Choo. Down to your left. Hurry."

No further explanation was needed. She swung after him, barely finding a new handhold before reaching out to the next. Rock exploded by her ear. The guards had spotted them and were firing. Choo-Choo pivoted around the edge, hiding from the shots. Yara followed, jamming herself next to him. The ledge was only wide enough for half their feet.

"Jam your hands in the crack."

She shoved both hands as deep as they would go, tearing away skin and cracking nails. Yara ducked her head behind the knife-edged rock as the countdown fell to seconds.

The explosion hit them like a two-by-four, slamming her head into the rock wall. She nearly loosened her grip, thinking the worst over, when the second one triggered. Loose stones bounced off her head and shoulders, while blood ran into her eyes, but she didn't dare wipe it away, so she kept them squeezed shut. When the rumbling stopped, she risked leaning back to see the entire elevator structure was gone. A hole in the side of the cliff was matched by another where the building had been. Tents were flattened for hundreds of meters. From the farthest side in the part of the camp unaffected by the blast, a black-clad team of men and women came running.

"Go!"

She nudged Choo-Choo, who shaking away the worst of the blast. Her ears were ringing and the first couple of handholds came with stabs of vertigo. The explosion had damaged her inner ear, making it harder to climb. Choo-Choo pulled himself onto the ledge first, and as she caught Tick's hand for an assist, bullets pinged off the rocks. Yara threw herself over the edge and behind the wall as the mercenaries fired on their location.

"This isn't going to make escaping easy," said Tick as he led them down the tunnel to the lower cavern.

Yara checked back before she followed, seeing dozens of mercenaries and guards gathering. Someone in charge was shouting and pointing towards the tunnels that would intersect with theirs.

"No. No it isn't."

Forty-Six

Pandora's arms pinwheeled outward as Noctus' punch knocked her over the edge. The impact reverberated in her chest, exploding the air from her lungs. The spiked arena floor rose quickly towards her.

She kicked out both feet, finding opposite poles, halting her fall as she slid for a short distance until she could stop her momentum. The splits stretched the limits of her muscles. Stabilized, she threw herself to a pole and monkey-climbed upward until she spotted Noctus lurking above. The second she reached the top, he'd be on her. Rather than continue the climb, she rotated around, leaping to the next pole, but Noctus followed. She kept up her monkey-like traverse until she could drop down on a platform.

The crowd gave her begrudging applause for the escape, while Noctus prowled above, clearly contemplating his next move. When he leapt, she scrambled across a field of poles to the place they'd started their fight, relishing the room as he sauntered onto the platform like a predator who had trapped their prey.

Pandora risked a glance to see her grandfather watching passively from his perch. She wondered what he would think if he knew that it was his kin in the tournament. The answer came right away. Her presence would only be meaningful if she won. That was the maetrie way. Win at all cost. No one cared about the losers.

Noctus' careful approach woke her from the thought, but she hadn't shaken the meaning. She was trying to fight fair against Noctus and he had the advantage of strength and speed. A possible path to victory appeared in her mind, based on Hylakane's teachings. *In a fight between the faeila and knavth, it's the terrain that decides the winner.* She would have liked to have believed she was a wraithhawk, but in this fight she was a knavth trying to match punches with a dolgant.

She eyed the arena, looking for the proper location to spring her trap. Before Noctus could engage, she leapt to a higher location, springing across the tops like a zephyr until she reached the highest point, which was a cluster of poles with no platforms nearby. The Brodarian warrior followed cautiously, sensing a purpose to her choices. When he was three poles away, he hesitated.

"Giving yourself more chance to stop your fall when I knock you off?"

She smirked at his attempt to lure her strategy into the open. "I thought this spot would make a better spectacle for the crowd. We wouldn't want to deprive them."

"Spoken like a true city fae," he said as he surveyed the surrounding poles, clearly looking for a place to make his assault.

Pandora checked over the edge. She was sixty feet above the arena floor and only twenty feet from the ceiling. The truncated stalactites that Kuma had run through to defeat her in their duel years ago were off to her right.

"There's value in spectacle," she said.

"As a diversion."

"Or I wanted to raise the stakes."

He chuckled. "It's the stakes that make this more interesting."

Unlike her, he had no way to slow his descent if he was knocked off. The longer the poles, the less stable they were, so she watched the one on which he was standing for signs of shifting.

The barely detectable quiver announced the resumption of the fight. As he strode across the poles, she slammed them with her sapphire at the same time she retreated two spots. Pandora danced across them as she shook the surface of their battle, never remaining in the same place. The enormous Brodarian struggled with the shifting poles and keeping up with her tactical retreat. To keep him guessing, she attacked him when he landed, but never stayed still long enough for him to counter. The guerilla warfare made him wary, but pushed him to extend himself, which was the intent of her strategy.

To anticipate his moves, she watched his eyes and the way his weight shifted, sending the pole to one side or the other, which made knowing which way he was going next as simple as if she had an amber. Pandora waited until he made a longer leap and threw herself in that direction.

Instead of aiming for her opponent, she flew like a spear towards the shaft of the pole about six feet below the top. The impact sent a loud crack throughout the arena as the wood splintered, sending Noctus over headfirst. The enormous Brodarian managed to grab a pole, swinging around, where she met him with a foot. The battle continued apace, not on top of the poles but along the shafts. She used her sapphire to push them around, making them sway like bamboo in stiff winds. Their back and forth slowly brought them closer to the spiked sands. Her nimbleness combined with the uneven terrain gave her the advantage, which she pressed with sundering kicks and devastating punches. She landed a half dozen blows as he tried to escape to the floor.

Noctus leapt, but Pandora caught him with a knee to the head, sending him tipping into space, headed straight for a pair of sharpened spikes that would puncture him. Using a Pull, she flung herself past him, exploding the wooden spears with a targeted Push. The Brodarian landed on the shards of wood, sending out plumes of sand upon impact. Before he could rise, she kicked him solidly in the back of the head, knocking him out.

The crowd was on their feet, quiet as death, stunned by the sudden turn of events. After the required timing of unconsciousness, the judge declared her the winner. Pandora resisted the urge to check on Noctus as it was something Lady Saha would never do. Instead, she strolled back to the competitor area with the haughty disdain she'd grown up with in the Eternal City.

Forty-Seven

The three of them ran full out, barely ahead of the mercenaries. Choo-Choo leapt a rocky outcropping, landing in a stream that crossed the fungus-illuminated cavern. The staccato pulse of gunfire echoed, bullets pinging against the rocks as he threw himself into the next tunnel.

"We can't take them back to Vasy," he said to Yara, who was in the lead.

The former Razor member hesitated, then cursed under her breath as she veered the opposite direction, taking them towards the southwest.

"They have stones," said Tick. "We can't outrun them."

"Give me your backpack," said Choo-Choo.

Awkwardly removing himself from the straps, Tick tossed the pack, which Choo-Choo caught and immediately unzipped. Holding the brick of explosives and attaching the detonation device while running made him slower and he fell behind the others. He set the timer for fifteen seconds, and when they passed through a narrow tunnel, he dropped it behind him.

"Go!"

He made it to the opposite side of the cavern before it blew. The concussive wave knocked him off his feet and slammed him into the ground. Pain shot through his shoulder as he tried to climb to his feet, but his legs wouldn't work. Yara appeared at his side, hauling him up.

"You set it too low," she said, her voice coming through muted. His ears rung. Choo-Choo wiped blood from his nose as Yara led him forward.

He thought he'd lost the backpack until he realized that Yara had it. They ran for another half hour before she let them rest. The moment he was no longer moving, Choo-Choo lost the contents of his stomach.

"You're concussed, you idiot."

"Did we lose them?"

"Yes. I'm not sure if you killed any, but they had to go around the collapsed tunnel. It worked."

"We need to get back to Vasy," he said, trying to stand, but she pushed him down.

"You can barely move. We've been moving at a rock slime's pace for the last ten minutes. I need to take a look at you."

Choo-Choo tried rising, but she held him down. He felt like a child, even though they had equal stones.

"Lean back, let me look into your eyes."

He did as he was told. She sighed. "Concussed for sure. We're waiting here until you can stand without looking like a drunken fool."

"But Vasy—"

"You're not going to do her any good like this."

"Then one of you go," he said. "Or both. I'd rather you save her."

Yara and Tick exchanged glances, the latter lifting a shoulder.

"I could go," said the diminutive waku. "With Koro, I'm best equipped to make it without getting caught."

"Except you can't carry her with your stones," said Yara with a heavy sigh. "It'll have to be me. You can wait with Choo-Choo until he's better."

"Thanks, Yara," he said, burying his head in his hands. He wanted to lie down and sleep for a century. A pounding headache was making his vision blurry.

Tick forced him to drink water and rest, but after an hour he stood up, focusing on not wavering.

"I'm going."

"If we run into the mercs, you're a dead man."

He forced a smile. "I can't wait here."

Tick put a hand on his arm. "Emilio..."

"You can either come with me or not, but I'm going."

Tick sighed. "Fine, but let me scout."

He was relieved to have Tick stay in front where he didn't see his struggles as he moved through the caverns and tunnels. He'd never felt so useless. At the pace they were moving, the finals would be over and Pandora would likely have lost without their help. Not that he could do anything right now. Lying down and sleeping for a year was all he wanted to do, but he kept moving. For Vasy's sake. For his clan. The one that didn't exist.

Tick led them on a circuitous route. Choo-Choo had wanted to check on Vasy's location, but they had to assume that Yara had found her. Returning to the Terreno took three times as long as reaching the waste-lands and that was without the normal patrols they'd had to avoid in past times. Either the bulk of the Alliance was at the tournament or some-where else entirely. They certainly weren't in the caverns.

The hidden tunnel they'd used to get out of the Terreno was directly ahead. Tick froze at the edge of the cavern, sending waves of concern through Choo-Choo. He hurried to his friend's side, spotting what had brought the unease. A single shape lay unmoving on a bed of moss near the back of the cavern wearing the clothes that Vasilisa had been in when he left her.

Choo-Choo ran ahead, fighting through the lingering vertigo. He threw himself at his sister's side and tentatively placed his hands on her shoulder, fearing that the body would be cold. He had a gun barrel in his face before he realized it.

"Shadows below, Emilio, I almost shot you."

"Are you okay? Where's Yara? Did they get her?"

His sister was pale, dark circles around her eyes. Her clothes were soaked through with old blood.

"I couldn't move anymore. Carrying me kept opening up the wound and crawling through the tunnel was out of the question. She went to find someone with an opal, even if she had to bring them back at gun-point."

He let out a quivering breath. "I'm was afraid that, you know..."

"I know, Emilio," she said, putting a hand on his arm. She screwed up her face. "You look like shit by the way. Not as bad as me, I imagine, but you should probably sit before you fall over."

He plopped onto his rear next to her. "Hey, Tick—"

"I'm on it. No one will get within a quarter mile without me knowing what they had for breakfast."

Choo-Choo leaned against the mossy wall and Vasilisa leaned against him. Time slowed down as they sat in absolute quiet. He could hear her shallow breathing and the slow beat of her heart. None of it would have been worth it had she died. He slept for an unknown time, waking when he felt his sister shifting into an upright position.

"Did you really blow up their entire camp and the elevator?" she asked after sitting quietly for a time.

"Yeah," he said, chuckling as he pulled a water bottle from the backpack, noting that two bricks of explosives yet remained. "Would have been cooler if we'd been at a safe distance, but I think we successfully pulled off the distraction." He paused. "What time is it?"

"Morning of the finals."

"Shit. Where's Tick?"

"He checked on us a short time ago," she said.

"Poor bastard. He didn't get to sleep."

"You needed it. You could barely stand without wobbling." She checked her watch again. "If you have to go, I understand."

"No," he said. "I'm not leaving you if you're not healed. Your shirt is wet. You've been bleeding again."

Vasilisa said nothing. The corners of her lips twitched, but refused to curl into a smile. She laid her head on his shoulder and they stared into the darkness waiting for help.

Forty-Eight

Kuma paced through the suite while Pandora sat on the couch with the wraithhawk mask in her hands, staring at the gift from Hylakane. He couldn't stand still and kept checking the clock on the wall.

"It's an hour before the fight. Where are they?"

Without looking up, Pandora said, "We have to assume they're not coming. Something must have happened."

"I don't know if we can do this if it's just you, me, Camina, and Adrenalynne."

"You go into battle with the force you have, not the one you want," said Pandora soberly. "It's not like we technically need them. If I win the final, I'll have a shot at killing my grandfather and ending this. The Alliance will fall apart without him."

"But you'll be dead."

"I might get away," said Pandora with a blank expression.

It was a lie, but he couldn't bring himself to call her out. She had too much to worry about already. He couldn't imagine what she was going through and was surprised he hadn't seen her counting primes. Was that a good or bad thing? He didn't know.

"The distraction worked at least," he said, trying to bring a positive mood. "I saw Titus leaving by the southern exit earlier."

Pandora said nothing as she stared at the dark mask. The face covering unnerved him due to the wispy shadows that drifted from the surface like mist.

"Are you planning on wearing that during the fight?"

"Do not forget from which it came, or why it was made," said Pandora, repeating the halting diction that Hylakane often spoke in.

"What does that mean?"

She shook her head. "I wish I knew. Or why he gave it to me."

"I should find Navos," he said suddenly. "I know Choo-Choo wanted to reach out, but we're out of time."

"How will you get to him?"

"Choo-Choo said he doesn't come all the way from the headquarters with him. Navos and the other bloodstone guards wait outside the arena until your grandfather arrives."

"You should go, then."

Kuma gathered his gear, strapping on the curved blades that had been his weapons since he was old enough to hold them. The wooden handles were scuffed from the years of battle and the edges were recently sharpened. He laid them carefully against his flesh so he didn't accidentally cut himself while walking. As he opened the door, Pandora called out, "Don't forget your mask."

He grabbed the knavth mask from the table, sliding it into the pack he wore and approached Pandora. Her jaw pulsed and her brow furrowed with thought, so he kissed her on the forehead before leaving.

The energy in the Terreno was electric. He could hear discussion of the fight on everyone's lips. The crowd was rooting for Victor, but no one counted Lady Saha out based on her previous performances. Beating Noctus had turned some in her favor. He wondered what the crowd would think if they knew who she really was.

The main entrance to the arena was blocked. They would start letting people in shortly, but that's not where Kuma needed to be. He snuck out of the Terreno using the exit behind the old Razor bar and circled around to the northern entrance to the arena, where he hoped Navos would be waiting for Dominion, but he didn't recognize any of the guards. Kuma crouched in the shadows and fingered the blade hidden in his uniform.

Forty-Nine

The wraithhawk mask refused to give up its secrets no matter how long she stared at it, so she shoved it into her bag along with the curved blades that she'd learned to use at Drops Academy. A contingent of Alliance guards waited outside the Night House to escort her to the arena without being mobbed.

The crowd shouted obscenities at her, calling her a "gray-faced bitch" or a "pale sorceress." The most inventive one she heard was a "statue fucker," which almost made her crack a grin. A few yelled encouragement, but they were the minority and quickly drowned out.

They'd just started letting the fans into the arena. People were climbing over the rows and hurrying across the paths to reach the seats closest to the floor. She was brought in through a separate entrance. Her eyes fell upon the platform at the center. They'd removed the entirety of the obstacles from the previous fight, and replaced it with a circular stage twenty feet above the sands. The spikes that had been a worrisome feature of the last two battles were no longer present. She wondered what her grandfather had in store for her this final round.

The competitor area was already full. She was almost the last of the final eight and received quite a few nods from the others upon her arrival. Valor had not yet arrived, clearly choosing to delay until the arena was filled. She settled into her area after shoving her bag under the chair. Getting the blades onto her person before the ceremony might be difficult, but she hoped there would be ample distractions.

"I need to talk to you."

Pandora was startled to find Sophia Botez glowering at her side. The dark-haired twin looked like she'd swallowed a bug.

"So talk," she replied menacingly.

"Privately."

Pandora nearly told her to leave but the intensity of Sophia's expression had her curious. She walked to the corner of the competitor area as Sophia leaned into her ear.

"Valor cheated."

"A little late now."

Sophia checked over her shoulder. "He's taking a whole bunch of elixirs—"

Pandora held up her hand. "This is not news. While your kind is not as clever with their cheating, I expected as much."

"Not just that," said Sophia, clearly distraught. "He poisoned me. During the fight. I don't know how it happened, but towards the end, I didn't feel myself. I was dizzy and had double vision. That's when he got me."

Pandora hadn't been watching because she'd been talking with Noctus, but she had no reason to think that Sophia was lying.

"Why are you telling me this?"

"I hate that man. He knocked out my twin and he's an arrogant twit masquerading as the man of the people." Sophia screwed up her mouth. "Look, I'm no fan of you city fae, but at least you don't hide that you're a stone-cold bitch."

"Your warning has been noted."

Sophia blinked before sensing she'd overstayed her welcome. She returned to the others, glancing over her shoulder. Poison wasn't a surprise. Pandora should have guessed some of the competitors would have tried it. It was ironic that the full human half of the match was the one competing in the maetrie way. Given that the fight would be hand to hand, the likely method of administering the poison would be through fingernails, or as a contact liquid.

A raucous cheer went up, interrupting her thoughts. Valor Drux had entered the arena. He waved to the crowd and shook their hands. The crassness angered Pandora. The Undercity had been a place of honor; now it was a gaudy sideshow. She wanted to beat Valor not only for the chance to kill her grandfather, but to show the world he was a pretender.

When he reached the competitor area, he marched up, towering over her by half a foot. The crowd ate up his posturing display. He jabbed a forefinger in her face.

"I'm going to break you over my knee."

He winked as he brushed past as if to let her in on the joke. The lack of respect for what the Undercity once was burned in her veins. While she hadn't been born here, it'd been the first place since her father's death that had truly felt like home.

The opposite gate opened as flags bearing the Alliance sigil were waved furiously. Cheers grew in crescendo. Pandora stared at the empty space, waiting for her grandfather to arrive.

Fifty

Camina stumbled into the cavern behind Yara with her head on a swivel, expecting a patrol to unmask her rebellion. A headache at the base of her skull warned her that the programming she'd been under was not completely gone.

"They're over here," said Yara, leaping over a rocky wall.

Choo-Choo and his sister were sitting next to each other. Vasilisa was covered in dark blood. Camina could smell the wound, which was never a good sign. She didn't know Vasilisa well, but she smiled in greeting as if they were old friends.

"You're lucky they don't have much need of me lately," said Camina as she knelt before Vasilisa.

"I found her before she made it to the Terreno," said Yara. "The tunnels are strangely empty."

As Camina peeled away the bloody garments and bandages, she said, "They took more of my students recently. The number's grown so large it's been hard to ignore."

"What are they doing with them?"

"I wish I knew," she said, then to Vasilisa, "This is going to hurt. I need to see the wound. It'll make it easier to heal."

Tears formed in Vasilisa's eyes as Camina pulled away the cloth which had become stuck to the wound. As the last pieces ripped away, a blob of blood plopped out and rolled down her arm. Her shoulder looked like a ruin.

"Is it fixable?" asked Vasilisa.

"You're lucky I've spent the last two years healing my idiot students. I've fixed more broken bones and stab wounds than an ER unit in the city," said Camina as she held her hands over the wounds in front and back. "This is going to hurt. Try not to scream."

Choo-Choo used his knife to cut a section of strap off the backpack, placing it in his sister's mouth. Repairing the wound took Camina ten minutes, mostly because she wanted to make sure she didn't miss any internal issues. Luckily, the body knew how to heal itself given the boost from her opal. When she was finished, Vasilisa spat the strap out and exhaled deeply.

"Thank you. Can you take a look at my brother now?"

"What's wrong with you, big man?"

He screwed up his face. "I'm fine."

"He got his noodle scrambled from the explosions," said Vasilisa.

"Concussions are trickier but I'll do what I can."

When she was finished, Choo-Choo looked better, but not back to normal. He climbed to his feet, grabbing the gun that had been lying on the stone.

"We need to move."

"Move? Like that? You look like war refugees. You'll never get within a hundred miles of the arena," said Camina. She nudged the bag of clothes she'd brought. "I grabbed these in case something like this came up. I had to guess at your sizes."

They switched into the Alliance uniforms while Camina stood guard, feeling like a patrol would come along at any moment. As near as they were to the Terreno it seemed criminal that one hadn't come by. Which only made her wonder what really was going on.

"Let's go," said Choo-Choo when he was dressed, grabbing his pack and starting off in the opposite direction.

"Whoa. Let's talk a second," said Camina. "What's the plan now?"

"Emilio," said Vasilisa. "Let's not be stupid."

"We were supposed to be back hours ago. I never got to talk to Navos," he said.

"Rushing into danger isn't going to help anyone. What are we doing?" asked Camina.

"We need to be there after the ceremony. When Pan attacks her grandfather, all hell is going to break loose," said Choo-Choo.

"Hell's already broken loose," said Yara. "We're trying to stuff it back in its hole."

"The Terreno is filled with Alliance waku. While ninety percent of them are newbies who can barely hold a knife correctly, let alone use it, the other ten percent are decent enough to cause issues, and since none of us have black diamonds, their guns can easily take us down. Once the awards ceremony starts, we need to be able to block off the arena."

Choo-Choo lifted his backpack. "We have a few bricks left. I could bring down the ceiling, block us in. That would leave only one other exit."

"It could work," said Camina.

"It *has* to work," he replied.

Fifty-One

Slipping out of the Terreno to the northern tunnels to circle around was far simpler than Kuma expected. The Alliance guards were huddled in groups, talking quietly, checking over their shoulders, but not actively seeing. He knew the look. They were afraid and he couldn't understand why, but he wasn't interested in that mystery. He needed to find Navos.

The northern entrance to the arena was well lit. Like a lot of the caverns adjacent to the Terreno, it was illuminated with stringed lights, and the paths had gravel, making for an easy traverse. The homey feel made him miss the Machi, which he heard had been abandoned months ago. The houses were probably rotting as the insects and other critters took over. When Vasilisa had mentioned it, he'd pretended not to care. He'd already lost his family. Why would it matter if the buildings were no longer in use?

Crunching across the gravel, he circled around to the barred gate. To his surprise Navos was actually standing guard, expressionlessly staring forward. Kuma almost raised his hand in a wave as he approached, forgetting that he was Aman Crownline, rather than a former clanmate. The only sign Navos gave that he was watching his advance was a shifting of the eyes.

"Navos..."

Kuma had practiced a speech in his head, but standing before the stoic former Drops member had him questioning his strategy.

"The proper entrance for the arena is on the south side. Please return before I deal with you in a manner equal to your disobedience."

The robotic, emotionless tone shocked Kuma. Navos has always been free with a grin, even when they were enemies. The blond waku had often looked out of place in the Undercity based on his lanky height and absence of obvious malice. He'd made a good counter to Choo-Choo's angry demeanor. Kuma checked over his shoulder and lowered his voice.

"Navos. It's me, Kuma."

His gaze slowly shifted, coming to rest on him. Kuma tried to give him a welcoming smile, but the lack of friendly response left his stomach in knots.

"We're going to hit back. We have a chance to flip the table, taken the Undercity back from Dominion. We need your help."

For a fleeting moment, Kuma thought he saw an anxious cry for help in Navos' eyes as if he were a prisoner in his own head, but his expression quickly changed to intensity.

"Navos? What's wrong?"

Kuma grabbed Navos' forearm to trigger a reaction, but it was like grabbing a statue. The former Drops member barely moved.

"Can't you talk? What have they done to you? Come on, we can do this. Join us." Kuma leaned back. "Why aren't you talking? Is this something they did? Drugs, spells?"

Navos closed his eyes, squeezing them shut as if he were in pain. He slowly opened his eyes and mouthed a word. No sound came out. Kuma wasn't a good lip reader, but it appeared to be two words.

"What is it? Can you say it again?"

The whites of his eyes shone before fluttering back to normal. The second time a whisper of voice came out, confirming what Kuma thought he'd heard.

"Blood...stone."

The gears clicked into place, followed by a chill that went bone deep. Bloodstone. The faez crystal had somehow changed Navos. Kuma gave Navos a once-over, looking for signs of the stone. While they used to wear their stones in places that couldn't be seen, the trend for the Alliance, having control of the entire Undercity, was to wear them prominently. Navos had liked his jewelry and tattoos, often looking like a rock star rather than a waku, but Kuma couldn't find it.

"Where is it? Is that what's happened to you?"

Navos appeared in great pain as he lifted his right arm, pointing to a spot on his left. Kuma frantically pulled up his sleeve to see a lump under the surface of his pale skin.

"I don't understand..."

Kuma ran his fingers across the lump. It moved beneath his fingertips, making him recoil.

"It's a typhid, or something like it," he said with realization. Navos was being mind-controlled like he'd almost become in the Eternal City, until Hylakane had removed it. There was no bloodstone. The truth made certain things clear that had confused him before. No faez crystal attuned instantly and gave multiple abilities.

"It's a trap. The contest is a trap."

The purpose of the competition became clear. Dominion was recruiting more deadly warriors for his employ. Rather than wait for his waku to get trained up, he'd lured grand masters to the Undercity with promises of wealth and increased abilities, but that's not what they were getting. The top eight would be turned into mindless zombies who did everything Dominion Thule said.

Kuma reached for his blade to cut the typhid, or whatever it was, out of Navos' arm. He was so lost in the realization, he hadn't heard people approaching from the opposite end.

"Hey! What are you doing?"

A group of six Alliance waku approached. Kuma spun around, twirling his blades as a show of skill, knowing at a glance he could easily take them. Not a single one appeared to have a gun. But he wasn't ready to fight yet. They were supposed to wait for the ceremony, but if Dominion was going to infect them with a method of mind control, maybe he needed to act now.

"We were having a conversation," he said. "I suggest you head the other way and forget that you even came here."

"Hey, he's one of the competitors," said one of them in back, eliciting a round of nods and concerned comments under their breath. Half the group looked open to his idea, especially because they looked relatively new. But the older one in front that Kuma thought he might have recognized from before scowled and pushed his sleeves up as if he were preparing to fight.

"I'll dance if you want to," said Kuma.

The waku chuckled. "Are you opposing the Alliance?"

"You're not my friends, if that's what you're asking."

Kuma had a sense he'd said something wrong when the older waku smirked.

"Navos. Grab him. Take his weapons."

The idea that'd he'd screwed up became clear when Navos' iron grip latched onto his arm. Before he could twist away, his other arm was pinned and the waku surrounded him, easily taking his blades. Kuma struggled to get away but it was like being trapped under a boulder.

"What do we do with him?" asked one of the younger waku.

The one in charge shook his head. "Let's stash him away until afterwards. I'd rather not upset the big boss while all this shit is going down. Besides, the last thing I want to do is get noticed these days."

The others nodded.

"Is something wrong? What are they doing to you? I know that trainees have gone missing."

"Shut him up," said the older waku.

"Look, if you don't do something, this will be you—"

Before he could continue, a rag was shoved in his mouth. The waku pulled out zip-ties and bound his wrists and ankles. He was hoisted on someone's shoulder and carried out of the cavern like a sack of potatoes.

Fifty-Two

Thunderous applause began the moment Dominion stepped into the arena surrounded by a cadre of bloodstone warriors, including Navos. She hoped that Kuma had been able to reach Navos in time, but there was no space to worry about that now. Pandora hid her distaste for her grandfather behind a mien of intensity. She had to focus on the final fight, but her mind wanted to skip ahead to the moment she would have to thrust the blade in. Her mother followed behind, but slipped to the back of the platform, not wanting to take any of her father's adoration.

Pandora wasn't sure what she was going to do about her mother. She might try to interfere, but without stones her mechanical enchanted arm couldn't do much. The cheering went on for a long time. *Is this what you want?* She didn't think so. The love of the people was only useful so far as you could exploit it. *I'm going to take your bloodstone and turn it against you.*

The thought curled the corners of her lips. Her grandfather gave a short speech, but Pandora wasn't listening. She barely remembered to wave when she was announced, recognizing the moment not because she heard her name, but the jeers and hisses that followed.

Valor Drux was given a hero's welcome. She saw families wearing T-shirts with his face on them. People held up signs in support. There were signs about her, but all of them negative, except for a small group of college-aged kids wearing the outfit she'd fought in during the weapons round. The high collar and crimson cloak stuck out in the crowd. She would have been flattered if she didn't hate the way the Undercity had been turned into a carnival.

"No place for you to hide here," said Valor, nodding towards the contained platform in comparison to the previous rounds when the arena was an obstacle course. "Winners don't run."

She didn't deem he deserved a response and stared back with contempt. The judge led them to the center of the platform where he gave them the unchanged rules. As the judge moved away, preparing to start the fight, Pandora recalled Sophia's warning about the poison. Most likely it was under his fingernails, or another part of his body that might strike her.

"Begin!"

If Valor had hoped that the fight would be easy, she quickly dissuaded him of that idea. He moved fast. Whatever elixirs and other magics burned in his belly, they made him a blur. He attacked with windmill strikes, his lanky arms coming at her with the power of a sledgehammer. Pandora caught him with a kick to the stomach, sending him flying backwards, aided by a Push. He landed on his feet, but stumbled backwards from momentum before he was able to stop.

Valor glowered, so she waved her fingers at him dismissively.

He attacked with fury, the reckless strikes a blatant attempt to strike her with his fists, which was where she assumed the poison was located. Pandora blocked five, seven, eleven attacks, before sending him spinning away with a hooked kick.

"Getting tired of winning?" she asked.

The blood rushed to his face as he charged. Using a carefully timed twisted Pull, she spun him around, tangling his feet and landing him on his back. He was good. She'd give him that. Better than most waku she'd fought.

But she was better.

He approached cautiously the next pass, having had his momentum used against him. The elixirs burned bright in his eyes, and unlike the young Alliance waku, he had the skills to back up the enhancement. He attacked with patience, content to spar while staying ready for her sapphire.

The attack was clever. Valor feinted a right hook, then threw himself feet first in an attempt at a leg lock, which exposed him to a counterattack. She punished his mistake, catching him solidly in the chest. He bounced off the platform, eliciting an in-breath from the crowd. Before she could leap away to keep him from entangling her legs, he reached up and raked the back of her calf with his fingernails.

Pandora scrambled to a new position, checking her lower leg to find bloody lines. The smirk on his face was enough to signal that she'd been poisoned, even if she hadn't felt the effects yet. Valor approached slowly, head tilted as he waited. *Maybe this won't be so bad.* She advanced, pulling him in with her sapphire and throwing knees and elbows that caught him across the chest and thighs.

Then she went for a right hook and found her swing missing by two inches, which was a gulf in her mind. The world shifted beneath her feet and her lips felt numb. Valor's eyes lit up as he watched her stumble backwards. He went on the offense, catching her with multiple kicks and punches. When she tried to knock him away using a Push, the weak effort barely knocked his hair back.

"You're mine now."

As she tried to block a punch, her arm coming up too late, she feared that he was right.

Fifty-Three

The whiskey was empty, except for a few drops of amber liquid at the bottom which Deacon sucked dry before smashing the bottle in the corner. Glass exploded across his bed, but he didn't care. He checked himself in the mirror. His right pec was covered in knotty scar tissue. Kneading his fingers into the rough flesh brought no relief to the ache that kept him awake most nights.

The other intact plate whispered to him behind closed eyes. He could hear voices. Inhuman cries like the dead trying to escape the

Veil. When the plates had been whole, he'd sensed their calls distantly, but since that bitch Yara had blown one to bits with a handgun at close range, they screamed in his head constantly.

His cheeks were gaunt. He traced his fingers across his ribs, proof that he hadn't been eating, even though sometimes he dreamed he had. It was the creatures in the metal. The black plates had protected him, but now that one was gone, they were eating him from the inside. Dying. He'd known it for months, but the bill was coming due. Sooner than he wanted.

Deacon slipped into his black suit with the gray shirt. He'd liked the way it looked when he first put it on, but now that he was pale and emaciated the clothes made him look like a second-rate maetrie.

"Fuck you," he said into the mirror.

The handgun fit into his inner pocket. He grabbed the hooked blade from the wall and marched out of his apartment, which was the largest space in the area. But as he looked to the top of the elevator where Dominion and his private maetrie army lurked, he knew that no matter how well he performed, he'd never reach the level he aspired to.

But disobedience wasn't an option. He knew what would happen. Dying didn't scare him. Living under the blade did.

The neon lights of the Eleventh Gonka buzzed, drawing him towards the sweet embrace of the whiskey he knew he could get inside, but Dominion had tasked him with a specific role in his little adventure.

As much as he wanted to blow off his maetrie master, he knew doing so would be a mistake. He'd seen what happened to people that disobeyed. It was easier to comply.

"Yo, Deacon!"

His hand twitched towards the handgun. He was in no mood for banter, but the black-clad mercenary under Titus' leadership made him stay his hand. Deacon mumbled a response.

"You heard?" asked the guy, preening as if he'd made the world himself.

Deacon stared back until the mercenary swallowed and checked over his shoulder nervously.

"They found it."

It needed no explanation. Dominion had been throwing resources and manpower at the dig site in the Dark Depths to acquire the lost Tear. Deacon shuddered at the power contained within that weapon, but he'd likely never have to worry about it. Even Dominion, as powerful as he was, would find it hard to subdue the Tear. Deacon had heard Titus talk about it on more than one occasion, speculating that their boss wasn't trying to acquire it for himself due to the difficulty of unlocking its power, but as trade. Deacon didn't think so. He'd learned that Dominion's ambitions knew no bounds, but then again, he didn't know the Eternal City native as well as Titus.

"Hooray," Deacon deadpanned, brushing past the merc.

"What the fuck, man? I thought you'd be happy to hear that."

Deacon speared him with his gaze. "You have no idea what a fucking mistake that was. You can't spend coin when you're dead."

He headed to the elevator. Neither guard dared stop him. They looked terrified that he might decide to take their heads off with the hooked blade. He'd almost forgotten he was carrying it. At the top of the elevator the maetrie guards acknowledged him only by their absence of performing their duties.

The interior made his skin crawl, reminding him of his time in the Eternal City. Dominion had found a way to pump the weird air of his realm into this little corner of the Undercity.

When he entered the assembly area, he found one hundred waku lined up in groups of twenty in a resting position. They bore the blank-eyed expressions that he'd first had after his modification. Those early days were like living in a hellscape that only existed in his mind. Deacon touched the remaining plate on his chest, wishing the voices would quiet.

He marched up to a woman in front with dark circles around her eyes and a wicked scar on her chin. Deacon flicked her in the throat, but she didn't react. He considered licking her face, if only to prove to himself how far gone they were.

"Attention!"

The entire hall snapped into the stance with the precision of a timepiece.

"Fucking hell," he muttered.

Deacon had seen the recruits perform at the Academy and they couldn't have managed that feat after a hundred attempts. But he shouldn't have been surprised. He knew what had been done to them because it'd been done to him. He hadn't known exactly what it was when it first happened, but after the plate had been shattered, the barrier between him and the creatures they'd installed inside his head had broken down, leaving him exposed to their attentions. He was being devoured from the inside by a winged cancer that had come from the Eternal City. How they'd managed to capture and convert the wraithhawks into a form that gave him superior abilities would be an eternal mystery. He looked over the hundred modified waku, their dead eyes staring back without a trace of emotion.

"Time to put down a rebellion."

Fifty-Four

The kick probably broke a rib. Pandora spat blood on the platform and rolled away from the next, catching a grazing blow. The world was distant. Her limbs felt like she'd slept on them. Pandora used a Push to climb to her feet, then another to throw herself out of the way. The stones were the only thing reliably working.

The crowd was on its feet, anticipating the end of the fight was near. Valor was taking his time. He had multiple chances to knock her out, but let her escape each time, drawing it out for the cheers. They were chanting his name. She sensed he would take her down soon and she wasn't sure she could stop him.

Her grandfather stood at the railing, watching passively. He didn't care about the fight. It wasn't part of his plan, only a means to an end. Yet she felt some deep-seated need to please him. Prove to him that she wasn't the failure that he'd sent back from the Eternal City.

Pandora used her sapphire to interfere with Valor's approach, but he waded through the Pushes as the stone seemed to work best on herself with the poison coursing through her veins. She wondered what the crowd thought as she jerked around the platform, using the sapphire to move her body like a marionette when her limbs wouldn't cooperate.

A missed block nearly took her head off. His foot connected with her shoulder, spinning her to the edge of the platform. Pandora wiped the blood from her lips, climbing unsteadily to her feet. The poison had wrecked her. It made the idea of losing to Valor even worse. She was a quarter maetrie, not him. She should have been the one looking for unfair advantage. Hylakane had admonished her inability to utilize that part of herself. Be an alloy. It sounded good in theory.

She dodged out of the way, backing across the empty space in a full retreat. Valor didn't bother chasing. He sauntered her direction with the arrogance of a lion. *If I could just get rid of this poison.* She held her fists up drunkenly, which brought laughter from Valor. *Get rid of poison. Get rid of poison?* As Valor approached, she burned her opal, turning her body into a furnace in hopes of burning away the toxins. Sweat dripped from her forehead. The agony of her muscles on fire made her debilitatingly weak. She kept moving away in slow steps, her limbs revolting from the abuse, and then the fever broke. Pandora was left panting, covered in sticky sweat.

Not wanting to give away the change, Pandora kept her head down and moved jerkily. She feigned dizziness as she stumbled across the platform. The corner of his lips curled upward in expectation of final victory.

Valor set his feet, looking like a kicker addressing the ball. He came flying towards her, arm cocked back in a leaping punch.

Time slowed down. The entire crowd was in a frenzy of anticipation.

As his fist hurled towards her jaw, Pandora snapped upward, throwing herself past his blow. Surprise registered on his face, but it came too late, as she used his momentum against him. Knuckles caught him cleanly under the jaw, aided by a Push that helped her explode upward. She flew in a high arc, spinning and landing in ready pose, but it was unnecessary.

Valor Drux collapsed onto the platform unconscious. The thud rang through the arena, which had grown silent. Not only had she fooled her opponent, but the entire crowd.

The small group of supporters dressed like her cheered raucously, breaking the rest from their stupor to applauded mutedly, or give half-hearted jeers.

As she stood over her unconscious opponent, waiting for the judge to declare her the winner, she couldn't help but bask in the self-satisfied smirk from her grandfather. He stood at the railing, a slow smile growing at the turn of events. She hated herself for caring what he thought.

When the judge approached, she lifted her chin defiantly.

"The winner of the grand tournament is Lady Saha!"

He handed her a huge silver cup. The trophy was symbolic as she, like her fellow competitors, was more interested in the bloodstones and black diamond as prizes. But she lifted the cup, allowing herself an awkward smile. The crowd applauded more enthusiastically than she would have expected. It'd been a good match, even if the ending had been a surprise.

Under normal circumstances, she might have basked in the attention, but the unsavory task that awaited left her stomach in knots. *How can I kill him? Don't get cold feet now.*

Exhausted from purging the poison from her veins, she made her way to the competitor area while trying not to vomit. The others congratulated her and gave her private, if unbelievable, assurances that they'd been rooting for her the entire time. A few minutes later, Valor stumbled back, his eyes unfocused with his chin tucked to his chest.

The crowd filtered out of the arena while the competitors milled around, chatting about their favorite moments from the tournament, all while clearly anticipating the gift of the bloodstones. Pandora used a wet rag to clean the toxins from her skin, using the moment to covertly slip her blade into the sleeve of her uniform. Then she attached the bag that held the wraithhawk mask to her hip.

When there were no spectators in the arena, the eight competitors were ushered onto the platform and situated in a straight line at the center point. They stood at attention and Pandora couldn't help but feel like she was back at the Academy, waiting for the acknowledgement of the instructor.

Dominion climbed onto the platform surrounded by his private guards. Pandora eyed the stoic Navos wondering if Kuma had reached him before the event. She checked around the arena, catching sight of Camina and Adrenalynne, standing guard near the platform.

Pandora's heart thrummed with anticipation. Her grandfather was only twenty steps away with Selena at his side.

Be an alloy. Don't let him hurt your friends any more.

"Congratulations, competitors," said Dominion, applauding softly. "This was a tournament for the ages and that final fight, I don't think anyone expected such a brutal reversal. But such is the way of war and conflict. Sometimes when you think you've won, you find everything you thought you understood was a lie and you learn that you are not the victor."

Her grandfather gave her a sour smile while inclining his head. *You're not the only one who thinks he's won.* She returned the gesture.

"Selena, my favorite daughter, would you make the presentation of the bloodstones."

Wearing a silver-and-gold gown that matched her arm and half-skull, Selena approached the far end of the line as a waku carried a tray of eight darkwood boxes. She gave the first box to Angel Chen, who received it with a smile, but did not open it. Pandora's heart thundered in her ears as her mother approached and then before she knew it, Selena was standing before her.

"You made our people proud today," said Selena as she handed over the box.

"I do not fight for pride," said Pandora reflexively, adding a ghoulish smile afterwards.

Her grandfather had a glass of champagne in his hand. He lifted it high.

"To the victors. May your reign be long!"

As he drank his champagne, they opened their boxes. Pandora was the last to open hers. The stone surprised her with its beauty. Crimson and black striations glinted. She grabbed the bloodstone between fore-finger and thumb, holding it up against the light as her fellow competitors attached the stones to their flesh.

One last step...

Pandora pulled back her jacket from her chest and stabbed the catch into her skin, anticipating that the true victory was about to arrive.

Fifty-Five

The plastic ties held his wrists and ankles. More than once he'd wished he'd been attuned to a topaz. Now more than ever. They'd thrown him in the break room to a guard station on the path that led to the Alliance HQ. He was attached to a closed hook on the wall and every yank bit into his flesh.

He'd been in the room for twenty minutes, which meant the final match was in full swing. When it was over, if he couldn't reach Pandora in time, she'd accept the bloodstone thinking it was a faez crystal only to become enslaved. Their rebellion would be over before it began.

Kuma pushed his feet against the wall, straining to snap the plastic ties. He was afraid his wrists would sever before he could break the plastic loops. The stones he had were useless in the current situation, but at least he'd spit the dirty rag out of his mouth.

"Think," he admonished himself, checking the room for tools he might commandeer to cut the ties. The little kitchen was on the opposite side of the room. While they hadn't removed his stones, believing his Aman persona, the ones he had weren't helping him escape. If he had a sapphire, he could have pulled sharp objects over to cut the ties. The only way he might accomplish that was if he could use his ruby on a waku who was actively using their stone. That way he could borrow their abilities. But no one was around. Once they'd dropped him off, they'd forgotten about him.

"Hello?" he called out at the top of his lungs. "Hey, you wayhos, you forgot about me!"

Kuma listened with his amber, hoping to detect the approach of the Alliance waku. Nothing. He growled under his breath and continued yelling. The exercise was beginning to feel futile until he heard the crunch of footsteps on gravel.

"Why don't you shut the fuck up or would you like us to cut your throat?" asked a dark-haired waku, who strode into the room with two others that had been outside. "Where's that rag?"

Kuma was sitting on it. He reached out with his ruby to find none of their stones active.

"You wayhos are too afraid of me. You know what that means, right? It means you're a dumb, cunty lighter. Too stupid to live in the shadows. The only reason you've survived this long is because your master doesn't let you off your leash or you would have died already."

He got part of the reaction he wanted. The waku shuffled over and decked Kuma with a right hook hard enough to bring spots to his vision. His jaw wasn't broken but it would bruise. The ruby detected no stones being used. The punch was unaided.

"That's it?" asked Kuma, mockingly. "I've taken bigger hits from my little sister. You might as well work at one of the hostess clubs. Pouring my drinks is all I'd let you do if you were in my clan."

Two more blows came in quick succession. Kuma couldn't avoid them, trapped against the wall. His head rang from the impacts and he was no closer to escaping, because no one had used their stones yet. Despite the pain and the blood running from his cut lip, Kuma started laughing hysterically.

"What the fuck is wrong with this dude?" asked one of the others.

"He fought in the tournament. Nearly beat that ugly ogre, Noctus. Maybe someone knocked his brains loose."

"I thought he wasn't from here? He called us wayhos," said the third waku.

Kuma realized his mistake, but he wasn't sure he cared. "Nah. I ain't from here, but I heard people talking. They call you Alliance fucks wayhos behind your backs in the Terreno. The vendors know you fake crystal. Pretenders playing at being warriors."

The two that had been standing in the back surged forward, pummeling him with their fists. He caught a kick to the ribs, leaving him bent over, but still no stone use. The laughter that came out was half deranged.

"I think a hostess I insulted at Club Onyx punched harder than you," said Kuma.

The taller one stepped forward, cracking his knuckles. He looked like the kind of guy Deacon had run with in the Crows, with two gold teeth and more chains than a dog pound.

"Oh really? Big mouth on this one. You want me to punch hard? I can show you hard, but you might not have any teeth when I'm done."

Sitting with his back against the wall and his bound hands in his lap, Kuma grinned at him.

"Give it your best shot, Princess."

Rage burned in his eyes. As he reared back, Kuma caught the whiff of a topaz burning. The young waku didn't know how to properly access his stone, but Kuma didn't care. It didn't matter how much, only that he had. Before the punch was thrown, Kuma snapped both sets of plastic ties and deflected the strike with an open hand. He exploded upward, a fist catching the tall waku beneath the chin and sending him across the table. The other two reached for their weapons, but Kuma was faster. He broke the wrist of the first and then caught the second with a heel kick to the temple. The Alliance waku with his wrist bent at an odd angle was screaming. Kuma leaned over and knocked him out with a single punch, unaided by the topaz since its user was unconscious.

"Thank you for the use of your topaz," he said, leaning down and removing their stones and dropping them in his pocket. He found the zip-ties and bound their limbs and connected them to each other. Using rags he found under the sink and some tape, Kuma made sure they wouldn't be able to call for help. When he was finished, he found his curved blades on top of the refrigerator and took two handguns, which he belted around his waist in overlapping straps.

Fifty-Six

The bloodstone was warm under her fingertips as Pandora pierced the skin. Almost alive. She couldn't decide if it was her mind playing tricks on her, or the aftereffects of the poison. No matter. This was one more step she had to take before her grandfather would invite her forward and then she could plunge the blade into his chest, ending his schemes forever.

She hesitated with the pin slipped through her flesh. The other competitors had completed the attachment, and all eyes were upon her.

A commotion near the northern entrance, the one the Alliance used exclusively, brought everyone's heads up. Two guards tumbled into the arena unconscious, crimson lines across their chests. When Kuma appeared, a blade in one hand and a gun in the other, Pandora didn't know what to think.

"Don't take the bloodstone!" he yelled. "It's a trap like the typhid!"

At the last word, she ripped the pin from her flesh. The crimson-and-black stone shifted like a tiny egg. She dropped it on the platform and smashed it with her heel. The other competitors looked in various states of agony as the creature hidden in the bloodstone was taking control of their bodies. She looked in horror at how close she'd been to succumbing.

The guards running in Kuma's direction stopped when two of their members fell to the blades of Camina and Adrenalynne. Then an explosion ripped through the gate, dropping rock and debris, blocking the exit that went towards the Terreno. Her fellow conspirators led by Choo-Choo appeared out of the dust, sending the entire arena into chaos.

With everyone distracted by the sudden change of fortunes, Pandora surged forward, pulling the curved blade from her sleeve. She had a direct line to her grandfather, who hadn't noticed her yet.

Before she could reach him, Selena threw herself in the way, pawing weakly at her knife arm. The distraction provided enough delay that Navos and the other bloodstone warriors formed ranks around Dominion, snapping to attention with their weapons at the ready.

"You traitorous bitch!" cried her mother, trying to grab the blade.

Pandora smacked her away, then seeing the approach of the other guards, she grabbed Selena's shoulders and put the blade to her throat.

"Move and your daughter dies."

The battle was in earnest. Her fellow competitors were writhing on the platform, fighting against the creature in the stone that was slowly taking control. Off the stage in the sands of the arena, her friends were quickly overwhelming the inexperienced waku, leaving Dominion's personal guard as the only remaining obstacle. But as she stared into her grandfather's eyes, she didn't see the devastation she'd expected, but the thin-lipped patience of a predator who had finally sprung their trap.

"You won't do it," he said coldly. "You're not that cruel."

Pandora pressed the blade against her mother's neck, letting it split the skin slightly. A drop of blood beaded up before slipping over her collarbone and beneath her dress.

"I'll gut her like a pig."

"I seriously doubt it. *Pandora.*"

The name sent waves of shock through her and her mother. "Pan?"

"Shut up," she said, shaking Selena and pressing the blade harder.

"You didn't think I would figure it out? I'd watched you fight a thousand times at my estate, seen the promise that you held as a young *human* child. I always knew you'd be great, even if it took time for you to see that. Pity you didn't take the bloodstone. It would have made this much easier, but we can force what you weren't going to do willingly."

Dominion snapped his fingers. "Valor. Sophia. Rise and serve me." The ex-military warrior and the twin snapped to attention. "The ones who think they are the strongest are often the weakest. See how quickly they succumbed? Now, my dear Valor, my dear Sophia, take control of my granddaughter before she hurts someone."

"I'll kill her," she said, pressing the blade harder. Her mother let out a soft cry.

Dominion held up his hand and the two warriors stopped a few feet away. A ghoulish smile formed on his lips.

"Ahh...there he is."

She didn't know who Dominion was talking about until she saw Deacon march into the arena ahead of two lines of stoney-faced warriors. They kept coming, their numbers quickly exceeding the rebellion's. Her friends fell back to the blocked exit that led towards the Terreno as the new warriors spread out across the sands in groups of twenty. Deacon gave a half-hearted salute.

Not only were the other competitors becoming slaves to Dominion, but the overwhelming numbers of lesser warriors made the battle into a farce. They'd lost. Completely. Absolutely. Her world had turned to ashes. Her grandfather had out-strategized her.

"Don't feel so bad, Pandora. It came close to working. It took me until the recent fights to see that it was you and make appropriate countermeasures. Your disguise was impeccable. How did you do that? I'm impressed, child. There's no reason not to tell me now, because you'll be mine soon enough."

"The Eternal City," she said absently.

Dominion licked his lips. "A productive visit. Maybe all you needed before was to feel the danger of our home, know that death lurked on every corner. It's a wonderful teacher."

"I hate you," she said, but the emotion barely came through as she continued holding the blade to her mother's throat. The threat felt impotent, but she didn't want to give up the illusion of control.

"Why? This is proof of how great you could be under my leadership. I have such plans for this realm and many others."

"I know about the Tear. I know what you plan to do."

He chuckled as he strode up arrogantly. "I doubt it. I am not wanton with my violence like you." Her grandfather stretched his arm towards the arena. "What a perfect venue for this moment. You bested so many great warriors. Why not join me? You've always sought power like me. Not like your weak mother."

Selena sagged in her arms, so Pandora pushed her standing. "I don't want to be you."

Dominion steepled his fingers, his crass smile mocking her answer. He was only a few feet away, but she knew she could never reach him before the others would stop her. Valor and Sophia lurked in range like dead-faced automatons.

"There are two alternatives. The first is that you submit to me. Take the bloodstone if you don't believe you can be faithful on your own accord. If you do, I'll spare your friends' lives. They can take the bloodstone as well and we can forget this nastiness."

He took another step towards her, daring her to strike.

"The second choice is for you to fight and lose. Those that aren't lucky enough to fall under the blade will be brought to the Eternal City and made to conform. Their treatment will make what happened to you look like a spa day.

"But it need not be like this. Join me, granddaughter. I promise you that you won't regret it. I'm not the monster you make me out to be. Look what I did for the Undercity. It was a place of constant warring. Wasted deaths. Think of all the great warriors who perished under the old system. I ended all that, made the Undercity a safe place, a destination for the people in the city. Join me, Pandora, and we can rule the realms. I promise."

The offer was more enticing than she would have liked to admit to herself. She could temper her grandfather's worst impulses. Be an alloy. She could do that. Maybe that was why he'd lived in the human realm for so long. He knew that the maetrie way was unsustainable.

Then she looked to her fellow competitors. Seven warriors enslaved to her grandfather through trickery. He'd taken their free will and chained them to his wrist. He would pervert their abilities, make them a mockery of who they really were.

"What is your decision, granddaughter?"

Pandora hesitated. She needed more time to think. He snarled his lips.

"If you can't decide, I can help."

Dominion snapped his fingers. Deacon held up his hooked sword in salute.

"Kill her friends."

Fifty-Seven

The explosion rattled his head, but nothing like the detonations at the wastelands. Choo-Choo strode forward with his blades in his fists. Three Alliance guards sprinted towards him. They were leaning too far forward, exposing their midsections. He slipped past them—one, two, three—slicing them across the chest with deep cuts.

An Alliance warrior to his left had him dead to rights with an automatic rifle. When it went off, Choo-Choo flinched, finding himself intact. He checked behind him to see Vasilisa with a shotgun under her arm, reloading the barrels.

The tight group of four took down the incoming warriors easily. Then Camina and Adrenalynne jogged over, having dispatched their opponents.

"What's happening on the platform?" asked Yara with blood splattered across her face.

Choo-Choo could see Navos' pale blond hair and the back of Pandora, who looked like she had her mother by the neck with a blade to the throat. Kuma appeared a moment later, reloading a handgun.

"Shall we make an assault on the platform?" he asked.

"Something's going on," said Tick with his eyes rolled back in his head. His flying snake, Koro, hovered in the upper part of the cavern, giving Tick a good view.

"Who cares, let's kill that gray-faced bastard," said Adrenalynne. The tendons on her neck stood out and she had blood smeared on the side of her head beneath the neon green Mohawk.

Before they could take the first step towards the platform, Deacon appeared on the opposite side as he led an army of Alliance waku into the arena. Choo-Choo prepared to defend himself but Deacon halted them about a hundred feet away on the sands. The waku lined up in five groups of twenty, standing at crisp attention like a military parade examination.

"What the fuck is wrong with them?" asked Yara.

"I think it's the same thing they did to Deacon in the Eternal City," said Camina.

Realizing they'd trapped themselves in the arena when they blew up the entrance to the Terreno, Choo-Choo said, "We need to get out of here."

"We have to get Pandora," said Kuma.

"I think it's too late for that," said Choo-Choo. He extended his amber towards the platform in time to hear Dominion's final words. The army of modified warriors led by Deacon raised their weapons.

"Back to the entrance," said Choo-Choo frantically.

"But we're blocked in."

"It's a defensible spot."

As the hundred warriors raised their voices in a war cry, Choo-Choo led the group up the stairs to the mangled gate and boulders strewn about the concrete. The steep stairs and railings provided barriers.

"Grab the gate with me," said Kuma.

They maneuvered the twisted metal to block off their left flank while Yara pushed boulders to reduce the lanes on the right. Dozens of dead-eyed Alliance warriors ran up the concrete stairs in huge leaps. Gunfire erupted from his sister's position, taking down the first two, but the others crashed into them.

In a matter of seconds, Choo-Choo was fighting for his life. The Alliance waku moved with power and speed. The only thing keeping him alive was their lack of skill. He wasn't sure how long he could keep up the fight. A blade sung through the air, kissing off his shoulder, opening a deep cut.

Choo-Choo cut a hand off with one blade, sinking the other into the chest of a young waku. The weapon went into the flesh next to a metal plate exposed by his open uniform. Black smoke leaked out, threatening to coalesce into something alive. He wanted to back away, but the blade was stuck between two bones. The black mist eventually rose into the air before dissipating. He spotted other signs of similar black mist in the battles nearby.

Dodging a thrown knife, he sank his weapon into a waku that had overextended, seeing the others in the same awful predicament. Even if they survived the first assault, they'd never last against a hundred juiced-up warriors. They were dead. It was only a matter of time.

Fifty-Eight

Pandora had never felt so hopeless in her life. Even when she'd been trapped in the metal box, faeila feasting on her flesh, she'd believed that she'd eventually be freed. Her friends were being overwhelmed by the warriors modified like Deacon. It felt like she only had one choice. She didn't want to see her friends die, but she didn't want to see them enslaved either.

"One word and I'll make it stop. Submit to me. Your friends will live, but not much longer. They fight valiantly, but they will lose. You should be able to see that. You're not blind."

She'd turned halfway, holding the blade to her mother's throat. Her friends had made a defensible position against the old gate, using the debris and metal railings to create a pinch point. The Alliance warriors were dying in twos and threes, but Dominion was right. She could see they couldn't keep it up forever, and even if they did, then Deacon and the other bloodstone warriors would finish who was left.

The only thing she didn't understand was the black mist rising from dead waku. It was familiar.

Then it all made sense. Hylakane had named them creatures from an older realm, and few were as old as the Eternal City. They were magic incarnate and Dominion had found a way to use their essence to give power to his weaker warriors. It's what they'd done to Deacon. Not only did she understand they were wraithhawks, but she knew what she needed to do to save her friends. The only problem was that she was surrounded by enemies and the moment she reached for the mask on her hip, they would have her.

"Make them stop or I'm killing her. I don't care who she is. I prefer my friends to my own blood. Once they're not under threat, I'll talk concessions."

Her mother broke into a deeper sob, forcing Pandora to hold her up. She wished she could tell her that for all their differences, she'd never actually kill her, but she needed her grandfather to believe the lie.

"Please, Pandora, please. I've always loved you. I'm sorry it's been so hard. Just give in and we can all be together again."

While her mother begged for her life, Dominion bore his gaze into her. She felt exposed. Then his hard expression cracked. He pulled a handgun out of his jacket. The explosion startled Pandora. Wetness had splattered across her face. The weight in her arms became extremely heavy.

"I'm finished with negotiations. Grab her."

Pandora tried to knock Valor and Sophia away with a Push, but they grabbed her arms before she could stop them. The power in their limbs made her feel like she was trapped by iron manacles.

She watched her mother's lifeless body crash to the ground, limp and unmoving. Her relationship with her mother was complicated. The abuse and gaslighting had been horrific, but there was some connection based on blood and a shared history that made her death a shock and a heartbreak. It was like breaking an expensive vase she never knew she had. The hole in her heart where her mother should have been had been filled with other people.

Dominion gave the corpse a last look before tossing his weapon to Navos, then reaching into his jacket pocket, producing a little box, the same kind that had held their bloodstones.

"Hold her. I want this over with," said Dominion with uncharacteristic annoyance.

The other competitors had risen to their feet, surrounding her like mindless zombies. The mask on her hip was so close, but with Angel and Valor clamping her arms tight, it might as well have been halfway across the world for all she could do about it. She struggled, sending out waves of Pushes that knocked them around, but did nothing to keep her from being held.

Dominion popped open the box. The bloodstone sat in the velvet catch like an engagement ring.

"You should kill me," she said through gritted teeth, yanking and pulling her arms to no avail. "I'll find a way to break through that thing and put a blade in your back."

Her grandfather gave her a cold, but amused glare. "A fighter until the end. Not like your mother. One can never tell how the blood will flow." His lips curled into a ghoulish grin. "Hold her now. I don't want interference."

The bloodstone was a bright sun before her eyes. She could see nothing else. From behind her, she could hear the cries of her friends in battle. Alive, but not for long. She fought harder, sending out waves of alternating Pushes and Pulls, trying to break free. The warriors surrounding her undulated like high grasses in stiff winds, but never broke.

"Make her stop. Now," growled Dominion, showing his true face without anyone around other than his bloodstone slaves.

The enormous Brodarian waded through the others, reaching down and picking her up like a sack of potatoes. It was like getting caught in a great machine. She couldn't wriggle or move. He held her like an offering while the other competitors backed away. Noctus had been the strongest and now with the bloodstone he was a frightening giant.

"Let me go!"

She spat in his face, knowing that her free will was about to end. To her surprise, he flinched slightly and then she remembered something he'd told her about his resistance to magic. Pandora checked over her shoulder to see a smear on the ground where Noctus had been lying. Confirming her realization, he winked and said, "Now."

Dominion was two steps away. He heard Noctus speak and was in the process of shouting when the Brodarian launched her high in the air and over his shoulder. She flew like a gymnast, flipping and landing on her feet on the far end of the platform.

"Get her!" screamed Dominion.

The other warriors, having no free will, had not acted immediately. Noctus barreled into the group, knocking them over while she used her sapphire to leap down to the sandy arena.

As she landed, she donned the wraithhawk mask. The cool interior slipped over her nose. As the artifact connected with her mind, it felt like her entire brain had been dipped in mint. She felt alive.

The battle at the destroyed gate was in earnest, with dozens of warriors trying to kill her friends. She felt the kindred creatures trapped in the plates, providing the supernatural abilities. Pandora reached out her hand and commanded the wraithhawks to obey her.

She hadn't expected immediate results. Hylakane had never explained how the mask worked. The only clue he'd given to its purpose was the cryptic phrase, *Do not forget from which it came, or why it was made.* She understood now. The mask had been made to observe and study the ethereal creatures; and it was the maetrie way to control. It was why Hylakane no longer used it. He'd learned how to live in harmony with the creatures.

But now they would become her flock.

Some of the bloodstone warriors had dropped to the sands, expecting an easy capture, while the rest battled Noctus on the platform. Even in their mindless advance, they realized something was wrong as she sent the modified warriors against them.

Pandora spotted Dominion escaping the arena with his personal guard, checking over his shoulder in his haste to flee. She reached for her weapons, but remembered that they'd been taken, so she stopped a wraithhawk warrior and made him hand over his weapons. With the blades in her fists, she burst after her grandfather.

Fifty-Nine

Choo-Choo didn't know why they stopped attacking. He'd been knocked over when a group of warriors hit the old gate, sending the metal bars into his shoulder. A warrior with half his ear cut off loomed over Choo-Choo, ready to plunge the knife in when he stopped.

When the entire group turned and headed back to the sands, he was confused. More than confused. He wasn't sure if he'd been poisoned with hallucinations, but seeing his friends equally unsure made him realize it was really happening.

"What's going on?" asked Yara, covered in blood.

"It's the mask. The mask," said Kuma breathlessly.

"We can take the fight to them," said Camina, limping after the others. "Let's finish this."

He turned to Vasilisa, who was scavenging shells for her shotgun from the fallen.

"Stay here. I don't want you hurt."

She fixed him with a heavy stare. "It's too late for that."

At first he thought she was wounded, but then he remembered what had happened to Andelei. Choo-Choo turned back to the arena to see Deacon fleeing after his master along with the bloodstone warriors, which included Navos.

They chased Dominion and his guards into the next caverns. Choo-Choo ran at top speed, looking for his friend. The bloodstone guards were turning occasionally to provide defense for Dominion. Choo-Choo tackled Navos off a rocky outcropping, landing hard on his friend, but he kicked up, knocking him off despite the topaz advantage.

"Navos, stop! This isn't you."

Choo-Choo had managed to kick one of the blades away, but Navos still held another and he looked ready to plunge it in his chest.

The rest of the fight was moving on, but Choo-Choo refused to let his friend go. Navos kept glancing towards the northern tunnel as if his master was pulling him in that direction.

"Navos."

The blond waku stared back intensely without sign of recognition. Choo-Choo tried to dodge in and grab his wrist, but took a cut across the thigh for his advance. The wounds from the earlier fights were adding up. His shirt was covered in blood.

His friend turned to follow Dominion, but Choo-Choo circled around and prevented him from fleeing that direction. The entire wraith-hawk army was in the way.

"I'm not letting you go. You're my friend. I can't let him take you. I've lost too much already. Please, Navos, wake up from this nightmare he's put you under. This isn't you. He's controlling you."

The tension in Navos' shoulders dipped slightly before the blade came up. Choo-Choo set his blade onto the rocks and advanced slowly with his hands up.

"I'm not here to hurt you. Put that down."

Navos jabbed it forward menacingly. His mouth was twisted and he wore an expression of great pain.

"Remember all the time we spent as kids, running through the caverns, playing in the canyons, staying awake all night even after Mami yelled at us for being too loud? Come on, Navos. You have to remember."

As he stepped forward, Navos went backwards as if he was fighting the command to kill.

"It's just you and me, buddy. You can do this. Put down the blade and I'll cut that thing out of you. I saw what happened to the others. It was a trick. That time is over. Dominion is fleeing. You don't have to protect him anymore. He's probably dead already."

The blade, which had dropped low, suddenly came up as Navos was reminded of his task. Choo-Choo sighed.

"Navos, you're my best friend. I love you like a brother. Stab me if you want, but I'm not letting you leave."

Choo-Choo closed the distance. For a moment, he thought Navos was going to drop the blade, but then he struck, plunging it deep into his chest.

Sixty

The walls blurred past as Yara bounded through the tunnels after Deacon. He'd broken away from the main group, heading northeast towards the old Razor lands. She knew it wasn't smart to pursue him alone, but she didn't care. He'd taken everything from her including her father. While he hadn't been the one to put the blade in, his betrayal had led to his death.

Hatred that she'd long thought faded fueled her pursuit. A litany of reasons why he had to die by her hand repeated in her head, including when he'd thought she might switch sides after the betrayal. Her father, uncle, friends, and family. Her *clan.*

A massive multi-level cavern shone with faint fungal illumination. She didn't see him when she burst into the airy space. A tickle in the back of her neck alerted her to the danger before her mind caught up. She threw herself to the left as a knife spun past her head, bouncing off the rocks and slipping into a crack, disappearing forever. Deacon stepped out from behind a set of stalagmites that climbed to a cathedral-like structure.

"It would have been easier if you hadn't avoided that," he said.

Yara stood on an elevated position. Blades were in her fists, but she didn't remember drawing them. Sweaty hair stuck to her face. Deacon's hooked blade rested on the stone as if he were too tired to carry it. She knew that wasn't true, but there was something hollow about him. His cheeks were gaunt and the swagger that he wore like a cloak was tattered and threadbare.

"It would've been a lot easier if you'd just died when I shot you."

He cracked an easy smile, which reminded her of why she'd fallen for him. He was everything the clan wasn't. She should have seen that betrayal long before it'd happened. Deacon pulled open his shirt, snapping buttons and revealing the mangled flesh where the dark plate had been.

"Maybe you did, it's just taking me a while to realize it."

"You fucked me. Fucked my family, my life."

"I thought you liked it when I fucked you," he said, his smile faltering at the joke.

"You could have had it all if you hadn't betrayed us," she said, lips curled in anger.

Deacon glanced askew. He closed his eyes. "I traded honor for subservience." His lips broke in a rakish grin. "Suppose it's too late for forgiveness?"

"I'd sooner give Tick a hand job."

"That bad, huh?"

The anger that had carried her in pursuit seemed to dissipate upon observing him up close.

"You look like death."

"You're not wrong." He pulled back the rest of his shirt, revealing the remaining plate, and rapped his knuckles on the dull metal. "I hear them calling me."

"I'd be happy to help you along," she said, holding up her blade horizontally.

"Don't. I don't want to kill you."

"You could let me sink my blade into your heart. I'd make it relatively painless and then all this could be over. Face it, Deacon. You lost. You picked the wrong side."

"Even if I'd won, I picked the wrong side. But you know I'll fight back. That's why I've survived this long. I don't know when to give up. I can't stop fighting."

He looked on the verge of tears. The vitality that she'd fallen in love with years ago was absent. He was a pale shadow of his former self. Any sympathy she might have had for him was lost to time.

"I have to kill you. I hope you understand that," she said.

He closed his eyes briefly while nodding his head.

"At least your father won't be around to grieve your death."

Yara moved into a crouch. It wasn't a natural pose, but it felt appropriate for their fight.

Despite Deacon's emaciated body and haunted gaze, he shifted forward with the grace and power of a python approaching an unwary prey. The hooked blade had her on reach and he was faster than sin, but she'd never felt more ready. Deacon attacked, using his hooked blade like a sledgehammer. Sparks flew as she countered his blows, slipping away before he could corner her against the wall.

"You've gotten better."

"I never understood my father's skill until recently. I thought he was a mythical warrior, but him dying proved that anyone can be beat."

Deacon arched an eyebrow. "I'm not even sure I could have beaten him."

Yara leapt with Lightness, coming down with a flurry of blows that would have eviscerated a normal foe, but Deacon moved with equal speed, keeping up with her attacks until he kicked her in the chest. She backflipped, landing on a ledge twenty feet away, a growl on her lips.

For the first time since she'd known him, he wore the mantle of doubt. He seemed to recognize that his skills had atrophied while hers had grown. He'd been measuring himself against the weak waku of his new clan, while she'd been honing herself in the shadows, waiting for the right moment.

She threw herself at him in another blurred exchange of strikes and blocks. When the pass ended with him retreating to a lower level with his skin flashing back from steel gray to pale cavern dweller, he checked his jacket to find a slice through the fabric. Deacon slipped out of the outer garment, slapping it on the stone. Blood ran down his forearm. He'd switched to black diamond too late.

The doubt burned away, replaced by unrepentant anger. He came at her like a whirlwind and it took all her skill to keep his blade from her throat. It was like fighting against a dozen foes at once. She never knew where the blade was coming, acting on instinct born from constant training. She managed to kick him in the thigh, giving her a chance to retreat to a different ledge.

"Two to one."

She didn't understand until she noticed the cuts. One on her thigh and the other on her side. Neither were deep enough to worry about, but they bleed into her clothes.

"I should have seen it when you put Camina in the hospital," she said. "I should have known right there you were rotten."

"You're not wrong," he said, stern expression breaking. "All I have left is survival. It's the only thing driving me."

"It must be miserable."

"It is."

Yara circled around, giving herself the advantage of terrain. In the last fight, she'd noticed a hole in his defense. The missing plate made him less flexible on the right side, either from scar tissue or the pain from its loss. She saw the path she had to take to kill him and hoped that he'd use his black diamond too late again. He wasn't using it as frequently as she'd seen in the past, which suggested he lacked the energy or hadn't kept up with his training. Her tactic would expose her to a fatal counter-attack, but there were no safe fights in the shadows.

When Deacon turned his head slightly, as if he'd heard something, Yara used the distraction to attack. She flew at him like a thousand knives, forcing him to defend on his back foot. Deacon leaned to his left with an awkward twist, so she attacked the hole she'd seen before. Her blade sliced through his shirt, opening up a gash along his ribs, but he'd turned ever so slightly, avoiding a fatal plunge. The overextension left her open to the hooked blade, which she deflected slightly, but it hit her across the shoulder. Her entire left arm went numb and she dropped the blade. Before she knew it, Deacon slammed his shoulder into her and she landed on her back with him on top. He held her wrist with the remaining blade while she fought with his other arm to keep him from slashing down with the hooked sword.

"You shouldn't have come after me. I would have been much happier dying without having killed you."

"You killed me when you murdered my family," she said through gritted teeth, knowing she was slowly losing the battle for position. He was on top and his maetrie-given strength was stronger than her topaz.

"I'm sorry, Yara."

He wrenched his arm away from her grip and raised the hooked sword. She hoped it would be quick.

A blast threw him off. Deacon tumbled off the short ledge, landing on the rocks below her. A bloody and soot-covered Vasilisa marched over as she reloaded the shotgun.

"Are you okay?" she asked.

Yara checked her shoulder. The cut wasn't deep. "I'll live."

Below them, Deacon lay on the rocks awkwardly. He was breathing in heaves. The side of his skull was pulpy. Yara dropped down and kicked away his weapon, then helped Vasilisa down the rocky slope. Deacon stared up with fear in his eyes. He looked like he wanted to speak, but he'd landed on a protrusion which had pierced his chest from behind. His skin rippled steel gray as if he were still trying to protect himself with the black diamond.

"I—"

A blast ended his attempted speech. Vasilisa threw the shotgun down next to the bloody mess that was once his head.

"I didn't want to hear another fucking word," she said.

Yara crouched down, grimacing from the wounds in her shoulder and thigh. She tried not to look at his missing face as she removed his stones, placing them in a pocket before joining Vasilisa for the return.

Sixty-One

Pandora led her army in pursuit of her grandfather. She'd expected resistance but none was given until they reached the Alliance caverns. The majority of the warriors stood arrayed in a semicircle blocking the path that led to the elevator, while others were on the terraces and balconies of the apartments and businesses. Even the ones that had been enjoying the local bars had come out, still holding their drinks.

Clothes were ruffled and sweat covered Dominion's forehead. She'd never seen him so disheveled. When they burst into the cavern, he'd been about to ascend to the Nest. He turned, chest heaving and hot with anger.

"Kill them. Wipe them from this fucking world," he spat.

There had to be almost two hundred Alliance waku standing between her and her grandfather. They had the numbers, but wore their doubt like a heavy cloak. The wraithhawk warriors standing with her had been their companions only a few hours before and she was known as a fierce fighter. The mask only added to her mystique.

When not a single one of them moved to attack, her grandfather grabbed one of the waku in back, a young kid who looked like he'd joined mere weeks ago, and pushed him forward. The young waku stumbled, falling to a knee and staring back in horror. The mask of the cunning businessman that Dominion had cultivated had been ripped off. Her grandfather had revealed his true, awful self.

Pandora climbed onto a rock and slipped off the mask, holding it tight in case she needed to use it again. The bonds to the modified warriors remained even as she wasn't wearing it. She checked back to her friends. Kuma was staring up at her expectantly. She took a deep breath before reaching into herself to change back from Lady Saha. After living in her skin for months, the return was difficult, but she managed to slip back into herself. The crowd gasped at the change.

"Some of you know me from before. But for those of you new to the Undercity, I am Pandora Thule, granddaughter of that wretched being who has called himself your leader for these last few years. I was sent here to infiltrate the clans and help him take control of the Undercity, but after living amongst you, I saw that he was wrong. The Drops clan, and all clans eventually, became my family.

"He doesn't care about you. Look what he's done to your brothers and sisters. Turned them into mindless slaves. He's been using you to acquire powerful artifacts hidden in the Undercity, while profiting greatly from the faez crystal trade. How much have you benefited from the hundreds of millions of dollars he's extracted from the Undercity? I see by your faces that you've not seen a penny except for the meager salaries he offers."

"She lies!" shouted her grandfather. "She would turn the Undercity into a battleground again. Look at the stability, the safety, I've created. Me! You owe it all to me! I've poured my profits back into rebuilding this place into a second city to match the one above."

"For whose benefit?" she countered. "You made yourself rich on the backs of their labor. Their steel. Their heart." She paused. "I would know him best. He killed my mother, *his daughter*, when her life grew inconvenient to his power."

The warriors, who'd been listening intently, turned towards him. Dominion took a step back.

"She lies. She was a spy sent to sow discord. She has no honor. She's a wretched liar."

"And who taught me? He's right. I admitted it already. I was a spy, but I found something that he can never offer. Family. Honor. A place that treats you with respect. I turned against him when I saw how wrong he was."

"You would prefer to die in the shadows?" he shouted. "You'd prefer a return to the wars that plagued this place? I'm the only one that can save you!"

Pandora gestured towards the blank-faced warriors at her side. "Look at your friends. Look at what he's done to them. He enslaved them using eldritch magics of the Eternal City. He was planning to do the same to you. In time, you'd all be like this. Mindless warriors that he'd throw at his enemies without regard. He doesn't care about your lives. How do I know this? Because he treated me the same, even as his granddaughter. It's why I know he must be stopped."

The focus returned to Dominion. He appeared indecisive, glancing back to his bloodstone warriors and then to the entire cavern of warriors.

Pandora dropped onto the floor and strode forward right into the midst of the Alliance. They parted as she advanced and her wraithhawk warriors drew in behind. By the time she'd reached the halfway point, the Alliance warriors had rotated towards Dominion. He backed away, then ran towards the elevator.

She could have given the order to kill him. The Alliance warriors would have obeyed her command. That much she could see. But it would have been a bloodbath against his bloodstone warriors, and Pandora didn't want to be like him. Dominion had killed *his* father to take control of his estate and make his place in the Eternal City. It was the maetrie way. She didn't want to be like that.

"What are you going to do about him?" asked Kuma, who had returned to his original form. Seeing the real Kuma brought warmth to her chest.

"He'll flee back to his estate."

"What about the Tear?"

She exhaled slowly. "He wasn't going to use it here. I think." Doubt crept in, but she pushed it away, finding certainty amid her whirlwind thoughts. "He hadn't been living here for decades to destroy it. I know that much about him."

"He'll destroy another realm then?"

A tightness formed in her chest. "I know it was the plan, but I couldn't kill him, Kuma. Or I'd end up like him. He killed my mother. I'm sorry."

"Lady Saha...I mean Pandora," said Camina with a smirk. "What do you want to do with all of them?"

The entire Alliance group was milling about waiting for her direction. She hadn't quite thought through the repercussions of her rebellion.

"I'll place the wraithhawk warriors around the elevator to make sure that they don't come back. Send everyone else back to whatever they were doing before."

"What about the Nest?" asked Camina, nodding towards the elevator.

"I'll give him an hour to flee and then we'll confirm he's gone."

The young warriors seemed surprised and apprehensive about the change, but they were new enough not to question the reversal. Most were probably happy not to have to fight a battle against their friends.

After the hour was up, Pandora took her friends up the elevator to investigate the Nest. The maetrie guards that stood outside the marble doors were no longer present. As they moved through the passages, she was surprised how similar to his estate in the Eternal City it'd become with statues of him in various poses of conquest, or ancient weapons on the wall. Some rooms had been stripped clean. She regretted not contesting him for every resource, but hadn't wanted to sacrifice more lives. The feeling of her mother's lifeless corpse sliding out of her grip still echoed across her fingertips. She rubbed her hands against her legs as if she could remove the stain.

When they reached the obsidian wall, Pandora ordered it to be destroyed. Her grandfather could come back to the city of sorcery through other means, but she didn't want to worry about him sending assassins through her back door.

Standing on the cliff's edge, she looked over the Alliance cavern, which had returned to its previous state of normalcy. It was strange seeing it revert so quickly, but most of the new warriors had no real allegiances, having joined to escape the lesser life of a gang member in the city above. To them, the clan was a place to belong and find shelter from the horrors of the world. She hadn't known it when she'd come to the Undercity, but it's what she'd been looking for too.

"What now?" asked Camina wistfully. "We've won. What does that mean?"

Kuma stood on the other side. They'd lost the others along the way to the Alliance. She hoped nothing had gone wrong, but there would be time to fix it. The weight she'd been carrying all these years seemed a little lighter. Then Kuma fell to his knees and she spun around in confusion. A breath caught in her throat as he put two fingers to his brow.

"I renounce my oaths and former allegiances, vow to protect my clanmates, both new and old, with my life. I agree with all my heart, knowing the shadows will rise up and claim my soul should I break my oath. I pledge myself to this new clan, the one led by Pandora Thule."

Shock left her speechless. She stammered for a moment. "Are you sure?"

His lips curled slightly. "You're the only one who can lead us now. It was your victory. Your speech."

"He's right, you know," said Camina with an eyebrow raised. "None of this would have happened had you not turned against him."

"But you were being trained by your father to be a clan leader. I'm a warrior. I don't know anything about leading a clan," said Pandora.

"Sure does look like it to me. Besides, I'll be here to support and advise you." He cocked a playful grin. "Among other things."

"I don't know what to say..."

"Then finish the ceremony," he replied.

The words were hard to find at first. She'd only heard Daraja say them, but when she reached back into her memory they were right there.

"Rise and be welcome. For the shadows do not care, but we do. We are your hearth and home, the blade that will not bend, the fist that will protect you."

Kuma embraced her as the first member of the new clan. Camina joined a short time later. In time, there were many more.

Sixty-Two

The Undercity seemed like a less scary place without Deacon. Vasilisa had made the journey back to the Terreno while Yara had gone to the Alliance area to see what had become of Dominion. Her shoulder still ached from the kickback. A knife to his throat would have been preferable, but she hadn't wanted to miss her chance to avenge Andelei. She'd thought there would be more closure once Deacon was dead, but killing him had only left a hole where her hatred had existed. It didn't do anything to erase the memory of Andelei's touch, the way he held her against his body, caressing her shoulders and thighs, making light kisses against her neck. The confusion of suddenly being turned on by her dead boyfriend brought a curt laugh and then she was wiping away snot.

There were no guards upon her return. She hoped that was a good thing. Vasilisa was going to head straight back to the Terreno, but decided to circle around the other way and froze in horror. She spotted her brother's body in the center of the cavern, entangled with another. He was covered in blood.

For a frightening moment, she thought he was dead. Then he erupted in laughter mixed with coughing and she realized the other person was Navos.

"What are you two idiots doing? You gave me a heart attack," she said.

Up close she saw they were still bleeding. Navos had a long gash across his upper arm, the center part of which looked like it'd been gnawed on, while her brother was holding his chest near his shoulder.

"Navos stabbed me."

"Then what did you do? Try to eat your way through his arm?" she asked aghast.

Navos stuck his finger into the meaty hole, grimacing and laughing at the same time.

"That's where the little bastard was until Emilio cut it out. You can see what's left of it on that rock."

She saw where he pointed. The pulpy blob looked like someone had skinned a lizard and then smashed it with a hammer.

"That's what was in you? Gross."

"Did a number on my brain. Even now I'm resisting the urge to stab you," said Navos.

"Once is enough today please," said her brother. He smiled in her direction but she could see the pain in his eyes. "Think you could find an opal for us? I've lost a lot of blood."

"Stay right here, I'll find someone."

"That's a good one," he chuckled.

Vasilisa ran into Camina in the tunnels and brought her to the two wounded waku. After a short session involving a lot of cursing and laughing, her brother and his best friend were patched up.

"I can stop the bleeding, but I can't give you new blood, so take it easy, you two."

Her brother winked as he limped off arm in arm with Navos in the direction of the Terreno. Camina was on an errand for Pandora, so she disappeared, leaving Vasilisa by herself. The Terreno wasn't as busy as it'd been in the last few weeks. She headed to Elani's shop, finding the older woman sitting behind her desk drinking a whiskey and smoking a cigar.

"You heard?"

Elani held up the bottle. "Want a drink?"

The amber liquid burned on the way down, forcing Vasilisa to cough.

"Is Pandora really taking over the clan?"

Vasilisa nodded. "All the waku at the Alliance area pledged to her. That's what Camina said anyway."

"What about you?"

"I don't know," said Vasilisa as the alcohol warmed her chest. "I killed Deacon."

Elani grabbed the bottle and poured more whiskey. "For not having a single stone, you certainly are racking up quite a list."

"The only thing I ever wanted to be was a waku."

"There's more than one way to be a warrior," said Elani, holding up her glass.

"I'll drink to that."

Sixty-Three

A crimson lizard the size of a small dog was snacking on a hunk of fur atop a low-roofed house in the Machi. Kuma picked up a rock and launched it at the creature, sending it scurrying out of sight.

"It doesn't look as bad as I thought it would," said Yara at his side. "A fresh coat of paint and some dusting and I could almost imagine it as it was before."

"Every building is probably rife with critters. Have to send Tick in here to run them out with his tiger's eye," he said with a sigh.

"I thought he was coming?"

"He's been in Darina's room whenever she's not working and she has three days off."

"So he *is* coming," snorted Yara.

Kuma turned his head. "When did you start sounding like him?"

"I spent two years listening to his quips. Some of it wore off I guess," she said, crossing her arms.

"I wish Niran and Brazio were here," he said after a long pause.

"I was so mad at him growing up for not teaching me his secrets. I thought he was holding back how to be a great waku. It took him dying and me having to survive in the shadows for me to understand he *was* trying to show me all those years."

"I'm sorry, Yara. I wish we'd been closer before. I was so stuck on making my father proud I never saw what you were going through," he said.

Yara turned. Her hair was pulled back into a severe ponytail.

"I never understood why my father didn't take the clan from Niran. He wasn't a waku and hadn't won the battles that Brazio had. But he never would have done that to his brother." Her mouth twisted. "Do you think they'd be proud of us?"

"They were *always* proud of us," said Kuma. "Even before all this. But it's hard to run a clan and be a parent at the same time."

"I wish I could see him one last time," said Yara wistfully.

"Me too."

"Is Pan going to let us rebuild the Machi?"

Kuma scratched the back of his neck. "She's not in favor of the idea. I guess Dominion had already sold the bulk of the faez crystals mined and there are fewer and fewer being found these days. We're already in a cash crunch with so many ineffective waku to feed. She wants the Pajot up and running first for those cash crops. But she's open to the idea that this can be the training grounds for the new waku. There's not enough room at the Alliance to put all their warriors through training."

"Alliance? I thought she was going to change the name," said Yara.

"Undecided. It wouldn't feel right using Razor or Drops, and no one wants to be Alliance," he said heading deeper into the Machi.

The bridges were solid under his feet. They chased off other critters, but nothing dangerous. At the center of the massive cavern, they found a set of wooden gallows. Without discussing it, they destroyed the structure with their bare hands. The splintering of wood felt cathartic.

The elevator that had been used by the Crows remained where it had landed, covered in rust, stones, and spiderwebs. The hole that went up to the old warehouse had collapsed partially. The bottom would have to be reinforced or the area would be unusable.

"Hey, I'm gonna check out—"

Yara jabbed her thumb in the direction of her old home. Kuma was standing on a bridge staring at the place he'd grown up.

"Yeah. I'll meet you after."

The home was in surprisingly good condition. He left his shoes on due to the dust. The sliding door opened smoothly, revealing an inner space untouched by critters. The shrine to his mother, Himari, had two old burnt candles sitting on either side. He entered each room, caught in a whirlwind of memories. Once he'd confirmed nothing was lurking, he grabbed a broom and began cleaning, starting with his mother's shrine. He worked until he was covered in dirt and a sheen of sweat. When the interior was immaculate, he removed his shoes and placed them on the mat inside the door and knelt before the shrine. In time, he'd add his father's picture. He'd given so much for the clan, including his life.

A knock on the pillar broke him from his trance. Yara was standing outside looking similarly disheveled. She peered past him with her mouth shifted to the side.

"Are you moving back?"

He hunched his forehead. "I don't know. But I didn't want to leave it dirty."

Yara lifted a shoulder. "Same." She glanced in the direction of the Academy. "Maybe I could help Camina with training. If Pan would allow it."

"Camina will need good instructors."

"Maybe I could learn to be one."

"Yara..."

She hung her head. "I'm serious. I've never taught anyone before. It's hard to see other people's issues when you're so angry at the world." Yara tilted her head. "What are you doing to do now? Besides be her fuck buddy."

"Okay, Tick."

"You didn't answer the question."

"Exactly," he said.

Yara arched an eyebrow then slowly nodded with understanding. "It doesn't get easier, does it?"

"Never does."

Sixty-Four

The tall Brodarian was standing with his hands behind his back watching the trainees move through basic forms. Pandora had been reviewing the facilities with Camina, listening to her complaints about having to pack so many young warriors into a tight space. Pandora understood the concerns, but splitting up the clan across the Undercity wasn't what she'd had in mind when she'd taken over.

"Noctus Prime," said Pandora as she joined him on the ridge. "I'm so sorry to keep you waiting. It's been nearly two weeks since everything that happened and I haven't had a spare moment to properly thank you for what you did on the platform. I wouldn't be here if it weren't for you."

"The weights of leadership are a familiar burden. You need not apologize." He shot a glance at the cadre of wraithhawk guards that lurked in the background. "Is this a social visit?"

"I'm sorry. Kuma doesn't want me unprotected. He thinks my grandfather will try to assassinate me."

"You don't sound convinced of his argument."

"I think he got what he wanted from the Undercity, or he would have fought harder to stay. Sure, he would have liked to have continued, but it was a tactical retreat."

Noctus furrowed his brow. "What *did* he get from this little adventure?"

Only a few select people knew about the Tear. Pandora didn't want the knowledge of the weapon to get out, because it might attract speculators who'd want to delve into the deeper sections of the Undercity.

"A small army of warriors, great wealth, and good will in the city. Very few outside of the clan know what he was really up to. His name is still spoken of fondly. He could easily return in a few years without suffering from the consequences of what he did."

"I grieve that our fellow competitors were ensnared by his deception."

Pandora nodded. Her grandfather had taken six of the eight final competitors into the Eternal City with him. Valor Drux, Angel Chen, and the rest of them wouldn't be touring the world as a traveling martial arts show as they would have wanted.

"They're not the only ones. He'd taken a few hundred men and women already."

"But he can't move against you because of your mask," said Noctus, nodding towards the silk bag on her hip.

"No, but there are realms upon realms to subjugate with his new-found resources."

"Will you go after him?"

It was a question that burned in her chest, but she knew the answer. "I can't. Not now. I've barely slept since we chased him away. Without his resources the clan is in shambles. I have too much to do here."

"Is that why you asked me here?"

The ever-present snaggletooth smile didn't match his gaze. Noctus was expecting a request, or invitation. She hoped he wouldn't be too disappointed.

"I owe you a debt."

"Hardly," said Noctus. "Supporting your escape aided my own freedom. Eventually your grandfather would have figured out the blood-stone didn't work and would have had me killed. Against so many there was nothing I could have done. By interfering, I gave myself a chance at survival, which I am much pleased was a successful gambit."

"Your callous evaluation leaves much to be desired," said Pandora smirking.

"How would you see the events of that day?"

"I saw a friend risking their life in service of the better side. While we're no heroes—these hands are covered in blood—my grandfather is orders of magnitude worse."

"That could be one version of it."

"What is another?"

Noctus lifted his chin. "Perhaps I see a kindred soul. Someone fighting with honor to protect the people they love. Your fight with your grandfather and mine in Brodaria have similarities. We strive to turn back the forces that would destroy everything in pursuit of unchecked power."

"In that I agree," she said. "Which is why I wanted to give you this gift."

Pandora handed over a small box. Noctus accepted the item, raising his eyebrows with curiosity. Upon opening, he marveled at the tiny gemstone inside.

"Is this…?"

She nodded. "The black diamond."

Noctus stiffened. "I am rarely surprised, but this is one of them. This is a gift beyond reckoning."

"It's a gift worthy of your act. You helped me claim my small empire, I thought I should give you the thing you believe would help you with yours."

His lips pursed together. "Then you must have found many of these."

"No. As far as we know, it's the only one. I should warn you that all previous users have perished."

"A cursed faez crystal?"

"No more than being a king invites usurpers," she replied.

"Deftly spoken." He bowed with the grace of a courtier. "I accept your gift and will cherish it in my homelands."

"May the shadows keep you safe."

"And the light blind your enemies," he responded. "I hope one day our paths will cross again and not upon the battlefield for you are a worthy opponent."

"As are you, my friend."

With no more to say, Noctus Prime left the Academy grounds.

Sixty-Five

The noodle shop was steamy from the kitchen and the congestion of tourists, leaving Choo-Choo to force his way through with Vasilisa right behind. He'd requested a private booth, but had gotten caught up in clan business and was running late. A waitress was shouting orders into the back as he passed the end of the counter. The sliding door revealed a surprising scene.

"Mami?"

His mother, Triana, rose from the bench, throwing her arms around him and forcing him to bend over so she could kiss his forehead. She did the same for Vasilisa, reviewing her for injuries which surely would have been blamed on him. But it wasn't his mother that had surprised him. Rather the person across the table, Yara Santos.

"Hey," said Yara apprehensively.

The half-drank beer on the table suggested she'd been sitting for a short while.

His mother made Vasilisa join her, so Choo-Choo took the spot next to Yara, ordering a round of beers when the waitress stuck her head in.

"I wasn't expecting to see you here," said Choo-Choo under his breath.

"I wasn't expecting to be here. I received a message this morning," said Yara.

Triana was clutching his sister's hand as if she expected her to be ripped away.

"I'm glad to see you're well," said Choo-Choo.

Triana scowled. "I heard you and Navos stabbed each other. What kind of friend does that?"

Yara flinched away, suggesting the source of the knowledge.

"It wasn't like that."

"Did your blade go into his flesh and vice versa?" she asked.

Choo-Choo recoiled. "Yes, but—"

"I swear you two are still the same children I smacked on the head for your foolish adventures," she said.

"Mami. He was being mind-controlled. It wasn't his fault and I had to remove the creature from his arm."

Triana blinked, before reaching into her purse and producing a newspaper article that had been clipped from the *Herald of the Halls*, an above ground publication. The headline read: "Chaos in the Undercity." The picture was the after effects of the explosion that he'd detonated. A cursory glance at the text showed it speculated on the fighting that had ensued.

"This." She jabbed her finger into the paper. "This is what I had to see three weeks ago. I nearly had a heart attack. Then it took you until a few days ago to finally reach out?" When Vasilisa smirked, she turned on her daughter. "Oh, you think you're blameless in this? You could have reached out too."

"I've been busy—"

"And I've been heartbroken thinking you're both dead. At least your friend was able to tell me what happened."

Choo-Choo reached out across the table. "I wanted to bring you down right away, but things were crazy. We wanted to make sure they wouldn't come back somehow. I sent a message, but it must have went astray."

It was a lie, he'd sent no message, and his mother suspected it because she flattened her lips.

"Uh-huh."

Triana grabbed the paper and stuffed it back in her purse. "I've been in the Terreno for three days now. I wanted to see how it'd changed. There are far too many lighters, but the place certainly has picked up."

"Three days?"

"I've been busy," she said, lifting her chin. "Amongst other things I ran into your friend Tick. He told me everything that happened."

Choo-Choo's cheeks grew red as he thought about strangling his friend for not warning him.

"Oh, Emilio, lighten up. I told him I'd make him regret it if he squealed on me."

Yara snorted laughter. "Now I know where she gets it," she said, gesturing towards Vasilisa.

When Triana speared Yara in her glance, she deflated and reached for her beer to hide behind a drink.

"I missed you," said Choo-Choo, hoping to distract her.

"I missed you both too. Even if you did make my life a living hell wondering if you were alive or dead."

"What have you been doing down here for the past three days?" asked Vasilisa.

"Shopping."

"Shopping?" asked Choo-Choo. "Clothes? Jewelry?"

"I bought a space in the Terreno. I'm opening a restaurant. A small one. Not too big that I can't handle most of it myself. It's on the second terrace on the back side, near the arena. The part you *didn't* blow up. After we eat I'll show you."

"You heard about that? Oh yeah, Tick. I'll strangle him later."

"Excuse me, ma'am," said Yara apprehensively. "Why am I here?"

The waitress showed up with the beers. Triana ordered four bowls of spicy ramen and a plate of fried lizard.

"I wanted to thank you for helping my daughter kill that bastard Deacon. I know our family has a history, but I believe that's all shadows in the depths now. We'll say nothing more about it. Now, drink up. I want to celebrate a reunion with my children."

Sixty-Six

Kuma checked his watch, wondering why Pandora hadn't arrived yet. The table was elbow to elbow. They'd had to bring in chairs from the main room of the Infernal Kitchen. Trays of pastries and other goodies remained mostly untouched. The rattle of ice and the sipping of water intruded into the uncomfortable silence.

"If she's not going to bother showing, I don't have time to wait. I have a business to run," said Leesa in her dark blue suit as she rose from the table.

"Leesa—"

Kuma had his hand out when Pandora burst in. She wore a black jacket and pants over a steel gray shirt. Even though she no longer looked like Lady Saha, the intensity of the maetrie noble remained.

"My apologies for being late. We had a problem at a dig site I had to deal with. Please, Leesa, sit. I promise you'll have my full attention."

Leesa hesitantly returned to her chair and folded her hands on the table, offering a pleasant demeanor.

"Now, how can I help...what is it now, the Council of Undercity Businesses?"

Leesa slapped her hand on the table. "Don't act like you don't know what's going on. You nearly tripled our taxes. Everywhere. Lazona. Big Dave's. The Terreno. I'm surprised you didn't try taxing the businesses in the city too."

"I would if they'd let me," said Pandora with a sigh. "At least the ones at the entry points. They profit on our labors."

"*You* profit on *our* labors," said Leesa.

He caught a kick under the table from Pandora, so he spoke up. "The construction of the arena, modifications to the tunnels to make passage easier, and safer, the manpower it takes to provide security, these don't come cheap."

"Your...I mean Dominion didn't ask us to pay for that," said Delilah, the owner of the Devil's Lipstick.

"That's because he extracted his profits from your labors and fled back to the Eternal City," said Pandora. "He never cared about your businesses and while he was mining faez crystals, he had little need for taxes and only collected that which had been historically taken for the sake of appearances. I should remind you that these tax rates are similar to the lighters', and that tourism to the Undercity has increased exponentially."

"Why not pay for these improvements with the faez crystals?" asked a businessman from Big Dave's with a scaled arm and claws.

"Dominion mined and sold everything he could find these last two years. New veins require more extensive and expensive mining techniques," said Kuma.

"I preferred her grandfather's leadership," said the businessman.

Kuma started to speak, but Pandora held up her hand. She leaned back to the guard at the door and after he approached, whispered something in his ear. A moment later, one of the blank-eyed warriors with the wraithhawk plates entered. The businessman sat tall in his chair. Kuma read his apprehension and fear easily.

"Do you know what he did to these poor souls?" asked Pandora. "He sent them to the Eternal City to be enslaved to a horrible creature called the wraithhawk. In return for their abilities, the creatures are slowly draining away their lives. I do not know how long they will live, but it won't be a normal lifespan." She pounded her fist on the table. "This is what my grandfather does. He drains away the assets until there is nothing left. He's a parasite. Eventually he would have drained you too."

The businessman swallowed. "But aren't you—"

"Aren't you what?" asked Pandora. "Related? Of course we are. I have not hid that. I'm one-quarter maetrie and have lived in the Eternal City, which informs me of my grandfather's behavior more than your desire for a little coin in your pocket." Her nostrils flared. "I was not born in the Undercity, but I made it my home when I turned on my grandfather during the Three Clan Wars. I'm not going to strip-mine the Undercity like he planned to. I want to make it a livable, profitable place for all. In line what Niran or Daraja intended had my grandfather's machinations not kept them at odds. When you talk about the peace that he brought, it was only because he no longer had the reason to meddle. He'd been pulling the strings for years, keeping the clans at each other's throats until he could make his move. Otherwise, Razor and Drops clan would have merged years ago and many families would still be alive."

Only a handful at the table could meet her gaze after the speech—Leesa, Delilah, Najani, and a few others. Kuma made note of them because it told him who truly understood and believed her intent.

"I do not intend to keep this high tax forever," said Pandora. "But until the clan can return to normal, operations and all, then the businesses of the Undercity must carry their weight."

"How long?" asked Najani, the owner of the Lime Duck in the

Lazona.

"I hope no more than a year, but I cannot promise that. It depends on how quickly we can spin up our operations."

"Why all the security?" asked Delilah. "Can't you pare some back and reduce the tax?"

"If I could we would," said Pandora. "But the faez crystal trade has brought a lot of outside interest. The Undercity isn't the same place it was three years ago. Before it was the outlands, a land on the edge of civilization. If you want to confine your profits to the clans only, then by all means, I can pull back my security teams, but if you want to reap the benefits of having wealthy university folk making trips to the Undercity, then I'll need those taxes."

Kuma leaned forward. "Since we don't have the same laws as the light and the Invictus PD do not count the Undercity as their jurisdiction, there are new shops opening up selling quasi-legal products that you cannot find above. I saw an elixir shop that opened in the Terreno during the tournament which sells D'Agastine knockoffs. That would never fly in the city, but it means more traffic down here. If we want to keep the Wild West mentality from before, we can do that, but I think you all prefer stability."

"Will your grandfather come back?" asked Najani quietly. As a fellow part-maetrie, she had a better understanding of the danger posed by the Eternal City.

"While I cannot guarantee that he won't in the future, I can assure you that he'd been making plans to pull back long before our insurrection. My grandfather came to the Undercity to exploit its people and resources, and now that he's got what he wanted, he has no use for the place. You know well, Najani, that this is the maetrie way. *Vyagragot*."

Najani nodded appreciatively. "*Vyagragot*."

Kuma tried not to smile. He was half certain that Pandora had planted that question with Najani, or at least, anticipated it due to their shared heritage.

"And if he does come back," said Pandora, "I'll beat him again. He's shrewd and cunning, but he's not a warrior. He always convinces others to fight for him. Are there any other questions?"

"Will you retain the Alliance name or return to one of the others like Razor or Drops?" asked Delilah.

A smile crept across Pandora's lips. Kuma wanted to know the answer too, but she'd been holding it tight to her chest.

"I'll let you know as soon as it's decided."

Sixty-Seven

The wall of the council room had a faint outline where the strange painting had hung in her grandfather's time. Like a lot of things related to him, she wished she knew the real story behind it. Despite being related, Dominion was an enigma. Whatever grand plans he had for his life and the realms, he kept his council close.

Pandora straightened the jeweled jacket. It was one of the gifts from Hylakane as part of her Lady Saha disguise and she'd found she enjoyed wearing it in the privacy of the Nest. A reminder of the expectations of her position as clan leader. When she'd come to the Undercity, it was the last thing she wanted, but now that it was hers, the weight felt comfortable.

The double doors opened revealing almost all the members of her leadership team. Kuma took the place on her right, and then it was Camina, Yara, Adrenalynne, Elani, Vasilisa, Choo-Choo, and Navos. The final chair remained empty. Only Kuma knew the identity of the last member because he'd been the one she'd contacted.

"May the shadows keep you safe," she told them.

"And the light blind your enemies," they replied.

The rattle of ice water being poured had her waiting. She wished she had Kuma's amber to read their auras, but decided that knowledge would be too distracting. The time for concern was over. No one had contested her leadership of the new clan, so she shouldn't be worried that they didn't think she belonged, even as she was the only one of them not born in the Undercity.

"Come in," she said after the knock on the door.

Striding into the room in a navy blue shape-fitting dress was Gabrielle Au, the former mage of Razor clan. Noises of surprise traveled through the room as everyone looked up.

"It's wonderful to see you all alive," she said, taking the empty spot between Navos and Kuma.

Kuma cleared his throat. "When Pandora asked me to find a clan mage, I was pleased to find out that Gabrielle was still alive."

"I wasn't at the Pajot when Titus Cabone showed up. I was in the city on business for Daraja. After everything that happened, I laid low until I heard about the rebellion. I hope you will accept me into the clan after being absent for so many years."

The uneasy expressions brought concern for Pandora. Gabrielle hadn't been a part of the fight to take the Undercity back from her grandfather.

"I have the utmost faith in Gabrielle," said Kuma. "She was an important part of my father's team. It'll be good to have someone from before around to help with the problems we've little experience dealing with."

"Welcome to the team," said Choo-Choo.

The others followed his lead and Pandora let herself relax.

"Thank you, everyone," she began. "I know these last two months have been chaotic, trying to stave off the many problems we were left with in the aftermath. I'm proud of how this team has handled those issues. I've spoken with you each individually about your new positions and the struggles that remain, but now is the time to formally begin as a clan. You might notice we have a much larger clan leadership structure than the simple ones the old clans used in the past, but I believe the scope of our operations requires it."

Pandora checked their faces for disagreement, then forged ahead.

"As we just discussed, Gabrielle will assume the role of the clan mage as she did before for Razor and as an assistant to Luscious Gaunt in Drops. But I want her to do more than she did previously. We're no longer the backwaters of the city. No longer overlooked by the mages above, except by those who want to hide their deeds in the shadows. The city, and the Hundred Halls, has taken an interest in our world. We need outreach, and Gabrielle, as an alumnus, is the perfect person to make those connections.

"This leads to the next position, which goes hand in hand with Gabrielle's. Kuma will lead the general fixer position. But this will be more than the clan used previously. He will be our connection to the non-mages of the city, namely the gangs and legitimate businesses which we might deal with, but also as our spymaster. We need to have eyes and ears in the city to ensure that we're not caught off guard by future problems.

"The Academy will be split in two. With a large influx of new members, we don't have the room in a single facility. Camina will take the newer recruits at the space near here, while Yara will instruct the older ones at the old Razor Academy." She smiled towards Kuma. "Which will require a small presence in the Machi, once certain security issues like the old Crow elevator have been dealt with."

The entire table chuckled lightly, leaving her to relax. She'd been worried about the meeting all day, but she shouldn't have been. Most of what she was going over, they knew about already, but this was a chance for everyone to hear about it at the same time and acknowledge each other's roles.

"On the security side, Adrenalynne will keep the three tourist locations, Big Dave's, Lazona, and the Terreno, safe and functioning smoothly, as well as the passages between."

"I'm here for you, boss," said the green-haired Adrenalynne, adding a wink for good measure.

"I've named Choo-Choo as the warleader with Navos as his assistant."

Gabrielle tapped on the table. "Excuse me if this has already been discussed, but with no rival clans, is the warleader position necessary?"

"A valid question," said Pandora. "The position has two roles. The first is to ensure that no gangs from the light decide to mess with our business, the second is to prepare the clan for the remote chance that my grandfather ever returns. And if not him, then the realms are full of other threats. I don't think we need a reminder as to the state of the Undercity eight years ago during the infernal invasion."

"Thank you, clan leader," said Gabrielle.

"This leaves our two remaining members of the leadership team. Elani will head the mining operations and all maintenance and construction for new endeavors, while Vasilisa will lead our logistics operations, keeping the flow of goods and equipment, which includes the harvesting operations in the old Pajot. Dominion had let it fall by the wayside, but we can't afford to lose those profits given the clan's financial position. Though we will not grow the illicit drugs, but instead focus on the common reagents used in elixir making. The profits will be less, but it will keep us in better standing in the community and make distribution easier."

"What *is* the situation?" asked Yara, frowning.

"The increased taxes from the local businesses have helped, but as I said, we need to revive the harvesting operations along with the faez crystal mining. In addition, we'll continue the regular arena fights, which will keep the tourism high. But as we appear more legit, our expenses will grow. We've already had inquiries from the city police. They were content to stay out of the Undercity when there was nothing to be gained, but now that things are happening, they're expecting to be compensated not to interfere."

"A bribe," said Elani, shaking her head.

"Invictus PD has political heft in the city which we can't avoid. In due time, we might be able to blunt their influence with some of our own, but for now, we need to stay off their radar. Especially as we expand into the city."

The last comment brought many chins up.

"Into the city?" asked Camina.

"All the clans had interests in the light before. But without the regular rivalries and wars, we can devote more time and energy into enlarging our business footprint," said Pandora.

Many parts of her plans had brought second-guessing, but not this part. She wasn't sure if she could truly call herself an alloy as Hylakane had wanted her to become, but the political maneuvering she'd seen her grandfather employ in the aphena of the Eternal City had been instructive. Like him, she knew that to stop moving was to invite challengers. If she didn't extend her influence into the city, they'd crush the new clan in its infancy.

Besides, the years of training in the clans had taught her that challenge brought new skills. It was why Duro had constantly invented new ways to train, because the old ones were becoming less effective. By forcing the clan to grow and adapt, she'd make them better at their jobs—or replace them with someone who could.

"I intend for the clan to become the largest legitimate and illegitimate business center in the city. Only by making ourselves stronger can we protect ourselves from future threats. But there are certain things we will not do. We will not murder for hire. Nor will we steal from the everyday citizens, or grow and sell drugs as we used to, which amounts to the same thing. Finally, we will teach our new recruits honor as was expected before, but was lost in the ascendancy of the Alliance. Do we all agree?"

Pandora checked with each member, waiting for them to nod or express their agreement. After she'd gone around the room, she laid her hands flat on the table.

"Are there any questions before I ask each of you to give an update into your responsibilities at the current moment?"

"Yeah," said Vasilisa, glancing around as if everyone had the same question. "What is the new clan called?"

A slow smile spread across her lips. Rather than answering directly, she reached into the silk pouch at her side, removing the item she'd brought back from the Eternal City. Cool black mist radiated from the edges, a surge of energy passing through her as she donned the wraith-hawk mask.

§ § §

ABOUT THE AUTHOR

Thomas K. Carpenter resides in Colorado with his wife Rachel. When he's not busy writing his next book, he's hiking, skiing, and getting beat by his wife at cards. He keeps a regular blog at www.thomaskcarpenter.com and you can follow him on twitter @thomaskcarpente. If you want to learn when his next novel will be hitting the shelves and get free stories and occasional other goodies, please sign up for his mailing list by going to: http://tinyurl.com/thomaskcarpenter. Your email address will never be shared and you can unsubscribe at any time.

OTHER BOOKS BY THOMAS K. CARPENTER

The Hundred Halls Universe

SEASON ONE

THE HUNDRED HALLS

Trials of Magic
Web of Lies
Alchemy of Souls
Gathering of Shadows
City of Sorcery

THE RELUCTANT ASSASSIN

The Reluctant Assassin
The Sorcerous Spy
The Veiled Diplomat
Agent Unraveled
The Webs That Bind

GAMEMAKERS ONLINE

The Warped Forest
Gladiators of Warsong
Citadel of Broken Dreams
Enter the Daemonpits
Plane of Twilight

ANIMALIANS HALL

Wild Magic
Bane of the Hunter
Mark of the Phoenix
Arcane Mutations
Untamed Destiny

STONE SINGERS HALL

Song of Siren and Blood
House of Snake and Tome
Storm of Dragon and Stone
Sonata of Shadow and Thorn
Well of Demon and Bone

THE ORDER OF MERLIN

The Order of Merlin
Infernal Alliances
Tower of Horn and Blood

www.ingramcontent.com/pod-product-compliance
Lightning Source LLC
Chambersburg PA
CBHW020617310726
48979CB00008B/1519/J

* 9 7 8 1 9 5 8 4 9 8 2 2 4 *